Heart of Gold

REBECCA NIETERT

Book by Small Press Department ~ Nietert Enterprises LLC

Nietert Enterprises LLC
Small Press Department
Published 2015
Lacombe, LA 70445

This is a work of fiction. Names, characters, places, and incidents either are the product of the author's imagination or are used fictitiously, and any resemblance of actual persons, living or dead, business establishments, events, or locales is entirely coincidental. The publisher does not have any control over and does not assume any responsibility for author or third party websites, or their content.

Heart of Gold - Published by arrangement with the author.

Printing History
The Trophy Abyss 2003 (No longer available)
HEART OF GOLD First Edition 2015

First novel in series of many more to come.

Copyright (c) under Rebecca Nietert 2003
Cover Illustration by Christopher Krieger
Editing Services by Katie Carpenter

All rights reserved
No part of this book may be reproduced, scanned, or distributed in any printed or electronic form without written permission. Please do not participate in or encourage piracy. Copying Copyright materials are an infringement on the rights of the author. Purchase only authorized editions.

For information please contact the author through the website at
http://RebeccaNietert.com

ISBN 978-0-9763815-8-7

Printed in the United States of America

TO ALL THE GALS
THAT HELPED MAKE THIS NOVEL SPECIAL,
YOU ARE TREASURED AND APPRECIATED.

THANK YOU.

ACKNOWLEDGMENTS

To my husband Scott, who told me that I could publish this and that people would want to read it. Your encouragement means the world to me. To my mother who continues to make my moments colorful and my heart fill with love. I love my children more than my own life, and I tell them all the time they make my life worth living. A warm thanks to the motivators who slaughtered the first drafts of this work and inspired me to finish it; I truly am grateful. To the many editors who painstakingly line by line led me to a stronger piece of work. To Katie who not only finally got the editing right, but lent her young voice to the work. Thank you Topher for making this cover design so amazing. I thank each and every one of you from the bottom of my humble heart.

Rebecca Nietert

1

People who come from poverty often say when they were growing up they didn't know they were poor. I knew. The pains in my stomach told me that I wasn't like the other children I saw. My tattered pair of jeans and only pair of shoes shouted that my life wasn't like other kids either. Not the other kids who went to my school. The hand-me-downs that my mother brought home were from the students I went to school with.

The kids knew wore their last years clothing and the torture of bullying began. My family had no possessions. We didn't have hot water and had to deliver it (after boiling out the yellow minerals), to the claw foot bathtub on the second floor of the apartment complex. The stainless steel barrel was too heavy for just one of us kids to carry. The wallpaper was almost as tattered as my jeans.

When I was a small child, the farm town farthest Southwest of Chicago was a sea of blue-collar men fighting desperately to hold down jobs. The violence, the drug abuse, the outright rebel against authority was so evident in my family that I could hardly escape its ripple effects.

When I was eleven, my mother managed to con one of the many men in her life into buying her a television. I watched The Brady Bunch show for the first time. I knew that Marcia Brady had things I would never have and my home certainly didn't look like hers. I understood the great divide between her life, and mine, I wanted hers instead.

On my fourteenth birthday I called the cops. My mother broke my jaw and arm because I had the audacity to answer a question she asked me. I didn't know it was rhetorical. When confronted by

Heart of Gold

authorities she promptly tossed me out onto the street. It wasn't as if I asked for it. The beatings and violence that surrounded me seemed to be a way of life. I was on my own and there wasn't any time for dating or silly kid things. I had to grow up. I had to eat. Had to figure out how to manage a life. Yet I was still just a kid.

I went to school for three hours under a new program called VICA. It was a vocational program designed to instruct kids who would never go to college on how to develop good work habits. Even though the program offered six weeks of training at several different jobs throughout the community, there were only about a thousand people in our small town.

We had two factories, a Dairy Mart, two restaurants, One grocery store, and about nine bars including one in a bowling alley. Working six weeks and then quitting was not a persuading argument to hire me. The rule was quit after six weeks and move on, but I had to break that rule. I had to eat. Fortunately, most business owners liked the idea of quitting after six weeks less than I did.

At the restaurant, I worked until four in the morning and then went to school since farmers got up that early. Two dollars an hour plus tips wasn't enough to pay the room under the house I was renting, let alone eat. The factories paid $4.25 an hour but no matter how desperately I tried, I couldn't keep up the pace.

I ended up working for another factory as an administrator and receptionist. I loved the job, my boss, and her family. The job paid $4.50 per hour and I thought I won the jackpot! Finally! I would have enough to eat!

One day that factory burned down. Then I was jobless and soon after, homeless.

Most people don't understand what it's like to be literally starving for food, and the gut-wrenching pain that never eases. Living in friends' homes and sometimes on park benches, out in the open; the continuous haunting fear of death whispering throughout the night. There's a deep yearning to survive until the next meal. That was my life.

When I was 18, a senior in high school, I worked at the bowling alley. I couldn't afford a formal education and my grades, that I was once proud of, suffered. Surviving became more important.

Headlines said that the oil business in Houston, Texas was booming. I saved every penny I made to travel twelve hundred miles from everything I had ever known in order to have the opportunity for success. Uneducated but determined, I packed my bags and put the money I saved, $250 dollars, in my pocket. In a matter of weeks after graduation I boarded the plane. I had no idea that my life was about to be turned upside-down. The only life I knew, a life of running from the pit of fire, was about to be transformed. The plane took off as I was whisked across the continent into a frenzy of grand luxury.

In 1985 I turned 22. That summer was blistering hot, but I had arrived in Houston, Texas. Home of the richest oilmen in the states. Gone were the days of waiting tables for one's and two's. After two bouts of homelessness, I would have done anything to put a roof over my head and food on the table. And that's exactly what I did.

As I gaze at my reflection in the mirror, I realize the glamorous woman before me isn't the girl I envision in my head anymore. Long soft golden curls frame my face, flowing gently over my shoulders. My grey-blue eyes are enhanced by the soft grey eye shadow I chose to wear for the evening and my salmon-stained lips reveal the perfect shape of a heart. My cheeks flush with the modesty of my choices. My lips tremble nervously as I make note that my simple prayer of beauty from when I was a little young girl had been answered. That awkward, skinny, flat-chested gangly girl with freckles over her nose and cheeks doesn't exist any longer.

The sherbet orange gown I now wear hugs every curve of my figure. Huge golden rings lace the side of the clingy gown which exposes small circles of my bare skin, announcing to the naked eye

Heart of Gold

that no other piece of clothing is hidden under the garment. Only I know about the very small pieces of fabric so delicately held together and cleverly hidden to shield the most secret places not yet exposed underneath.

I take another long look in the mirror and think for a moment. I need to put my smile on. When I do, I realize that the only semblance of the old me is the biggest and widest smile from here to Chicago. Past the suburbs and a hundred miles of cornfields is where I'm from. Or was. I often ask myself, where did that innocent girl that I used to be, go? Shaking my head, I pick up my things and head to work.

I have an overwhelming feeling that my life has changed in a direction I never wanted. I've made many wrong choices in life lately, and at times I'm absolutely convinced that the latest choice wasn't the best. I often wonder if I've made a grave error, sending me yet further down a path than I never imagined I would travel. Yes, I am dressed like a Hollywood starlet. Yes, I am about to go into a palace. But who cares? You do. I tried to quench that small whisper deep within me. I can't shake the feeling that men I meet aren't the kind of men I should associate with. Not for any dollar amount they make.

I stand in the main entrance under the huge crystal chandeliers hanging from the ceiling. I nervously scan the luxurious palace, feeling impressed yet overwhelmed by the beautifully decorated gold elegance and velvety-red fabrics. I stroll slowly into the grand room, and I can't help but marvel at the exquisite decor.

The chairs are draped in plush burgundy fabric so thick even the heaviest of men won't leave a dent after sitting in one for hours. The wall-to-wall industrial rug is spun in gold and green circles. The stage comes out onto the floor just under the huge chandelier. Velvet green curtains drape the back, ready to give the next performer closure until ready to be seen. The required attire for men is a suit and tie. The men who frequented Mack's are famous sports heroes, rich lawyers, doctors, and celebrities.

Rebecca Nietert

Mostly though, the clientele consists of Houston's men who obtained their wealth in the oil industry. The atmosphere is filled with a converged cliché of colognes, instead of the prohibited cigar stench. The lights are dimmed just enough to show the elegant moving of bodies throughout the room. Sexy love songs are playing in the background while men speak, sizing up one another. The attention to detail is obvious, even in the meticulous placement of the chairs, which sit next to the dark, masculine oak tables.

My boyfriend, Philip, chose this extravagant club for my new job. It was his decision to turn me into a dancer for profit. The club sure is very different from the home I come from, where floors creaked and the water never got above room temperature. The water had a mineral smell so obvious that it turned the wash yellow, unlike this place, which smelled of cologne and was flecked with gold. This place was warm and cozy, unlike my childhood where there wasn't heat.

I shudder, feeling that odd mix of trepidation and excitement adrenaline snake through my body just from walking into the club. The beautiful architecture of the building reminds me of the need to escape my former life in any way I can. I anxiously look around the room filled with half-naked young women, all of us searching for a reason to be here. Part of me has that small-town ordinary complex that will not go away. I can't rid myself of it no matter how hard I try! Great. I clench my teeth. It appears I still possess some genuine modesty. The only thing that cures it, to me anyway, is temporary inebriation. I head to the bar, strolling into the grand room on the way there. It was late, and the room was packed wall-to-wall with the Houston's finest.

I notice Lana, a good friend of mine, walking briskly toward me. Lana is tall and lanky. She's blonde like me, but hers did not come from a dye bottle. Some of the girls who work at the club think Lana and I are sisters, because to them we look so much alike. Lana has a similar background to mine. She too came from the wrong side of the tracks, through hard knocks and over

Heart of Gold

obstacles no young girl should have to endure. Over a short time we developed a kinship bond of trust unlike any other. That sort of friendship is especially rare in this business.

"Beverly! Where have you been?" Lana exclaimed, exasperated. "I have been waiting here all night for you! The room is hot tonight."

"Oh man! I just got here. Can't I put my things away?" I pause for a second, realizing that she said my real name out loud. "Lana! Call me Brooke!" I hiss. Not only am I not in the mood to work, I'm annoyed as well. I look longingly towards the bar. I still need my nightly transformation to take place before I can summon the courage to work the room. My makeover is steadily increasing to a fifth of Crown each evening to get the courage required. To say the least, I am not ready to work, and I know Lana knows this.

"Oh, I'm sorry." She flippantly answered. Then, as if she hadn't time for my cocktail, she shouts, "Hey, no way!" and waves over another dancer named Anita. Lana grasps the bag from my hands and gave it to Anita. "Take these. Put them in Brooke's locker!" She barked.

Before Anita could scurry off, I reach to grab my bag back. "Wait, Lana! I need to put my dancing shoes on!"

She giggled and helped me reach in the bag, handing the salmon colored 5-inch pink-lace stilettos into my waiting hands.

Like a chameleon, my dress of indecent exposure transformed my persona into men's fantasy for the evening. My dress is form fitting, tight, but also classy and falls under the cocktail dress code. My jacket was easily removable, which I gently handed to Anita along with my street shoes. I put on my dance shoes and shyly pulled my dress down as far as it could go. I whisper a quick "thank you" to Anita before Lana shoos her off with a wave of the hand. She then turns to face me.

"We'll get your drink at the table okay?" Thank goodness she understands I need that drink.

Rebecca Nietert

"Okay fine." I hiss, feeling rushed. I hate feeling like that. Somewhere hidden deep inside I still feel that high school girl, with "Bird Legs" typewritten under my name in the school yearbook.

Heart of Gold

2

I met Phillip, my boyfriend, a few short months ago through my younger sister. They were friends and she knew him to be a rather large income-producing man, so when she introduced us I was modestly apprehensive. After we discussed some decisions I had made in the past, and the challenges that stemmed up because of the decisions, he summed up effectively that I had created a huge mess of myself. He said it was because no one really took the time to teach me how to take care of myself. With his support my concern yielded and gave way to a new kind of courage. It was promise of hope that Phillip would undertake the enormous responsibility of caring for me by teaching how to become independent of everyone. In return, I would assist him in obtaining recording studio equipment for his song-writing career. I eagerly accepted.

"Take mental notes." He always said. So I did. I was taught the importance of studying how men respond to me. Little did they know how the details of their body language, eye contact and even tone of voice left unwritten clues? They tell me too much without even saying a word. He also taught me to fine tune my skills in order to motivate them by enchantment. Phillip often demanded that it mattered not what I thought about the men's lustful proclamations of love, which they boldly professed while leering into my eyes, but that they could look at me and tell both lies and truth. He warned me that no man in the clubs would want the real me. I've never known any man to want the real me, and frankly I have no idea who the real me was, so I believe him.

I was told that if I want to take control of the income I produced, I have to be the best. I need to be the one in demand

Rebecca Nietert

with the men I meet. I have to survive, but if I'm honest with myself, the truth is I want pretty things I have seen such as a fancy car and fancy clothes. I want the luxurious lifestyle I imagine the wealthy men have.

Most of all, I want to be able to drop a hundred bucks at the drop of a hat and not feel guilty for doing so. I want to know what it's like to feel secure in the ability to produce income that I won't have to worry about the fact that all over America people are truly poor. In a crumbling economy, how much money does one have to have to allow for the ability to waste cash on intangible objects? Part of me wants to believe that the end results would justify the means.

I truly believe that being with Phillip, who will one day become the songwriter he hopes for, will allow for all my efforts to finally be noticed. The other part of me hopes my prince charming is right around the corner, coming to rescue me. Do I want that to be Phillip? Yes. I want a man like Phillip to give me the promise of a life filled with the new things that I witness men possess.

I hear a distant voice say "Look!" I look to see Lana pointing to a table as her voice steadily grows clearer, snapping me out of my reverie. I need to stop thinking so much. "Toni has been looming over the table, about to strike, for almost half an hour. When she gets there, our level of performance has to raise a bar if you know what I mean? Nothing has been happening in here except at the table."

Toni is one of those girls who pose for big trade magazines in order to get more money for their table dances. She made it to Playmate of the Year status for Penthouse Magazine. In my opinion, she is way too pretty to be letting herself get sucked into that type of permanent labeling.

I take hold of Lana's hand defiantly. "Don't worry about it. Let's go on over." As we approach the table, the men look up at us. I scan the circle of men, reading their expressions very carefully, Lana whispers, "They can be loud, but they still seem nice."

Heart of Gold

I just smile and nod. "Would you boys like some company?" Their response was of course, typically encouraging, saying the least.

"What's your name, Lil' Lady?" One man spoke with a soft southern drawl from across the table. I look in his direction and size him up instantly. He's wearing a uniform from some branch of military. He announces, "I'm Joe." It's a shame I've already learned soldiers don't make much money.

One of the men next to him shouted, "You would really like that one wouldn't you Joe?!" I could tell they were talking about Lana, because like Big Joe, she is also tall.

"Whew!" I whisper as I watch Lana walk over to Joe and proceed to sit in his lap. I look at her, mouth softly when she caught my wide-eyed expression, "Big mistake," and tilt my head to the right. Her eyes follow my suggestion, and she slowly slid onto the lap of the gentleman next to Joe. She leaned in to whisper in the man's ear and I can barely hear him say "Donald."

Although shouting is prohibited, another man whistles at Lana and begins to raise his voice a few notches above the crowd. The other men at the table keep their attention on him, awaiting his next move. He looks at me and grows quiet for a moment, then smiles. I politely smile back. I guess they are waiting for his approval, and he's waiting for mine. Typical man. I gather up my courage and boldly sit on his lap. Where the hell is my drink?!

Mack's is a high-class membership club in the most affluent part of Houston. The owners believe their establishment is a high-class joint. It's not the kind of place where a man can act like an idiot. I'm a little surprised that these men are still here. There's generally no shouting or hooting at the girls, and those who choose to do so are promptly escorted out. They must have greased a few palms.

The man put his hand on my thigh. "What's your name?"

"Brooke." I answer.

"Brooke what?"

Rebecca Nietert

"Brooke White."

"Brooke, have you danced long?"

"No. Before last month I didn't know I could have this much fun." I lied.

"Only a month?"

I look directly at him. "Yeah, you got a problem with new girls?"

"Well, it is just that new girls don't really know how to dance yet."

"Try me." I respond as I catch the attention of a waitress passing by. "My drink please?"

"Okay I'll do that." He announced as the waitress scurries off. "But wait until a new song comes on. If I am paying twenty bucks, I want my money's worth."

I try not to glare at him. Men can be so rude.

We usually receive a standard twenty dollars for table dances. I watch Lana as she stands up and proceeds to dance between Donald's legs, as he remains seated. Even though I know that the dances should comply with Texas Alcoholic and Beverage Commission rules (the State Regulatory Commission), it doesn't mean they always do. The dancer is to be no closer than three feet to the customer. Like that actually happens. We break that rule every minute of the day! The only time we pay attention to it is when the owner, Doyle, comes in announcing TABC is in the house. That's when things get annoying. We are supposed to set the amount we wish to be tipped and usually state it before a dance. It's more common, however, for men to assume that everyone gets twenty bucks. If the customer doesn't want to pay more, then we can just leave. The best part is when a man decides to make a big deal about it, since he will be promptly escorted out and never allowed back.

We also get tipped for dancing on stage. A performance for each dancer is limited to three times per evening. Stage performances are in full costume and curtains are drawn on the first

Heart of Gold

song so that the dancers can shock the audience with their attire. Men love the element of atmosphere it provides, much like a stage show. Of course, we have to know how to dance too, specifically Burlesque-type dances. There are strict rules to follow. No sitting on the stage; no bending over, and absolutely no showing of a girl's secrets. The stage presence must be choreographed. Also, on the second song, a strip tease must be provided, allowing for the removal of all clothing except pasties on the breasts and a 2-inch wide minimum G-string. Some good news is that we get to pick our own music and become known for our individual acts.

When I began dancing I danced to Prince. I don't dance on stage though, simply because it's easier to pay managers each evening to skip it. I don't think I could ever get used to stripping on stage. Managers receive a nightly commission of all the money earned by each dancer. The standard rate is around twenty-percent, but I routinely tip above that to get my way. It's a win-win situation. It keeps them happy and it keeps me happy. Besides, singles, fives, and tens that men tip the stage dancers is too little money for that much work.

Talking at tables and dancing half naked in front of one man is a whole lot easier for this modest girl, especially with a little intoxication. I can feel myself growing steadily more impatient. Where is that waitress? After some idle conversation and limited introductions around the table, I learn Mr. LaDon is the name of the man on whose lap I'm sitting. I look over at Lana. Poor baby. The other men are keeping her busy, that's for sure. She's a hard worker and deserves every darn twenty bucks that comes her way. Like me, dancing doesn't come easy for her. She's not shy, but she does believe the good in people. It's a promise of hope she holds on to, despite what the men she met show her. I love that about her. I try hard to teach her how to manipulate as Phillip taught me, but she's just really down to earth, feet planted firmly on the ground. I often wish I can have that undeniable hope she has.

Rebecca Nietert

Maybe one day. A new song begins and I stand to dance without my cocktail.

Mr. LaDon looks up at me and whispers, "You're so tall, Brooke."

"Yes" I say, but nothing more. I am almost six-feet-tall in heels.

"Your skin and your hair look so soft. You're so elegant!" He starts panting as the words come out. "Your eyes are so blue. Your hair is so long. Goodness Brooke, you look like you're just not real!"

I don't respond. I can feel my heart pounding in my chest and think I just might to die of embarrassment. No matter how hard I try to hide my shyness or to appear confident, my disadvantage at times will seep through the cracks of my strategically placed outer shell. My modesty is not an act, it's a huge part of me. It shows my vulnerability, which makes me incredibly uneasy.

I can feel Mr. LaDon becoming restless as he tries to push me against him. I can tell he wants me to touch him.

"Touching is against the rules, Mr. LaDon. Would you have a new girl fired?" I say coyly, surprising him.

He thinks for a moment, then answers honestly. "No."

After the last song finished, I put my lips against his ear. "I told you I could take your money." I whisper, reaching out my hand to receive the money.

"How many dances was that?" He asked.

"A few in a row. Give me what you think is fair."

He takes a wad of cash out of his pocket and hands me two hundred dollars.

"Thank you. I'll be back after I take a short break." I close my fist tightly around the money.

"Please come back?" He asked.

I smile and nod in affirmation, though I know I'm not going back. I walk down the plush carpet path that gives entry into an enormous dressing room. The dressing room is almost as nice as the rest of the bar. Glamorous lit-up makeup stations line one side

Heart of Gold

of the room's long wall. Each station is cluttered with various hues of blues, greens and browns in makeup pods. Shades of red splashed with touches of gold shimmer on sticks help keep the illusion each woman wishes to create for her own character on stage. Rows of lockers stretch along the other wall, each one large enough to fit a gym bag. Inside the lockers are many costumes, each one custom-designed for the evening charade.

    I remain in the dressing room, hiding for about an hour. I'm tired. Tired of what exactly, I do not know.

    I jump as Lana lunges through the door, squealing and laughing.

    "How do you do that? I saw what he gave you! I just now made as much as you did from one man." How can she be so inspired by such a small amount of money? All I can think is how the endless dancing and constant compliments make me so tired. A month ago I would have been so happy having that much money, but tonight night I can't shake the feeling that I have made a terrible decision to begin dancing. Yes, I need to eat, but this money just seems so…dirty and cheap.

    "Here's your drink from the waitress." She hands me the glass, which I take a swing from all too eagerly. "Now that I've caught up with you again, I need your help."

    "Sweetie, go on without me this time. I'm waiting for a regular to come in." It's a lie, but I don't have the heart to tell her otherwise.

    "Oh great! Once again you are going to beat me aren't you?" I could feel the excitement mixed with competitive frustration.

    "No. I have what I needed to make. Go ahead. I will catch up with you later."

    After she turns and talks out the door, I follow her down the corridor just far enough to see the whole bar. Exhausted, I learn against a wall and watch Lana walk back to the table we were at earlier. I take another sip of my drink. Sometimes it's more fun to watch the show than be the show.

Rebecca Nietert

The manager, Mark, walks up behind me and begins to rub my shoulders. I'm thankful he's become a good friend of mine.

"Rough night?" He asks softly.

"No, it is not that. I don't really know why, but I am in a rather odd mood."

He began to whisper something in my ear, Toni appears and starts dancing up to him. She flips up her skirt at the same time Mark whispers in my ear, so I couldn't hear what he had to say.

She inched closer to him. He whispers something to her. Even though I can't hear what was said, I know it's sexual by the way be looks back at me as Toni leads him away. I guess it's time for her nightly disciplinary action, which usually involves him calling her his bad girl.

Out of the corner of my eye I spot Mr. LaDon walking towards me. I pretend not to notice as I walk briskly toward the back of the club. I have to get out of his sight. I can't give him any more tonight than I already have. Men can be so demanding. And draining. I need to escape. As I stand by the back door, I notice the door is slightly cracked. I inhale the coolness of the night air laced with smoke. Smoke? I peer through the crack and spot Wilma, another dancer, smoking a cigarette. I call her Wilma because she looks exactly like Wilma Flintstone. She notices me and opens the door. I smile and stand next to her as she lets men in and out of the club. She has the smallest waistline I've ever seen and the most fake boobs that project from a set of shoulders boxers would die for. She has hourglass hips, skinny legs, but what really solidifies her Flintstone reputation is the bright red hair in a bun, along with a huge pearl, white necklace she wears every night. It's rumored in the club that she runs a prostitution ring for the owner. Even though we've talked a great deal, almost to the point of friendship, she's never conveyed to me her extracurricular activities. I don't ask either. A girl like me doesn't draw that kind of attention to herself. I need to be under the radar. I've learned at a much earlier age that if

Heart of Gold

people want to jump out and be froggy, well let them. They're the ones who will always end up paying the price and paving the way.

I scan the room, watching the entertainment, I notice a guy at the bar, attentively watching me. He appears to be in his seventies with gray hair and light-colored eyes to offset his tussled grey suit. I pay him no real attention until he moves to a nearby table and Mark approaches him. The guy gets a little heated as they talk, then hands Mark a bill, who lifts it up to the light and smiles.

"Good!" Mark mouthed before he walks away. It isn't long before Toni walks to the older guy's table with a few girls in tow. Throughout the next few hours, as I slowly make my way between the backdoor and the bar, I spot several instances where girls had approached and left the older gentleman's table. Each time he handed them hundred-dollar bills. As I continue watching the activity Lana walks up to me, panting something about someone tossing around hundred-dollar bills. Someone's popular tonight. "Do you know who he is?" I nod and gesture toward the older gentleman.

"You're going over there, right?" Lana looks at the table eagerly.

"No." I realize my voice come out dull and flat. She looks at me, confusion written all over her face, then shrugs and walks off to join the table. I've already earned enough and I'm not interested in begging for hundreds.

What I am interested in however, is another drink. I need to loosen up. I try to squirm through the multitude of bodies but the bar area is jam-packed. Do I really have to go around this crowd? As I pass the gentleman's table, I hear Lana say "She has the best body in the club! If you have any sense you'd get to know her." I cringe and try to blend in with the crowd. I can tell he notices me when he asks, "Who is the wild spirit that will never be tamed?" Lana laughs and grabs my arm, pulling me in.

"This guy says he knows you." She smiles but her tone was borderline mocking.

Rebecca Nietert

"Really, I don't believe that I know him." I mimic Lana's tone as I turn to face the gentleman. They both smile and I seize the opportunity to study the gentleman up close.

"You're not from Houston are you?"

"No, just driving through, looking-" He stopped mid-sentence, clearing his throat.

"Looking for one of these girls?" I gesture around the table at the surrounding girls.

"Well...yes" came the slow reply.

"I'm sure you're very nice, but I don't like egocentric men who do this sort of thing much." I don't care if I sound self-righteous; it's easier to be that way.

I start to walk away when he shouts sarcastically, "We have a saint, Girls!" The others laugh.

I do not like being provoked. If he wants me to just sit with him, then fine! This is a game and I know it. I've played it many times. The man has to know I'm not easy like the other girls. I have to build my worth. I'm a good girl I tell myself. "Tell them to go, and I will sit down." I demand as I wave the other girls off. Of course they are instantly outraged, but I don't care. I sit down as the gentleman waves them off.

"Why me?" No sense in skirting around the issue. It's better to get to the point anyway. The sooner this is over with, the better. I find this game nauseating.

"You did not come over!" He victoriously whispered, smiling.

"I'm not easy or cheap. I can live without your money." I slam my hands on the table and stand up.

What a waste of time!

"That is what I noticed about you Blondie." He cajoled. "Please tell me your name?"

This is too exhausting. I give up. "Brooke." I consider the chair I just vacated, not wanting to admit that there is something about this man which plagues my curiosity. How can he toss away money so frivolously? More importantly, how can I get some?

25

Heart of Gold

"Brooke, do you have a last name?" He inquired.

"Why is it that you all know we create these fake names, and yet still ask me for my first and last name?" I can feel my impatience getting the best of me, so I take a deep breath and slowly exhale. Calm down, this will be over soon. "You cannot have the last name, Sir."

"You seem to watch and analyze people." How observant.

"Yeah, so?" I sit down, feeling irritated he's not moving this along quicker.

"I want you to watch me with a few of those gals." He points into the crowd. The very thought of his answer was more than sickening. I want to get up, leave, and never come back, but something inside makes me stay.

"Just watch them dance for me." He looks into my eyes, voice barely a whisper. I don't know why I'm wasting time on such outrageous requests. After all he hasn't promised me any cash to sit and stare. I don't care what he thinks. I am not his girlfriend. It's about the money.

"Do you know any girls that would go out with me?"

"No Sir, I don't. But there's a gal named Wilma who might be able to help you out. My friends and I don't do that sort of thing for money."

"Really?" His eyes widen as he leans forward. "You're a Saint and a leader? It seems I scored big."

"Believe me, you've scored nothing!" I snap. I can feel the tension between us, and it makes me need to get away from him even stronger. "What do you want with me?" Why am I still sitting here? This doesn't make any sense!

"Here is what I propose–" He starts to say. Immediately, I raise my hand in objection, and look away.

"Wait, before you go on, I'm not cheap. It doesn't work that way for me." I look at him and continue. "I watched you tonight. You really like these girls all over you. You know they don't care anything about you; they only care about your money.

Rebecca Nietert

Why do you do it?" Why do you care, Bev? He's just like the rest of them!

"Because I have the money, Babe. Besides look at me!" He gestures to himself. 'What woman would want me without the money?"

I can't tamper the wave of empathy that washes over me for his lack of confidence. I remember spending my childhood as a wallflower, waiting desperately for puberty to hit. I don't know if it's the empathy or my curiosity that got the best of me, but I can't help it. I have to ask. "How much are you willing to pay?"

"I am willing to pay you and them five hundred dollars each. Does that change your mind?"

"Not in the least." Even though it's a good chunk of change, I won't miss it; simply because I can't imagine how a woman can be bought for her most prized possession, the most intimate part of her. That was one part of me that I only shared with those I cared for.

"You give me what I need, and I will give you what you need." He tried again.

"I don't need your money!" I spit back, this time enraged.

"That's a shame."

A few more girls came up to the table after hearing the rumors. He offered the cash to them for services after the doors closed, and they eagerly accepted. After they leave, he leans over to me, whispering, "When do I get you in bed with me?"

"I'm sorry Sir, but that will be never." As I stand to leave, he grabs my hand and places a wad of hundred dollar bills in it. I don't fight him or give it back. He looks into my eyes, gaze intense. "There's more where that came from if you change your mind." He lets his hand slip from mine.

As I walk away, I can't help but look at the cash he had given me, then back at him. He's still intently watching for my next move. I grip the hundreds tight in my hand and walk to the dressing room,

Heart of Gold

hoping no emotion is showing on my face. I count the money as I reach the dressing room. He had given me seven hundred dollars.

Somehow that money felt different than the dancing money I earned. Deep in my gut it felt wrong, but the wad of cash felt good. Having that disposable cash is what I want.

I'm contemplative on the drive home. I can't help but think about how hard it is for me to put aside my modesty, when other girls can do so easily. Why is it so hard for me to accept cash given to me by a stranger, in hopes he would change my mind? The reality that there are men all around me with so much money that they could just give it to women for nothing, astounds me. I want to be on the other side of that fence. I want to live like the customers so badly I can taste it.

I never really wanted to be a dancer, and if I could figure out how not to dance I would. The moment he handed me that cash I knew that I wanted more than just dancing for $20.00 table dances. I have no idea how or what could make that happen, but I have to try.

Rebecca Nietert

3

The next morning I was partly asleep and partly awake when Marilyn Monroe brought me my morning coffee. When my eyelids lift slightly, I can see her a little more clearly. That's right; not Marilyn. It's Donna, I remind myself. That's Donna's perfume. I sniff at the light complex blend of spicy musk fragrance that gently makes way into my nostrils. I look up at her bottle-blonde Marilyn Monroe hair, and am once again amazed at how effortlessly she pulls off her desired look-a-like.

"How was your evening, Darling?" She softly whispers, handing me my morning coffee. I can't help but be jealous at what a handsome woman Donna is. She has beautiful green eyes, her brows are perfectly formed and the way she wears her makeup is flawless. She's small-breasted, shorter than I, yet has very full hips to emphasize her small waist. I'm envious of her, since my appearance is hard to keep trim.

I met Donna as Phillip's live-in girlfriend, a fact he revealed to me after we started dating. They were together long before I came into the picture and I often wonder how they came to be together. She respects Phillip, but takes care of him much like a mother would take care of a young boy. They love each other in a very different way than the other couples I had known. I have never known anybody who loved like them and I honestly feel lucky to be included. To me, love didn't really exist before I knew them. Most of what I know about relationships is from extremely selfish and emotionally immature people.

Only after my family rejected my plea for help did the three of us become roommates. When I arrived, I had just been rejected by a man that I probably should've never been with. The relationship turned bad when I became pregnant, resulting in the abortion of the

Heart of Gold

child along with my dignity. All because the doctors told me it wasn't a fetus. The recovery took quite a toll on my young body, leaving me exhausted and unable to work. Before long, I was on my own and starving. I reached out to my family who'd recently moved into the Houston area, but they would not help me. Feeling abandoned, I reached out to Phillip for help. He introduced me to Donna and we've been roommates ever since.

Our friendship is instantaneous. I love Donna. She's kind, decent and her honesty is innately transparent. She's also sensitive and very in tune with her emotions.

Donna and Phillip are similar in nature, but they approach situations in opposite ways. Phillip isn't as emotionally driven as Donna is and can be quite aloof. Like Donna, he is exquisite to look at, but there's an air of arrogance about him. His lean body is rippled with muscles. His skin is a dark golden brown and he has strong arms and long legs. His waist has never been larger than a size twenty-eight. His v-shaped back complements any silk lined shirt he chooses to wear. His skin was a dark golden brown. His hair was jet black. His magnificently white teeth were perfectly aligned. His high cheekbones accentuated his large, dark eyes. He's more than an attractive man; he's stunning. People will stop talking as he walks by.

Smelling the strong earthy roasted coffee, my brain fog begins to clear and memories of last night push their way through for my attention.

"Thank you for this coffee." I accept the cup. "It's just what I need."

I softly blow against the steaming brew, tilt the cup to my lips and carefully sip. I have an idea, but I'm afraid I will be criticized. I have to speak to both of them at the same time.

Biting the bullet of confrontation I decide it's now or never. "Where's Phillip?"

"In the kitchen, why do you ask?" Donna a raises an eyebrow, concerned with my quiet tone.

Rebecca Nietert

"I have something to tell the both of you." She reaches out her manicured hand for mine, sensing my nervousness. I take a deep breath and gratefully grasp it as we walk together into the kitchen, hand-in-hand. Our home is a two-bedroom flat, just on the outskirts of River Oaks, a prestigious neighborhood on the east side near Montrose. Phillip and Donna share a room while I have one of my own. Our community consists of several millionaires who frequent Mack's. The movie Terms of Endearment was filmed in one of the million-dollar homes.

"Good morning!" Phillip blurted in his deep masculine voice. "Been a long night hasn't it?" It was. I can feel the warmth of the sunshine shinning in our kitchen as I think about what I need to say. I have to phrase this very carefully.

Remembering last night, I know I need Phillip now more than ever. There are rules to our threesome though: the money is shared by all three of us, no other men are allowed, and any change has to be agreed by all participants.

It was his idea for me to dance. He figured while I was young, to turn me into someone who is good looking and can score big enough to pull in megabucks. The money is great and the little daytime I have to myself is even better, but I can't shake the feeling that I hate to shed my clothes. I often feel like my work is torture. I desperately want to make enough money for us, and to not have trade skin for cash to do it.

Phillip taught me everything I know about dancing and manipulating men. Donna helped him teach me about what men expected in the club. I'm convinced that without Phillip I would be nothing. He's the reason I make money. Sure I struggle some nights more than others with the humility of dancing, those nights my conscience overrides the greed. But in order to stay here, my income needs to stay consistent, no matter what. I can't come home empty-handed, or I'll lose them. Then where would I go?

I can feel my throat going dry and swallow hard. I need to tell him. I can feel the emotion written on my face like a banner on my

Heart of Gold

forehead. Unfortunately, I've never been able to hide my feelings from the people I truly care for.

Phillip barely glances in my direction, sensing my uneasiness. "What's wrong, Beverly?"

"Something happened last night." I manage to answer in a low voice.

He turns away from cooking breakfast to face me, frowning. "What?"

I can see the anger quickly building as the darkness of his black pupils start to dilate through his calm exterior. Uh-oh. I know that reaction all too well. He always gets like this when I do something against what we talk about. Rules…the rules. I have to remember them. I'm not trying to panic; I just need him to understand how I feel about dancing, even though I've said so many times before.

It feels like every time he calms my nerves it sets me back on a path of his choosing. Well, not this time. Hopefully. Why am I so afraid to tell him? Is it because I need to feel accepted and not criticized, or worse, rejected? I can't help but hesitate, looking at Phillip for a while. "I found a new way to make money." I feel the words rush out of my mouth before I could stop them. I can't believe I'm actually telling him!

"How?" His eyes narrow with suspicion.

"Being a madam." Again, the words were out before I can stop them. What did I just get myself in to?

"A madam!" He shouts. I flinch, bearing the weight of his wrath. "What? Are you nuts?!"

I can't back down now. I have to try! "No! Hear me out, Phillip!" I tell him about the customer last night, hoping to change his mind.

"Tell me you did not have sex." His voice was cautiously flat, eyes wide, signaling me to be careful.

"No! You know I would never do that." How can he think such a thing? There are rules!

Rebecca Nietert

"Okay." I can feel his anger fading, replaced with a curiosity. "Are you telling me that girls would work for you? Do you know clients who would pay that kind of money?"

I tell him and Donna about the events at the table regarding the older gentleman last night, but finish with a lie. "He's coming back into town again."

"He's going to call you when he comes to town?" By now he is incredulous, but also very fascinated. "You're going to arrange everything?"

"I think that's his plan." I respond boldly, then quickly catch myself. "Yes, I will!" I can literally see Phillips brain ka'ching with dollar signs in his eyes. That was close. I stifle a small smile. This just might work.

"Do you have his number?"

"Yes." I lied, looking away for a split second. I need to get better at this whole lying thing!

Thank goodness he doesn't seem to notice.

"Do you think other clients will pay you too? Can you really make a business out of it?" With each question, Phillip's voice registered another notch in decibel. My, he is excited! This worked out better than I'd hoped!

I can feel a new sense of adrenaline rush through my veins. I've got to think fast! "I'm smart enough to figure it out, Phillip." Wrong move. I soften my voice. "You know I despise taking my clothes off for these guys. I will not have to take them off anymore." That's more appealing to me. I anxiously wait for him to respond as he remains silent, thinking. If I'm honest, the main reason I want him to agree to this is so I can have more control over what I do and how much I can make. "It would benefit the girls as well. I could make sure the ones who want to do this, get top dollar." Two smiles shoot my way and I am about to burst with excitement.

To my surprise, Donna blurts out, "I would work for her too, Phillip!" Really? I can't help but smile. She has a wild side to her that she only allows Phillip access. I know about it because she

Heart of Gold

discusses her sex life with Phillip openly with me. She's the type to try everything and has very few inhibitions. She's a free spirit, and I admire that about her. If I can be a little more like that, I can make a whole lot more money than I do now. When Donna dances, she often finds it difficult to 'get in character' while on the floor. Her honesty and transparency are the two qualities that don't mesh well in a club environment. Because of that, she's often disillusioned in men's reactions. I can relate, since that idea is as great of a solution to her as it is to me.

Phillip is obviously as shocked as I am by her declaration. We both turn our heads abruptly to look at her. "Is that what you want to do?" Phillip's voice echoed a deep rumble.

"Yes!" Came the high-pitched squeal. "I can be one of her best girls who will receive the highest price! Who doesn't want to sleep with Marilyn?" Phillip and I look at each other wide-eyed, shocked into silence. His brows are as lifted as mine must be as we connect understandably with our glances. Breakfast was eaten in silence. Each one of us carefully considering what this could mean to our future. After we finish and stack our plates in the sink, I finally brake the silence. "I will check it out when I get to work tonight."

"Okay, Beverly. But, be careful! If Doyle finds out he will have your head on a silver platter!" Phillip warned, his voice deep and serious, reminding me of last night. Oh, what a night that was.

"I know. I will be." I flippantly answer as I head to my room. Now I need to purchase some new dancing clothes. Thinking Donna and Phillip can use some time alone to talk, I spend some time alone in my room getting ready for the day. I like that Donna never convicts me for the sins of my past. She doesn't judge me for getting pregnant and being unmarried. She accepts me with all my faults and she helps to turn me from an enraged individual into a calmer hopeful person. I had discussed many topics about life in the timespan of being transformed from skinny and awkward to what I see in the mirror every day, bold and beautiful. I feel like Donna honestly gets me, sometimes more than Phillip.

Rebecca Nietert

When I left I walked around the pool area, through a corridor to the parking garage, I notice Donna leaning against the wall next to the car.

"Hello Donna, what's up?" She raises her head, startled, staring at me for a moment. "You are going to steal my boyfriend and take everything I have away, aren't you?" I can feel the slap of her accusatory words. What's gotten into her?

"No, Donna. You know I would never do that!" Surprised and hurt, I try to eliminate her despair. "I love both of you and wouldn't hurt either of you for the world!"

"Well, you may not mean to." Her voice sounding apologetic, then quickly filled with jealousy. "But you're different! You're good at what you do. I can't pull off this dance thing and you know how he is about money. He wants that recording studio so badly he can taste it. I can't give it to him yet you can." She started to cry.

Embarrassed, I step forward to comfort her but she pushes me away softly. What if Donna saw the shocked looks on our faces and felt rejected? I just want to hold her, tell her I love her, and fix what's broken. I honestly had no idea that Donna would want to have sex with men for money. Did I just open the door for her to be able to do it without feelings of remorse? Had she been wondering how to capitalize on obtaining income from being an escort all along? If that's the case, she is right. I opened the door to something much more than any of us expected.

"I'm sorr-" I start to say but am interrupted by soft sputters of sadness, "I have to go." She hurries off, leaving me to stand there, watching her walk away. What just happened?

I understand that my heartache, born out of a life filled with the fury from selfish people, isn't something I can just easily convey to someone who has never had to endure more than a common sorrow. When one's acutely aware of human suffering it's hard to be amiable to those who are blind to it. I really haven't given any thought whatsoever to how my actions could hurt anyone else.

Heart of Gold

I've been so wrapped up in trying to survive that I haven't taken the time to consider the relationships I'm in. My friends have feelings and emotions I'm not prepared to deal with. If Donna is just helping me because she knows how uncomfortable it is for me to take my clothes off, then I don't need her to make that sacrifice for me. Even though the thought of her being hurt by my ability to do something better than her makes me feel guilty, part of me feels solidified to move forward, despite how she feels.

Oddly, I miss the days of my youth when things seemed hopeful.

I remind myself that I really have no time for insecurity and self-doubt. I need to remain clear on my purpose; because without it, I'm sure they'll put me in a white straight jacket, because I will actually lose it. I'm not sure how easily broken I could become but I am quite aware of how shattered my life has become.

Rebecca Nietert

4

I can't help but feel ominous after my talk with Donna. Her words reverberate over and over in my mind. I can't concentrate on anything! They echo all day and into the night. I see her crying as she walks away in my mind's eye and can't help but feel guilty. Like I could have done more. I shake my head. It doesn't matter; I have to pull it together. Money is the only thing that will save us now. I slide in the car and drive to work. I'm already late!

As I walk in the club, I make a beeline for the bar. I can feel the Crown cocktail beckon me. I need it, badly. After grabbing my drink, I head down the corridor to the dressing room. There, I transform into my nightly necessity. I slip into a dress that has a slit clean up my hip, put on expensive necklaces, slide my feet into heels too high for my liking, and finish the look with so much mascara it could pick up a stiff wand. The transformation takes maybe 10 minutes tops, but it feels like an hour by the time I'm done.

I look in the mirror and can't even recognize myself, just like the first time I started dancing. Why do I feel so pathetic? I'm still the same small-town Bev…. Right? I study myself for a moment, feeling like a cheap fake. I hate this! I can feel the despair creep slowly in my utmost being, but I tamper it out. No! This isn't a mistake. It's just a way to make a lot of money in a short amount of time.

Once Phillip gets his studio all set up, I'm done. Even though each night is harder than the one before, I can't help but wonder how I'm going to talk to men about their lustful desires. I can feel the tears start to form in my blue eyes. No! You have to go through

Heart of Gold

with this! Get out there and own it! I can feel the shift in mood from embarrassment to impatience.

I reach for my courage and gulped the remains of my glass. I'm going to become a madam and nothing will stop me. I look up to see Lana's reflection in the mirror, standing behind me. I can read the concern written on her face.

"Someone has been trying to reach you on the house phone all night." She sounds as concerned as she looks.

"Do you know who?" I question in a false bravado, not bothering to turn around. It's probably one of those impatient men wanting their nightly fix. I almost laugh. As if they're going to get me like that!

"No, but they are really anxious to talk to you."

"Huh." I remark dismissively. "Hope it is not a customer. I'm not that easy."

"I don't think so." She pensively replies. This isn't the Lana I know. I look up with one eyebrow raised as our eyes meet in the reflection.

"I think it is someone from your family. After Mark got off the phone, he was really sad. That's why I thought you would want to know right away."

"Duly noted, thank you." I know I overcompensate for my indifference to Lana, I can hear my voice sound dismissing, but I have to regain some sense of composure. Hearing about potential news from my family somehow managed to boost my gumption to the level I need to work. I wonder what they want from me, the outcast. Probably money. I can still feel the scars from their abandonment.

Sometimes I can't sleep at night, the anger and denial creeps into my soul when no one's around. I can't let that happen here. I will myself to stay numb, to feel nothing, but the anger starts to creep through my facade. Where my family is concerned, I somehow don't possess that power. It's like all of the energy is sapped out of me.

Rebecca Nietert

I could care less that Mark is troubled. What really irks me is that my family, for some reason, wants to contact me. They have the nerve to call me after everything they've done! Ignoring the small voice whispering that it may be something important, I check my Barbie makeup, Bon Jovi inspired hairdo, and walk out the room.

My family's judgment and contempt for what I chose to do for a living not only increases a growing shame, but it also reminds me of their rejection. Denial is something I've cultivated my entire life. Their hostility is the last thing I need tonight. I proceed to leave the sanctuary of the dressing room and head into the lion's den of the club.

I take a deep calming breath and place my show face on. It's game time. I walk out the door and into the grand room. I talk with every man I can find, trying to match names with numbers and faces. I just need to find the name and number of a certain first-rate gentleman who wants girls after hours. I have to find him, but also have to be cautious. I can't get caught the first night I'm out sightseeing, trying to figure out how to profit off other dancers. I pause for a moment, gathering my surroundings. Is my choice to become a madam right? I shake my head. Of course it is!

I'm honestly shocked at the ease of finding men who are eagerly willing to pay a small fortune for a girl of their choice. In the same way, I've found communicating my plan to be an effortless adventure to some of the girls who regularly offer themselves to men. It's as simple as offering candy to the ladies.

I see Mark approaching as I'm about to move around the room again. I feel my heart land in my stomach and brace myself for what could be my last night. Does he know what I'm doing?

"Got a minute?" How did he figure it out so fast?! Wait, hmmm. He looks a little worried. Not quite like a man who's about to fire someone.

"Yes." I can feel my breath trapped in my lungs. I have to be cautious. "Everything okay?"

Heart of Gold

"Not exactly." He said uneasily. Great, just what I need.

"Someone has been trying all night to reach you and they just called again." He watches me closely, gauging my reaction.

Two can play this game. "They say what they want?" Why are they so freaking persistent?! Can't they just leave me alone? It shouldn't be that hard after all of these years!

I can feel the restlessness starting to kick in as I see valuable potential customers start to leave, some I hadn't even approached yet. I can feel the money slipping through my fingers. I have to end this conversation as quickly as possible.

"No, but it sounded urgent." Mark squinted, noting my impatience.

"They leave a number?" I ask. My tone disconnected. It's taking everything in me to keep my foot from tapping. Really?! The men are leaving! Can't he tell me this later? I take a deep breath. Breathe. Just breathe.

"Yeah." He paused for a second. "It's a Herman Hospital number," then lowered his head. Utter silence halted my thoughts. I feel as if the wind was knocked out of me, frozen in time. Then all hell breaks loose.

"You're just now telling me this?" I snap. "What is wrong with you?" Whatever I didn't want to hear Lana tell me now rang loud and clear. I feel nauseous. I've got to find out what happened! I snatch the piece of paper from his grasp and race to the dressing room. I open the paper, scan the information written, and then run to the pay phone on the wall in the locker room. My hands are shaking as I stumble to dial the number to Herman Hospital. A lady answers in a proficient manner, "Intensive Care Unit."

"Room 350 please?" It was written on the note. I beg, reading the information on the note as my heart races. I'm sure the lady on the other end can hear it too. She puts the call through to the room. LaNette, my sister, answers the phone.

"Hello." She sounds like she's been crying. I hear an alarm ringing in my ears; I seldom hear her cry.

Rebecca Nietert

"Hello, its Bev. I finally got the message you called. What's up?" I can't hide the worry in my voice.

"It's Shirley!" LaNette started to cry again.

"LaNette, she's going to be okay. She always is." I can feel my head start to spin. I have to be strong!

"No, Beverly. She's not." I'm surprised at the impatient tone she's using with me. If everything isn't okay why didn't they contact me sooner?!

"We could not get a hold of you all night at that strip club!" She shouts disapprovingly.

"I'm sorry! I was busy okay!" I shout back defensively, wincing. "What happened? How bad is it?" I can't allow myself to hear that Shirley might not be okay. I refuse to believe it.

"Shirley and this guy, Gemini, have been dating." LaNette began. "He's a dancer too. You might know him." The contempt and spite in her voice echo what I feel inside. I can feel the bile rising up my throat. What the heck was she doing with someone from this kind of scene?! She doesn't deserve that!

She somehow managed to calm herself and continues a calmer tone, "They were in his truck, racing, when they hit some water. She wasn't wearing her seat belt so when the truck flipped over it pinned her pelvic area before rolling off. According to the boyfriend, she stood in an attempt to help him but collapsed as she did so."

Everything is spinning; I can barely hear what she's saying. "When life flight got there they pronounced her dead. The medics revived her, and now they are checking to see if there is any brain activity." I feel my knees give way as I start to sweat. I'm trying to breathe but nothing is coming out. My knees had begun to buckle while I listen, sweat starting to form on my forehead. I feel like I've been shot in the heart, left alive but unable to breathe. I feel the phone fall from my hand as my body gives way. I feel the impact of the ground, exhaling the breath I'd been holding. I can barely hear

Heart of Gold

the shuffling of feet, shrill voices growing dimmer by the second. I hear something about help before everything went black.

"Oh! My God! Get her up!" I hear a voice cry as a cold, wet object is pressed against my face. A towel? The voice continued, "Where do we need to go? Who do I need to call?"

Is that Lana's voice? I can feel the darkness creeping up on me once again. Trying to fight it, I focus on the alarmed voices. Yes, one has to be Lana. But-I never finish the thought, feeling the comforting cocoon of darkness once more.

I awaken in the backseat of a car. Gathering my surroundings, I notice Phillip and Donna looking at me. "Herman Hospital" was all I could muster. On the way there, Donna explains how Lana found Phillip's number in my locker and called him for help. She was worried because I was unresponsive and even cleaned me up by putting my regular clothes on for me. She's always so thoughtful.

By the time we arrive at the hospital I feel almost catatonic, but as soon I set foot out the car door I feel a surge of supernatural strength wash over me. I run through the entrance doors and up to the reception desk. "Where is my sister?!" I can't hide the fear and frustration in my voice.

"Someone wants to speak with you first." The nurse said, with her eyes lowered. No! I have to see her now! I can feel my brain turning to mush. I watch her dial a number and speak into the phone softly. Oh God, No!

Within a matter of seconds a man dressed as a pastor walks up and asks me to follow him. I can feel myself trembling furiously. I don't have time for this! Donna must have sensed my frustration and put her hand in mine, trying to comfort me. I can feel the fear's death grip embracing me as we walk into the room, which happens to be a hospital chapel. I immediately spot my family sitting together in the chapel pews, who look up at us, startled.

The first thing I notice is my father holding my mother's hand, something I've never witnessed before. I feel my gaze flow from their hands to my mother, who won't return my gaze, head hung heavy with grief. I see her exchange shocked glances with my father. I don't blame them; I haven't seen them since I was a small child. They shouldn't have called me if they're going to subject me to this kind of treatment! I see disappointment slowly creep across my father face. My heart feels like it's being squeezed as the familiar pain of rejection hit. LaNette walks up, her ferocity so evident that I actually feel worse, if that's even possible.

"Where the hell have you been all day?"

Her eyes are red from crying, voice full of contempt.

"Doing what I normally do, LaNette." I hear myself snap. I don't have time for petty arguments! "What did the doctor say? What happened?"

"The doctor just told us that Shirley is dead!" She snapped back, eyes aflame.

I look at her, then at my father and mother. I can't find the compassion to offer them comfort, it's not like they'd accept it anyway. They don't even accept me! Life isn't all about them, I have feelings too!

My father walked up beside us, then grabbed my arm, pulling me forcibly to the side. "Look," his tone aggressive, "Your mother needs you right now. Shirley. Is. Dead." He spit out the last part.

I can't believe this! I didn't do anything wrong! I'm here, just like everyone else and yet somehow, I'm the bad guy. Again. I jerk my arm away from him. Why am I always the one to blame? I'm sick and tired of everyone's immaturity, dumping their crap on me to make them feel better.

As if he heard my thoughts, my father hissed, "Everyone is hurting, and they don't need any crap from you!"

I blink shocked. I can't believe that after all this time he would still reject me like this! I clench my jaw. I should have known. The nerve of him to judge me! I can feel his indignation feeding my fury. I can feel the colossal distain he has of my choices as he looks at Phillip as if he's Satan and Donna and I are his pawns. It's like he

Heart of Gold

thinks we don't have a mind of our own! Oh, how little does he know?

"Don't pretend that you know me or how I feel!" I hiss back. I can't do this anymore! I should have never come back to this! What was I thinking? That maybe we'd be one happy family, reunited through my sister's death? A fool's dream!

My father runs after me as I stormed out the door, pleading. "Beverly, wait! Your mother needs you."

"I'm just trying to understand what happened!" I can feel my body trembling, but not from the cold this time. His words, his tone and the way he looks at me, infuriates me. I look him in the eye. Why do I still allow him to bother me? "Whether you believe it or not, I am doing the best I can. It's not like you're helping or like you've ever helped me." I don't have time to waste on this crap. I just need to see Shirley! I quickly turn away from him and walk back to the nurse's station in ICU.

"Can I see my sister?" I ask the sterile nurse. She nods and points to a room. I walk in and see the doctor taking one last look at Shirley. I guess he's going to be the bearer of more bad news huh? He steps out to meet me, a firm look on his face.

"Immediate family only, Miss."

"I am her older sister." I can feel the sadness echo in my words. "May I see her?"

"Yes," his voice more compassionate now. "But we are about to turn the machines off.

"The only reason we've kept her body alive this long, was for organ donation, but her mother declined. Her brain has been dead since the accident earlier today. I am so sorry."

I can tell from the look on his face that he's genuinely sorry as he slipped past me to walk quietly down the hallway, leaving me alone with my sister. With what's left of her anyway.

I nervously walk over to the hospital bed, standing over my sister. The woman in the bed before me looks absolutely nothing like the girl I remember. The innocent teen girl's expression is

Rebecca Nietert

absent, replaced by a cold shell. It feels like I'm looking at a figure in one of those wax museums. I can't help but feel shocked as I'm staring at her beaten and torn corpse. Tears start to form as I look at her once-beautiful face now bruised. This is what's left of my baby sister. I can feel my heart restricting as the tears start to flow. I don't bother to stop them. I've never felt so numb in my entire life.

No experience with men or dancing could prepare me for what I feel now. How can I feel both pain and numb simultaneously? So…detached? I can't find an answer.

No matter how much I will her to move, she just lies there, stiff as a board.

I've never experienced death in such a personal way before. It's overwhelming! Why can't I do something? I feel so helpless! I can't believe she's gone! I will never speak to her again. I can feel the tears streaming down my face. She will never tell me another stupid joke, or ask for my help again. And there's nothing I can do. I feel the reality sink in, my heartbeat slowing down. She's gone…forever!

I hear myself yelp, as if someone's slapped me. I can feel my body giving way and soon enough I'm on the ground again, curled into a ball. I gasp for air, but can't feel anything. I'm drained of air, of life. I too, feel dead.

Everything's so surreal. I remember my mother working all the time. We never really felt loved by either of our parents. We would often discuss how emotionally abandoned we felt. Our father's abandonment added to the resentment of our family, which in time, turned towards all men. For some reason, my parents loved LaNette. They always showed her favor and left me and my sister to fend for ourselves. Maybe it's because she's the oldest. The lack of attention from our parents left us to need people's affection.

Shirley needed unconditional love from men. I needed it from her. She craved their attention just like I craved hers. Her ridiculous obsession with getting love from men often left her alone and disappointed. Just like how I'm feeling now, alone and broken-hearted.

Heart of Gold

    I remember how I spent the better part of our childhood trying to save her from committing suicide. I'd watch her like a hawk, pulling knives out of her hands, rushing her to the hospital to pump out the sleeping pills. Her disappointment in the sins of others often ran rampant, causing her to have bursts of fury that she only allowed those she trusted to witness. I was one of the lucky few. I often thought she got angry because she was mad at herself, but now I think it's because she lost faith in everyone. She needed her family to bail her out so many times because of her choices. The weight of burden fell hard for the rest of us to fulfill, I understand what that feels like now.

    All Shirley wanted was to feel loved, just like I do now. After my pregnancy, she was very verbal that I should have kept the baby in my pre-dancer days. Just this past year she told me that she wanted children, that a baby was God's greatest gift to us all. She would finally have someone to live for.

    I force my trembling legs to stand, bracing against the hospital bed for support. I look down at her precious face. Is this God's way of punishing me for killing my baby? By taking my sister from me? I lean down to whisper softly in her ear, "You got your wish. I hope you're at peace." With a kiss on her cold cheek I turn away and walk out the room. I can't help but look back one more time. Goodbye. Exhaling a sigh I turn back and walk down the corridor.

    I walk back to the chapel where everyone is waiting to see Shirley. I can't contain the rage inside. I look at my mother, focusing all of my feelings onto her. It's your fault! If you hadn't treated us like you did, Shirley would still be alive! She had a miserable life, no thanks to you! As if she heard my thoughts, my mother looks up at me, and with that my words rush out like a snarl. "I cannot save her this time."

    Donna rushed to my side, taking my hand. "We don't have to stay if you don't want to. You need to grieve however you want to."

    "Thank you Donna." I look at my family as they watch me in silence. "I don't think I'm very welcome here anyway."

Rebecca Nietert

They don't say anything to refute my statement. I'm not expecting them to either. Seemingly to them there's no love-loss. I can see the condemnation and rejection in their eyes. What could I have done that was so horrible? What could I have done so badly to cause them this much hatred?

I can feel tears start to form so I turn to Donna and whisper, "Let's go."

Heart of Gold

5

Upon arriving home I walk straight to my room and collapse on the bed. Shirley's death and my family's rejection weigh heavily me. The nights events swirl into a soup of frenzy and fear. I feel I may never really get what I truly want. My past hauntingly washes through my thoughts.

I can feel my body shutting down out of pure survival. I need to feel nothing; I need the illusion of nothingness. I feel the blackness cover my vision like a veil as I drift off to sleep.

"Are you ready to see the Doctor Miss?" I hear a nurse ask. The questions ripped themselves from me, attacking with furry.

"I don't want this responsibility. I don't know if this is a boy or a girl and this thing in my stomach makes me so sick. You're sure that this isn't a baby yet? You're sure that I am not killing my child?" An overwhelming sense of confusion sweeps over me. Do I want to do this? Why am I doing this? It's because he wants it, isn't it? What am I going to do?! "No, wait! I can't do this!"

The doctor 's voice is calm as he straps me down, "It's okay Darlin', your reaction is typical."

"No, I don't want to! It's our baby, Rob!" I plead, tossing my head back and forth to find an empty chair. I can't believe it! Rob isn't here. I feel the familiar pain of abandonment all over again. That's right, he doesn't want me, much less want a baby with me. I'm not Jewish, what would he tell his mother?

My head tossed, because Rob said he didn't want a baby with me. I was confused, and then I remembered he doesn't want me. I'm not Jewish. What would he tell his mother?

"Ok, I'm ready now." I can feel my body shaking uncontrollably.

Rebecca Nietert

"Okay. You can change your mind any time up until you hear this machine turn on. I'm giving you a shot to open your cervix. It will be all over soon." His words must have been the standard disclosure because I just asked him to stop. I told him I had doubts. I don't want to do this! The room begins to spin as I start to panic. "It's okay. That's just the sedative we gave you."

"No!" I whimper, but no one seems to be listening! "I can't do this!" Shirley walks into the room, begging, "Please, Beverly, don't do this. I'll help you."

"It'll be okay Shirley. We will be fine." I whisper as I feel a shot straight into my cervix like a sting I hadn't ever known. I suddenly realize that I can't go back now, no matter what.

"Oh my God...What is happening?!" My body took over, shaking as I sob uncontrollably.

"It will all be over soon." A nurse said in the distance. The pain is excruciating! I hear the machine kick on. Then I hear one big swoop.

"That's it Lil Lady, it's all over!" I look up at the doctor as tears sting my eyes and begin streaming down my cheeks. He was smiling.

I can't believe it! "You took my baby!" They stole my baby! Mine!

"It's okay, it's okay. You wanted to abort the baby." The nurse assured me.

I was still dreaming, tossing back and forth, when I hear Donna's voice, "Wake up. Wake up, Baby." I slowly pry my eyes open, panting. I try to sit up, but fall back down. My clothes and body are drenched in sweat. Am I still dreaming? I remember Shirley waiting in the room where they took my unborn child. She would've never witnessed that procedure in a million years. She always told me that I would be murdering my baby. She was right.

"Can you close the curtains, Donna?" I can't even think. She promptly walks over to the windows and shut them, then came to lay down with me in bed. She wrapped her arms around me,

Heart of Gold

cuddling me close. I feel the warmth of her embrace and it feels nice. I curl up into her arms and feel her brush my hair from my face. She kisses me softly on the forehead while rubbing my arms gently. I love that she's doing everything she can to comfort me. I look into her eyes, seeing a reflection of sorrow. I shut my eyes. I'm not used to this kind of vulnerability! I can feel Donna's genuine sadness radiating off her skin onto mine, resonating so powerfully.

Before I know it, she kisses me on the lips, she whispers, "Let me make you feel better." Her voice is low, deep and full of sentiment. Her words hanging like a whisper after the words she spoke are already gone.

I can't respond, can't feel anything. I let her hands make their way to my breasts, unable to move. At any moment I'm certain that I will sob uncontrollably, but the tears don't come. My body isn't mine to command anymore. I feel her hands caressing me softly, her touch stirring something deep inside that I never knew existed before. I feel paralyzed emotionally, but physically I'm more alive than ever before.

"I love you dearly," She whispers as she plants slow, soft kisses right under my breasts.

I inhale sharply, feeling myself giving way, bit by bit. I've never been physically intimate with Donna before, but I've always loved her, just like she loves me. I've always been profoundly attracted to her beauty and thought she felt the same way, but after feeling that first kiss, I have no doubts about it now. I lean my head back on the pillow, willing her to take the pain away from me, even if only for a moment.

"You're so firm and strong, Bev." Her breath is hot against my stomach. I arch my back, running my hands through her hair. I say nothing as she lowers herself gracefully down my body, careful not to put any weight onto me until she settles between my legs. She places her hands on my chest, and then she slowly traces her fingers down to my stomach and around my hips. I can't breathe.

Rebecca Nietert

She leans down and kisses between my legs, her mouth warm and hot. Oh my God! I grab her hair and push myself up to her mouth even more. She begins to work her tongue with such amazing expertise. I lean my head back and can't help but moan in ecstasy. My head is spinning! She stroked so gently around the opening of my vagina, and then caressed my inner thighs. Slowly, painstakingly slowly, she slipped a tiny finger inside me. Why do you tease me like this?! I want to cry, but the words won't come out. Before I know it, we are moving as one. I want her more than I've ever needed a man. Her luscious lips are bringing me to a place of no return. The pleasure of the moment replaced the sadness for a brief moment as I reach a climactic orgasm, crying out in pleasure. It is the first time I have ever experienced an orgasm. Although I have been with a few men, I've never felt like that with a man.

The pleasure only momentarily lasts before the shockwave of sadness washes over me twice as hard.

The three of us don't live by moral rules or social norms. It's not unusual to hear stories of women sleeping with other women, or men with men. Especially in the field I'm in. I just never thought I'd get so lucky. I love Donna. For me, the intimate acts aren't something to be embarrassed about, since I've never really gave it much thought, until now. You cannot help who you love. I certainly love Donna. I want to please her just as much as she wants to please me. That's as far as sex is concerned between us. Once I'm feeling better, I will be back for more.

My thoughts are interrupted when Donna pulls herself completely on top of me, forearm resting on my chest as she looks into my eyes. "Baby, today is Shirley's wake. We have to get ready to go."

"I can't, Donna, I just can't. I still can't believe she is gone." I look back at her; the tears in her eyes haven't fallen but are still welling inside her beautiful features. She wants to help, and I love that about her, but she can't. She doesn't know how to. I don't have the wherewithal to tell her how to help me either.

Heart of Gold

"Come lay down next to me again." I don't want this moment to be over.

"I want to help you so badly. I know you're really hurting." She doesn't move.

"I know. There's nothing you can do." I put my hand to my face and whisper. "I can't go."

"Pull yourself together. You're going. You'll never forgive yourself if you don't." She abruptly stands. She says a little sternly as she rips open the curtains to let the sunshine in. Before she leaves, she announces that she and Phillip are coming too. I smile. I can't say no, because I truly need both of them.

A little while later, Donna, Phillip and I arrive at the funeral home. I walk to the front, sitting on the front row titled 'Reserved' as they sit in the back. My parents don't even look at me when I sit next to them, my sister pretends not to notice me, and my brother Eddie, who flew in from Chicago ignores me also.

After what seems like forever, my mother leans over and asks, "Do you want to go and say good-bye?"

I already said good-bye at the hospital. I can't bear to see her in a coffin too. "No." I respond. I can feel my body trembling. The ceremony is torture. I can't wait to get out of here!

On my way out I notice Rob, who was in my dream this morning. He notices me at the same time, grabbing my arm as I try to walk fast past him.

I look at him, jerking my arm away. "What do you want?"

Any trace of pervious sorrow was now replaced with Indignation, his jaw clenched. I know that look all too well.

"You know why this happened, don't you?" I've got to keep this short.

"Yes, LaNette told me how it happened."

"I asked why, not how, it happened."

"No, and I don't care." I start to walk away.

"God took a life for a life! We made this happen."

Rebecca Nietert

I stop in my tracks. Rob left me not so long ago, because he said I had 'no Religion'. I'm not Jewish and he is. He often talked about his abundant knowledge of the 'written Word'. I'd never read the Bible, never gone to church, and didn't know much about this "God" that I've heard of before. I can't imagine a God that would kill my sister because of what I'd done. Rob's words proclaim the worst kind of God. Wouldn't Rob know a lot more about what God would do?

The thought that I may have caused Shirley's death, shot right through the center of my heart, like a bullet of guilt. The tears start rolling down my face; I don't bother to stop them. It feels as if he had struck me on the cheek again.

"You're a sick man, Rob!" My body is shaking, bearing the full weight of his words. Judging from the look on his face, he seems pleased with himself. His eyes turn more golden brown, showcasing that he'd hurt me as much as he had intended.

"Have a nice life Beverly!" He hisses as he walks away, victorious.

I can't get his words out of my mind! What if he's right? What if I really did kill Shirley? Had I angered this God so profoundly that He would take something so precious away from me? A life for a life? Would He use the rest of my family to continue punishing me? How could a God who professes to love unconditionally be the same God who would spite my whole family? It doesn't make sense! But then again, my family is a heathenish bunch, deserving of any form of punishment beyond comprehension. It would be justice!

Something deep inside snapped. I can feel the heartbreak, an inexplicable cold rush filling every fiber of my being. There's no hope or faith left. If I had taken one of God's children and He had taken one of my family's children, then we are even. End of story. I don't owe this God anything and He doesn't owe me. Why hasn't this supposed God been there for me all these years? He hasn't

Heart of Gold

saved me, hasn't brought my father back. Instead, He'd left me with a woman who beat and tortured me.

Rob's god had the audacity to take a life that meant something to me because I did one thing wrong? No! He's wrong! It's my life and I'm going to live it the way I see fit; not from His perspective or anyone else's. If it's going to be this way, then I accept what I've done and will cause as much pain to others as I need to.

I waken with a strange sense of resolve: to die. Everything I have ever known is taken from me, why do I want to live anymore? No more pain or guilt. Freedom. Peace. That's what I want. I don't want to feel anything anymore. No sadness, guilt or rage entrapped within is going to save me now.

I've been way too innocent for far too long. I need a real education, to be as knowledgeable as any man. I need to hold on to something, some unwritten values. Something like, 'do unto others as you would have them do unto you.' Except that I don't believe in that rule anymore. I deserve to be as selfish as everyone else around me. I want to be like everyone else, void of empathy or human decency. Seemingly not caring for anyone else other than myself. I'll be that person who won't feel any more pain. It's just me, myself and I. I don't need anyone's help. Who cares what they think? I'm ready to begin a new chapter in life. I can't wait to get started!

In the next few weeks I went to work each night setting up rendezvous between girls and guys. I don't bother paying attention to what Donna and Phillip do anymore. I flip cash to Phillip as I walk in the door and pass Donna as I walk to my room. This new business and my new is more profitable than I'd ever imagined!

For some reason, I no longer feel inhibited by getting naked. Doing so only means that I'm one step closer to my goal, a means to an end. It means that Phillip will get the recording studio soon; I will keep a good portion of the new profit, and will soon be out of the business. I can do whatever I want.

We finally moved into a town home on the upper West side of town. As time passed the money increased. Philip finally began to

Rebecca Nietert

buy items for the studio: guitars, receivers, speakers, microphones and keyboards. Everything is so expensive! As he dwindles in his latest collection, Donna and I sneak off to have a little fun.

Work, long nights of teasing guys and the constant stories of rendezvous from the girls, gets so exhausting! I love being able to watch her hourglass figure. She is like a dream come true! Her supple, soft breasts drive me insane! The thought of her sharing herself with someone else makes me feel sick. Why can't I have her all to myself? She's so priceless. Oh, what a great love affair we have!

I make a sizable profit from working for people who would pay for sex. I've hit the jackpot! I don't have to hook. They come to me. Being a middleman and getting paid for it is amazing! What Phillip had taught me all of these years finally paid off? The Long hours of training back then, is now second nature to me. If there is ever a problem I know Phillip will handle it.

He turned me from a gangly schoolgirl into a woman every man desires. I owe him everything and will give him anything he desires, except the part of me Donna owns. As time passes, Phillip and I grow increasingly closer as he and Donna begin to drift apart. Phillip and I are friends; I love the fact that Donna is so accepting of us spending time together. Sometimes she even admits that she welcomes the break. Yes, I have has sex from time to time with Phillip, but she doesn't need to know that. Of course she gets jealous, as she should. If she can share herself with anyone, so can I. Sure it feels like I'm being tossed from one to the other at times, but I make them both feel special; it's like a high. No, it is a high.

Despite my attempts to reassure Donna that she is my one truest love, I can't help but notice signs of jealousy begin to emerge. Even though she drinks a lot, I've caught her drinking in the daytime. I've also noticed that she will have sex with any man who will pay the slightest attention to her. Which is unusual because she's usually picky. No matter how I tried to comfort her, nothing

Heart of Gold

helps to pull her out of the deep despair she's in. I wish I wouldn't care so much, but I do.

One evening when she slept with a man I thought was kind of seedy because he paid attention to her, in a fit of rage I lied to her. "I can't do this anymore. Nothing else matters anymore but me." I hear her crying as I slam the bedroom door in her face. I don't have time for her childish attempts at getting attention anymore.

We were both naïve, small-town kids. Dancing changed us both, but it changed me for the better. Her existence spiraled into an empty pit of drugs, booze, and sex. There's nothing I can do to stop her, which makes me mad. I'm losing her and it's breaking my heart. Sure her actions remind me of my mother's self-absorbed, twisted way of doing things. Sure she hurts me, but I can't bring myself to tell her that. At least she doesn't throw me out on the street. I hate how she uses the drugs and alcohol in place of us. They've won her over and I don't think she's ever going to return. Every time I try to talk to her outside of work I get rude comments that slap me in the face. I can tell Philip feels the same as I. We both have discussed many a night that her drug usage is the ultimate slap in the face for us. How could this happen to us?

When I try to confront her about her drug addiction, she snaps at me.

"You're not the same woman you once were!"

"What do you mean? I've always been this way!"

"No, you have a black heart!"

Great, the drugs are talking again. "Sure." The indifference in my voice shocks me. Why do I show her I feel…nothing? I watch as she gets in the car, slams the door, and leaves. As I walk inside I notice Phillip staring out the window, watching Donna drive away.

"Good riddance." I mutter under my breath, unsure I mean it.

"No, we have to bring her back." He insists.

"What?! Why? She's been hurting us the whole time!" I walk up to him and grab his face, making him look me in the eye. "Now it can be just you and me." I smile as I plant a kiss on his lips.

Rebecca Nietert

Tears start to form when he doesn't respond. He never cries! Sure I was cruel. Okay I give her that. But so was she. We can't help her deal with her emotions; she's got to learn to fend for herself. There's no turning back now.

I keep myself occupied by going to work. Day by day goes by, still no word from Donna. Oh well, life moves on right? Tonight's going to be fun. I walk in and see Donald, the gentleman from LaDon's party. I try to walk past him but he stops me. "I remember you."

I guess I'll have a little fun with this one. "How so?"

"We met that one night with Mr. LaDon. Don't you remember?"

"Hmm...Is that all you know about me?" I can't contain a smirk.

He starts to fidget. He's getting nervous, good. "No."

"And what else do you know about me?" I look him in the eye. You're not getting out of this one. "What did Donna say?" What?! I can feel my heart skip a beat. Regaining my posture, I manage to choke out. "What has she told you?"

He looks around, and then he leans close. "Well...I know you're a madam for the girls here. Also, I know that you give all your cash to a black man."

I begin to tremble.

I can feel the rage creeping in with every word he says. First she tries to destroy my feelings, now my income?!

"You got a problem with who I am?" Damn! I hate being the woman any person, let alone a man, can make feel again. I want so badly to be angry with her for what she's done, because she wants to make me suffer. She wants to hurt me, and that's the only reason she's told any man who I am. She wants me to hurt like she does.

I get it. I love her and I hate her all at the same time. For some reason I feel humiliated. How can a stranger make me feel this way? I turn my head away, feeling vulnerable for the first time in a while.

Heart of Gold

As if he can feel my vulnerability, Donald softly answers. "No, not at all. I think you're beautiful, but have you thought about what you're going to do when you burn out like Donna?"

I feel my brow furrow for an instant and turn my head to face him, regaining my composure. "Listen, I don't know who you think you are. I am not Donna and will never be like her. I would appreciate it if anything she told you is kept to yourself!"

His eyes sparkle. "Then I can take it that what she said is only partly true?"

"Yes." I hate him toying with me. He knows he just threw me off my game. He smiles broadly this time, teasing me. "Are you what she said you are?"

I tilt my head, about to go off on him when I feel something bump into me hard. I fall right into Donald's lap. I snap my head up, about to go off on whoever did that, but see Lana instead. "What the heck was that for?!"

"I am so happy! Guess what happened?!" She's practically bouncing up and down. I lean back against Donald, raising an eyebrow and shrug my shoulders. His muscles are hard as a rock against my back. I shiver as he puts a secure arm around me, holding me tight. I wonder what else is hard.

"I got a new puppy! His name's Alphy and he's a Pit Bull. He's a little underweight but we love him. Just love him!"

I smile and nod. "Lana you remember Donald?"

"Yeah, but listen!" I roll my eyes as she continues to tell me about how excited she is that she got this puppy. I can't help but be mesmerized at how a puppy can make a person so happy. I love listening to her; she can always make my day brighter. She seems so…innocent. Lost in her story, I feel my body loosen in Donald's arms. Uh oh. Big mistake.

Donald leans forward and softly whispers in my ear, "There appears to me more to you than I thought." I quickly compose myself as I push Lana away and stand. His soft words just whispered on my neck make every muscle in my body flinch. I feel more than defenseless, something that I'm not ready to feel. I turn to face him. "Lana is naïve enough to listen for a drink. She is nice enough to care." I get off of him and walk away, leaving them alone.

Throughout the night I keep an eye on Lana. She is a treasure and I can see her and Donald hitting it off. She has mentioned that she likes his rugged shoulders.

He does take great pride in his appearance, and even I have to admit that he is good looking. I can't help but wonder what he feels like.

Wait, what? No! He's just another man, who cares? I shake off the thought and soon head home.

Once there, I found Phillip waiting up for me. After reiterating what Donald said, to me we decide to visit the club where Donna is rumored to be working. We both have our reasons for wanting to know why she would do such a thing.

We walk in and see her on stage. She spots us and glares as we walk up to the stage. Even though I don't agree with her decision, I don't hate her. Seeing her brought back all the love I ever felt. I pull out two fives. "Hello, Donna."

She bends over and whispers, "I don't need your dirty money!"

"What's gotten into you?!" Even though her rejection hurts I still want to try to work something out.

"I heard you slammed me to Donald. He just left here." I didn't see him leave Mack's. Damn, you really can't trust a man, no matter how sweet he spears to be.

"I heard you told Donald some things about Phillip and me. I can't believe you would do that! And I can't believe you would believe that I could say anything bad about you!" I'm trying to keep my anger in check but can feel it seeping out.

Donna puffs her chest out clenches her jaw tight. "Well, I just told the truth. I told you that you would steal him away from me." She points at Phillip, furious. "You took everything that mattered to

Heart of Gold

me! You think you're so great. Well, I have news for you; you're not. You have no conscience!"

"Donna, you've got it all wrong!" I know she's right. I'm used to feeling nothing most of the time. But now her words shatter that shell, even if for a moment. Sure we hurt each other, but for some reason all I can feel is pity for her. I feel like an idiot standing here, looking up at her like a child to a mother.

"No, I don't! If you and that traitor don't leave here now I will have you thrown out!"

I flinch, realizing that there is no way to mend this wound. Phillip and I look at each other knowingly. It's over. I meet him in the middle of the club and we talk towards to exit, leaving Donna behind for good.

Rebecca Nietert

6

The months seem to drag on and on. I do everything I can to not think about my sister's death. Work, help Phillip, sleep, rinse and repeat. Day in and day out. I have to keep her memory at bay. The constant barrage of emotional bullets against a strategically placed security façade is starting to get the best of me. I can't help but think of Donna, and of our unconditional love, of life before Shirley's death, of that night when she died. It's all a blur, like it was another lifetime. No! Don't think about that! I have to be strong. I need to be a formidable individual; capable of doing anything I need in order to earn my living. Earn my life back. I don't want to be a dancer anymore; I've learned to hate being a broker for love.

As I begin to re-organize my office, I notice a sealed envelope that seems to have been tossed unceremoniously into a drawer. It's not addressed to anyone. Hmm...I look at the doorway. It's probably Phillips.

Our relationship developed into tumultuous at best. Even though I feel like I owe him for saving me from starving to death, there's still some resentment I feel about the way he treats me. Still, a peek can't hurt. I mean what is he going to do, fuss at me? If that's the worst that'll happen, fine by me. What if it's a secret lover, or maybe a family letter? Even though I have no Idea what it could be, I don't feel jealous. Hmm...that's odd. Why am I not jealous? Maybe it's because I just don't care anymore? Then my heart stops as I open the letter.

"Happy Birthday to the best sister! Many days we have spent together fighting with each other. At times when I thought I would be mad forever, I remember that you are my beloved sister and that I will always love you unconditionally. Beverly, don't worry about your baby, it is with God now. He is watching her until you or I can

Heart of Gold

go be with her. Remember to keep God close in your heart so that one day you may see your blessed child again. Remember that I love you, too. One day soon, Beverly, you will have a wonderful life!"

I re-read the letter a few times, shaking my head. I'm so confused! How did this letter get in the drawer? Why hadn't anyone told me? "Phillip!" I watch his face drop as he enters the room, seeing the letter in my hand.

"You were so sad. I just didn't think you needed to read that after she died two days after your birthday. I know it's a birthday card, and I know she meant for you to have it but giving it to you just seemed too cruel given everything you were going through with your family and all."

"Oh, okay." I pause to read it once more, then look up at him. "She said I have to believe in God. What do you think that's about?"

Phillip sighed in disgust while giving me a stern look, "Beverly, you did what you had to do to take care of yourself. God hasn't taken care of you so far has he?"

"I don't know Phillip. It's just so odd that Rob said what he did, and now she writes this?" I wave the letter in the air.

"What?" He said dismissively, not paying attention. It's as if he's lost in his own little world, like this is just some random letter that 'just so happened' to be in a random drawer. The nerve of him! "Never mind! Just leave me alone."

Is my sister now with the God who killed her? If she is, and if there's a real afterlife, would I ever be included? Didn't Dante's Inferno say there were different levels in Hell for different sins? I guess it shouldn't matter but oddly it does.

Shirley is gone and I will never be able to see her again. I can feel the tears start falling down my face as I stare at the letter. I haven't cried over her since the week of her death. That shell I've so strategically placed is beginning to have larger cracks of consciousness than I want to allow. I can literally feel the despair crawling back in. I can't believe she's still gone! It seems like it was just yesterday.

Yesterday...what happened again? Well I want to work...I pause, head snapping up. Work! I'm going to be late! I run to my room and apply makeup over my swollen eyes and red face, trying to cover the tracks left by my emotions. This is hopeless! I can't believe that I forgot about work! I grab my keys, run to the car, and stomp on the gas pedal.

I spot the policeman from LaDon's party as I walk into the club. What's he doing here? I watch him for a few seconds, then casually make my way to where he's standing. "Well, hello Joe."

"Hello Brooke." He turns to face me, eyebrow raised in confusion. "Say, have you seen Lana? I have a few questions to ask her."

"What kind of questions?"

He smiles broadly. "Some police rumors. Brooke, don't worry. I really like her."

My natural instinct to protect Lana kicks in. "Is she in some kind of trouble? She tells me everything and is way too nice of a girl to be getting into anything with the law. If you knew her you would know that."

"Look, I can see that you care about her, but she is a big girl you know. She's a survivor. Maybe right now she doesn't need to be around you much?"

Huh? "What's that supposed to mean?"

"There are rumors that there's a prostitution ring around this club. I've watched how you work the room; how many girls come to you for advice. I would wager that if you're not in it, somehow you know all about it."

I blink rapidly, processing the information. What?! How can he know about that! I can feel my head spinning. Surely he doesn't think I'm guilty...Right? I've got to regain my composure. Fast. There is no way I'm going to end up in jail. I manage to muster a sneer.

Heart of Gold

"You're wrong; we all just do our jobs here. If you have questions I'll answer them, but only when there's evidence."

"Still the same Lil' Lady huh?"

Good, he's done. My turn now. I smile at him playfully. "Yup, still the same. What about you?"

"Same old, same old." He throws his head far back and laughs. "Lana told me about your little gift."

"Really?" I lean in closer, placing a hand lightly on my hip. "Which one?" Did my voice really just come out as a whisper?

"I'm not getting put into one of your finely-fit categories of men. I like Lana but really don't want to piss you off."

"Don't bother then, I already know which one." I force a smirk as I state the half-truth. I can read the uncertainty on his face; can feel the war between doubt and desire.

"Do I take you up on your offer, or do you walk away?"

"You're clever, I like that. Tell me what you want." I whisper in his ear as I slowly slide my hand up his back side.

I've already analyzed him anyway. "Ask and it will be given to you, seek and you will find." Rob's face suddenly appeared in my mind. What did I just say and why does it sound so familiar? No! Not now. I need to focus!

"Why do you need to put men in a compartment?"

"Wouldn't you like to know?" I tease. Like I'm actually going to tell him how my training helps me make sense not only of men but also of myself? How it's helped me to make sense of what I already know to be true, that people act certain ways based on what they've been through? Oh no! I'm most definitely not going to tell him how I pick up on that information and use it to my advantage. He's a cop for God's sake!

"I've learned that men aren't all that different from one another."

I can feel his curiosity, a hunger for more. "Brooke, please!" He looks at me, exasperated. "Do you really hate men as much as Lana says you do?"

Rebecca Nietert

"Yes, sometimes." I look away, pausing for effect before I look back at him. "Other times..." I lean in, voice barely above a whisper. "I wish I had one of you for my own."

He swallows hard. I read the struggle on his face. He doesn't know whether to feel pity or compassion for me. Hmm...there's something I can use later. But...why do I feel so uneasy from the weight of his gaze, and those eyes. Damn! I can't let him get to me like this. He's just a customer in a topless bar, even if he's a friend of Lana's. Who cares what he thinks? That's the last thing I need. Speaking of need, how about that drink? It's way overdue. I turn to walk away but feel a hand on my arm, stopping me.

"I need something from you."

"What can I do for you sir?" I keep my tone warm, void of any clue to the turmoil raging inside.

"I'm curious. Please, tell me what you decided about me?"

Hmm...just maybe.... "What would you do if I am on target?"

"I will give you your first fifty dollars of the evening." That's a lot of money for him. Someone's desperate to know how I surmise a man quick enough to con one. I've got to make this quick.

"Now we have a deal." I smile, settling back on the high back bar stool while grabbing a drink. I love being in my element, being in control. I watch his face change, void of any emotion as if he's playing poker. I try not to laugh. It's odd to see a man really care how I think about him, especially when his ego is at stake.

"Well, you had a girlfriend recently. Probably a dancer, but nonetheless she worked in clubs like this. You loved her and she recently left, probably for some other guy. You have a military background but now you're a cop. You're too stubborn to have a roommate so you live alone. You make a good wage but don't have a lot of extra money. You have no pets but have children, presumably girls, and don't spend any time with them."

I pause for a moment to look at him, his eyes wide with amazement. "Even though you have a lot of friends your life is in limbo." I pause again as if I'm actually thinking heavily, and then

Heart of Gold

finish with a serious sigh. "You're searching for something or someone but haven't found what or who that is yet." I need to stop, this kind of thing puts people off. I feel like a clairvoyant at times, which is something I don't want to be known for.

"Shall I continue?" I look at him, his face incredulous.

"I'm a trained cop, and I can't do what you just did! How do you know so much about me?" He laughs while shaking his head. "Did Lana tell you all that about me?"

"Actually, Lana and I make it a point never to discuss any man that enters the club unless it is financially beneficial to the both of us. It's our rule so we never get too attached."

His creased brow line suggests that his question wasn't just a normal one. "So, Lana doesn't consider me more than just a customer?"

I can't help but feel a little sorry for him. "I can be so callous with my words." I say gently. Wow, do harsh words really come out that easily? "To tell you the truth she probably does. Lana is just really sweet, but she wouldn't tell me because she knows that I won't care."

"Wow, you do keep that wall up don't you? Has anyone ever made it come down just a little?"

"No, no one has ever been good enough to even crack it." I lie.

"Are you angry with me for asking you to do that?"

"No, I'm just frustrated with the way the whole conversation is going. Look, I like you and think you're a nice guy. Thank you for the warnings but I have to go to work now. Do you want to know about how surmised that or not?"

"Yes, please tell me."

"I know you were in the military because when we first met you were wearing a military uniform, remember?" I wait for an affirmative now before continuing. "I also met you with some pretty diverse friends; hence you have a lot of them. Then I saw you in this police uniform, so enough said there. I surmised that you were the kind of man who needed to feel like a knight in

Rebecca Nietert

shining armor; hence you're trying so hard to protect Lana from me. You seem to have some genuine compassion for Lana so I figured that for you to feel that much sincerity you have either dated a dancer or that a dancer hurt you recently. I read the level of pain on your face suggesting the latter of the two. I also deduced that since there was so much pain there, it must have been very recent."

I take a sip of my cocktail and continue, "Your limited patience with me and your stand-offish attitude leads me to believe you can be quite stubborn. You're usually here instead of home, leading me to believe that you have no roommates and are searching for something similar to what you had before. I've seen you here on several after hour occasions even if we never said hello, meaning you either have no pets to go home to and take care of or have no reason too.

Now regarding children: I said girls because of the way you talk to a woman. Men who have only sons are crass and rude. You're not. Maybe you have only sisters too, or you never would have considered dating a dancer. You seem to take woman for what they are. Now, may I have my money so that I can go to work?"

"Brooke, you are something else!" He laughs, shaking his head. "Here's your money. Have a great evening, but remember to tell the madam running the joint I'm watching."

I smile, my heart skipping a beat. If only you knew. "Thank you." I accept the payment and leave him sitting alone.

Heart of Gold

7

I watched Joe the rest of the evening out of the corner of my eye, making absolutely sure he doesn't witness anything I might be doing that's illegal. I see Lana approach him at one point, to which he smiles and winks over at me.

Just before the club closes I call a meeting in the back dressing room. About twenty girls showed up. I have to inform them of the danger; it's my duty to protect them from harm. I briefly convey my suspicions about what I know and who could be the person behind the rumors.

"No more going it alone guys?" I state in closing.

Toni speaks up, "Wait a minute. You're telling me that we have to go through you for our hook-ups or not hook at all?"

"Well Toni, let me put it to you this way. One, I can get you more money than you can. Sometimes I can get double what you negotiate. Two, I have a lot of clients who will continue to want you. Three, all of the men that I know, we've used before. I will screen new clients so that we don't get an undercover cop in here anywhere. Finally, all the regular clients will know that I am the one to go to. That means the price will rise for each occasion. The harder you are to get, means they have to pay an increased price. We can corner the market so to speak."

"Can we renegotiate your split? How much do they pay you anyway?" Toni asked.

Wow, the customers have been true to me. "You mean none of you know how much I get for each one of you?"

"No." Came the unison reply.

"Okay, here's how it works. I get so much per girl depending on her status. Status has variable factors: big breasts, playmate or penthouse pet, long legs or whatever the client's preference determines what he pays. Like Toni, she gets about seven hundred each time. Toni, how much do I give you?"

"Five hundred."

"Bobbi is so wild. She gets about five hundred. Bobbi, how much do I give you?"

"Four hundred."

Toni shouted, "Hey! How come you only take $100.00 from her and take two hundred from me?"

"Toni you need a lot of constant attention. For instance, throwing things, using props, then getting me into trouble. It all pays."

"Gee, thank you for putting that so gently." She sneered.

Ignoring her, I continue. "See, girls, my job is to make sure that you are taken care of. If anything ever happens to any one of you I would feel awful, so this is my way of helping. I've got to make sure I get compensated. After all, I'm a dancer too."

"I'm sorry I asked you to renegotiate. Looks like you're giving us most of the pie, thank you." Toni states flatly.

Anita chimes in, "Hey Brooke, how come you don't turn tricks yourself?"

"I'm happy with things just as they are." I've just found a way to keep a lid on the situation while keeping my cash flow alive. Yes, I'm taking advantage of women who put their faith in me, but I can't change who they are or what they want to do. It's their decision to trust me or not. Profiting may not be the most ethical way, but right now it seems to be the best way.

Lana approaches me as the others leave to go home, worry evident on her face, "You really need to get a handle on this Brooke."

"I think I just did. I can't go back to dancing for twenties again."

"Sometimes you are such a snob! I miss competing with you every night."

Heart of Gold

"I miss that too." I lied. "But I don't miss the money. It's so little compared to how easy it is to make what I do now."

"Money is not everything. You taught me that, Brooke."

"That's very true Lana, thank you." I hug her affectionately as we leave for the night.

Even though Lana and I don't talk about what I do for a living anymore, her words hang heavy on my mind. After several invites to lunch everything returns back to normal. "Lana I love having lunch with you. I love that I can just be myself and that you accept me for exactly who I am."

"I feel the same way." She smiles that sweet, sincere smile I wish I can have. "So, why did you start dancing anyway?"

"I started because I was hungry and angry. I met Phillip, and he approached me with an offer that made sense. We made me a deal."

"Like a deal with the devil?" She asks facetiously.

What?! Phillip is not the devil by any means! I phrase my words carefully. "No. He gave me a dream, a purpose, a reason for living. He said he would teach me everything I would need to know about making money. I'm able to talk to him whenever there's a problem. Sure sometimes it feels like my words are his words, like I'm a wooden puppet who mouths them, but I really need him."

Lana leans forward eagerly, "What is Phillip really like?"

"He's so handsome, has amazing muscles." I paused.

I thought, *he takes care of me*. "He motivates me when I need it and listens. He picks me up after a bad night by bringing me hot tea and drawing a bath. He judges people, because he thinks people judge him. He's always in a serious, rather dark mood. Sure he's selfish, but somehow he manages to make absolutely sure that my day is stress-free. He's my savior, my protector, my provider. He's my everything." I pause for a moment. Wow, I've never stopped to think about how much he does for me!

"Go on." Lana presses, taking a sip of water.

"I don't see him much, which I like. I like that he lets me do whatever I need to do. I spend most of my days preparing for the next day. I'll get tanned, do my hair, nails, get facials, extensions, whatever I need. The only bad thing about Phillip is that he's doing it all so that I'll buy him the recording studio. He wants to be a musician. He's doing it for me." He is doing it all for me…right?

"Why is that so bad? At least he wants to do something."

"I have a bad history with men."

"Well, what happened?" Even though I don't really care for divulging the sorted details of the painful decisions that leave me weakened, I trust Lana.

"I dated a guy named Tim and fell madly in love. I was so crazy about him. I learned that he needed a girlfriend who would have sex. At 15 I thought I wasn't ready, so he left. I was still stuck on him when I met a college guy named Todd. He was my sister's boyfriend's best friend so we all hung out together. He was so romantic, but I couldn't get over Tim. Todd ended up leaving me too, but not before I screamed my head off in a back alley behind the college somewhere. How embarrassing is that?!" I laugh and Lana joins in, the sweet music of her laughter edges me on. "I assure you that it was the last time I ever did that! Anyway, to make matters worse I went to a bar in Wisconsin to drink since I was underage in Illinois."

I stopped to sip some of my water then continued. "I met this guy who was tall, handsome and charming. He turned out to be Tim's younger brother, Terry. At the time I had no idea. So, Terry and I began seeing each other and decided to move in together."

"How crazy is that!"

"Then I found out that Terry lived in the same house with Tim. By this time I thought I had gotten completely over Tim, but I was stupid. Lesson learned: never date the brother of a lover."

"Please don't tell me that Terry got suspicious of you and Tim?" Lana's eyes open wide with excitement.

"Terry decided to follow in his father's footsteps and get his woman 'back in line'. I was tortured for well over a year before I broke free. My mother of all people helped me get out. She got me

Heart of Gold

a waitressing job and I hopped on a plane with two hundred bucks in my pocket and ended here, in Houston. The rest is, shall we say, history."

"Did you know anyone in Houston when you landed?"

"Yes, my sister LaNette followed her high school sweetheart here about a year earlier. She was struggling financially, so I used that as an excuse leave Terry. It was right after my birthday, which was the day Terry asked me to marry him. I think he thought I would come back if he asked."

"Wow! He asked you to marry him? What happened when you got here?"

"I was in here for about a month or so when I met this guy and fell pretty hard. I always knew I would send the engagement ring back but I was terrified to see Terry, so I mailed it."

"I would have mailed it the next day!" Lana laughed.

"Trust me, I wish I had. So, one day this guy I liked came to my apartment that I shared with LaNette. She invited us go out to the pool so we went. My white gangly body could not measure up to her curves. He took one look at her figure and that was that. He asked her out." Lana's jaw dropped in shock. "Yep, the man I was crushing on and had been on one date with asked out my big sister."

"Did she go?"

"After getting to know him better, she asked if it was okay if she went out with him. Can you imagine?!"

"Your sister dated your boyfriend?"

"Yep. I'm not sure if she did that often, or if she just toyed with them, making them think that they have a shot. I think she liked making me feel as if I'm not as worthy as her. She has this ritual of hurting me, something I've grown used to."

"I hear you, I have sisters like that."

"One night I went to one of her parties that she had for this guy, Chris. It was in his honor and I met Dave, one of his friends. He was a nice guy and I really liked that he had a steady job. He told me all about college and his dreams. We connected on what I thought was a positive level so I let him take me home. When we got to my apartment and I asked him in, he raped me."

"Oh. My. God. You're kidding, right?!" I don't think I've seen Lana look so mortified. I take a deep breath.

"Nope, I put myself in that situation and never saw him again. There wasn't anything I could do. He was huge and overpowered me. I never really got over it. To this day I go over it in my head. 'Why did I ask him to come in?' Sometimes my thoughts make me feel guilty."

"Did you report the rape?" She asks, exasperated.

"Nah."

"Why on earth not?! He could do that to someone else, Bev!"

"When I was younger my mother used me for her punching bag when she was angry. I can remember telling my grandparents, my aunt, my uncle. When I was sixteen she beat me so badly that she broke my jaw and dislocated my elbow. Do you know what the cops did? Nothing!" I slam my hands down on the table, causing Lana to jump. "No one saved me then, why would they now?"

My contempt for cops seems to unnerve her. "I'm sorry that happened to you." Came the soft reply. "I can understand being raped, because I was several times. I've been on my own since I was twelve. I went from one semi-truck to another in hopes of finding someone who would take care of me. Most of my youth was spent in fear jumping from one hell hole to the other."

My brow lifted. "Really? That's just so sad! At least I was able to wait until I was nineteen before I left everyone I knew."

"My mother is a schizophrenic and my father isn't much better. I had to go."

"I'm so sorry. No wonder we get along. How old are you now?"

"Twenty-two."

"I just turned twenty-three." Our birthday talk must have reminded her of my sister's death.

Heart of Gold

She asked, "So you've been dancing a year then. Do you think about your sister?"

"Every minute of every day. In fact sometimes that anger is all that keeps me going."

She was about to respond when the waiter interrupted to ask us what we would like to order. Our standard order is two Crawfish Etouffee meals, bread with butter and two ice teas.

"Okay now," Lana smiles as the waiter leaves. "Tell me about the guys you dated after the rape? I know you hate taking off your clothes and you must have like a billion dollars by now. Why don't you quit?"

"The only thing I can tell you is that I dated this guy named Rob who didn't want me because I was not Jewish. That's the man I think was the father of my unborn baby I terminated. He left me in a horrific way but I can't go there."

"What's wrong?" She looked me in the eye. I can feel the tears start to form, so I clear my throat and shake my head.

"I can't talk too much about Rob, but I will tell you I'm torn between getting a real job and staying in this business to own up to my promise. Phillip needs his recording studio. I give him all my income and he spends it as fast as I can make it. It's mostly on himself but sometimes there's some left over for us. I love having a beautiful home filled with nice things but I'm tired of being responsible financially for a man. I owe him though, so until my debt is paid I can't do anything. I owe him whatever he asks of me."

"You don't have to take care of him. You've done all right by him already. It's been a long time, and if he can't get that studio by now, maybe it's because he doesn't really want that to be the end of you two."

"I haven't really thought about that. You know what, part of me treasures him. I really do. But the other part of me doesn't love him romantically the way I should. I mostly feel like I owe him."

"You'll find out some day you don't owe him as much as you think you do."

Rebecca Nietert

"Lana, I was on the brink of homelessness again when my sister, Shirley, introduced us. I was waitressing at this club, had just terminated an unwanted pregnancy and couldn't stay on my feet enough to work all night. There were complications and I was not right physically."

"I understand. I've been there." Her eyes were filled with sorrow. "So tell me more."

"I can't." The tears begin to swell in my eyes again. Hearing myself speak of my pregnancy termination brought up all kinds of memories. The look in Lana's eyes doesn't help much either.

"Hurts too badly or don't want me to know?"

"Both I guess. You see the baby was Rob's. At Shirley's funeral, Rob told me that God had taken Shirley's life because I had taken the life of our unborn child. He never wanted the child. The abortion was his idea. The doctors told me it wasn't a baby so I had it terminated. It's a choice that still pains me."

"That's the most horrible thing I have ever heard! What a terrible thing to say to someone at her own sister's funeral. Does he have a heart?!"

"No, and I was very angry when he said it." I sigh. This is so exhausting!

"I bet you were. You know that's not true, right?" Feeling very uncomfortable with where the conversation was going, I change the subject. "Hey, where's that waiter?"

"The food is coming. I'm sorry; I didn't mean to make you feel uncomfortable."

"You didn't, but thank you." I lie.

"Whatever happened between you two?"

"We had a blast dating! There were plenty of good times that he and I shared. I wanted more of him, but he told me that I had to be Jewish or he couldn't marry me. He already married a woman who was not Jewish and their marriage didn't work out so he didn't want to chance it again. He said it would break his mother's heart."

75

Heart of Gold

"And this is the guy who did not want you even when he found out you were pregnant?! I would be mortified."

I lowered my head in shame and mutter, "Yes." Why did I tell her all of this? She's not even being really sensitive about it!

The waiter arrives with our food and places it in front of us. Lana looks at me. "You once told me that you met Phillip when you couldn't walk. Did your physical problems begin right after the termination? Is that why you feel so loyal to Phillip?" There are so many questions! My head feels like it's going to explode.

"I think it was a combination of things. I had to take some time off from work for the recuperation. After I went back to work I thought things would get better. I made a good bit of money from waiting tables but then my mother asked me to loan her some money for a new truck. You should have seen the car she was driving; it was horrible. I didn't think anything serious about loaning her the money since I was a successful waitress. I also thought the complications of the termination would be temporary."

"How long did the recovery take?"

"Months. Anyway, she asked me for the money and I loaned it to her. It was only six hundred bucks. She promised to pay it back when her taxes arrived in a few weeks, which I thought would be fine."

"It was not was it?" Lana took a bite of bread.

"Nope."

"What happened?"

"When I called to collect I was literally starving. She told me she didn't need to repay it 'after everything I've done to her', whatever that means. It really wouldn't have been so bad but my bleeding wouldn't stop and I was constantly in pain. The stress just made it worse. I ended up not making enough money and that's when Shirley introduced me to Phillip. At that time I was homeless again."

Rebecca Nietert

"Your mother sounds a lot like mine. Hold on, I need some more tea!" Lana stood up and got the waiter's attention. After her tea was poured she looked back at me, "Go on."

"Before long I looked anorexic. Shirley told Phillip that I was having a rough time so he purchased groceries for me. He brought them over one evening and Rob was there. Rob was trying to get me back since he felt like he had let me slip away after the pregnancy. He took one look at Phillip and slapped me, called me names and left. I didn't care because Phillip was the one who bought the groceries, not him."

"You're still that grateful girl, aren't you?"

"Yes, I've been that way ever since."

"I admire you Beverly, I truly do." Lana's voice softened. "One day you're going to realize that he's using you."

"He's the reason I make the money I do. You just don't understand." I understand where Lana's coming from, how she's looking out for me. I appreciate it, but now I feel bad for ever saying anything bad about him. My conscience is modified by behavior and choices. One think I love about Lana is that she makes me feel like I should put myself first. I know that when somebody cares about you, their focus is derived from your words, for the benefit of your future. Somehow, I think of my mother when someone tells me that I need to consider myself first.

When I was a child, my mother was the epitome of self-centeredness. She's spent her entire life making choices for her benefit only. From the Coca-Cola bottles that she refused to share with us kids to the random appearances she used to make, I don't think that woman thinks about anybody else but herself.

I've spent most of my adult life running from memories of my childhood. It doesn't make sense for somebody who truly knows me to tell me to think about myself first. Anybody who truly listens to what I have been through will understand. That's the worst thing I can do.

Heart of Gold

I'm so diligent about making sure that my life isn't self-centered. Yet somehow I feel as though the last years events have created this void of selfish behavior that is all consuming. I have all this ability to earn an incredibly large income and yet I am still at the mercy of Phillip. No matter what he commands, I do and no matter how I feel about it I do nothing.

Sometimes I believe I've entered into the rubber band effect, going the exact opposite way, away from being anything like my mother. In doing so, I've made myself the doormat. It's a wonderful thing being introspective, but it's awful to analyze oneself to the point when driven mad.

I can't help but wonder how do I balance my feeling of being a doormat with the sometimes confidence in my own ability. Emotionally I feel as though I am being ripped apart at the seams.

Rebecca Nietert

8

I take a week off from work to relax. Luckily, my job affords me the luxury of not having to go in each and every day if I don't want to. Normally Phillip and I take that opportunity to reconnect with each other. Lately, though he's been absent. I didn't mind. Rather than having him micromanage my successes and failures I welcome the distance between us. I use the time to run a hundred errands I don't normally get to do and shop. I spent a lot of quiet time catching up on some reading too.

I notice a voicemail from Lana, saying not to come back to work for a while. Odd. I call back. "Why not?"

"Look, Beverly, some of the girls got busted last week while you weren't here for prostitution. Word is out that you're the madam! If you come in, you've got a good chance of getting busted too."

"What?! Oh please, Lana. They haven't got anything on me."

"You do know that running a prostitution ring is more than just a misdemeanor, right?"

Really? "What did Joe say?"

"I can't tell you, he asked me not to. Just promise me you'll call him, okay?

"What's the number?" I shout, not meaning to. I grab a pen and paper, fumbling to write the number as fast as I can.

"I'm not going into work for a while."

"Okay, great. I've got to go now. Thanks again, Lana." I hang up before she can say anything and dial Joe.

My mouth starts spitting out words before Joe can even say 'hello.' "Joe we need to talk. I just got a hysterical call from Lana. What's going on?!"

"Go to dinner with me so we can talk. Some place public."

Heart of Gold

"Dinner?" What does he think this is? Does he truly believe this is an opportune time to go on a date?

"Yes, but don't worry I will be the perfect gentleman. Meet me in the parking lot across the street from the club at 6:00."

"Deal. Then will you tell me what's going on?"

"Yes, I'll tell you everything but be careful; your phone might be tapped." Why did he warn me?

"See you tonight." Isn't that going to get him in trouble?

As soon as I hang up I run into the living room where Phillip is watching TV. After I tell him what just happened he looks at me like I'm just a child. I know that look. I hate that look.

"Beverly, you can't just leave these people hanging! You told them you would help them, right? You have future appointments. If you abandon these customers you will lose them forever. You can't go to dinner. You have to go to work! You have to set it straight. Tell your clients to hold out for a while till things cool off. You have a responsibility here."

"I see your point, but what if they already have a warrant for my arrest? I could go to jail!"

"They have to prove it, Beverly. They don't have a case yet, or they would've already come here."

"Okay, if you think that's the best way to handle this." I sigh, not feeling very reassured.

I leave for work immediately. The club's packed with clients as I walk in the door, just like Phillip said. Why do I doubt him? Of course he knows his stuff when it comes to this. I've got to get the word out. Fast. I spot one of my favorite clients, Sonny Rigatoni. I make a beeline for him, only to be stopped by his friend, Mickey Goldman. Mickey and I do a lot of business for Sonny together. He arranges all the girls for Sonny. After a few times, I learned that Sonny likes his woman strong enough to knock down. His demeanor terrifies me so I normally set his things up through Mickey. Mickey and I became friends, even exchanging gifts on special occasions. He's the local representative for an alcohol

Rebecca Nietert

distributing company, which is all I know about him. All I need to know anyway. It isn't good business to get in too deep with your customers. Mickey is just the arranger, not bothering to take part in festivities. I guess I'd better go say hey. I walk over to Mickey, who laughs after I tell him what happened earlier.

"I can't imagine who would've squealed! No worries, I'll talk to Sonny and get things taken care of."

"How can Sonny take care of this?"

"You have no idea who Sonny is, do you?"

"He's just a client. Why should I?" I try not to stammer but fail miserably. Apparently I looked just as dumbfounded as I sound because Mickey grins at me. "Let's just say he's connected."

"Connected?" He laughs wholeheartedly again, confirming that my nerves are showing on my face. Why can't I keep my cool?!

"That's why I love you, gal! You're so sweet. Let's just say that if, and I mean if you get busted, Sonny won't let anyone hurt you."

Like child I whisper, "Sonny's the mob isn't he?"

"No fear, Darling. You need not worry about that kind of stuff. I'll take care of it."

"Is he married?"

"Yeah, his wife's name is Jane. Why?"

"Does he have a mistress?"

He pauses for a moment, eyes narrowing in suspicion. "Her name's Ellen. Why?"

I've got to shake him off. "He just seems like the type. How come you never partake in the festivities?"

"My wife would kill me!"

"How would she know?"

"Oh, she can tell. She's really smart. I just walk the line and don't get into much trouble. Besides, I am one of the lucky people. I happen to love my wife."

I wondered what that feels like, to be loved by a man. I wonder if that can happen to someone like me. "I'm glad for you Mickey."

Heart of Gold

Probably not. I smile while giving him a big, bear hug. "You make me hopeful and really make me smile."

"You can be a princess. Some day it'll happen."

I almost laugh. He says that like he thinks that what all girls like me need to hear. I try not to roll my eyes as we kiss goodbye on the cheek. As I turn to walk away I feel a hand on my arm. I turn around expecting to see Mickey but see Joe instead.

"Hello Brooke!" Why does he seem so upset?

"Wait! Before you yell, hear me out."

"The bets are off! Friend or no friend of Lana's, I can't protect you anymore!" I can feel the sting of his words as I let him walk away. Why is he so upset with me? It's not like we've had a relationship or anything. I don't owe him. All I need is for him to be a friend to Lana and give me the inside scoop. Oh well, as long as I know the truth from Mickey I'll be just fine.

I look around and spot Mickey walking up beside me. Speak of the devil. "I need you to complete a transaction for Sonny." His eyes dart around the crowd, scouting out the place. That's what they come for right?

"Give me a minute. Who's his preference tonight?"

"Toni."

"Fine." I walk away, only to be almost knocked over by Joe as he flies around the bar. Gees! What does he want now? "What do you want?" He wraps his hand around my arm and drags me to the front of the club. "Ouch! Let go of me!" I yank my arm away.

"Do you have any idea who that is?!"

"Yes. I just found out tonight. Why do you care?" I take a look at my arm, which is red and starting to swell.

"You haven't read today's headlines have you?"

"I don't read the paper or watch TV. What is wrong with you?"

"Sonny is the head of the mob. Don't you get that?! He's the head of organized crime!" His voice raises an octave and I push him.

Rebecca Nietert

"Be quiet! You're going to get both of us in a lot of trouble! I just found that out tonight from talking with Mickey."

"And do you know who Mickey is?!"

"Yes. He's a liquor distributor who sees Sonny gets what he needs."

His eyes slit narrow with anger. "He also orders hits for Sonny."

"Okay. So what does all this have to do with me?"

"Jane Rigatoni was murdered two days ago."

"Sonny's wife?" I scream softly, putting my hand over my mouth.

"Yes for Pete's sake, his wife! Guess who did it?!"

"How would I know that?" I snap.

"His mistress, Ellen. She's been arrested for Capital Murder!"

"Do you think Ellen and Sonny planned it?"

"We're investigating. You're being watched as we speak. You'll be called to testify if you don't get yourself out of here now, and I mean quick! They'll use you being a madam against you so that you testify against Tony."

I suddenly feel weak at the knees, my stomach is tumbling in knots. "Oh my God."

"You need to wrap this up and hit the road, babe." I nod in agreement, rushing inside to organize the meetings. I run around, not caring who gets matched up with whom, as long as someone has a prospective date. Once done, I rush outside to my car. I see the limos parked by the front door, a luxury spot. I glance into the side mirror on the nearest limo to see Joe walk out of the building behind me.

Mickey pops his head out of one of the limos, motioning for me to come over. I swallow my fear and walk over, hoping he doesn't see me shaking. This is too much to handle! I see Mickey looking behind me, noticing Joe. "Darling, how would you like a vacation? You've worked so hard, that you've earned it. How about for a month?"

Heart of Gold

"Oh, I know. What does a guy like me know, right?" He laughs, looking over at Sonny, but I know he's serious. He abruptly turns towards me, jaw clenched, his steel blue eyes meeting mine. All laughter stops. "Someone from our organization just told Sonny your friend is investigating him. I saw you talking to him by the bar tonight. He's here to bring you in for questioning, which can't happen. You can't tell anyone what you do for him or what you know. How much will it take?" He asked me again.

"Ten grand!" I look him straight in the eye, hoping to look more confident than I really feel.

"Done." I watch as he leans in the car, searching through a briefcase. He pulls out a wad of bills, counts it, and then hands me the cash. What?! Is he actually giving me TEN grand?! I can't help but stare at him, dumbfounded as he blows a kiss, rolls up the window and drives off. I can't believe he has that much money in his car!

"Go home, Brooke. Just go home." I look up to see Joe standing a few feet away. I nod, hands shaking. I get in the car and stomp on the gas, not bothering to look back. Once home, I run to Phillip, slamming down the cash on the table as I stare at him sitting in the chair.

"What the hell, Phillip?!" The color drains from his face. "Why didn't I know until now?!"

He looks up at me and sighs. "Do you remember Daryl, my cousin who attends the University of St. Thomas?"

"Yes?"

"He has two friends who are brothers; both were arrested tonight for murder. It seems Ellen hired the younger brother, Max, to commit the crime. Matt, the older brother, found out about the plan and went to warn Jane. But Jane saw the two of them in her house and freaked. She ran to call the cops so Max panicked and shot her."

"Wait a minute; I don't know any such thing! I don't know this guy or his brother!"

Rebecca Nietert

"Do you think that matters?!" Phillip jumps to his feet, causing me to flinch. "You know me, I know Daryl. You know the husband, Sonny. I just put it together when you came home. It never occurred to me it was the guy you provided with prostitutes! Plus you know Mickey, and he is probably the one who ordered the hit. Why do you think they asked you to leave?"

"I had no idea I would be getting girls for a syndicate boss! How could you have dragged me into this mess?"

"If you had listened to what I've taught you, maybe you wouldn't be in this mess!"

"Oh, so now you're telling me that you would've been able to spot a mob man?"

"Yes, now we have to get out of here. Just the two of us."

I cross my arms defensively. "Why?"

"Because I love you and want to keep you safe." I feel his fingertips brush against the side of my cheek. "You're the most valuable possession I have." I can't help but fling myself into his arms. How does he always make everything make sense? I'm not sure if I need him to talk or realized a new appreciation for him. Maybe it's both. It doesn't matter. He's here with me and that's all I care about. So much has happened this past year. Everything else feels like a dream. "What can I do?"

"Well, I'm always up for something a little different." He smiles that pearly white smile and I can't help but melt into his arms. I grab his face and kiss him. I whisper, "What's your pleasure?"

I feel his hands slowly make their way up my sides. "How about a blow job?"

I can't help but smile back at him, taking his hand as I lead him to the bedroom. "That would be my pleasure." His hands pull me closer as we fall onto the bed. I don't waste any time unzipping his trousers while passionately pulling them down.

The music of his laughter rings in my ears. "You must really feel bad tonight."

Heart of Gold

I look up at him and smirk, "Oh I do." I take his long shaft in my mouth and work the magic I know I have. I touch his sensitive spot over and over until he grabs me feverishly and tosses me on my back. I'm wet with anticipation as I watch him tear off his clean white shirt and reveal those amazing muscles that secretly wait for only my eyes. I feel the tension between us as he rips off my clothes, then climbs on top of me. He enters me quickly and so generously lifts the weight of his body off me so we can move in unison. It seems like hours before he finally jerks out and splatters his sperm all over the front of my body. Good thing he got out. I'm not on birth control right now. He lets out a huge sigh and rolls over, facing me.

"I have to tell you Bev, when you get back things are going to be different." He whispers, stroking my cheek. I nod, knowing he's right. Nothing will ever be the same. I don't know how I've gotten mixed up in this mess to begin with! Was it before or after I started dancing? Was it before or after I met Phillip?

He takes my hand and looks into my eyes, "Let's get going." I get up and before I know it we are packed and heading out of town his seventies model Camaro. Good thing we decided to take his car rather than the Porsche, no one at work knows about Phillip I told myself.

Rebecca Nietert

9

Phillip and I always look for the best hotels when we travel, preferring towns where neither one of us had been before. Maybe now the authorities won't find us. Unfortunately, people aren't as nice here than they are back home. They don't seem to take too kindly seeing a black man and a white woman together.

"What about the children?" The question rings in my ears, asked inconsiderately by random strangers. It hasn't even been a week and I'm sick of hearing that. We aren't even married! It isn't any of their business!

My mind goes back to the police officer, which stopped us on the side of the street, accusing Phillip or kidnapping me. Phillip, being the gentleman he is, replied that he would never do such a thing. What right do they have to ask about such a thing?!

As we walk into a restaurant a woman at the counter, who shouts, "Hello Ma'am", greets us.

Finally! Someone is being nice. I flash a smile. "Hello."

"Are you in some kind of trouble?" Her brow creases, eyes showing concern.

What? "No. I'm not. Why would you think that?" I look back at Phillip, who is looking around the room. He leans in, eyes scanning the room, and whispers "Because of me, Blondie."

"No! I am most certainly not in danger." I can't keep the anger out of my voice this time. What is wrong with you people?! "Are you going to take our order or do we have to leave?"

"Well, Miss, I was just making sure…" came the snotty reply. God I just want to smack her!

"No need." I force a smile, trying to keep my cool.

Heart of Gold

All of a sudden she turns her head to look towards the back of the building and screams, "Donald!" In moments a man with a knife in hand appears out of nowhere, running towards us. Phillip grabbed my hand and in an instant we were in the car, tires screeching as Phillip turns onto the road, flooring the gas.

Catching my breath, I turn to face him. "Are they judging us based on the pigment of your skin?"

"It happens." Came the reply, his eyes never leaving the road. Does he go around town with other white women?

"People come at your with a knife?"

He laughs, shaking his head. "Well your mother did when she found us."

I smile, chuckling at the memory. "Yes, I remember that."

"I have female friends that I know from other clubs. I go in to check out your competition; to make sure you're in the right club to make the most money."

When Phillip pulls up to a stoplight I look right, spotting a huge four-by-four pickup stopped beside us. I look over, spotting the driver and feeling strangely uncomfortable. Before I can say anything to Phillip, the man rolls down his window and shouts "Hey lady! You with that black man on purpose?" I quickly look at Phillip, who was watching the light, ignoring them. Warning bells ring in my head, my instincts screaming danger.

"You like big black men?" The man shouted again. I look over, about to flick him off when I notice there are two men, one who's driving and the other, pointing a twelve-gauge shotgun at me.

"Phillip!" I scream. Not waiting to be told twice he slams the gas, not waiting for the green light. The sound of gunfire quickly followed by the smell of smoke fill my senses as my head slams against the headrest.

"Where is a cop when you need one?!" I scream. I can feel my heart racing at a hundred miles an hour. We were just shot at! I clutch the dashboard as Phillip clutches the steering wheel, trying to stay steady as we swerve all over the road. The pellets must have hit

Rebecca Nietert

the rear of the car. From the rearview mirrors I see the truck closing the distance. I look around, searching desperately for a cop, but there is none in sight. I look to my right again to see the truck pull alongside us. My scream must have startled Phillip because he tried to run them off the road, but the attempt is futile. We are no match for a four-by-four. I see the gun flash, aiming towards me.

"Stop!" Phillip slams on the brakes and the car starts to spin. I hold onto the dash for dear life, before finally slamming back into my seat as we skid to a stop. Another gunshot. More smoke fills my nose, flowing into my lungs. This time I know we're hit. I lurch forward as Phillip slams on the gas again, driving as fast as he can in a different direction.

"Where are we going?!"

"To find population!" He shouts back.

When we finally get into town, Phillip parks the car in a full parking lot. We jump out of the car and run into the local shopping plaza.

"Are you okay?" Phillip asks, slowing down to let me catch my breath.

I look at him, incredulous. "No! I am not okay!" How can I ever be okay again?

"You will be fine."

"Some white man just tried to kill me because the man I was with had a different color of skin than he did!" I hiss, trying not to draw too much attention of others around us. The thought of so much ignorant hatred pisses me off!

"How could people hold the color of someone's skin against them when they don't even know who they were? Or for that matter who we are to each other?"

"I know, right?" I shake my head, slowing my pace while taking deep breaths. Is this real life? We spend some time walking around quietly, mostly observing the surrounding area. After making sure no one was following us we head out to the car and get in, looking at each other in sheer disbelief.

Heart of Gold

"I can't believe this is my life!" I can't hold it in any longer, the tears start falling down as I begin to sob. It was then I noticed I was bleeding. A couple pellets had hit my torso. I don't know if it was my contempt for the men or my adrenalin from trying to survive such hatred, but it didn't hurt.

We went back to a hotel, cleaned up the wound. Both of us never saying another word about what just happened. I feel Phillip take my hand and look up at him. "Let's go home."

I nod, squeezing his hand. "Yes."

On the way back home we stop at a local store just outside of Texas. A black woman working at the counter looks up to see Philip with me. "Look lady, there isn't a great many decent black men around. Why you got to go on takin' one of the good ones away from the black community?" She put one hand on her hips and scolds me with the other.

Can't she even consider the fact that we could be just friends? I look up at Phillip, who lowers his head. He's ashamed of me?! I stare at him, feeling as if I was just punched in the stomach. Not only have I witnessed prejudice against him but he's turning around and inflicting the same kind of prejudice on me! Did I not just stick up for him? Did I not just save our lives?!

The ride home is silent. Any inclination of a strong, respectful bond that we've had faded as I realize that we've never really been truly in love; just have affection for each other. Sure there's things we don't like about each other, but the things we do like far outweigh the rest. Or so I thought.

I've never noticed the color of Philip's skin, not even after my own mother pointed it out, until now. Now I see him as a black man. Now, I feel like I have an invisible scarlet letter hanging around my neck just by being with him. Not just from strangers but a sort of reverse prejudice coming from him. Whatever the letter means is obviously important, seeing how he treats me when I'm around him in public.

Rebecca Nietert

I can't help but feel affected by the whole incident! What would I do if I had another accidental pregnancy? I'd always assumed that he would want to keep it, but now I'm not so sure. I can't keep a child in a world when they could get shot. I look over at Phillip, his demeanor calm as usual. What is it about what that lady said that makes me want to flee from this man? Hasn't he protected me and provided for me all this time together? How could one woman change all of that? I have to do something, anything, to end the hatred.

Sadly, I feel compelled to make Phillip's life better. No matter how much his rejection hurts. I look out the window, trying to think of something to help not only him, but also myself feel better. Nothing comes to mind. Why do I feel so helpless?

Somehow, that lady changed my world. I now see color where there wasn't any before. I can see the differences, why people view the differences. I now understand why African American men and women feel the way they do. Not much has changed for them in the eighties in rural America. That lesson is one I would've been happy never knowing. I feel persecuted and protective all in the same relationship.

I call Lana right as I get home. "Hi Sweetie, what is going on? How's that beautiful animal of yours?"

The first thing I did when I got home was to call Lana to see if anything was going on. She answered the phone. It was really good to hear her voice.

"Fine. Gosh I've missed you!" I smile. It's so good to hear her happy. "Where have you been?! You dropped off the face of the Earth! Tell me what you've been doing!"

This is the first time that we've spent a long time apart without being in constant communication. Staying in touch is hard to do out on the road. Pay phones cost money and hotel phones charge an arm and a leg to make long-distance calls. Besides, I can't put her in danger. She has to be as far away from this whole issue as humanly possible.

Heart of Gold

"I've been traveling all over America." Then I proceed to tell her about everything that happened the night at the club. Including the men who shot as us, and the lady who scolded Phillip.

"...You're kidding me, right?" I can hear the shock in her voice. "People shot at you?"

"Yep, happened just like I told you, Lana. Honest."

"I can't believe that someone would be that stupid! Bev, I don't know how you keep on going. I truly don't."

"Well I'm glad to be back. Phillip said that this town is the safest place to be for our kind of relationship."

"Well I haven't thought about that. It's probably best that you're back. What are you going to do now?"

"What do you mean? I'm coming back to work."

"That's not a good idea, Bev."

"Why not?"

"Well, after the one-hundred-girl arrest, Doyle found out who was behind it all."

"Oh no! You're kidding, right?" I can't believe what I'm hearing!

"No Ma'am! He is out for blood. Thinks you owe him all kinds of money. He's really pissed and is on the lookout for you."

"Well are you working tonight?"

"Yeah, why?" She asks carefully.

"I've got to set the record straight. I can't work in this town without doing that first. I need a job! Will you let him know I'm in town and ask if we can talk?"

"Yes, but be prepared. He is Sonny's friend, who told him everything. He knows why you left town."

"Don't worry, I'm prepared. Call me from the club and let me know when and where. I'll meet him anywhere."

"Will do." She hangs up.

My eyes fly open as a loud blaring ring bursts. I look at my caller ID. It's Lana. Didn't she just call? My eyes flick over to the time. What? It's that late already?! I must have fallen asleep. I quickly answer, hearing her voice before I can say a word.

"Hi, Darlin. Doyle says he will talk, but only on the phone. He says he can't leave the club, and you're not welcome back in it so you'll have to call him."

"Thank you for the update, Lana." I blink, trying to steady my voice. "I'll call right now." I shake my head, whether it's from the events or the fogginess of my brain, I don't know. I can't believe my life is so turned upside down! Here I am in fear for my life. Again. I know I have to make a change. Something has to give. Maybe I need some coffee to wake up? I stifle a laugh. Yeah, like that's going to fix everything. I have to get out of this business, to move on and do whatever I need to do. I want a real life, and this is my ticket there.

"You take care. Call me when you figure out what you're going to do."

"I will, I promise. Now, go take care of yourself. I'll see you very soon." I hang up then dial Doyle's number.

"Hello?"

"Hey, this is Brooke. I heard you're looking for me. Before you talk I want to say how sorry I –"

"I bet you are!" He interrupts. "Brooke, what you did in my club was wrong! Do you realize how wrong?"

"Yes, I do, and I'm so sorry. How can I make it up to you?"

"You can't. I have cops coming down on me like rain. Sonny told me you are under his protection. Now I have a renegade lawyer throwing my company into receivership. I don't need this right now!"

"What can I give you to make up for what I did?"

"Short of all that money you stole from my pocket? Nothing. Brooke, I liked you. I thought you were tops. Now I can't trust you, and I can't do a thing about it either. Do you have any idea how mad that makes me?"

"Look, I still have some money. I can give it to you."

Heart of Gold

"I don't just want your money, I want your respect. I thought I had that. Now none of my gals respect me either. What you did was ruin every good thing I had. It'll take a long time to fix this!" I can't help but wince as is voice raises several volumes.

"I'm so sorry, I had no idea you would feel this way. I was wrong. If there is anything I can do-"

I stop, suddenly realizing what I've done.

"You're a decent kid. Get out while you still can." His voice suddenly doesn't sound so harsh. It sounds almost like pity. Does he really pity me?

"I will." I can't keep my voice from cracking.

"See to it that you do. Don't worry about me. Take care of yourself. I wish I could say come back to work. You were one of the best, but I can't. You've made your own way now Babe. Good luck to you! Have a great life!" He hangs up, as if he doesn't want to hear another apology.

I suddenly feel the full weight of the impact of what I've done. It was all-just so I could make more money. I realized that I turned into a far worse person than I could have ever imagined. In the past few months a mob boss threatened me. I had swindled men out of money so I could eat. I had offended the entire female African American population, and I was almost shot by a redneck. This was not the life I signed up for.

I turn around to notice Phillip sitting in the room. Had he been listening the entire time? I look over at him, unable to speak. I will never be allowed back in Mack's. I can't do anything else but dance. I'm not educated and don't have the skills to get out of dancing. There's nothing for me out there, only here. Besides, I still owe Phillip his recording studio.

Phillip isn't empathetic to my feelings; I can see it on his face as he approaches. How I wish he would hold me and tell me everything's going to be okay. Instead, he pulls my hair back. "Put Brooke on." I look down and nod. He knows the money is almost gone, but is that really all he cares about? What about me? Have I

Rebecca Nietert

been deceiving myself this entire time; mistaking respect for whatever this is?

Performance sex isn't real romantic to me. Other than sex there is nothing romantic about Phillip and my relationship. Yet somehow, it's understood that neither one of us will date anyone else. I wondering how long it will take to pay him back. I am willing, but that doesn't seem to be enough.

What I know is that I'm building a growing hatred for the choice I made to dance. The worst thing about choosing a lifestyle like dancing for a living is that it gives you all the freedom in the world. You don't have to go to work if you don't feel like it. Your income is based on your ability to perform and when you do it well, it's intoxicating to know that you have that much freedom over your own life.

When I sit down and think about getting a real job or changing my options, I can't help but think about how easy the money comes to me now. The money is so addicting. I look at the hard-working stiffs around me who get up at the crack of dawn to put a suit on. They go to work every single day and have to put up with snotty attitudes and whatever their boss tells them they have to do. It's obviously frustrating and full of pressure, seeing as several clients have told me so. My job isn't like that. I go to work and get to socialize and talk to some pretty amazing people. I get money for doing that and in all honesty, I show less skin then a teenager shows on the beach.

As mad as I get at Phillip, I have to remember that I made this choice for a reason. Yes, I was starving. But I chose the tougher road because for me, life has been so difficult. I just really want options I can control after having spent so much of my life in the control of others. It's a comfort zone. I am used to it. At least I believe I am in control, but lately I am feeling like even that's slipping away.

Heart of Gold

10

Phillip and I drive all over town from one topless establishment to another, looking for the perfect club. Finally, I'm able to talk an owner into a job at a club named The Gentleman's Club. It's in a new building and has a brand new owner who doesn't know anything about me, except that my reputation as an income producer. Apparently that is legendary.

Of course the first argument is over my stage name, Brooke. Another girl is already using it but the way I see it, it belongs to me. I've earned every dime from the infamy of it and I am mad as hell that someone else is riding off the skirt tales of my efforts.

The manager promptly informs me that he isn't going to make her change her name. His reasoning is that I'm new to the club and the other girl had been working every day. If I want his respect I have to earn it.

Fine by me. I listen as he rambles on about many girls switch clubs because the clientele isn't like Mack's. This is blue collar and the girls "can't handle it". Sure it's more difficult to make a living with blue collar, but who cares? I'm the best he's going to get and I think both of us know that, but it is a new club.

I don't know if it's the shooting or the loss of my job, but I suddenly feel a random sense of humility. For some reason I feel...thankful? I'm thankful that the manager has given me a chance at the new club. For the first time, I find myself looking forward to making money and the ability to leave everything else behind. Somehow dancing with my top off doesn't seem so bad anymore. The thought of prison time changed my perspective on what I should do to create income. From now on, everything I do will be completely legal.

Rebecca Nietert

I have some time off before I start back to work, so I see my OBGYN for our annual physical. Upon recommendation, I take a mammogram as well as blood tests. I'm very conscious about my health, considering the environment I work in.

I spend the next few days sleeping, eating, but mostly trying to forget about anything that has happened up until this point. Forget about Donna. Forget about what Lana said. Forget she made me doubt everything I've known about Phillip. Phillip found me a new job. Although I believe everything will work out eventually, sometimes, I honestly just want to stay asleep and not wake up.

I hear the phone ring and check the caller I.D. It's so cool that phones just came out with the ability to identify the caller. It's the nurse from my OBGYN's office.

I click answer. "Hello, is this Beverly?"

"Yes, is everything alright?"

"I have the results from your mammogram. I need to set up an appointment so you can speak with the doctor."

"I don't have time to come in to speak with the doctor. I start my new job soon. Can't you just tell me what the results are?"

"Ma'am, I can't tell you that. Confidentiality reasons. You will need to come to speak with the doctor."

"Well, I'm not coming in, so you'd better just put the doctor on the phone."

I hear a deep sigh, then a mumbled "Just a moment."

"Is this Miss Beverly?" Asked a deep voice.

"Yes."

The doctor cleared his throat nervously.

Uh-oh.

"Your mammogram results came back positive for a possible tumor. We really need to run more tests. I don't want to alarm you, it's just a formality. We need to get an ultrasound done as soon as possible."

That's why the nurse couldn't tell me. "When's the earliest time we can schedule?"

Heart of Gold

"How about tomorrow?"

"Perfect."

I walk into the crowded waiting room of the doctor's office, looking around. Is everyone here for the same reason I am?

The wait to see the doctor normally takes about an hour, but it took only about five minutes before someone walks out to greet me. She kneels down by where I'm sitting and asks if I'm ready. I nod, feeling alarmed already.

As we begin to walk in the back I can't help but ask. "How common is it for someone as young as I am to have a tumor?"

"Have you had anything to eat or drink today?"

"No, neither." Aren't nurses supposed to answer your questions?

We walk back to the exam room where the technician has the machine all ready. He proceeded to examine my breasts by smashing my breasts and then snapping shots with an mammogram. He sighs as he finishes, looking at me sadly.

"Don't be afraid." He attempts a smile. This is making me absolutely terrified! I suddenly remember Rob saying that God had taken a life for a life. What if it's my life instead of my sisters? After all, I'm the murderer. I just want to run out of here!

The technician leaves to get the doctor. A few minutes later they both emerge. The results are on the wall.

The doc doesn't hesitate to move toward the results. "This is large, but it may not be anything more than fatty tissue." He said as the technician nods in agreement.

"What if it isn't fatty tissue?" I look from the doctor to the technician, then back to the doctor. "What does that mean?"

"Well first we're going to do what we call a biopsy. We're going to take a needle and place it right where the mass shows on the sonogram. It will hurt a little, but it will be over quickly. We'll send it off to a lab, then wait a few days and see what the results tell us. Please be patient with us."

Rebecca Nietert

It's been a week. The thought of the unknown is tormenting! The fear is overwhelming; the vision of my sister in the hospital with no life haunts me. I don't want to die!

I can't work or eat. Sleep escaped me and I don't really feel like talking with anyone. The days drag on until a phone call from the doctor finally arrives.

"The cells don't appear to be cancerous."

I let go of the breath I didn't realize I've been holding. "Thank God!"

"But, they can still become cancerous if we don't take care of it. The test results show a small center of calcium, which is a sign for a possible beginning of cancer."

"I want this out but I can't be lopsided. Do you know what I do for a living?! I'm a dancer. If you take my breast it will ruin me!" I responded anxiously.

"I'll contact a friend of mine, Dr. Gerald Johnson, head of the Plastic Surgery Association. He can consult us on what needs to take place."

A few days later I'm sitting in the office of Dr. Judy and Gerald Johnson. I see some celebrities in the lobby waiting for their treatments. He must be well respected to have so many famous people visit. Farah Faucett walks next to me in chase of her three-year-old son Redman. She's a very small woman, about a head shorter than I am. She's probably a size zero too. Her hair is as perfect as any picture I've seen. Her tan skin looks stunning, like she's from a wealthy family. Noticing me watch her, she looks around, and then walks over to me.

"Please keep an eye on him for me? My mom is in there and I need to make sure she's okay."

"Sure." I responded.

She eyes me suspiciously. "You know who I am, don't you?"

"Yes. I won't tell anyone."

She nods in appreciation. "Thank you, I will be right back."

"No problem."

Heart of Gold

In about an hour Farrah reappears with her mother, scoops Redman up by his hand and leaves. I've met many celebrities and sports heroes in the clubs but none had the kindness that Farah displayed. She's a class act for sure.

After the consultation I realize that I'm going to be just fine. Dr. Johnson talked me into having an augmentation to adjust my breast a size larger so that no one would see the lumpectomy taking most of the breast tissue. We schedule the surgery for the next week.

All week I feel apprehensive about the surgery. I try to get Philip to talk but he's being unusually silent, saying that he's trying to "keep me focused." We finally get to the hospital and soon my world goes black.

I open my eyes, voices swirling all around me. I pick up on a nurse saying something about outpatient surgery. The nurse mentions something else about going home. I try to move but can't. I look down to see a bandage around my chest. I try to breathe but it's too tight. I fumble for the button to call the nurse, gritting my teeth.

A nurse rushes in. "What can I do for you?"

"These bandages are too tight. Can you help me loosen them please? I can't breathe."

"No, Darlin. I'm sorry, but those are not to be touched."

"I can't breathe!"

"You have drainage tubes in the bottom of your breasts. Those bandages are pushing all the nasty stuff out through those tubes. I can't loosen it, and you mustn't either. It is for your own good."

Breasts? Wait? "When do I get them off? Before I go home?"

"No, Darlin. You wear them for a week. Didn't the doctor explain that?"

"No. Okay, I can do this. Where's Phillip?"

"He's in the waiting room."

I look down and take in the view of my new chest size. "Um...do I look little swollen?"

100

Rebecca Nietert

She laughs, "Everyone is a little swollen afterward. We had a problem with the bags you chose. One of them broke. You were under sedation so Dr. Johnson asked your husband what to do. He selected a bigger size because we were out of the smaller ones you chose. He said you both talked about the bags."

"What?! Husband? Who?" I can't help but stutter.

"Phillip. Isn't he your husband?"

"Oh my God. No! He's my friend." I hissed feeling very afraid of what he's done.

I can't believe I called him nothing more than a friend. What is wrong with me? Maybe it's the meds… "Let me get this right…the bag that the doctor and I agreed upon broke so now instead of just one, both are bigger?" I ask, pointing to my breasts.

"Yep. That's what they decided." She smiles then leaves the room.

I struggle to sit upright in the bed, trying to look at my breasts. If they've taken too much tissue then that means they won't look normal. Now I have both breasts done. Only one was supposed to have the augmentation. I have a reputation and thanks to this it's going to be ruined! I don't want people to know about this!

The nurse walks back in, followed by Phillip, then leaves us alone. "We have to go home.." He states as he begins collecting my belongings.

"Home? Now?!" I can't keep the shock out of my voice. "But I just had surgery!"

"Yes. You're an outpatient, so that means you have to go home now." This is very un-ceremonial.

"By the way, I hear that you and the doc decided to increase the size of my breasts."

"She told you that huh?"

"Yeah, so what's up with that?"

"It was either that or leave you lying on the bed without any breasts."

"You're kidding right?"

Heart of Gold

"Nope. I had to do what I thought was best for us. After you take off the bandage I think you will be pleased."

I can't believe this! I close my eyes, whispering, "Please wake up? Please wake up." I hope this is just a dream.

"Come on Sleeping Beauty," I hear Phillip's deep voice. "No sleep for the wicked. Get to your feet. Come on over to this wheel chair and let's get going."

Before long we are on our way home, neither of us having much to say. Phillip tries to speak but I'm not listening. I can't breathe, especially sitting up in a car.

Phillip received sedatives from the doctor in case I had any pain. The rest of the week consists of him putting the sedatives in my food or drink. He keeps saying I need the rest. After a few days I can finally wake up feeling refreshed. It's time to remove the bandages.

I go back to see Dr. Johnson, who takes the bandages off. When I look in the mirror I can't help but raise my hand to my mouth. There's some blue marking on my skin but beyond that there isn't any bruising.

I blink a couple of times, unprepared for what I see, and then look at the doctor. "They're so big." I manage to whisper shocked.

"Yes, but the swelling will go down some."

"Some? You're kidding me, right? How big are these supposed to be?!"

He walks over to a table and picks up a plastic bag, just like the ones he placed inside my chest. "This is an implant bag, filled with saline. There is a ball of silicone on the inside that will keep your breast up. The saline makes it feel natural."

I touch my skin. "It doesn't feel natural to me."

"It won't for about a year. It has to gradually set to your body. The most important thing you can do is to massage them often to keep the scar tissue from building up around the bags."

I turn and face Phillip. "Why did you decide to go bigger, Phillip? This is embarrassing!" I whisper the latter as if someone's

Rebecca Nietert

going to hear me. "It was a mutual decision between you and the husband." I remember the doctor's answer. I know it's not his fault, but that doesn't dissipate the anger I feel towards him. I begin to shake uncontrollably, just realizing that he has no way of knowing that Philip isn't my husband. Phillip must have told him we were married or else he wouldn't have done the surgery, unless the nurse says something. Still! I can't wrap my mind around why Phillip did that to me, without any regard to how I might feel!

Once we arrive home I try sitting in a chair but am still unable to get comfortable. I can't help but look at the new breasts; they are right in my line of sight when I look down. My stomach has disappeared. I feel disgusting, useless.

This is a life-changer and he seems so cavalier about the choice! Now, I'm going to feel too humiliated to show my face! Sure I was scared to death I almost had cancer. That doesn't give Phillip the right to decide my medical issues. I would rather he chosen no breasts, than to give me these monstrosities.

Yes, I'm apprehensive about working in a new club, but for the first time, and now I have to show up to work deformed.

The surgery took every bit of confidence I have about my body. I have absolutely no idea how the men are going to feel about this addition. I have always been a natural beauty and now this enhancement just screams fake!

I looked into the mirror in my room. My hair is dyed blonde, my nails put on by a German technician, my tan is a fake and bake and now my chest is fake. I put my hands up to my face and I lowered my head to sob into them. I was more than stripped of any dignity that remained. I was absolutely humiliated.

No wonder I have no idea who I am. I am trying too damn hard to please men I care nothing for, and paying a high price of changing everything about me to do it.

Heart of Gold

11

None of my blouses fit anymore and forget about lying on the bed. I can't move to the side or lay on my back because it feels like someone put's a 10-pound weight on my chest. I'm furious with Phillip!

I tell myself, "I'm going to be okay." I stare at my face in the mirror, willing myself to believe those words. I can't believe I'm going to work in a new club with this stupid deformity! None of the swelling is down, but we need the money. The cash I got from Sonny has long since run out after paying hospital bills. Phillip and I are broke.

Why do I keep telling myself that everything's going to work out, especially when I don't really believe it? I begin to wish I can stop dancing to have a regular job, one where I can actually cover my expenses with intellect. Of course, I don't have the academic capacity to do such a thing. One can dream right?

One thing I do know: if I want to succeed I'll have to earn it. Sure, it would be nice to have a job where I don't have to deal with humiliation and embarrassment on a regular basis, even money can't deter those feelings; but this is the life I've chosen.

Philip keeps reminding me that it's the beginning of a huge economic downturn with the abandonment of neighborhoods left and right. He keeps drilling into me that someone with a college degree has lost everything they have. Presidents and officers are standing on street corners, begging for money, yet the clubs are full. Packed every night with Houston's elite who doesn't fluctuate in cash flow. I need to count my blessings. I don't feel that way though.

Rebecca Nietert

Tonight's the night I begin my new job. When I step into the club I'm introduced to a few girls. Bobbi, one of the girls from Mack's, had moved over here as well. It's so nice to see a familiar face! We sat at the bar a long time while I try to muster enough courage to walk on stage again. I haven't taken my clothes off in so long I'm not sure I can do it, especially with the new change in appearance.

When it's my turn on stage, I do exactly what's expected of me. Maybe if I don't think about what the customers are thinking I'll be fine. Maybe I can even pretend I'm not really on stage. I can't help but feel humiliated I keep my back to the crowd so they can't see the shame of my new breasts. I've put stage makeup on my scars but I am sure if I turned around everyone would know anyway.

I wish I could fake confidence, just like at Mack's. Wait a minute… It's nearing the end of the song when I gather the courage to face the crowd. To my amazement, the men don't seem to notice my new monstrosities in the way I thought they would. I receive more tips on the stage than I have at any other time in my dancing career. Although I feel a little boost of confidence, I also feel confused.

After I finish walking around the room to size up who might or might not be worth approaching, Bobbi pulls me over. "I know you're going to do great here!"

I can't help but smile. "Thank you!"

"There's a guy asking about you, his name's John. You have to meet him!"

"Sure!" When we arrive at the table John smiles at me.

"Hi."

"What's your name sweetheart?"

"Barbie." I look over to see Bobbi move closer to him and put a hand on his shoulder. He doesn't seem to notice or care.

"No it isn't. What is it for real? I've seen you at Mack's haven't I?" Bobbi rolls her eyes, gets up and walks away.

Heart of Gold

"At Mack's my name was Brooke. Now it's Barbie, even though it's really Beverly. Do you have a problem with that?"

"Not at all." Maybe it's the sound of his voice or the look in his eyes, but I find myself caught completely off guard. Why did I just tell this guy, a complete stranger, what my real name is? I sit down next to him; unable to figure out what it is about him that makes me feel almost...at ease. For some reason, I decide to spill my entire life's story on this poor soul. I divulge everything except my relationship with Phillip.

I'm getting really tired of pretending. I don't want to hide anymore. I want someone to see the real me. The real question is why him of all people? Either way, he doesn't seem to mind. Why do I trust a man with all the secrets that I've been trying to hide my entire topless career? I've got to end this, fast. I feel uncomfortable.

"Time's up." I open my hand to receive the money. He slaps two hundred dollars in my hand. I start at it, then at him, incredulous. Is that all I'm really worth? My fall from grace washed over me. I made only two hundred dollars? I haven't made this little money since I've begun dancing!

I slam the two hundred-dollar bills on the table in front of Phillip as I walk in the door. He stares at it, and then looks at me. "That's it?"

"Yep." *Wrong move.* I thought after I spoke.

"You're supposed to make more money now, not less."

I blink confused. "When did how much money I make ever become an issue? We have enough to eat for a few days. I'll make more."

"You need to make more tomorrow. I have a gig and I need that money."

"A gig? Where? For what?" He never had a gig before.

"Me and the boys are going to a studio to cut a demo. I need a new guitar. The money that you were supposed to make tonight was going to pay for it."

"Wow! Okay, can't you use one of your other ones?"

Rebecca Nietert

"I can't. I gave those away."

"Look, I've given you thousands of dollars this past year. I've given you far more than enough to have your studio built! It should be up and running. Where is all that money?"

"I spent it on stuff for you and for this house. I spent it on our lifestyle, Beverly!"

I can't back down now. The usual fear I would have at his raised voice is gone. "Listen, if you spent all that money then the fact that you don't have a guitar to play is your own fault. What are you doing giving away your equipment anyway? Frankly, I don't feel I owe you anything more. I've done what you asked of me and much more than that. When you did this to me," I pointed to my breasts. "That erased our commitment. I would never do anything like that to you without your permission."

I didn't see it coming. In a blur of motion Phillip left his chair and was suddenly grabbing my arm, shaking me. His voice an octave higher than it was a few seconds ago. "You owe me your life! You will do exactly what I tell you when and how I tell you to do it!"

I can't believe he just spoke to me like that! What's worse, I can't help but feel as if I'm looking into my mother's disappointed eyes all over again. If I figured out a way to leave her and a boyfriend who beat me, I can sure figure out a way to leave Phillip!

Can I really trust him anymore? For some reason I feel…afraid? Am I afraid of Phillip? No way! I jerk my arm away and look him in the eye.

Maybe Lana was right. Maybe he's just using me after all? I turn and walk to my room, feeling his eyes on me the entire time. I lay down on the bed and shut my eyes.

The next morning, I open my eyes to see a silhouette of a large black man. I blink, unable to help the jolt that shocked my body. His arms are crossed, feet standing apart. It's Phillip.

"What are you-" I shake my head and try again. "Why are you standing there?"

Heart of Gold

"We have to talk. Now." I watch as he turns and leaves the room.

What? I get dressed and walk into the kitchen to see Phillip sitting at the island, looking towards me.

"What's this about?" I grab the coffee pot and pour some of the dark liquid into a cup. "The money?"

"No. Your attitude." I look at him and take a sip, waiting. "I asked you to do something for me and what did you do? Nothing! You're ungrateful, that's what you are. After everything I've done for you!" I watch as he begins to pace back and forth, as if he's the father and I'm the child. "I made you who you are and you have the nerve to speak to me like you did last night?"

"You're using me." I try my best to keep an even tone.

He stops and turns to face me. "I'm using you?" I look him in the eye and nod. I can see the anger burning in those black, lifeless orbs. "How dare you tell me that I am using you!" I wince as he puts his big hands on my shoulders and shakes me. Hands that used to caress me are now punishing me. "You asked me to help you, remember? I picked you up. I brought you home when your family turned their backs on you." I can't back down, no matter how much this hurts. "Do you not remember that I fed you when I had very little to feed myself. I taught you how to dance. I taught you how to walk like a lady. I taught you how to dress. I taught you what men really want from you. You can't even get through a single night without asking me what to do."

He's right. I was the one who begged him for help. How could I have accused him of using me? He's the only person on the planet who truly cares about me. Everyone else just uses me. How could I not owe him? I owe him my life and so much more. Maybe the breasts were really for the both of us. So he could have his studio. So we could be rich when he sells his songs. How could I not understand it was for us?

"You're right." I whisper, feeling his eyes on me as I look at the floor. I feel the shame start to creep up my face. "Why do you stay with me when you could've had your recording studio a long time ago? You could be well on your way since you're so talented."

"Because you big fool I love you!" I feel him take my hand and look up as he kisses my hand, his proclamation shocking me. "I don't understand."

"Bev, I could have bought a recording studio that would take all my time. But you needed me, and I've been there for you. Do you want me to stop helping you?"

"No, not at all." I admit. I looked around at all the expensive things we've bought that adorned our lovely home. I love our luxurious lifestyle.

"I want to marry you some day. When I become famous everything's going to change." His eyes change to a soft caramel brown. They pierce my soul. I try to shake the confusion that's been looming over me. Do I or don't I want to be with Phillip? I am not sure what to do.

He's right. He's the only reason I have any success at all. All the times I've called, asking what I should do, begin to play in my mind. I can't imagine my life without him.

"Would you prefer I left you all alone?" He asked.

"No, but I would prefer that you don't grab me like you did, that you treat me with respect. I would prefer to not be a dancer and you be okay with that. Isn't that what you want from a wife?"

"There is nothing about us that's conventional. We've been through hell and back this past year and have a long way to go to get back to where we were financially. We work together, don't you see that?" He kisses me and for a moment I'm lost. Lost in him, in his world of possibilities. I wrap my arms around his neck as his hands move slowly to my waist. I run my hands down his chest as he pulls me closer. I press my body into his as he begins to move against me. I kiss his neck while running my hands up and down his body. I can feel his breath against my ear as he whispers softly "I'm here for you."

Heart of Gold

I stop and look up at him, smiling. "I know and I appreciate everything you do for me." I plant another kiss on his lips and whisper, "I truly do. I am just not sure this arrangement is working anymore. I'm so tired of it all."

He stops and looks at me straight in the eye, then whispers, "I will make sure that you're completely alone if you change one thing about our relationship."

I suddenly realize how tight he's been holding me. I'm completely crushed against him. I push against his chest and he lets go, his gaze not leaving mine. His words rattle me even more. Something just clicked and for some reason I get it.

I step back, and I look at his piercing eyes. I realize that's not love. That's manipulation. That's what I do to men. Something deep inside me breaks and the trust I had was all gone. His threat caused the exact opposite aftermath he expected.

I am the master manipulator with men though, and I remain calm. I cannot let him know that I feel this way. My eyes have to remain cool and not as surprised as I actually feel. A huge part of me no longer feels the loyalty I promised to him anymore. I don't know if it's what he said or how tight he held me, but something changed the way I feel about him. I back away further and walk as fast as I can to my room. It's not like I have a choice, but I do need time to think. Alone.

When I get off work I call Phillip at home just to see if he'll pick up. No answer. Hmm…that's odd. Where else would he be after professing to always be there for me? I go the bar and see Bobbi walking towards me. "Are you still working? It's late."

"I just got off." I responded. Dancers have shifts and some of us get out sooner.

"What are you going to do now?" She asks.

"Find out what my boyfriend, Phillip, does at night. Why?"

"Be careful. You might not like what you find."

I look at her, sensing she knows more than she's letting on. "You know, I don't care anymore."

Rebecca Nietert

"Yes, you do."

"I need to be clear so that I don't feel I owe him." I say softly.

"I don't understand, but okay." She shrugs and walks away.

I leave the club and head to the Building of Zeus. It's the next most popular topless bar. After convincing a gentleman to escort me inside, I walk to the bar and order a drink. The bartender asks I want a job. I refuse, and for some reason, tell him I'm looking for someone. He asks for a description, which I gladly give.

He points me to a back corner, where I spot Phillip and some of his friends.

I lean against a pillar so he can't see me and watch him. He's concentrated on a stage performer with a boa constrictor wrapped around her neck. What an amateur. Why on earth is he so interested in a side show rather than what he's got at home? I walk over to his table and stand directly in front of him.

"Baby! What are you doing here?" He sings.

"I came here to see what you're up to every night." I don't know why it matters?

He sputters out a few words I can't understand, then mutters about not attending this club in a long time. "I'm just having a night out with the boys, blowing off steam after our talk." The song ends and we stare at each other. It's as if he can't believe I'm not on stage working and I can't believe he's looking at another girl on stage other than where I work.

The stage girl who must have shed her enormous snake runs past me, pouncing in Phillip's lap. She's a petite brunette whose green eyes compliment her dark skin. She's very exotic looking and energetic. She's smiling while adoring Phillip.

"This is Kelly. My friend." He absurdly comments.

She gives me the up down, the look that a woman gives another woman that looks just like they ate something horrible as they view her from top to bottom. As if the woman intruded in their territory. I shoot it right back.

"Who is she?" Kelly asks Phillip.

Heart of Gold

"His, you know, girlfriend." I dismiss.

Her eyes grow grew wide with shock. "I'm his girlfriend too!" She sasses, trying to throw me off-guard.

Phillip bolts out of his chair tossing her up in the air and stands her abruptly next to him. He grabs her by the arm. "If you want to be a friend of mine Ky you'll watch how you talk to her. Now go, I need to talk to her."

She looks at him, then at me, and finally makes up her mind to walk away.

Phillip sits down and looks at me, taking my hand. "She means nothing to me. She's just play I use to let off a little steam, just like other men you know. I won't let it happen again if you ask me not to."

I don't know what to say. On one hand, I don't want to tell him he can't have fun. On the other, I don't want him with anyone else. I need answers that he can't give me.

"Ky, Phillip?

"Yes, she goes by Ky Kelly." He said with a wide grin.

"That's disgusting. I would appreciate that. I'll be back." I walk away and head to the dressing room. He doesn't even try to stop me. I have to talk to this girl.

When I walk through the door I hear her voice. "Can you believe his girlfriend came in here? I did not even know he had a girlfriend?" I felt a little bit of embarrassment for eavesdropping, but nonetheless I waited where she couldn't see me before I fully entered. When she finally realizes someone is there she moves and realizes it's me. Her face turns red but I don't think it's from embarrassment. I think it's because she's angry. I guess we are both surprised to find out about each other.

"So…what's going on with you two?" I ask her.

"We've been out a couple of times and he comes in here to see me. He tells me I'm his girl."

"Have you slept with him?" Funny that's what he calls me too. His girl.

112

Rebecca Nietert

"Yes." There isn't a single trace of hesitation in her voice.

"Do you know about me?" I choked out.

"No. Are you a dancer?"

"Yeah. I worked at Mack's before and now I'm at the Gentleman's Club."

Her eyes got wide. "You're one of those fancy dancers! What's he doing here then?"

"To see you I would imagine." I don't know what irks me more, the fact that she just called me 'one of those fancy dancers' or the fact that he's cheating on me with some low-life snake dancing wannabe. Crap! Now I am angry.

"You know, I've been to his house and I didn't see a single picture of you anywhere." She questioned.

It's true; we don't have any pictures of us together. In fact, we don't have any pictures of each other at all. She's been at my house and I didn't know it? It's never occurred to me that Phillip may be seeing others. In everything I've done for him, what is there that I couldn't provide? For some reason, I'm not as concerned about Phillips indiscretion as much as I am about the manipulation he's been mastering?

"What does the house look like?" I interrogate.

"It's a town house, the one with the big fancy black satin couch. It's decorated in black and white." She paused waiting for confirmation.

She described it perfectly. I feel sick, as though my world is slowly breaking apart. I feel a mixture of fear, anger, but most of all betrayal. I looked at her with all the contempt I could muster. I shook my head. This just cannot be happening!

I leave Kelly and march up to Phillip. "We need to talk."

He turns to his friends, "Give us some space guys."

After they leave I lose my cool. "I can't believe you brought that whore to our house! You jeopardized everything we have meant to each other because you were 'bored'. What? I can't believe you'd spend your time with such a nasty girl who can't even dance! You

Heart of Gold

have me! I can dance for you or give you a lap dance or whatever the hell you want! You're supposed to be at a studio, working on your career! Not sleazing around in this whorehouse! If you want to see a dancer, come see me!" Everything just keeps coming as if it's from somewhere deep inside. I sit in a chair and look at him, exasperated. "How could you do this to us? What the heck is this all about?"

I never realized I had so many questions for him. At this point I'm not even sure I want to know the truth. I see all of these girls at work whose boyfriends are pimps and I was so grateful that I didn't have that. I've always believed our relationship was based on clarity. Each of us knew their part in the relationship. I worked while he saved to build a life for us. While he worked? While I worked? The master of destruction is what I was living. I realized he set me up. I am just as gullible as the men I have conned and the women I have contemptuously watched. Women just like me who were sucked into believing one thing and who ended up being betrayed in the worst kind of way.

How could this happen to me? I've gotten smarter. I listen to what the men say. I pay attention to everything that goes around me. I focus on everything I need, except what Phillip wants or needs.

I suppose I thought he would always be there. Now, I find out I am wrong about everything? Am I? Is everything a lie?

I've always been grateful that he picked me up when he did, and dusted me off. I am grateful for what I have learned. Now that gratefulness is diminishing, and I'm not sure what to think anymore. Deep down I realize that this isn't just about how bad I feel Phillip is, it's about how bad I feel about myself. Sigh, I am confused yet again.

Rebecca Nietert

12

We left the bar so that we could have a serious discussion in our home. He humbly walked into our home as if he was a pup who had just done something terribly wrong. I am not sure if he knew it was wrong but he definitely knew that I thought it was wrong. He spoke, "Baby, you can't believe anything that girl says."

You have got to be kidding me. "No! I don't believe anything you say! From now on things are going to be different. I'm not giving you any money. Whatever I have is mine." I insisted still feeling like I needed his constant work-related encouragement.

"You need me." He retorted. "You can't dance without me."

I felt he might be right but I continued, "You betrayed me. Right now, I would rather be homeless again!" I spit out and his pupils shrink. Did I really just snatch some of his power away? I'm in as much shock as he seems to be.

"Listen, whatever you ask, I'll do it." He whispers, eyes staring into mine.

"We're going to set some ground rules here. If you break them, I'll leave. You'll be left with nothing! I'm not afraid of my credit going bad. I'm not afraid of you hurting me anymore. Let's just say I got my wake-up call."

"Fine! Anything." He's getting desperate. I like this side of Phillip. How ironic would it be to have power over the man who taught me everything I know about having power over any man?

"No more other girls."

"I promise."

Let's see how long that one lasts. "As far as we are concerned, I'm not marrying or sleeping with you. That part is over."

"Aw come on baby. You can forgive me? I need you sexually too."

Heart of Gold

"If I find out about another girl we are finished. Do you hear me?"

He nods. "Where did all this come from? How come you came to that club?"

"I'm tired Phillip. You've drained me long enough. I can't do this anymore. I care about you and want to see you happy, but I can't do this anymore." I was honest.

"Yes, you can. You're a rock. Come on now, let's go to bed."

"I'm not 'a rock' Phillip; I'm a person who never wanted this in the first place."

"Yes you did. You were starving and I taught you how to care for yourself."

"Enough!" That's not enough anymore. Yes, it doesn't give you license to hurt me.

"I know." He muttered.

I'm more than confident he won't ever go back. I can tell by the way he waved goodbye to Kelly when we left. As it should be. It's his fault neither one of us are happy. For some reason, finding him with another girl left me more so angry than hurt. I had kept my end of the bargain. Most people would say leave him, but I just can't. I feel he keeps me safe from harm. Sometimes I can't help but wonder when the deception began. Did he ever plan on having that studio or was that a ruse to keep me working hard? I don't think I'll ever really know.

Saturday night I arrive at work. Not only do I hate working Saturday's, there's a contest going on throughout the club to win a chance to be a dancer in one of Eddie Murphy's upcoming movies. That's one way to get out of this life right? For some reason, I don't want to enter the contest. Sure the money will be out of this world, as will the fame; if that promise comes.

That night was one of contests for the best dancer. I am set to get off early and miss the shenanigans.

Me, I want a real life one day, with kids. The thought of them seeing my body on screen, dancing half-naked, makes me feel sick

Rebecca Nietert

to my stomach. I'll have enough horror stories to tell them, no sense in them actually seeing me in the act. I begin dancing, moving from table-to-table, guy-to-guy, I overhear bits of information here and there. Soon I'm able to piece together that the producers will be in town for a few days and are gathering as many girls as possible for the try-out. Too bad they'll be missing out on the best one: me. I smirk as I head out the door, done for the night.

I start my car; lean my head back against the headrest, and let out a sigh. It was a good night overall. I made a considerable amount of money, not the best but not the worst I've done either. After a short drive, I walk inside the house and immediately notice that Phillip, who's been behaving himself, is in a rather foul mood.

"Where's my money?" He doesn't look up from the pile of paperwork at the kitchen island.

He's probably getting stuff ready for the studio. Finally! "I made a grand tonight. How much do you want?"

As I reach into my backpack to pull out some money he jumps up from where he was sitting and in the blink of an eye, snatches my backpack. "Liar!"

"What are you talking about?" I let him take the bag, unable to do anything else.

"You made more than that, I will bet my life on it!" He rips the bag open, shoving his hands into it, words coming out in a fury. "That contest was tonight. You had regulars come in to tip you, right?" He dumps out the bags contents on the floor. "And you tell me you only made a grand?!"

"I didn't dance in the contest. What is wrong with you?"

He throws the bag on the ground, grabs wads of cash and shoves them in my face. "You would dare lie to me?!"

I step back, letting him count the money. He usually doesn't get like this. "I assure you there's only a grand." I hiss.

"There's twelve hundred."

"Yes. I told you it was about a grand. What's wrong with you?!" I pick up my backpack and start to shove my belongings back in.

Heart of Gold

"Someone's stealing from me." He answers flippantly.

"You think I'd steal from you? I give you everything Phillip!"

He ignores my comment. "We all know when we do something wrong we tell the truth right?"

"Yes?" I'm so confused.

"Good. Let's hope you never break our trust forever." His arrogance takes me by surprise. I let him walk off, cash in hand. I don't know what just happened, but I need to get out of here. Soon. I walk to my room and stuff a few hundred-dollar bills he missed in my shoe, just like at work. I sit on the bed, in a daze. I need help, someone to help sort through my emotions. I call Lana, tell her what happened, make plans for lunch tomorrow and fall asleep.

We end up at our favorite restaurant. It's Pappadeaux. I sit down across from Lana.

Lana asks. "How are you?"

"Fine, I guess." I say softly.

"I love this place." She looks around at the old vintage décor. "When we're old we're going to be sitting on rocking chairs laughing about these times!" I can't help but smile at the thought.

Lana smiles back. "There, now see that was not so bad." She flags down a waitress. "Two glasses of white wine please?" Normally we don't have alcohol this early, but it's a special occasion.

"Water too?" I ask. Better safe than sorry. Who knows how much I'm really going to end up having.

"Bev, you don't look okay." Lana looks at me, her eyes piercing into my soul. "Really, how are you?" I hate how she has that effect on me.

"Sad, but I don't know why. Hurt and tired. Angry. Nothing seems to go my way. Plus I really miss working with you."

"What it's like at the G.C.?"

"It's a blast. I work hard like you do for every dollar believe it or not. I bust my butt on stage twice a night. I work the room just like we used to and really don't mind doing it. I thought I would,

Rebecca Nietert

but I'm meeting some pretty down-to-earth people. Not all snooty, like at Mack's. I like that I can do my job, get my money and go home without my work following me."

"No madam?" She looks at me, both of us understanding what she really means.

"Not making that mistake twice."

"Good for you!" She takes a sip of wine, seeming genuinely happy.

"You warned me. I'm sorry about that."

"I know sweetie, thank you. I bet that was hard to say."

I take a long sip of wine. "See! Now I have something else to feel guilt about!" I blink a few times, unable to stop the tears from forming.

"Bev, what's really going on?"

"I don't know. I'm sad all the time, all I want to do is cry. I'm talking more now to men than ever before. In fact, one of them is actually becoming my friend. What's that all about? I can't figure it out!"

"You're just searching for truth. Good for you."

"What truth? All I know is that I have a river of emotion I can't seem to handle. It makes me volatile towards Phillip. I'm not sure how to fix this."

"Well, start from the beginning. Tell me about this guy."

"His name's John. I can't figure out why I opened up to him. He was nice but I'm not attracted to him. He's three times my age! I don't know what it is, but he makes me feel like. . . I don't know!" I take another sip of wine. Maybe that'll help a bit.

"A respectable lady?" She offers.

"Exactly. He tips me without making me dance for him. We talk a lot. He gives me money to sit. I don't have to hustle him. He thinks I'm way too smart to be doing this. Everything he says to me is respectful and really nice. We talk about books and museums." I can feel myself starting to smile. Great, just what I need.

Heart of Gold

"He sounds wonderful." Lana says softly, looking intently at me.

"I know! He knows I like Van Gogh, Monet and other impressionistic work. He bought me a book and gave it to me so I could learn more. Anything I tell him I'm interested in, he finds a book somewhere to bring it in, so I can read about it."

"What else does he do for you?"

"You know how it's really hard for me to understand why people do some of the things they do? Like laugh when walking by or talking behind each other's backs?"

"Yeah? I don't understand those things either."

"Well, he explains social behaviors and the causes and effects in a more profound and untainted view than Phillip. He helps me understand more about what women think than I could've ever learned from Phillip. He says that there are levels of appropriate conduct. He says there's a behavior for each certain situation. I don't like it but at least I get it now."

"It sounds as if you like who you're becoming. If that's true, why are you so sad?"

"Because of Phillip!" I can't help the sudden outburst of emotion. At this point, I'm not sure what I feel. "I care about him, I really do. I feel as though he's the most genuine friend I have, even though I owe him for teaching me how to take care of myself. Even though it feels like he only wants my money, which hurts, money isn't what my life with him is about. At least, it's not what I thought we were about."

"I've had many men promise one thing and deliver another. I suspected this."

"He's just so…angry all the time. He rips the money out of my hands, as though everything we've shared is now gone."

"You put Phillip in the position he's in." She pauses as I blink at her, then continues. "You made it so that he doesn't have to work. You allowed it to become all about the money and now you're surprised that it's like that?"

Rebecca Nietert

"Yes. I guess that I thought we had something uniquely different. I thought that I would buy his studio in exchange for the teaching me how to be independent and then both of us would sail into success. He would have his career, and I would be done with dancing, but the way John explains things, what I get is that he's just using me. When I told Phillip that, he turned it around and made me feel bad for telling him I felt that way."

"Maybe Phillip sees how happy John makes you. Maybe he's really jealous?"

"Phillip, jealous? That's ridiculous!"

She raises her eyebrows. "I think where he's concerned you don't really know what's going on."

"What do you mean?"

"You don't love Phillip. You don't watch him or pay attention. There's no way for you to know how he feels or what he does. You don't really care."

"You know, you may be right. I remember being so obsessed when I loved someone. I knew what their favorite colors were, where they loved to go; everything about them. I know nothing about Phillip except what he's done for me. I guess I didn't want to become obsessive again."

"You needed and God provided, that's all you did. You don't owe him any more than what you've already given. You've handed him so much of what he's requested of you that it makes you exhausted. I'm exhausted just looking at you!"

"See? These are the kinds of conversations that I need. I don't know about the whole God thing but I do know without you I can't seem to clarify things. Please come to work with me?"

"Speaking of guys, I have a new boyfriend!" Lana blurts out, then puts her hand over her mouth as if she's done something awful.

"Sorry, I've been babbling on about me this whole time. Tell me about him."

Heart of Gold

"His name's Kerry. He's the guy that I adopted Alphy with. I thought he wasn't going to work out but he did. We're moving in together!" I can't help but smile at her excitement.

"Are you happy?"

She shrugs. "What is happy anyway? He makes me feel good, drives a convertible roadster. We travel to the beach with our pup. Yeah, I think I am happy."

"I'm happy for you." I force the words out even though I can't help but feel jealous deep inside.

"Can we rekindle the competition between us? Honestly, I'm not making the money I was when you were around. Apparently I need you to help me too." She smiles.

"I've always been able to inspire you? You're too funny." I laugh then look at her, unable to keep the question from coming out. "Do you think that I should leave Phillip?"

"I think we should eat and talk about something other than him."

"I have this feeling that my life is about to change. Again." I sigh.

"What crossroad is this now? Number two?"

"Yep."

"You know Bev, you need to remind yourself that you have courage. Every time we take our tops off we have to mount up more courage than anyone thinks is possible. You can do whatever it is your heart desires, you just have to want it badly enough. You're strong; a rock. I just wish you believed that."

I can't keep the tears from forming. "Sometimes I'm on top of the world, other times I'm so far under that I can't seem to climb out. I'm tired of this emotional roller coaster. I just wish that something would happen to show me the truth, so I can jump off."

"You're loyal, I'll give you that. Don't worry about it right now. Everything will work out."

The next night at work, Lana walks in for a job and (since I put in a good word) is hired immediately. We made plans to be there at the exact time so we can work together. I sit against the far wall at a table, figuring we could have some drinks until she's acclimated enough to work. John arrives and joins us. We are busily talking when Lana decides to ask how my roommate is doing, loud enough for John to hear.

He turns to me, seeming confused. "You have a roommate?" I look at Lana silently hating myself for feeling so comfortable that I had forgotten we aren't in a bar. I face him, putting on my best show face. "Yes I do. I live with a guy who's a musician and his brother is coming to stay with us for a while. I just found out about that news today actually."

Lana looks at me, confused. "His brother?"

"Yep. I'm helping out two brothers who are homeless." I look back at her, hoping my eyes tell her to shut up and keep up the lie. It's not really a lie. Phillip would be homeless without me. His brother really is moving in with us...sort of. I'll fill her in on the rest later.

Lana smiles and turns to face John. "See? I didn't even know that about her."

He laughs, seeming to be enjoying himself.

I don't know if it's the drinks or the fact that there's a listening ear, but Lana and I both say how much we both want to stop dancing. His compassion for our plight is written all over his face. He seems surprised. "Neither one of you enjoy what you're doing?"

"No. Honestly, would you?" I laugh, trying to shake the feeling of self-pity.

He laughs. "Well when you put it that way, no."

Lana and I looked at each other and then back at John.

"Finally, a guy who gets it!" Lana laughs and turns to me. "You're real lucky."

"Yes, I am." I smile at John.

"I have been thinking about that too." He looks back at me, eyes staring into mine.

Heart of Gold

"Thinking about what?" I bite my lip, unable to help the tingling sensation that's coursing through my body. I love it when he looks at me like that.

"Giving you money not to dance." He takes a sip of his drink.

"Oh, well...I've been down that road. Don't get me wrong, I haven't slept around or anything, but I took money I didn't deserve and it got me into a ton of trouble. So, I'm not prepared to get into what you think you deserve if you give me money."

His eyes widen. "What are you talking about?"

I suddenly feel stupid. Really. Stupid. Why did I open my mouth? "Umm..."

"I wouldn't think you're that kind of girl!"

"Oh." I sigh in relief. ""I'm not."

"I hear you say that you hate this business and I want to help. My wife just passed away and left a sizable fortune, as you already know. Listen, you have to realize that some men during your lifetime are going to love you. When they do and they offer you a way to improve yourself you take it. They want you to take it. It's because they are being unselfish. That's what real love is. The sooner you understand that, the sooner you'll find that happiness you so desperately seek."

He sounds so wise to me. I want to accept what he said as truth but the look on Lana's face makes me pause. Red flag warnings keep going up. I'm not sure what to do. I don't want to dance anymore and he's giving me an opportunity to get the money without strings attached. Or is it really that simple?

Mack's Club was a gentleman's club for the rich. It is private and mostly the clients are celebrities and famous athletes. Rarely is a blue collar man invited let alone show up. I never really felt like working there was equivalent to working in topless bars like The Gentleman's Club. When I was a small girl I wanted to be a teacher, not a topless dancer. I never envisioned I would ever wind up making a living the way I am no matter how much money it pays. I don't want the money anymore. I just want respect.

Rebecca Nietert

I can't help myself. His sentiments touch my heart. "Okay, deal."

"We've got to get to work, but will be back." I grab Lana by the arm, pulling her out of the chair.

"You two go have some fun. I'll order dinner."

After we tell him our order, Lana and I walk into the sea of men. We approach one table after another, dancing for what seems like hours. By the time we walk back to the lockers to put our cash up we are both exhausted. Still, it was a fun evening that's for sure.

"Can you believe him? Giving me money anytime I want?"

She pauses, and then nods. "Yes, I believe it. You have got to be the luckiest person on the planet!"

"I've been honest with him. I guess we've developed quite a friendship."

"I think that this guy will, in time, think he has paid for you, owns you?"

"Owns me?" I slam the locker shut. "I don't think so."

"Bev, you don't get something for nothing, okay? Not even you. Eventually he will fall in love and will want you all for himself. Eventually, you will loathe him. I know this because you can't fall in love with someone who gives you money. It's not possible."

"Why are you being so harsh? He is so nice and just wants my time. How can that be a bad thing?"

"Mark my words; there will come a day when many tears will fall because you should just do your work. Come in, do your job, go home and take a shower. Pretend you never danced that evening. That's what you should do."

Her words hit me like a ton of bricks. Even though I respect her honesty, I'm not used to her judging me. I sink down on the bench next to the lockers, soaking it all in. Did I just make another horrible decision?

She sits next to me. "You keep looking for that guy who's going to save you. You want a guy who will make your life mean something to you. You're searching for your 'Knight in Shining

Heart of Gold

Armor' but it just isn't going to happen. That's a fairy tale, not real life."

"Okay, Lana, I get it! I'm not going to be saved." I snap, then sigh. "But does that mean that for a few nights I can't just sit back and be entertained by someone whose company I enjoy and get paid for it?"

"I will be here for you no matter what okay? If you fall, I'll be here. When you hurt or when it all doesn't make sense anymore, I will be here."

I nod. "I know. Thank you." We hug, then head back to the table where John is still sitting waiting for the both of us.

We talk for the rest of the night. John asks a lot of questions, seeming to want to know everything about me. It's flattering. I tell him about me dreams, future plans, how I want a family. I somehow end up telling him about my unborn child. He knows more about me than any man who's paid me money. For some strange reason I connect with this man. I am okay with trusting him with knowledge of my personal life. I find it shocking, but I genuinely like him.

"Think you'll want to visit everyone in Chicago?" Lana asks. I pause, feeling my heart become heavy at the thought.

"Yeah, I miss them. Want to join me?"

"I wish, but I need to stay here. I doubt they'll let me have vacation this early."

"I'll be more than happy to go." John announces jokingly.

Lana and I look at him, then at each other. The three of us burst out laughing. Of course that will never happen.

Rebecca Nietert

13

The next weekend seemed as though nothing bad had transpired between Phillip and me. Everything seemingly returned to normal.

Phillip and I often shop at local flea markets in downtown Houston. This market has plenty of fresh fruit and vegetables. The two of us have a restricted diet, mainly to keep my body in shape. We enjoy the market because there are generally a lot of people.

While there Phillip introduces me to his friend, Ernie, and Ernie's girlfriend, Tanya. She's a beautiful woman, dark and thin. It feels odd to be in the presence of primarily African American company. I look around, noticing uneasy glances from bystanders.

After traveling around a bit with Philip and the disapproving stares, which never bothered me before, suddenly became a huge issue; the uncomfortable feelings are evident. For some reason I'm acutely aware today. Not only do I feel the stares, I suddenly feel the hairs on the back of my neck stand out, as if something's off. Phillip and Ernie walk off to talk, leaving me with Tanya. We get to know each other and as we meet back up with the boys she mentions how she wants to be a dancer.

Ernie looks at me. "Any chance you might talk with her?"

I can feel Phillip's breath in my ear as he whispers, "Yeah, this may be just what you need. She doesn't need your aloof attitude either. You can be quite hard to take."

I look at Phillip dismayingly, "Sweetheart contrary to what you may believe, some men think I am captivating to be with." I smile up at him, bringing on my A-game.

He says, "If you're going to help anyone it should be Tamara, a girl at Zeus. Poor thing can't make a hundred bucks a night."

Heart of Gold

Where did this come from? "Whoever thinks that I am a teacher for these girls needs to think again." I can't imagine that he brought up a girl's name out of the blue. Either Ernie is interested in her or Phillip is. However, I still can't imagine how he can say her name in front of us, two supposed girlfriends, not a good idea.

Phillip pulls me aside and looks into my eyes. His attitude diving for the worst, he grasps my arm hard. "I think you're getting too big for your britches! John brings you all kinds of books and now you think you're better than me?"

I jerk my arm from his grasp. "I don't think I'm better than you. Where did that come from?"

"Sometimes you're such a snob!"

"I don't want anyone to have to learn what I do!"

"I don't care if you help Tanya but you better help Tamara. Just talk to her. You're so good at what you do; it's the least I can ask you."

"Is Tamara your new girlfriend?" I look at Ernie and Tanya. Oops, was that too loud?

"No, she's his girlfriend." He points to Ernie whose face is white.

"He's cheating on Tanya?" I whisper, trying not to be too loud this time. They both start to look around at various venders, trying to give us some space.

"Yes, he wants to quit his job. Tamara wants take care of him by dancing. That's why I need you to help the girls."

"He's going to have two women working for him? Phillip, he's short, not that good looking and apparently has no real talent. Why on earth would two women want that?"

"For the same reason you do, Beverly." His words feel like a slap in the face.

What?! "I don't work for you. I work because we made a deal: you help me and I help you. What is he going to do for these girls but take their money?"

128

Rebecca Nietert

"Once you teach them to do what you do, he's going to do everything for them that I do for you."

I can't help but stare at him. I meant nothing more than a whore?

I can't help the tears that now sting at my eyes. Even after everything we've been through, he's been using me this whole time? I suddenly think about how I don't call Phillip from work anymore, especially not when John is there. Could it be that I really don't need to depend on him? I am so confused! I gather as much courage as I can muster. I will not let him see me cry. "Just what exactly do you do for me?"

That made him angrier. "I taught you everything you know. You wouldn't be making a dime without me. You might not call me as much but that's because I taught you how to be strong. All I'm asking is for you to teach these two girls the same things I taught you."

I can't help but laugh. For the first time the thought of me owing him something is somehow hilarious. "Why don't you just teach them? According to you, it's all about you."

"I can't; they won't listen to me. They want you to teach them." He walks off to where Ernie and Tanya are standing, looking some fruit stands.

"Well at least they might be smart." I mumble as I follow. He doesn't hear me.

"Are you going to help us or not?" Ernie disrespectfully asks.

I don't bother paying attention to Ernie's desperate plea for help. Instead, I choose to focus on Tanya, who's looking at me with pleading eyes.

"Please, I work in an office. I make six bucks an hour and have a kid. I can't make it on my own anymore. I need this."

Sure I've taught many people about what I do; Lana is my main girl and my best friend. But for some reason I don't want to teach this girl. Her story pulls at my heart, but the idea of someone raising a kid while being a dancer scares me. I've known quite a few people

Heart of Gold

who have done so throughout my short-lived career, so why do I feel so different about this one?

I look at her. "How on earth are you going to raise a kid and dance?"

"The father's out of the picture. I can be with her until eight or so at night and then go to work so she doesn't know that I'm gone. I can also hire a nanny."

That makes sense. "What about when she gets older?"

"By then I hope to be retired with enough in the bank for her college. I figured I'll save what I can, so that when she got smart about me being a dancer, I will be able to quit. Besides, why do you care about what happens in my life?"

Good question. Why do I care? Part of me wants to believe her, but I can't help the feeling in my gut that all of her money will go to Ernie, just like mine goes to Phillip. Well, went to Philip; that's not happening anymore. I don't see a way out for her if she chooses to do this. Still, I can't shake the feeling of guilt, knowing that I'd turned someone down at making a good living. Even if it's something I personally despise, it just might be the life for her. "Fine, I'll teach you." I can't look her in the eye.

After we get home, Phillip and I get into one of the biggest fights we've ever had. I can't help but feel awful for helping a woman into a profession that I now loathe. Thoughts of what he said earlier are running circles in my head. They won't stop! His voice is getting louder.

"How dare you humiliate me in front of Ernie!"

I shout back, not caring anymore that he's so much bigger than I am and can hurt me. "Talk about humiliating?! You treated me like a common whore. You have no respect for me!"

"How did you get that? I said you're getting too big for your britches! You fight with me about everything now!"

"I fight because you treat me so badly. Now you want this girlfriend of his to dance to make money for him?! That's just wrong and you know it."

Rebecca Nietert

"What makes it wrong? He loves this girl and she loves him. He wants to make her happy since she isn't happy at her work."

"Love? I don't think you know the meaning of that word. Does he even work? When she dances for him is he also going to buy a recording studio?"

Phillip laughs, shaking his head angrily. "It doesn't work that way, Babe. Women go to work, and men stay home."

His statement enrages me further. "What are you talking about? I work because you're a musician. Is he talented like you are? Does someone believe in him the way I believe in you?"

"Who cares? That's their deal."

"I care! I'm the one who is going to help this girl give him money, and for what? What is he going to do for her?"

"Pick up her groceries. Do the stuff on a list, just like the ones you give me."

"I haven't given you a list in a long time."

"I know but they love each other. It's not like you and me."

What?! I can't help but stare at him, shocked by what he just said. He's right; I can't define us anymore. I may not know what kind of relationship we have, but he obviously does not love me anymore.

"Is that all I am to you? Just a paycheck?!"

"You give me freedom to do what I need to do. I promise, when I get my recording contract I will give all this back to you." He seemingly calms. He walks towards me and strokes my face. I stare into his eyes, wanting to believe him. Suddenly his hands are at my neck, and I can't breathe. His voice transformed into a menacing growl. "But I swear to you now that if you ever disrespect me like that again in front of my friends, I will leave you so fast your head will spin."

He just answered my question. I can't help my stomach from forming knots, twisting and turning. I feel like I'm going to throw up. Could Lana possibly have been right? No, of course not. I've made a living conning some of the smartest men in Houston. No

Heart of Gold

way will I let Phillip get the best of me. Once I'm free, I can keep the money all for myself. I look back into his eyes and nod, feeling a dim, faint hint of hope for freedom for the first time in a long time. The man I look at each morning doesn't seem appealing anymore. I decide not to fight it anymore.

Over the next few weeks I find myself dreaming of freedom. I begin formulating plans on how I can be free. I also begin listening to the music of my past in the house, country and western. When Phillip complains, I just turn it up louder.

Very much like I did when I had just turned 19, I call my mother to ask if it's okay to come talk with her. She said she would really like that, so off I go.

"It's good to see you." She opens the door and hugs me tight.

"It's so good to see you too!"

"Want some coffee?"

"I would love some, thank you." I step inside. She owns a 900 square foot house in West Katy. It's as small as a cottage house. Her carpet is a marbleized blue and white, her furniture a Paul Bunion oak style. The furniture is so big that it overpowers her living space. Somehow, she's managed to decorate in such a way that it still feels like home. Her furniture is covered in out-of-date orange cushions; most of the wood throughout the house is engraved with ducks. Her house is an eclectic blend of all the things she loves; nothing matches but it still feels like home.

"What is the problem?" I sit at the dinner table as she pours coffee, looking concerned.

"Mom, do you ever think about Shirley?" I don't know why I just asked that. I guess I need some kind of closure, although I'm not sure which issue I need closure for.

"Every minute of every day." I see tears start to fill her eyes as she looks at me. "Have you cried yet?" Instantly I wish I hadn't asked her that question. I didn't mean to make her cry.

Rebecca Nietert

I pause. I guess she noticed I didn't cry at the funeral. "No, not really. I remember some tears but I keep thinking that she's going to walk around the corner. It just doesn't feel like she's gone."

"Is that why you came here, Darlin'?"

"No, I'm sad. I cry all the time about Phillip but yet I can't seem to cry for my sister."

She tilts her head, looking at me intently. "You're not happy?"

"No. I promised Phillip I would buy him a recording studio in exchange for him teaching me how to live on my own. I don't regret that, I truly don't. What I regret is where our relationship has gone from there. I'm so confused."

"Beverly, have you kept your promises to him?"

"I think so. I honestly believe I've given enough."

"Why do you stay?"

"I have no choice."

"You always have a choice."

"Really? What choice did I have when I was starving?" I can't help but snap back.

Doesn't she realize what she's done to me?!

She stares at me, dumbfounded. "What do you mean you were starving?"

"Do you remember when I gave you that money for your truck?"

"Yes." She looks at her cup, playing with the handle nervously.

"I never told you, but I really need that money to be repaid."

"What do you mean? I got the money and spent it on the truck."

"I know but you never repaid me."

"You were making a lot more money than I was at that time."

"No, Mom I wasn't. I had such a hard time after that pregnancy termination. I was in trouble and needed some quick cash. I couldn't work and soon was homeless and starving." She didn't know?

Heart of Gold

"I'm so sorry Sweetheart, I had no idea. You know you never think that the things you do directly affect your children." The pain etched on her face makes me tear up.

"They do affect us. Look, I didn't come here to make you feel bad; I'm fine now. I just never understood why you were always so angry with me."

"I was angry that you called me for money because I thought you were doing fine. I figured after all you would put me through, I kind of deserved to keep it."

"I hear you, but I was starving."

"I would have repaid you if I had known. I would die for you!" She proclaimed.

For some reason, I believe her. "I hate that we've grown so far apart. I miss you. I hate that it was Phillip who had to pick me up instead of my own father. You might think I'm a lunatic, but you have no idea how many nights I've dreamt about that man coming to my rescue."

"Honey, I don't think you're a lunatic. Your father will never come." She looks down, her face worn. I can tell she's trying not to cry. "He never has." She whispers, then shakes her head as if clearing her thoughts and clears her throat. "So, Phillip fed you?"

"Yes. Sometimes I think I've made a pact with the devil. He won't buy what he needs and release me from my debt. He spends all the money on everything but his studio."

"Surely he can purchase a studio on his own by now right?"

"You would think, right? I don't know what's happened to him. He's become angry and resentful. He wants me to train two new girls; it all just makes me sick."

"Honey, you don't need this kind of money. You've had real jobs before; you're a survivor. You don't need his help or his influence. I know you can get a real job somewhere else."

"No, I can't. I can't go back to a life where I'm struggling for five bucks an hour. I can't make a life with that. I have no skills; I don't know how to do anything else. I'm afraid that this is all I can do. All that money is all gone now." I slump back in the chair, exhausted.

I found it odd when my mother who taught me that no man will ever want to take care of me said, "Find a rich guy and marry him." I snap my head up, looking at her in surprise. Did that really just come from the woman who taught me to never let a man take care of me?

"I can't do that." Even though such an idea sounds nice, that's all it is; an idea. One I can't entertain.

"You, my darling, can do anything; I've seen you. I know you don't know this, but I truly respect your courage. I think you're smarter than you give yourself credit for. You pulled this off when your family told you that it was wrong." She pauses briefly, pouring more coffee before continuing. "I wish I had half the courage you have. It takes guts to go against everything you were raised to believe. I hear you're living in this beautiful town home and drive a Porsche. No one has to know what you do for a living."

"Thank you. I know what I do for a living and to tell you the truth, I'm exhausted. It's painfully humiliating. It's on my credit report; on the application for my car. Everywhere I go people know who I am and what I do for a living. I hate it! I don't like knowing what they think of me."

"The only thing that matters in this world is what you think. Do you really think that these people care about you? If you had a normal job these people would like you anyway?"

I blink, taking in what she's saying. "Well yeah, I was kind of hoping they would."

"You're tall, gorgeous and blonde. When a woman looks at you, the first thing she thinks is: 'hide your man.'" She laughs then continues, "When a man looks at you, the first thing he thinks is: 'how can I get her into bed?' There is no way that people are going to look at you and think you are trustworthy or respectable. It's not really their fault either, you set yourself up that way."

I wince. "That's harsh."

Heart of Gold

"That's the truth. You're so busy trying to get everyone to like you that you forget that you have to like yourself first."

"I hate myself sometimes; hate what I've become. I hate that I am in this kind of relationship. I hate dancing. I hate that I have no choice and the more I think about it the angrier I get!" I can feel myself shouting, letting the words fuel my anger.

"And that's what's going to help you get out of it." She finishes softly. I stop and look at her, tears coming to my eyes. I let them fall and nod.

The rest of the afternoon we talk about Shirley and how she accepts responsibility for her part of the past. For mom, that's huge. I appreciate her patience and willingness to be there for me in a way she never has before.

After leaving I head home, not wanting to go to Zeus to train the girls. They can wait. After mulling it over for a few days I finally decide to meet up with them. When I arrive for my appointment with Tanya, Tamara is also there. I soon learn that Tanya had no idea what Ernie has been up to. She didn't know about Tamara or that she would be sharing him with another woman. Although we didn't discuss the matter, I thought several times that I should say something, but I keep my mouth shut. I begin to teach them what I knew about the business. After a few hours, Tanya leaves because Tamara opens her stupid mouth and spills the beans about her and Ernie's relationship. Oh God, here we go. I'm not sure if Tanya left because Ernie is such a jerk or if she truly is a good girl after all. Either way, I'm glad that she got out before it's too late. She seems to have a good head on her shoulders, even if she did pick Ernie as a mate.

Tamara on the other hand can't wait to have Ernie all to herself. She seems extremely young and when I asked how old she is, she said 21. I don't believe her, but I don't question her either.

The next evening I meet Lana at work. After some idle conversation she asks, "Are you going to join Phillip later?"

"Why would you ask me that?"

Rebecca Nietert

"I saw Phillip at the store. He was buying some beer and told me he was going out to a dance club tonight. He said that he had a date so I assumed it was with you. When you were late I thought you were coming in to make some money and then go out later. You've done that before so I thought you were going." She shrugged her shoulders.

"You're kidding, right?" I stutter, not believing what I'm hearing.

"No? I wish I were." She looks confused.

"Where would he be?"

"I heard that the Rosemont was hosting a dance." She offers.

"Isn't that a ball dance where all the men in the oil business go every year?"

"I think so. Some of the others were talking about it being sometime this week. I guess it's tonight."

"How would he get tickets to that? How do I get tickets?"

I didn't mean to voice my thoughts out loud.

"You're going to crash it?"

I nod. "Yes."

"Seriously, do you think he would go there?"

"It's the hottest gig going tonight and he's all about being at the hottest event in town." I can't keep the lump in my throat and knot in my stomach from forming.

"I don't think they will let him in. He's not in the oil business."

"Well he's thinking about the cash, that's for sure. In my head I'm thinking I need a reason to leave him and I think I know what he's up to."

"Call John and see if he can help." She looks at me, worried.

Good idea. John works in the oil business anyway. I call him. I go to the back payphone. I ask John, "Hey, are you going to the dance by any chance tonight?"

"I got the tickets but I'm not going."

"Well, I want to go and I need a date…" I let my voice trail off, biting my lip.

Heart of Gold

"Oh, well then I'll come pick you up. Where are you?" I can't help the smile that comes over my face.

"At work."

"Be there in fifteen."

I hang up and turn to Lana. "I need your help getting ready." She and I bought a dress out of the costume shop. It's a white flapper dress with spaghetti straps. It falls just above my knees.

When John and I arrive at the dance, he whispers, "You fit right in here, Beverly. You are the most attractive lady here."

"Thank you, you make me feel like a lady." I smile.

"Why did you want to come all of a sudden?"

"I wanted to be with you." I gush, batting my eyes at him. He smiles, then I let the truth slip. "I also have to find my roommate to tell him something. I hope you don't mind?"

"It's fine. Are you sure he's here?"

"No, but he said he would be." I look around the plush Victorian-style room. I see Sonny and Mickey as well as several clients from various clubs, but no sign of Phillip.

John suggested that we should walk around a bit. I agree. As we are walking, a guy I knew only as being on the soap opera, Days of Our Lives, walks over to chat. I've seen and spoke with him many times at Mack's. He recognizes me, seeing as his version of "hello" is to take several bills out of his pocket and folded them as if to tip me. He hands it out to me and I back away, looking at John, embarrassed. I smile nervously, trying not to draw attention to my face that is shouting how he's treating me like a whore, even in a public place. John tries to protect me but the man is fast and shoves the money between my breasts. I take the money out and shove it back at him, then run to the ladies room and disappear inside humiliated.

I sit down on a stool, catching my breath. The money tore my skin and the red blood is now oozing onto the lovely dress I just bought. Have I made a mistake by coming here? After what just happened, I have no right to judge Phillip for being with another

138

Rebecca Nietert

girl, even if I do find him. A man I don't even know just humiliated me in front of someone I highly respect, all because of what I do for a living. I am not respectful. I don't deserve to be here. I am trash. I know it. Suddenly I hear a familiar voice. "Bet his girlfriend wishes she had him now!" I wipe away at the tears that started to form.

"He dumped her last week. He's running off to Florida with me." I sit quietly and listen. She talked about having sex with the man and how he professed his love for her. She even said how sorry she feels for the girlfriend left behind. All of a sudden, it hits me. That voice. Kelly. The girl from Zeus.

"I heard he's still dating her. Are you sure they're no longer an item?" The girl with whom she was conversing asks.

"Cathy, Phillip said she's dating an old guy now and he's tired of it."

This is more than an affair! My heart stops at the sound of his name. I didn't even think it could've been about him until now. Lana had suggested that Phillip was jealous of John, but I thought he had too much confidence for that kind of jealousy. I was dead wrong. The thought of him sleeping with her makes me want to throw up.

Before long a girl that John had sent in to check on me asks if I'm okay. She opens the stall door. I whisper that I'm fine, then close the door. I hear Kelly and her friend leave. I sit back, suddenly feeling betrayed all over again and it hurt. I don't want to be here anymore. I want to run home and pretend that tonight never happened. I shouldn't have come. I get up, and clean up as best I can.

When I walk out of the bathroom, John is immediately by my side, concerned.

"What happened?" He looks at the blood stain.

"My heart is broken." I hear the words rush out before I realize I've said them. Crap! "I don't want to talk about it okay?" I see tears fill his eyes and want to wipe them away. I want to say I'm

Heart of Gold

sorry for everything and ask if we can start over, but the words won't come.

"Can we leave?" He nods. On the way out I notice Kelly and Phillip talking intimately by the front door. I look at John. "How do I look?"

"As beautiful as ever." He looks straight ahead.

"Thank you." I say sincerely, looking up at him, then back at Phillip as I approach him. He notices me right away, tried to retreat but realizes there isn't anywhere to go. Realizing he's trapped, he leans against the wall casually, trying to look inconspicuous.

"Hello Phillip." I try my best to keep my voice calm.

"What are you doing here? I thought you were working tonight."

"No, for your information I have just told John all about you. I thought you should know that because I want you out by tomorrow. He's going to hire a lawyer if you don't." I lie and turn to leave.

Phillip grabs my arm with one of his big, meaty hands as he pushes Kelly away with the other. "You're not going anywhere!"

Kelly stumbles, surprised by what he just did. "You said you left her!"

"Shut up!" He yells, looking disoriented.

"I don't owe you anything anymore. Whatever it is that you think we had, you just lost it." I look him straight in the eye. "I even gave you the benefit of the doubt. I told you; don't let me find out about it. I'm done." I jerk my arm away and turn to walk off completely unaware that our display has left John with numerous questions.

"I love you Beverly! Please don't do this, she means nothing to me."

I turn back to face him. I don't feel angry or sad. I feel numb, the betrayal scarring me with indifference. I don't feel anything for him anymore. "For something to mean so little she took everything

Rebecca Nietert

you had. I hope she was worth it." I walk away, silence filling the air.

"Beverly!"

I hear his booming voice. The voice that used to have so much power over me now has none. I take John's hand and walked out of the building.

During the car ride John and I don't talk. There's nothing to say. It's like he knew I haven't been honest. Still, there's a difference between thinking you know the truth and actually knowing the truth. I feel he's got to be so disappointed in me. Heck I am disappointed in me how could he not be?

Love or whatever Phillip and I had was just that. I wonder how it could have been so good between he, Donna and I? I wonder whatever went wrong? Did my life become all about the money? Was that tearing me apart? Had my desire to live extravagantly somehow changed Phillip? I gave all of my money to him! I feel sick. I want to cry but cannot do so in front of John. Well, one thing's for sure: I've got to start my life all over again.

Heart of Gold

14

After several days of contemplating the situation I calm down a bit. The problem with my situation is that I'm living with Phillip. I have taken care of him for so long that I don't think he would be able to ever take care of himself fully. After the anger subsided I realize I'm not the kind of person who will turn her back on someone in need. Not even after what he did. We still share the apartment after the other night because I told him I would until he packed and left. I'm a woman of my word, unlike him. I'm paying for everything so the house, car, and everything else that was bought on my credit is mine when he leaves. Of course, he disagrees. The arguing never ends! Finally, I snap.

"How could you have done all of that to me?" I finally ask.

"Kelly didn't know you were in the bathroom?"

"No, I went in before she did. She never saw me." Why won't he just answer my questions instead of beating around the bush? His new trick is to avoid my questions and ask one instead. It's so annoying.

"Well it isn't true. I never slept with her. Frankly, I'm surprised you would think I would. She's just a distraction, that's all."

"How can you tell me she means nothing to you? You probably wanted her to make money for you too."

"How did you know I was going to that party?"

"Lana told me you had a date. Why would you tell one of my closest friends that? Do you even realize how humiliated I was? I asked you not to let me or my friends find out. I thought I made myself crystal clear? Honestly Phillip, I think if I never found out about you two I would probably still want to help you."

"I didn't know you were looking for me!" He shouted softly.

Rebecca Nietert

I can tell by the sorrow on his face that he feels the pain of his own betrayal. No matter what we've been through, I don't feel comfortable hurting anyone.

"You can trust me now. I want you, not her. I don't have anything to do with her anymore and you have to believe that."

"Actually I don't have to believe anything you say anymore, Phillip. I think you've been using me for a long time to get whatever status you think you need. Frankly, I'm sad it took me this long to wake up."

"I'm sorry." I think he's being genuine.

"Thank you." I'm not about to admit how good it feels to hear him say that. I turn around and walk out the door, leaving to find an apartment of my own. Once he's gone, my income will decrease. I need to protect myself as well as my stuff. Phillip will never leave, not at this rate. I've experienced his angry outbursts as well as his violence. He would hurt the things I care about to make me stay. I've got to be careful about this. After I find a place I go home to start packing boxes. He isn't home so that makes it easier to keep the apartment a secret from him. Life will be so different without him. Can I really make it in this world on my own? Soon I've packed everything that means a lot to me. There are some things that if he took, would devastate me.

At one time I had the most respect for him than anyone. The emptiness I now feel seems so real that it's consuming me. I can't think about work. I barely give Phillip any trouble when he's at the house because I stopped paying attention to what he's doing. The weekend he's out on a week-long family vacation is the time I make my move: bringing everything I've packed into my new place.

After I get my treasures in the new place I take a look around and let out a sigh of relief. That was a lot more work than expected but it was worth it. I can already feel a sense of freedom stirring in my stomach.

My phone rings. I look at the caller I.D: it's Lana. I answer and before I can get a 'hello' in, she starts talking a million miles a

Heart of Gold

minute. I sit in a chair and patiently listen as she tells me how she's broken up with her boyfriend but is seeing a new guy. She rambles on then finally explains that her ex is kicking her out and she needs a place to crash for a while. I tell her about my new apartment briefly and let her know that I will leave a spare key for her to come and go as she pleases.

A few days go by. Phillip called to leave a message on the old apartment answering machine. He said that he's going to be staying away longer than expected, so I go to the new apartment. I've been going back and forth between apartments gathering mail. I want to see Phillip face to face to tell him decisions I made.

When I walk in the door, I see a person sitting in a chair, head down with shoulders slumped. If I didn't just hear the words "Hello Beverly," backed with a familiar voice, I would have screamed bloody murder.

I sit on the floor next to Lana. Obviously something's wrong. "What's going on?"

"I don't know, it's all so terrible!"

I wait for a few seconds, letting her have some space. She finally opens up. "You know my ex wasn't working."

"I'm so sorry. No, I did not know that."

"Well, I was supporting him. He hasn't got off his ass to look for work. He thought that I needed to work all the time so he could have this new car he wants, with all this other stuff." She pauses, takes a deep breath, then continues. "I cooked. I cleaned, and did all the laundry. All he did was drive me to and from work. I wish I hadn't let myself be used like that. It sucks."

Tears sting at my eyes as it hits me: the realization. I don't know if it's the way she said it or the words that were used, but its like clouds fell from my eyes. I can see everything so clearly now. Not to make her pain about me, but I'm clear that's exactly what Phillip has been doing this entire time! I suddenly feel warmness in my heart open up, for both of us.

Rebecca Nietert

Although she was sitting in my living room hurting all I could feel was the pain deep within. The deep sadness that hit is indescribable for the both of us. No woman or man should ever have to feel so used. I can't believe I've done so much for someone who cared so little for me. What's worse, she's going through the same thing! Are there any other women who are going through the same thing we are? Who am I kidding, there has to be. The thoughts cause my mind to wonder.

"Oh my God!" She shouts. I almost fall over at the sudden shout.

"Wha-" I start to say as I look at her, but the words are taken out of me.

She helps me steady myself. When her face lifts I can see her clearly. I stare at her, and at the bruise. I can't stop staring shocked. The angry roar that comes next. I stand up, looking intently at her face. "What did he do?! I'll kill him!"

"Huh?" She looks at me, confused.

I try to keep my voice calmer this time as I take a deep breath. "Where did you get-?"

"Your face!" She interrupts. "Those tears aren't for me, they're for you. With everything I've said to you all this time, it took me going through the same thing for you to finally get it?"

"Stop avoiding the question!" I snap.

She reaches up to touch her face. "Oh this? That was him." She shrugs. I stare at her in disbelief. How can she be so casual about such a thing?

"Where is he? You didn't fight back? You're a big girl. You could do some damage?"

"Don't worry about me, I'm a big girl, you're right. People say you should see the other guy but seriously, you should. This isn't the first bruise and it won't be the last."

"Lana, I could kill the jerk! Does it hurt?"

"No, stop! It's fine. I'm here now. Can we talk about something else?"

Heart of Gold

I let out a sigh. There's no use; she's just as stubborn as I am. "I don't know why I can't take care of myself the way I take care of you." I ask.

"You can! I'm so happy for you." She hugs me.

I shake my head, feeling the tears coming back. "What do I do now?"

"You will be fine." I look at her and smile wearily.

"Hey," She looks me in the eye. "You are my hero. I had the courage to leave him because I know you."

I can't help but stare at her, dumbfounded. She used me as an inspiration? Someone who can barely get out of her own sucky situation? How is that possible? I need air, need to clear my head. Unable to speak, I nod appreciatively and walk to the door.

"Don't go!" her voice stops me in my tracks. I know that sound, the sound of heartbreak.

That's the sound of abandonment. I've used that same voice with Phillip. I turn and face her.

"Don't worry; I'm just going to get some stuff out of my car."

"I'll help. That is what we will do first."

"What will we do second?"

"Get drunk." We both laugh. I open the door and let her through. After we got the rest of my stuff in the apartment, Lana pours some wine and we sit on the floor.

"You know Bev, all of this stuff isn't much." She gestures around the apartment. "How can you have so little when you make so much? You make twice as much as I do."

"I don't know." I look around the studio, at the tiny kitchen, small bed and small closet space. She's right. I really don't have anything. "I've tried keeping the money but Phillip would have none of it." I kept as much as I could for payment for this place. "This isn't exactly all of it either. I left him stuff he wanted that we purchased. I split our things fairly. I don't want that stuff anyway. There are some things I left there. I'll get them when I tell him that I have my own place.

Rebecca Nietert

We both pause, sharing a moment of reflection of our past, of our failures. I share the memories of the numerous beatings, all the yelling, and the lies. The pain.

"How could I have been so naive?" I didn't mean to whisper the words, but out they come.

"We all are. I think you felt like your money would buy his love."

"Maybe so?" I take a sip of the wine and lay back, looking at the ceiling. "I can't do this Lana, I just can't. I am alone again. "

"Yes, you can. Before you know it, you'll be on top of the world again. You're lucky that way."

"Thank you. I hope you're right."

She lies down next to me. "Look, why don't you just bunker here for the week? Take some time. Sleep it off. Next week you can decide what you want to do."

I let out a sigh. "I can't. I spent all my money on this apartment and need more if I'm going to take off for a whole week."

"How much do you have?"

"A couple hundred dollars. That's hardly enough for dinner all week!"

Lana laughs. I look over at her, confused. "Oh girl, you've been living way too high for way too long! Come on down to the poor side of town."

"I don't want some junk food, if that's what you're saying."

"Not at all! I'll teach you to make delicious stuff for very little money. I can come here after work and cook before I leave."

"You promise it's not going to be like...nasty?" I remember the days I was homeless. When I had food, it was awful. I'm not going back to that again.

"Promise. Let someone else take care of you for a change. Please let me do this?"

"I need some time alone to think. Are you going back to get all your stuff?"

"Later this week I am. I've got to wrap up a few things first."

Heart of Gold

I take her hand and smile. "Thank you, Lana. I can't do this without you."

"Yes you can. You are so much stronger than you give yourself credit for."

I squeeze her hand.

"So are you."

Instead of waiting, the next morning, I arrive at Phillip's place, still thinking about last night. There is something so incredibly wonderful about connecting with another human in such a way that, for a brief moment in time, we feel similar emotions.

Phillip's brother, Mickey, is home. I notice his car parked in our driveway as I walk to the door. I walk in and see Tamara and some other girl asleep on our couch. Ernie is knocked out on the floor. I walk by casually; none of them move. Obviously Phillip's trip was cut short?

I head into Phillip's room. It's been a while since I've been in here. I remember when I used to love it. The good old days when I would push him on the bed and we'd have fun. I miss the days when I wasn't worried about him bringing some chick home. I look at him sleeping. Would it be possible to go back to that, even if just for a moment? I lay down next to him, putting my head on his chest. I just want to be held. Even if he's hurt and betrayed me, even though I'm moving out, I want him to hold me one last time.

He stirs a bit and then opens his eyes. Blinking a few times he looks down, surprised. I don't know if it's because I'm home or because I'm actually in bed with him; something that hasn't happened in a very long time. "Hey there." He whispers sleepily. "Where have you been all night?"

"With Lana. What's going on?"

"Lana?" He bolts upright. "You were with another guy weren't you?"

I roll my eyes. "Phillip, look at me! I haven't even showered. If I were with a guy I would not be in these ratty old clothes. You of all people should know that!"

Rebecca Nietert

He looks me up and down, then laughs while raising his hand to his mouth. "No I don't suppose you would!"

I sit up, ready to leave but he pulls me back down, looks into my eyes and whispers, "But you still look beautiful." It's been a while since I've heard those words come out of his mouth, and honestly it feels good. I feel the smile that comes over my face, followed by a blush. Maybe there's some hope after all.

"Thank you." I stare into his eyes, those dark orbs that enchant me. I put my hand on his chest, feeling his muscles ripple at my touch. I love having this kind of power over a man. The ability to make him tremble at my touch; even Phillip isn't immune. I slide my hand across his chest to his side, just the way he likes it. I can hear his breathing get faster, his eyes growing a bit wider at the surprise of what I'm doing. I lean over and kiss his neck softly. Feeling him swallow hard, I smile, then kiss gently up his neck to his face. I run both of my hands up and down his sides softly as I kiss his jaw and stop just above his lips.

"I've missed you." He whispers as he kisses me softly at first, then more forcefully. I let him part my mouth with his tongue as I climb on top of him, pressing my body into his. I run my hands up and down his chest as he runs his hands down my back to my butt, massaging and feeling me. I feel his hands move up and down my legs, then up my body, taking my shirt with his hands as he moves them from my stomach to my chest. I let him take my shirt off and move down to kiss his neck. He starts to moan as his hands move to my breasts, massaging them.

"I've missed you too." I whisper as I move my hands down his chest to his shaft, feeling him. He flips me onto my back and looks down at me, then takes off my bra and starts to kiss and gently bite my breasts. I lean my head back and moan, lost in the moment. Lost in his touch. He takes off my pants as I run my hands down his chest to take off his boxers. I'm in awe at his manhood. He's so beautiful. I move down to kiss his chest, then lick my way down to his stomach, feeling him twitch and move at my touch. These are

Heart of Gold

the moments I live for. I want moments where I'm the one in control, not him. The moments where he's begging, willing to do anything I ask. I look up and him, at the face that's longing for my touch. I can feel his eyes on me as I take his shaft into my mouth and begin to work my magic, just the way he likes it.

"Oh, God!" His deep voice edges me on further. I kiss up his stomach and chest to his lips, and then gasp as he pushes himself against me. I let him. When it's all over, I'm left gasping for air. He collapses on top of me, breathing heavily.

"Bev, you're so amazing." He whispers in my ear. I shake my head.

"Tell me what's going on."

"Let me get dressed first, okay?" I nod. As I watch him get off of me I feel a sudden twinge of guilt. Did I really just do that? With him? The one who's been using me this entire time? I can't believe he still has the ability make me regretful even when he's just trying to be pleasant.

I get dressed silently and leave. I walk into the kitchen, grabbing some coffee beans to make coffee. I hear footsteps as I grind the coffee. Then I hear a voice.

"Hello, Barbie!" It's Tamara.

"Here, the name's Beverly, thank you." I can't help the quip from coming out.

"Oh, I'm sorry. Do you know what we are going to do today?

I resist the urge to roll my eyes. "No."

"Phillip is taking us to a studio at the University of St. Thomas. He said his cousin goes there and he can get us in the ballroom! We are going to dance in front of mirrors and he's going to teach us to walk with a book on our head so we can become just like you!" Her enthusiasm is piercing my brain. I feel sick. Phillip taught me to dance exactly the same way. Are her and the other girl on the sofa his next source of income? How have I ended up taking care of a man who has no respect for me or for the girls he just met?

"I suppose Prince is the music of choice?" I ask nonchalantly.

Rebecca Nietert

"Yeah! How did you know that?" I snicker at her reaction but don't answer. "You are so smart. I sure hope I'm as smart as you one day."

"No worries. One day you will be." I roll my eyes, not caring that the comment came out sarcastic. She deserves it.

Phillip walks in to the kitchen, dressed as if nothing had just happened between us moments ago. "Good morning."

Tamara turns towards him. "I told..." She pauses, looking at me and winks, "...Beverly, what we're going to do today." I almost laugh at the look of alarm that crosses over his face.

I look at him, taking a sip of coffee. "Good morning." I make sure to keep my voice light and pleasant. "Is there anything you'd like to share with me?"

"Beverly, you know the drill. I told you I was going to help these girls."

"I knew of Tanya and Tamara. Who is the other?"

"They all need help!"

I look at Tamara and smile. "Would you excuse us for just a minute?" I wave my hand back and forth to dismiss her.

After she leaves, I turn loose, hissing, "Just what are you doing?!"

"I'm helping these girls. That's all. Helping."

He looks me in the eye.

I can't believe that just a few moments ago he was all over me and now he's lying to my face!

I put my coffee down and walk up to him, smiling. Keep your cool Bev. "I saw the beauty on the sofa." I wrap my arms around his neck, making sure his eyes are glued to mine as I whisper. "She hardly looks old enough to dance. Is she yours? Or is she his?" I nod my head in the direction of where Ernie is still passed out on the floor.

Mickey walks in to the kitchen. I let go of Phillip and grab my coffee cup. "Good morning Phillip. Good morning Beverly. Who are the girls in the living room?"

Heart of Gold

I look at him. "There's never been a problem with you here, I hope you know that." I fix my gaze on Philip. "Phillip brought these girls here."

Mickey looks at Phillip. "What is she talking about?"

"I'm helping these girls make more money. I'm going to teach them how to dance."

Mickey looks at me, then back at Phillip. "Aren't you taking away Beverly's edge in the business?"

"No, these girls do not work at her club."

For some reason Mickey looks offended. "Well what if they decide to? What are you trying to do, man? Build some kind of dancer harem? Beverly is this way because of who she is, not because of what you made her."

I almost laugh. Mickey actually believes that I'm the sole reason I make the money I do? John has told me the same thing; that I'm so elegant that it doesn't matter what profession I have. I can succeed and be anything I want. I'm starting to think they might be on to something, though my confidence hasn't been proven.

"She is what I made her to be. She can't do anything without me. When I tell her 'Jump' She asks 'How high?'"

I made her!" Phillip boasts.

"I guess that's that then." I pour more coffee and leave the room.

"If you can't see how wrong this is, you are crazy!" Mickey shouts.

When I enter the living room, the girl on the sofa is awake. Tamara is sitting next to her. Both of them are very close to each other.

"Beverly, this is Kris."

"Hello Kris." I put on my best smile and crouch down in front of her so I can look in her the eye. "How old are you?"

"Eighteen." She laughs.

Liar! You look sixteen. I thought.

"How long have you been dancing, Sweetheart?"

Rebecca Nietert

"I haven't yet. I know Tamara and I thought I would try it one or two nights, that's all."

"Are you sure you really want to do this? It's a hard world in there."

She nods enthusiastically. "Duh, I need the money. Phillip said I can help him out by taking off some of your stress. He even said you might let me move in here. I have nowhere to go."

"I see." I stand up and shout. "Phillip!" Kris jumps at the sudden change of my voice. When Phillip arrives I give him the look that he hates. The one that says I don't trust him one bit...

"You're replacing me with her?!" I point to her, then put my hands firmly on my hips.

He pauses, and then slowly responds. "No, I am not replacing you. She is here to help you make more money, that's all. She's down on her luck. Her mother is a terrible mom and she needs a place to stay."

I glare at him. He knows that playing the terrible mom card might soften my defiance.

I laugh off my feelings. "I make more than enough. I make twice-" I hold up my fingers, "the salary of my co-workers. What makes you think she can help me?"

"She can take some of the burden off. You won't have to work so hard."

"And where does that leave us?"

"That's for you to decide."

Why can't he just get a job? Relying on all these women to make him money is ridiculous! It's a lot of work to train another girl. My shoulders slump; I feel defeated. Would he really be able to make it without me? What does that say about me? Am I really that useless, able to be thrown away like trash in place of some new toy?

"Man you still don't get it, do you?" Mickey shakes his head as he walks away.

Phillip shouts, "What's your problem?"

"I'm not the one with the problem." He retort back.

Heart of Gold

I go to my room to gather up a few more things when Philip enters the room.

"I'm sorry about today."

I don't bother looking up. "Uh-huh."

"Look, if you can drive the girls home I promise we will have time for us when you get back. I'm still driving the old Camaro and I'm not sure it can make it to Pasadena and back."

"Fine, but when I get back we need to talk, just us. No one else around." For some reason, no matter what contempt, pity, regret or disappointment I felt for Phillip, I still can't seem to lie to him. After what we just shared it softened my heart a little.

"Okay." He nods, then walks over and put his arms around my waist, hugging me from behind. I stop picking up things and let out a sigh. Why does he still have this effect on me after all these years?

"I really do miss you." I feel his breath against my ear and can't help but shiver.

I shake my him lose and then yell out, "Come on girls! I'm leaving! If you want a ride better hitch it now!" I walk away from Phillip, briskly head to the door and open it. Like a stampede of cattle they follow me out the door. Tamara called shotgun. Within five minutes I deem her Chatterbox. All she said all the way to Pasadena was nothing important or relevant.

We approach Kris's subdivision. It's not the greatest neighborhood but it's decent. Livable. Her house is a beautifully landscaped ranch style home. It was not very big. It was not in the greatest of neighborhood, but it looked decent. I know all too well the outward appearance usually doesn't match the inside. It's funny to draw that conclusion about something that's so similar to yourself.

I park and turn to Kris. "Do you want me to come in with you?" I ask because I am all too familiar with a violent mother.

"Yeah." She answers hesitantly.

Rebecca Nietert

Knowing that mothers can be unpredictable, I turn to Tamara. "Tamara I think it would be better if you stayed here. I'll leave the car running so you don't have to roll down the windows okay?"

Pasadena, Texas is filled with oil refineries, industrial and mechanical factories. The odor is overwhelming and of course, toxic. Phillip would kill me if anything happened to these girls. As we walk towards the house, I see what appears to be her mother watching from a foyer window.

The woman stands just behind the door so that when Kris closes it, she's standing very close to us. I back up quickly, unsure of what she will do. I try to put as much distance between us as I can manage. Kris and her mother whisper a bit, then Kris runs upstairs. Her mother grabs at thin air, and then turns to me, pleading. "Please. Don't take her with you."

"I'm not going to take her. I am here to drop her off. I'm a taxi, that's all."

"She's only sixteen! She needs to be in school! She needs to be at home!" She shouts. Her eyes focused on me, accusing.

"Ma'am she told me that she's eighteen." I sneer. Obviously it isn't the truth.

She briskly walks to a roll-top desk, tossing papers, in search of something. I stand back and watch.

"She lied. Look!" She hands me the birth certificate.

I pretend to assess it. I can tell by the way she acts she's younger than eighteen. That's all I need to know.

My stomach cringed. "I don't want to cause any trouble. Phillip asked to help her."

"That black guy I caught her with?"

"You caught her with a black guy?" I asked more alarmed.

"Yes, they were driving a Camaro." I am going to kill him!

"How long has Kris known this guy?"

"I don't know. I've seen them off and on for a year now. I think he's her boyfriend."

I choke on my words. "A year now?"

Heart of Gold

"Did I say something wrong?" She asked.

I manage to compose myself. "No Ma'am, but that guy is bad news."

"How do you know Kris? Do you work at that dancing place?" She asked me.

"What place?" I'm not stupid enough to tell her anything.

"Oh she hasn't told you about that. Well, she has the right to keep it to herself."

This woman seems to want the best for her daughter and has a hard time setting boundaries. Of course the girl is going to act out.

"Can you tell me anything about the place you're talking about please?"

"Miss I think that she should be the one to tell you. Besides, she gets so angry with me she hits me sometimes." She says it so softly I almost don't catch it.

"You let your daughter hit you?" I have a hard time believing her. When I acted out my mother would hit me, not the other way around.

"She has a mind of her own you know."

"You and her really need to work this out. There is no way that what she told me about you is the truth." I say calmly, then scream, "Kris!"

Kris runs down the stairs almost stumbling. She looks at the both of us. "What?"

"Have you hit your mother?" I'm tired of playing babysitter but I want answers. No mother deserves to be hit. Not even mine after all the terrible things she's done to me. She turns to face her mother, furious. "What did you do? Stop humiliating me!"

Her Mother just stands there, head down in shame. I suddenly realize that she's not the abuser but the victim! How can her daughter treat her like that? I suddenly remember the defiance I had as a teen.

"You're only sixteen?"

Rebecca Nietert

"So what?" She snaps.

I take a deep breath. "Have you slept with Phillip?" I'm trying to best to stay calm.

"Yeah, so?" Her voice is defiant as if it's no big deal.

I put my hand to my head, feeling dizzy. The room suddenly feels like it's closing in. I feel like I can't breathe. It feels like I'm watching a movie! Has this really been my life in only a year? Lies, deceit, and manipulation everywhere I turn? This cannot be happening!

"Do you know how old he is?"

"Yeah." Her eyes dart away from me. She's lying.

"Well what he did is against the law. You could be in serious trouble."

"Who cares? I've been sleeping with him almost a year. He said you knew and that you were okay with it."

"He did not tell you that." I can't hide the anger anymore.

"Uh...yeah, he did." Her hands are now on her hips, as if she's about to throw a temper tantrum.

"Why did you hang around if you knew I was there?"

"He said he was going to move me in at the right time after he helps me become a dancer, just like you do. Think about it, we could make so much money!" Her eyes are wide with excitement at the thought of making a lot of money.

"Oh my God, Kris, you're just a baby!" Her mother shouts, bursting into tears.

"No fear Ma'am. I wouldn't help her if you paid me."

"Thank you!" She whispers.

"You better take me with you! I'll tell Phillip if you don't." Kris shouts, glaring at me.

"Kris, if you were eighteen I still wouldn't take you." I turn to face her mother. "I want you to know I had no idea what he was doing, and I never imagined that he would have sex with an underage girl. I'm sorry for what he's done to you and your family and I wish you the best of luck in the future."

Heart of Gold

I'm enraged when I get to the car.

I'm also unable to tolerate Chatterbox anymore. I sit in the driver's seat and adjust my seat belt. I look at Tamara. "If you ask me I swear I will tell you!"

After a long silence I sigh. "How long has Kris been working with you?"

She giggles. "She's worked got about a few months now, why?"

"Why you didn't tell me that back at the house?"

She shrugs, so I try again. "How long have she and Phillip been sleeping together?"

"About a year now, right?" She looks at me for confirmation.

"That is what I thought too." I confirm.

When we arrive at Tamara's house, she bursts out, "Look! Mom's in the yard again!"

"Great, another mom." I mumble. As I stop the car she throws the door open and jumps out, then turns around.

"Come in with me!" I sigh and unbuckle my seat belt. She grabs my hand and pulls me out of the seat then takes off towards the house. I follow her and stop as she runs through a hallway, briefly explaining that the pictures on the wall are her model shots. Whatever that means. Once in the kitchen her mother walks in. Tamara runs past her mother and up the stairs to collect her things.

"Hello Ma'am."

"What's your name?"

"Beverly, nice to meet you." I answer, trying to sound as nice as possible.

"What are you and Tamara up to?" She eyes me wearily.

"Ma'am I'm just here to drop her off, then I'll be on my way."

"I am not old, so don't call me 'ma'am'." She snaps.

I nod, seeing that she's the confrontational type. "Was she showing off her pictures again?"

"Yes she was…" I almost say the word she hated again but manage to stop myself.

158

Rebecca Nietert

"Did she tell you how many pictures we had to take to get them all perfect?"

"No she did not." I fidget uncomfortably.

"Making her dress in one outfit after another all day until she gets what she wants. I think it's a little ridiculous."

"You took the pictures? All of them?!"

"Yes, when we played dress-up. She requires a lot of maintenance."

"Wait, you mean she was never a cheerleader?"

"Little Tamara? No, are you kidding me? She has no smarts. Poor girl thinks sometimes those pictures on the wall are real."

What kind of mom would walk about her daughter like that? Did mine ever do that? Chatterbox runs down the steps, feet stomping the whole way down. She almost knocked her mother over when she tumbled down the stairs.

I watch as her mother wipes some of the hair out of her face. "Tamara darling, it is a good thing you are so pretty. If you had to rely on your brains, baby you would starve."

"I can't wait to dance! Can you take me with you?"

"Phillip just asked if I could drop you off, so no. Good-bye Ma'am!" I smile to myself, proud of saying 'Ma'am' on purpose as we walk out the door.

On the drive home I am captivated in my own thoughts. Captured in my own world. What am I going to say to Phillip? Of course he would never believe what I've found out. He will probably lie and tell me it's all in Kris's head. Why does this matter to me so much?

Heart of Gold

15

After I take the girls home, I decide to spend the night in my new apartment. I'm too tired to talk to anyone, let alone Phillip. I need time to digest what just happened. I wake up and do small things around the house, mainly trying to gather my thoughts. Lana calls me in the afternoon. She tells me about her day, how she was out this morning picking up groceries and clearing things out of her apartment. She finished and then ends with "I have some bad news."

"What's that?" Can anything be as bad as yesterday?

"Last night I saw Phillip follow some girl in an apartment complex near the house I'm moving out of. They looked super intimate. I think he's got two apartments like you."

"Great. Of course." I pause then sigh. "Did she have blonde hair and look really young?"

"Yeah, she did. How do you know that?"

I tell her all about what happened yesterday. I also let her in on my suspicion: that it's Kris. She listens but offers no comment. After we hang up, I go to the town home to see if Mickey is still in town. He is.

"Hey, what do you know about Kris?" I ask him.

"Phillip told me all about her last night. He asked me not to tell you but I can't help it. I'm so sorry Beverly; he's replacing you with her."

I let out a sigh. It's not like I didn't expect such a thing, I was waiting for it, it's just one more nail in the coffin. For once I'm glad we haven't had a talk with him yet. Usually I'm itching to say something, but this time it's almost like one of those why bother because it won't change anything feelings. Besides, I would've left feeling as though I'm abandoning him, when in reality he

Rebecca Nietert

abandoned me so many times. He would have probably tried manipulating me into feeling sorry for him again. Like yesterday morning. I shudder. I vow never again. If anything, his betrayal solidified the sense of freedom that I felt I really desired from time to time, but couldn't quite grasp before. He's going to be just fine without me. In fact, I'm sure he'll even miss me, but not before the girls turn out to be something entirely different than he imagined.

I look at Mickey, who is staring at me, concerned. I ask, "Do you know where the new apartment is?"

He gives me the details.

"How long has he had the place?"

"She's lived there a month or so."

"Mickey, I am going to ask you one question and I need an honest answer." I look him in the eye and he nods. "How long has Phillip been trying to replace me?"

He shifts, obviously uncomfortable.

I close my eyes, exasperated. "Please. Just tell me."

"Ever since you left Mack's." Came the quiet reply.

"Thank you. I'm glad you didn't lie to me." I walk off before he can say anything else and lock myself in my room. His honesty hits me hard but I asked for it. I sit on the floor, lost in thought. Why haven't I noticed this before? I've seen this exact same scenario happen countless times in the clubs. Why did I think my situation was so different?

At one point, Phillip truly had helped me take care of myself. I had felt so much admiration and respect for him. Back then I was sure he was doing it because he found a quicker way to become the songwriter he always dreamed of. I was so sure that we would be friends forever.

How wrong I was. So incredibly wrong. The night we met, I made a pact with the devil himself! I bought, signed, sealed, and delivered the pact. Phillip never really cared about a studio. He lost sight of his dreams while I lost all respect for myself.

Heart of Gold

I stand. I walk to the wet bar that we made out of cabinets in the bedroom. I open a side drawer, revealing a cabinet that we keep liquor in. I pull out a flask of Crown Royal and sit back on the floor to drink the whole bottle. Before I know it, darkness surrounds me.

When I wake, it's morning again.

I pack the remaining things that I considered mine. I had my photos. I gathered everything into one bag. I take the bag as well as some previously packed boxes and bring them to my car. I walked back inside and take a look around. There's nothing else I want. He can have the rest. I head back to the car, get in and take one last look at the house. For some reason, I don't feel sad. I feel…relief? The sense of freedom that has been incubating inside me is itching to get out of here. I press the gas. I'm never coming back.

When I arrive at the new apartment, I notice Lana's boxes are all around the room. One of the boxes is open; inside is another flask of Crown Royal. I smile. Looks like I'm not the only one who needs some pain medicine. I don't want to feel the rejection, the humiliation. I want to be free from the fear that's wrenched deep within. I know I don't need Phillip, but he was my comfort zone. I take a swing from the flask. I need to relax. I drank another and then another…

Later Lana came home. "My God what happened?" Lana's voice pierces my ears. I can barely open my eyes. She pulls my hair from my face. I feel gross, sticky and smelly.

"Too…much…" I can barely get the words out. The light coming through the window is so blinding.

"You don't drink to get drunk?" Her voice is softer.

I can't say anything, so I try to nod.

"What happened after we talked?"

"Phillip…replacing me…"

"You have got to be kidding me!" I wince as her voice penetrates my skull. "With who?!"

"Kris…." I take a deep breath. "She's…sixteen…" The words come out in a slur.

Rebecca Nietert

"You are better off without him. You need to tell him what he did to you. Don't stand for someone treating you like that! If you don't you will always wish you had."

"Yeah...confront..."

"Beverly you have to tell him, so he will finally leave you alone!"

"He...never....leaves... alone."

"Girl, get up!" She shouts. I wince as she lifts my limp body and drags me into the bathroom. She starts the shower and props me up on the side. "Either you get in or I'll throw you in."

"Fine." I fall in the shower, lie on my back with feet against the side as the water washes over my face and body. It feels good.

"I got more to do today, but you take care." She says.

I nod. "It's daytime?"

"It is early but yes. Are you going to be okay?"

"Yes, thank you." I look up at her. "I appreciate you. I honestly do."

She giggles and leaves.

I get out of the shower and turn on the TV, trying to quiet my thoughts. It doesn't help. I can't pay attention to anything that's on TV. I've been used the whole time Phillip and I were together! Even Lana said so! I don't just feel like a victim, I feel completely played. I have to find Phillip and give him a piece of my mind. I turn the TV off, get dressed and jump in the car. After errands are run I head to the apartment building Mickey told me about. I look around but can't tell which apartment is theirs, so I sit in the car, hoping I'll see them walk by. The next thing I know, it's morning of the next day.

Ugh! Did I seriously fall asleep?! I get out the car and walk inside the complex. How am I supposed to find them now? I better suck it up and try again; I have to find Philip. I go up to the apartment building again and knock on every door that lined the hallway. Finally, a woman answers. I describe who I'm looking for.

She giggles. "You sound embarrassed."

Heart of Gold

"It's just that I've learned that it's difficult for a black and white couple." I'm sure being an older woman, she can relate to that. The apartment isn't in Montrose. It is near a suburb called Katy. Not a whole lot of mixed-race couples there.

"They live over there sweetheart." She points to a door on the right.

"Thank you." She nods.

When I arrive at the door, it's cracked open. I put my hand on the door and open it further. Inside I see Phillip sleeping on the couch. Time to wake up. I can't contain a smirk as I slam the door, jolting him awake. He bolts upright and looks wildly around the room in alarm. When he sees me, his eyes grow wide.

"What are you doing here?!" He shouts, scrambling to get off the couch.

"I came to see your new apartment."

"This is not mine, it's Kris's place."

"Kris's place?" I laugh. "Tell me Phillip. How does a sixteen year old girl get a place on her own?"

"Sixteen?" He retorts. "She's eighteen."

"Oh really? Her mother showed me a birth certificate when I left her at her mother's house. Didn't she explain that to you?" I stare at him, my voice dripping with sarcasm.

"That's why you left her there?"

"Of course. You told me to take her home not pick up things and bring her back to you. By the way, I'm not protecting you anymore. You are aware that if her mother wanted to, she could put you in prison for statutory rape right?"

"Now come on Beverly, no need to be that way." He pleads. I ignore him.

"It's not me who is going to call the cops, Phillip. Her mother has you dead to rights now."

"She wouldn't do that."

"Really? She was pretty mad when she found out what you were going to turn her little baby into."

Rebecca Nietert

"You told her?!"

"Maybe, maybe not. Oh wait...that's right." I snap my fingers, as if I forgot something. "This was supposed to be on the up-and-up but then again, you have all these secrets...so no, I didn't have to tell her. She already knew." He stares at me, unable to speak. I start to walk down the hallway. "Where is she, Phillip?"

He bolts from the couch and grabs my arm. "Don't do this!"

"Do what? Embarrass you? Humiliate you? Make you uncomfortable?" I look him in the eye and then continue my search. "You have been doing that to me since I've met you!" I don't see Kris in the bedrooms.

"Where is she?" I turn around and face him. He shrugs. I look to the side and notice a crack in the bathroom door. I open the door and see the light on. "Ah-ha!" I exclaim in triumph. Phillip is at my side in an instant. The moment is short-lived as we both spot Kris. She's in her panties, wearing a tiny t-shirt and nothing else. The sight of her slumped against the sink with a needle in her arm stops me in my tracks. Her lips are blue with white foam-like saliva dripping out of her mouth. Her eyes are partly open. I can't help but stare, shocked. "What...did you do?" I hiss.

"Nothing! What's wrong with her?!" He scrambles to pick her up.

"She has a needle sticking out of her arm Phillip!" I scream, beginning to panic.

He pulls out her arm so that he can see it. "A band is tightly wrapped around her upper arm too! Look at this!" The pool blood tricking onto the floor is coming from that arm.

"Beverly...is she dead?" He looks at me, his voice shaky. If we weren't in such a precarious situation, I would have fully embraced his fear. He deserves to be afraid after everything he's done.

"Put her down! Dial 911!" He looks at me. "Now!" I snap, which jolts him. He runs to grab the phone. I pull her up off the floor and sit her on the commode leaning against the wall. I check her throat and find a soft pulse. "C'mon, you can't die now." I

Heart of Gold

whisper as I place a nearby towel around where the needle is. I put her head on the side of the sink so she won't fall and stand, assessing the situation. Phillip rushes next to me, receiver in one hand with the other covering it.

"If they see me here, I'll be thrown in jail!" He pants. "What am I going to do?!"

"Face what you've done Phillip!" I hiss.

"I was sleeping. I didn't do anything!" He hisses back, looking at the phone cautiously.

"You've had a live-in relationship with a minor who's a drug user. You did something!"

"Beverly, help me!" He pleads, his black orbs trying desperately to pierce my eyes.

Suddenly, I get a sense of clarity and calmness. It's not my job to clean up his mess anymore. He's the one who replaced me.

"You know what Phillip? You're on your own; I don't care anymore. I already have a place of my own and will be taking the remainder of my mail this evening. I've contacted the landlord and I'm officially off the lease as of tomorrow."

"Beverly, please! Don't do this!" He cries.

I walk up to him. "I hope she was worth all this. When you do something horrible it's bound to come back to bite you. There is nothing you've done in the last year that is for anyone other than yourself. You and I both know that." I pause, making sure he's paying attention. His eyes are glued to mine. Yep, he's still listening. "As long as you hold on to being lazy, not caring about anyone but yourself, this is the kind of life you'll have." I walk to the door and open it, then look back at him. "This is not what I signed up for." I slam the door and leave.

When I arrive at the house, Mickey is still there. Phillip and Kris took his car so when I told him what happened, Mickey couldn't wait to leave.

"Can you drive me back to my moms house?" He asked.

Rebecca Nietert

"Sure, but if Phillip comes back I don't want to be alone with him."

That's between you two. I don't want any part of all this."

"Okay, let me make a quick phone call, then I'll take you."

I pick up the phone to dial. My mother answers.

"Hi Darlin'!" She sounds happy to hear from me. That's much better than any reaction she would've had before.

"I need your help."

"What's wrong?"

"I'm leaving Phillip and please don't say 'I told you so'."

"I won't. I am so glad, Beverly."

"I'm afraid of him." I can hear my voice cracking. I clear my throat, trying not to cry. "I need you to be here with me if he comes here. I have to pick up mail, lock doors and check that I got everything. I'm scared to be alone."

I want to hear what happened at Kris's too.

"Will he be there tonight?"

"Yes and he's going to be really angry."

"What happened?" After I explain she's silent, then sighs.

"I had hoped it would never come to this. Do you have a place to stay?"

"Yes, I got my own place." Like I had hoped things would turn out this way? I roll my eyes. "Will you come to help or not?"

"Of course, sweetie. When would you like me to come?"

"Well if you leave now I will meet you there after I drop off his brother at his mother's. I'll leave the door open so just walk in."

"Sounds great. I'm leaving as we speak."

"Thank you. I love you." I'm surprised those words came out of my mouth. It's not often I say 'I love you.' I can't even remember the last time I've said those words.

"I love you too. You will be all right."

"I know." I cleared my throat and hang up.

"Mickey! Ready to go?" I shout.

I took Mickey to his place and then I went back home.

Heart of Gold

As I pull in the driveway I see his Camaro in the driveway. Great. I was hoping to beat him here. I look at the car and sigh. Might as well get this over with. I've got to face him some time right? I walk to the door and start to put the key in when Phillip opens the door.

I jump in surprise. "You're not in jail?"

"Nope. No thanks to you. Her mom met us in the hospital and is pressing charges against me. I swear to you that I had no idea she was only sixteen."

"Uh-huh." I roll my eyes. You so knew.

"Why are you here?"

"I've come back to get my the remainder of my stuff."

"You were serious about that? After everything I've done for you?"

"What have you done for me?"

"I picked you up off the streets when you were begging for food! If it weren't for me you would be dead."

"Yes, you're probably right." I snap. "I would much rather be dead then what I am now."

"Just what did I do that was 'so bad'?"

"You turned me into a money-making machine so you wouldn't have to work. I can't believe I actually cared about you!"

"I gave you a life! A job, a roof over your head, food, clothes, whatever you wanted! I gave you a nice car. I took you shopping. What more could a girl want?"

Real love. "You just don't get it. You bought those things with my money. I would have been faithful to you until I died. Too bad you blew it on an underage girl."

I hear a door close and turn to face the direction the noise came from. It's my mother. She stands in the doorway of the kitchen.

"Now you're going to hide behind your mom? The one who abandoned you? Your abuser? The one who left you out on the streets to die?" Phillip let out a harsh laugh. "Wait, don't tell me. You need her to talk to me too right?"

Rebecca Nietert

"I need her more than I have ever needed you." I snap, glaring at him.

That made him angry. He opens a drawer and grabs a knife. My heart skips a beat. I instinctively step in between him and my mother. I look him dead in the eye.

"Put that down."

"Or what?" He sneers. "I have the power. This is my house now right? I can do whatever I want. Just like with Kris."

"You don't own me anymore." I'm trying to keep my voice as calm as possible. Knowing him, he's bluffing about the knife.

"You won't make it without me. I found out John's number and told him all about us. He won't be there for you to take his money anymore."

"Unlike you, he's not about the money. He actually, you know, wants me for more than just a good time."

He lunges forward and grabs me, turning me to face my mother with the knife at my throat. I freeze. He was serious?! Don't panic, don't panic. Just stay calm. Think! I can't look at my mother. The look of shock that's written across her face is too much. I look at the wall. C'mon! Think!

"You're never going to be rid of me." He whispers, his breath hot against my ear. I can't believe that this is the same guy who used to whisper 'I love you' while in bed. I have one shot at this.

"You know, there's one thing you've never realized about me."

"And what's that?"

"I'm a survivor." Now! I kick my leg back, connecting my foot with his groin. He drops the knife. I run towards the door, grabbing my mom's arm and race to the car. Phillip is hot on our tail.

"You little bitch! You'll never get away!" He screams.

I shove her in the passenger's seat, jump in the driver's seat. He opens my mother's door but she has picked up a bat that I have laying across the side of my car. I use it as protection.

Heart of Gold

She wields it without thinking and screams, "I will use it on your black ass!" She shuts the door when he backs up and I slam on the gas.

We head to the Rocky Mountain Men's Club. After what just happened, I can't work at the Gentleman's Club anymore. I walk in, apply for a job and am hired on the spot. I get back in the car and drive to my apartment. Silence fills the car. Did that really just happen?

The next day mom drives me back to the townhouse to pick up my car. I check every angle of the house before pulling in to make sure Phillip isn't home. I've got to be fast. If he finds out I'm here, he'll be over for sure to tie up what happened last night. I don't need that.

I walk around the house, checking cabinets and desk drawers. I came across the note that Shirley wrote me. How did I forget this here? Tears sting my eyes.

"How proud you must be of me now." I whisper, then shake my head. Focus! I walk over to the cabinet where the booze is kept and pour myself a pitcher of Crown Royal. I look at the note and take a drink, then another. I walk down the hallway to Phillip's room. I open the door and see a picture of Kris on his bed. He seriously has a picture of her after her mother is pressing charges against him? I laugh at the lunacy and smash the picture against the wall. Oops? I take another sip.

I walked over to his closet and see a locked box on a rack. I take the box with me to the bathroom sink, where he keeps his keys. Yup, there it is. I laugh. He's so predictable. I spot condoms in the drawer as well. We never used them. I slam the drawer shut. I open the box and see numerous pictures and notes from other girls. There were love letters, notes and pieces of hair. I almost close the lid when I see a piece of paper that seems different. I open it. There's a satanic ritual that describes placing women in the center of the room and chanting words for them to be under his spell. I can't unglue my eyes from what I just read. My mind's eye flashes

Rebecca Nietert

back to a time, years ago, when he said he had a special 21st birthday present for me. He had thrown me on the bed and kissed me, then said he had written a poem just for me. I look at the note. He had said these exact same words, claiming that it was a love letter. I, of course, felt flattered and we ended up having sex. The part he called 'desert'.

I close my eyes as the full weight of what happened hits me. I can't believe I was that gullible! How did I not see this? I take a big swallow of the Crown. I'm not sure who I'm more pissed at: him or my own foolishness.

"Why?!" I throw the box against the wall, the letters and pictures flying everywhere. I walk out the bedroom, down the hallway and back to the kitchen. I notice the black and white theme that penetrates every corner of the house. He has always said it was "his taste." I look around the kitchen, at the counter, sink and cabinets. Everything here is to par with 'his taste'. I finish my drink and throw the glass against the wall, basking in the sound of breaking glass. One down. I pull more alcohol out and grab another glass. I fill it to the rim, chug it, and then slam it against the counter. I don't want to feel anymore. I look down at the shattered glass and my bleeding hand. It doesn't hurt so badly. I walk over to the sink and grab a towel. I grab the First-Aid box and find a Band-Aid. I walk over to the counter and stop.

"Crap!" I look down at my foot, which now has a huge piece of glass stuck in it. I need to be numb again!

I hobble over the floor out of the range of glass and fall to the floor. I pull the piece of glass out of my foot and put the towel against it to stop the bleeding. After it subsides, I get up to get something to clean the wound. I grab a bottle of Jack Daniels from the counter and I pour it over my foot, then drink what's left in the bottle. I take the bottle of Vodka and do the same thing. Next is the Scotch, which I drink straight up. I grab a bottle of run and walk into the living room with the towel wrapped around my foot, soaked with my own blood. I slump down on the cool tile floor by

Heart of Gold

the front door. I put my head on the tile. It feels so nice. I decide to just lay here. Whatever happens-happens. I look at the ceiling. How did I get involved with Phillip anyways? Oh yeah...because of Shirley. They were friends.

"I miss you, Shirley. This one's for you." I lift the bottle of rum and take a swig. I sit back up against the wall and notice Phillips jacket hanging on the doorknob. I jerk it off and jump as a bag of pills roll out of a pocket.

"What the hell?" I pour them in my hand and popped them in my mouth. "No one will care." Then I take a giant swig of rum and lay my head back down on the cool tile flooring.

I wake up to a doorbell rang. I can barely lift my arm to turn the knob but I somehow manage despite not being able to feel anything. I'm looking up at a UPS driver.

Huh? "What's going on?"

"I have a package for a Miss White." He looks down at me, confusion etched into his face.

"That would be me." The words come out in a slur.

"Can you sign for this?"

"Sure."

He helped me raise enough to sign his electronic thing and then hands me the package. I slam the door, then throw the bottle of run against the wall. I drop the box and then kick it. That didn't feel good because the pain in my foot came back. I fall back on the floor, re-wrap the towel back around my foot and then crawl to open the box. Inside is a Panda Bear. It's just a lousy bear. I drop it. Then I notice the card at the bottom of the box.

"Wonder who this is from?" It's probably a girl trying to be cute with Phillip. I read the card. It says: "I love you. Your Father."

I drop the note, I look at the bear and suddenly I feel remarkably sick to my stomach. I hobble to the hall bathroom and heave everything I drank. I sit at the base of the stool, seeing the sunlight fading as the darkness creeps in. "I'm going to die." I rest my head on the seat of the stool, accepting my fate.

Rebecca Nietert

Hours later I awake to a crick in my neck. I cannot believe I am alive. I notice the blood on the floor. "What did I just do?" I reach down and unwrap the towel from my foot, seeing that the blood had clotted. That's good news at least. How did that happen? Oh yeah the glass. Then…I fell. Then…some guy handed me something…a bear. I stand as gently as I can and carefully walk back to the living room. I see the bear, pick it up and look around. Why hasn't Phillip come back? Surely he must've noticed my car or seen me asleep by now. I look at the bear and Shirley's letter on the ground. Who am I kidding? He's probably at some girls place. He's never given me anything. I pick up the letter, pick up the card and whisper "Thank you, dad." I scan the mess that I'd just made. He can deal with it. It's his place now. He's left more of a mess in me than I've left in this house. I open the door and leave.

Heart of Gold

16

The past few weeks have brought more than I'd bargained for. The oil business seems to be suffering. The clients I know from both clubs previously worked at will not come to a new club. I feel so alone. Sure, it's nice that no one knows me but it's also sad because I can't come up with the money I used to. I have to meet new people. Even the dancers are different. They're...a lower class. I don't know anyone, not even the bartenders, so I can't get completely free drinks anymore. The club doesn't even have an established clientele! Maybe Philip was right, maybe I can't do this without him. I'm even scared to call John, embarrassed because I don't want him to see me in a place like this.

The new bar where I work is even lonelier than I could have imagined. I let the humiliation of taking off my clothes turn into loathing for men who wanted to come into the topless bar.

Do the men have any idea who they're talking to when they approach me? No. They don't know my story, or frankly care to hear it. They have no idea who I am but are quick to point out my outside beauty. Their affirmations make me feel even worse. I need more than just physical reassurance. I hate approaching men now, and wait for them to come to me. I have no interest in flirting anymore. I just want someone to see me for me. Even if I hated me, I wanted them to know the real me.

I want someone to get to know me intellectually, not just sexually. I want someone like John, who actually wanted to know me and wasn't all about the money. Someone younger than John. I miss our friendship. I had to get a new phone number so there's no way for him to find me. Besides, he probably gave up on me, thinking I'm ignoring him or something. He probably believes that I

Rebecca Nietert

used him; I'm sure Philip had told him that to keep him away. Sometimes the pure irony of me taking my clothes off for a living and then expecting a man to think of me as something other than a trophy keeps me up at night. I can't see myself as anything more, why would a man? Maybe I'm wishing for something that will never happen, but I can't help it.

Often I find myself angry with Phillip for what he did to me. I begin to drink more; anything to get him out of my head and to ease the pain. Why do I feel so lonely all the time, even with guys fawning all over me, practically (some literally) falling at my feet? Sure Phillip and I had a faux relationship; we fell in lust, not love. Nothing had turned out like I had hoped and dreamed. I guess that's life. Can a man really love me forever? I can feel myself going in and out of the five stages of grief like a lost soul. I'm resentful, angry, emotional and fearful of men after Phillip. But ultimately, I can't describe how completely lost I am. It's like I'm flailing in the wind, trying to find out what went wrong.

I can't live my life anymore. I am consumed with being ashamed of what I have become. At what point did everything go so wrong? When did I realize how shameful a life like mine is? Why didn't I know that before I began down this path?

Lana and I have had long talks about the choices that I made. We can't collectively figure out why I chose a guy like Phillip to help me. She says that I'm more than capable of caring for myself. I'm not so sure about that. So far, I'm failing, much like I did before I met Phillip.

When I'm not working, I spend my time with Lana or trying to restore the still-strained relationship with my mother. I also tried a therapist, but that didn't work out because he couldn't help much. I've even tried dating again but most of the men that are open to dating coming in and out coming in and out only wanted one thing. I want a real relationship, not just sex. Of course I want the passion that comes with the love I so desperately crave, but in the end, all I want is for someone to stick around. I want a man who will put me

Heart of Gold

before his own needs. I want someone who truly understands me; someone I can rely on when times get hard. I want a man to puts my interests above his own. I guess I've never thought about what kind of man I want until now. The kind I really want, not just someone to have fun with on a weekend night.

Most evenings I now stand against the gold rails that line the sidewalls of the club and watch the people coming in and out. I imagine what their stories are; what their lives are like. I imagine who is abusive to his wife or cheating on her. I feel more alone than I have felt in a long time. The club remains empty more often than I have ever seen at a club before. The chairs don't hold many patrons; the girls are the bottom of the barrel too. I don't want to befriend anyone. Most of the girls do drugs, and the ones that don't are still not my cup of tea. I feel dirty just being in here. How did I create so much chaos in my life that it landed me here?

I long for the days of high-dollar table dances and of girls who trust me enough to set them up with John's. As much as I'm glad to finally be rid of Phillip when I feel lonely enough I desperately want to feel connected to someone again, even if that someone isn't good for me.

My shame keeps me from enjoying any monetary successes of independence. I've finally come to realize that my mother was right. I'm not meant to be a dancer; I just ended up this way. I don't see dancing as a courageous way to take care of myself anymore. Even though I was a tramp and had thought I was the best, I'm starting to realize that the highest bidder doesn't determine your real worth. I was never really in control, they were. Their money was a small price to pay for my attention.

I guess I had chosen the easy way out after all. This kind of career is a quick way to get a quick buck. All you've got to do is just show some skin and get paid. It's not that difficult. Sure the competition is difficult, but the work itself isn't that hard to do. All the pride I used to have seems to have vanished. If success really is about showing some skin to get some money, then I don't want

Rebecca Nietert

success. I want someone who will challenge me intellectually. If all I do is take my top off and get paid, is that really living?

My sister and I used to fight a lot; she felt like I had changed. She would often comment on how she didn't know who I was anymore. "It's like you're a completely different person!" She said as I try to explain what I'm going through. Every evening I look into the mirrors that line my new place of business and she was right. I don't know the woman staring back at me. Her words echo in my mind.

Loneliness is a disease that wraps the person in an unhealthy battle of insecurities. I can't get over whether or not the emptiness I feel is self-induced or because others can't really understand me. I'm trying to right the anger, trying to bury it within. I don't want to trust anyone or be trusted by anyone, especially not at this club. I find myself using gossip, slander, abuse, whatever I can find in my arsenal of weapons to wield off any potential human connection. There's no way out of this situation.

The memories of my grandparents telling me what a fine young girl I was vanish. Their favoritism is nothing but a distant memory. My sisters respect as well as my friendship with my mother are something I can only dream about. After she helped me with Phillip, she was done. I can't trust myself anymore. I don't know what's right or wrong. I can't help but dream of my life could be. I fell for Phillip and look what happened there! I remind myself men are good for one thing: getting what you want.

I want to feel again. I spent every day staring out into the crowd, doing minimal dances so I can fix dinner. Before long, I can't even put enough cash together to make rent. Forget the bills. I'm sinking in quicksand and there's no way out. All I do at home is sit in front of a blank TV. I can't think, can't feel. The times I want to die I can't.

Everything's a haze. Men try to talk to me but I can't hear them. I felt nothing; no hatred or contempt. If I just do what I'm supposed to, I can get paid and go home. I'm just playing the game

Heart of Gold

now. Laughing when appropriate, answering with a small "Uh-huh" and fake smiles to keep them entertained. I am just a shell of what I once was.

Late one evening, Lana and I discuss the possibility of my plans in getting a man I desire one day.

"You live in a fairy tale world." I look at her in shock. Yeah, she's blunt but not this much usually! People have reminded me how unworthy I am of real affection my entire life. My father didn't have to say it; he just left. My mother said that no man would ever want to take care of me every time a new blow of her violent tantrum would land upon my body. I thought Lana would be different. I thought she would be the friend who could actually believe that with me. I guess I was wrong. When will I learn to not trust anyone?

"Hey, I have a right to expect mutual respect from a man. Not now of course, but maybe in the future. It's not too much to ask."

"Men can't give you what you need. You just don't get that."

"Why not? They're just as capable as I am."

"That's where you're wrong." She sighs, giving me an exasperated look. "Men aren't capable of showing their love. You're looking for this perfect fairy tale man you saw in the movies. In real life they don't exist."

"I think you're wrong. Remember John from the club? He and his wife were married over 30 years before she died."

"Yeah and then he blew what she left him on you. For Pete's sake Beverly, he expected you to have a love affair with him because he gave you money."

"Well, that's because he was lonely."

"When you're lonely you make the worst mistakes of your life. It's when you're the most vulnerable you get caught up in the Phillip's of this world."

"Maybe. Why can't I find a decent man? All the ones at the club are so…repulsive."

Rebecca Nietert

"The problem is that no man is ever really decent, just like we aren't decent women. No man worth half his salt will have anything to do with either one of us."

Is that really true? Even after all the invitations I've received over the years? None are that respectful but at least they show interest right? Why couldn't they show the same kind of interest John has shown me? He didn't pay for my services. He paid me to talk. I hate wearing the shame and guilt, the scarlet letter on my body, visible for everyone to see. The fact that everyone views me as a tramp is sickening.

"You know, sometimes I think of how few men I have actually slept with in my lifetime. Why do I feel so dirty all the time?"

"Trick of the trade, girlfriend. Stop beating yourself up. You do what you have to in order to survive."

"I suppose you're right." I look down.

"Look, you made a choice. You feed yourself, take care of yourself now and no one has control over you unless you let them."

"Yeah. But geez, Lana, how am I ever going to find a man who will respect me for who I am on the inside?"

"I'm not sure you ever will. You're going to have to learn to live with what you can get. Make the best of it. That's just life. Honestly, that's all I expect."

"I'm just not sure I'm okay with that."

Heart of Gold

17

At first I don't pay much attention to him. A handsome man wearing a silver Stetson hat glides up to the bar. I think I've seen him before? I shrug. Probably one of the new regulars. I reach for my drink and take a sip. I need it, my courage. I grab my Crown and Seven and face the crowd again.

Moments later the tall man with the Stetson is facing me. He has crystal blue eyes that I find mesmerizing. His square jawline looks earned. I hear a crash and look down, not realizing that I had just dropped my drink. The glass shatters into a thousand tiny pieces on the tile floor. I have to blink a couple of times to bring myself back to reality. I struggle to collect my thoughts, finally realizing that it was me who has broken the glass. I can't help but stand there, staring at him. Completely awestruck. Those eyes. I look down. What is this…feeling? Wait! Feeling? No! I don't want to feel! I bend down and collect the broken pieces of the glass, trying to busy myself.

The bartender summons a bus boy to help. My body starts to feel warm as we work to clean up the mess. Everything in me wants to look up. No, don't do it! I see his shadow and can't help myself. I look up at the figure standing before me. The cowboy.

"Need some help, Ma'am?" His voice has a thick Southern accent that serenades me. I can tell he's from Houston. After being here for almost a decade, I can pick out the locals easily. I can't help but wonder who he is and why we never met.

He holds his hand out to help me up. "Thank you." I smile up at him, trying not to think of how strong his hand is. He smiles back, his eyes turning a darker blue with sparks flying through them. I can feel my heart skip a beat. I let go of his hand once I'm

Rebecca Nietert

standing, hoping he doesn't notice my palms beginning to sweat. What's happening? I am out of control again?

"You okay?"

"Ye-yes. I'm fine." I stutter.

He turns to the bartender. "Get this Lady another drink please." He tips his hat to me. "Anything else I can do for you?"

I've never felt as powerless from meeting a man as I do right now. Phillip made me feel powerless but this is…different. I can't help but notice the sparkle in his eyes. I did not imagine that. Or did I? But the way he's looking at me now… I swallow hard, about to answer when a girl comes up to him and kisses his cheek and grabs his hand. Of course it is too good to be true. I look away slightly not to seem like I am starring.

He pushes her away gently, telling her he's interested in talking to me. That makes me feel good.

"But you promised!" She whines. He looks at me.

"Oh?" I raise an eyebrow.

He tells her to leave and takes my arm again, looking into my eyes. "Don't worry about her. You sure there's nothing I can do for you?"

I let out a short laugh. "I'm sure. Go have fun." I pull my arm out of his grasp, grab a new drink from the bar and leave, not bothering to look into those smoldering eyes. I can feel him watching me walk away. I can feel him watching me as I dance. Sometimes I let myself slip and look back at him.

He hasn't moved from his spot at the bar.

Was he serious when he meant it was nothing with that girl? Every time I look at him he tips his hat towards me, making sure that I see him. Focus! I need to focus! Guys watch me all the time. What makes this one so different?

As I get off of work he's still sitting at the bar. I walk past him, but he stops me. "My name is Joseph and you're one pretty lady."

"Thank you. I'm Beverly."

"You're from Houston then?"

Heart of Gold

"No. I moved here when I was nineteen."

"You come here often?"

"Yes." I laugh. What a lame line. "I work here."

"Really?" He raises his eyebrows. I try not to roll my eyes. As if he hasn't seen me all night? He's playing with me.

"Why do you look so pleased?"

"I know where to find you now." He looks at his watch. "It's late. A buddy of mine and me are going head out but I'll be back."

"Whatever." I shrug.

"You and I both know it's not whatever. We'll catch up then."

I can't help the response that comes out. "That'd be nice." Did I really just say that?

"Now that's better." He smiles and tips his hat, then walks off, his friend joining him as he heads out the door. Suddenly I feel very alone. Like somehow the room is colder because he's gone.

Late that evening I realized he hadn't come back. I didn't know if he ever would. I wonder if the heat I felt with him was kismet. I wonder if what I thought I had with Phillip was just manipulation, because Phillip didn't stir the same desire.

I get in my car and drive home.

It's been two weeks since I've seen him. I can't help but be impatient. I hate this stupid feeling of actually wanting to go to work; the anxiety of hoping he's there.

When I finally see him again he seems apprehensive. It isn't anything like our first meeting. Maybe he doesn't remember me. I throw myself into my work. I finally head to the bar for a drink. He sees me and smiles, looking intently as before into my eyes. "Nice to see you again." He says softly.

"Didn't think you'd come back."

"Been thinking about me then?" He takes a sip of his drink, those blue eyes staring at me. I try not to stare back.

"Maybe, maybe not."

"Can I get you a drink?"

"Crown and Seven please."

Rebecca Nietert

"Seems we have more in common than just this drink." He holds his glass to toast me. I notice it too is a Crown and Seven.

"Why is that?"

"I can't get you off of my mind either. I haven't felt this many butterflies since I was a kid."

"Really?" I try not to show how flattered I am but I can feel my cheeks get warm.

"When I saw you it felt like I've known you my whole life."

I laugh. I wonder if he can feel the heat too. "What kind of cowboy are you?"

His eyes are dancing. "I have to tell you I'm no teacher. I don't preach, I don't tell lies and I don't want to be anyone's father. You're an independent woman. I respect that."

I can't help but look down shyly. I still can't think of myself as independent because I was barely scraping by. Joseph is handsome. The fact that he thinks I'm independent when I don't feel like it makes me feel a little bit hopeful. I can't let him get to me. "I'm not that independent."

"I bet you are more than you think. How much do you make a night?"

I hesitate. "Two hundred." I've never worked for so little! I'm so ashamed and I wonder if he can tell? I clear my throat. "Why?"

He leans against the bar and takes a sip of his drink. I stare at mine. "What if I was to pay you for a whole week up front to go out of this restaurant with me?" He looks over at me. Instantly I'm on alert.

"I don't do that." I grab my drink and start to walk away.

He reaches out his arm to catch me to whisper, "Please sit down. Let me explain."

"I can't." I can't help the tears that are forming. I can't believe he'd say such a thing. I can't believe I'm even wasting my time here! All men are the same. This one is no different.

He reaches out and tilts my head to force our eyes to meet. His eyes are soft, his manner calm. Somehow I feel safe and vulnerable

Heart of Gold

all at the same time. "Beverly." He wipes my hair back from my face. "I'm going to be honest. I want you." I can't speak. He continues, "But I also want to be fair to you. You don't make much money. I would be a cad if I took you from your only source of income without compensating you for it."

All I can do is stare into those blue eyes. I'm completely mesmerized. "You don't have to sleep with me. Let me get to know you out of here. Let me show you the real me, then we can see if we want to take it anywhere. That's all I'm asking."

He stands up, his body invading my space as he towers over me. He purposefully pushes his tall form against my body. I can feel the heat radiating from him. I can't help but wonder how hot he would feel without his clothes on. My mind is swirling; lost in the wonder of a promise so real.

I look up at him and whisper, "Yes, I will go out with you." I put my hands on his chest, trying to keep him at some sort of distance. "You can keep your money though. I'm not in it for the money."

Bad move. I can feel his heartbeat. "I will not keep my money, but I do promise that I will never think of you as anything less than a lady."

"Thank you." I look into his eyes, praying that he would whisk me in his arms and take me out of here.

Rebecca Nietert

18

We exchanged numbers and he did call me to set a date. I'm sitting on a park bench when he strolls up. His silhouette is unmistakable. His Stetson sparkles in the afternoon sun. It's different than the silver one he wore at the bar. This one was almost white and it was made of straw. The atmosphere is incredibly romantic as the waterfall of the Transco Towers trickle in the distance. Joseph sits next to me.

"Howdy."

"Hey."

"You look absolutely incredible."

I smile shyly as his eyes wander from my face all the way to my feet. I had dressed up a bit more than I usually do for the occasion.

"Thank you. You look quite fine yourself." He puts his arm around me and we watch the scenery together quietly for a few moments.

"Can I ask you something?" I blurt out.

"You can ask me anything."

"Are you a real cowboy?" I laugh nervously. "I mean, do you ride horses and have a ranch and stuff?"

He laughs. "Yes, I've ridden horses in the past. They're dumb animals and I won't be bothered if I never have to ride another one. And yes, I do live on a ranch."

I can't keep the excitement from my voice. "Really? How big is it?"

"About three hundred acres."

"What do you do?"

"I ride my dirt bikes on a self-made track. I live with Trent and John; they're my roommates."

Heart of Gold

"I meant what do you do for a living?"

He holds up a hand. "Oh! Now hold on, I love talking about my ranch. We have a real blast out there. There is a pond out back that I can show you. We fish too. It's stocked with bass from local fisheries. The ranch is its own island. We don't have to leave it if we don't want to. We fish outside the back, we ride our dirt bikes around a track, and we have tons of other guy stuff we do out there."

I smile, letting myself get lost in the images of him riding dirt bikes. He probably looks so good with no shirt on. there's silence for a little while as I soak it all in.

"How old are you?"

He laughs. "Forty-two. How old are you?"

"I'm twenty-six."

He thinks for a moment. "Does it bother you that I'm so much older than you are?"

"Bother me? No. I think you're handsome."

He laughs. "Darlin', I'm just a man with no aces in the hole." I've heard that phrase before and know what he means. Why does he think his life is on the downside? Suddenly my stomach growls loudly.

"Hungry?" He asks playfully.

"Yeah." I laugh, a little embarrassed.

He stands up, takes my hand and leads me to his white pickup truck. He opens my door and helps me inside, then walks around to get in the drivers seat. Before he starts the truck, he looks at me for a long moment. I look at him and can't help but smile. He smiles back then puts the key in the ignition.

"Where are you taking me for lunch?"

"You like sandwiches? I know a great place."

"Sandwiches sound great. Thank you."

We drive to Neil's Deli on the east side. It's not a part of town I visit often. He seems to know his way around pretty well, winding around back roads. He drives through traffic with ease. We talk all

Rebecca Nietert

the way to the restaurant. After he parks, Joseph walks around to open my door.

"I can open my own door. You don't have to do it if you don't want to."

"My father always said to respect a lady. I do it without question." I smile. I must admit, it feels nice.

He orders to-go for both of us. After a short wait, the waiter brings us our bags. Joseph pays, takes the bags and we head back to the truck. He brings me back to the place where we were earlier.

I take a bit of my sandwich and look at him. "What's next?"

"Well." He clears his throat. "What do you want to do?"

"I don't know. Would you think I'm crazy if I said I don't want this day to end? I'm having the time of my life!" I laugh.

He looks at me intensely. "Beverly, you have to tell me what you want. I'm not here to baby-sit. You have to know what you want to do and be able to tell me."

I take another bite, feeling uncomfortable. "I'm not sure how to tell you what I want."

"Okay." He pauses. "The Sheraton Grand Hotel is just across the street. We can get a room, then we can talk and see what happens. Are you up for that?"

"I'm not sure if I should be grateful for you taking me out or offended you just asked me that." I can't help the snap come out.

"Look," He pulls one thousand dollars from his pocket.

A sense of indignation washed over me.

He said, "I like spending time with you but I know you have to make your money. If you don't want to go to the Sheraton I understand."

I roll my eyes. What is it with men and money? "Listen to yourself! You just asked me to go to a hotel room with you, then you offered me money!"

"I'm not trying to offend you. I want you to take the whole week off for that cash. I really want to get to know you. I want to give you the power. We can do anything you want. Beverly, I want

Heart of Gold

you. I hope you know that. I don't want you to feel like I think of you as anything other than a lady."

"How nice of you." I can't keep the sarcasm from my voice. I take the money and shove it in the pocket of my jeans, then start to walk off. He quickly stands up and walks in front of me. He turns to face me and tilts my chin up toward him. His fingers gently caress my cheek before he let them slowly descend to my waist. He pulls me in close. I can't breathe. "You're beautiful Beverly! What is it that you want to do?" His eyes are a deep blue, his voice husky. I can't speak. He slowly bends his head gently to my face. He pauses, his lips just inches away from mind before he kisses me. His kiss is so soft and passionate. I feel my knees going weak, not wanting this feeling to stop. He stops and looks me in the eye and whispers, "Beverly? Tell me what you want?"

"You." I answer hoarsely. It's the only word that comes to mind!

He laughs softly. "Come on." He takes my hand and walks me to the truck. I can't say anything. This feels so surreal to me. Is this really happening? We drive to the Sheraton. Joseph goes up to the lobby desk and gets us a room. He pays cash then walks over, takes me hand, and leads me to our room.

Our room is amazing! It's beautifully decorated in pastel colors, mainly purple and yellow. There's a large hot tub decorated in blue tiles and a huge window that overlooks the Transco tower and Galleria area. The room is impeccably clean.

I suddenly feel an overwhelming sense of modesty. I take my clothes off at work and with a look or a move I entice men to want to spend more money. When I am intimate with someone they take all of me. Secrets that the men don't see in the club I consider tiny pieces of my soul. I don't give that freely, and certainly not for profit. That's the one bit of self-recrimination I have left. I will hold on to it tightly.

Rebecca Nietert

I don't want to treat him the way I've treated other men. I want this to be special. I don't want to ruin it. Before I know it, Joseph is unbuttoning my blouse. I can't relax. I put my hands on his chest.

"I can't do this!" He's so comfortable. I'm just a dancer who's trying not to manipulate a man for once in my life. I feel like I did back when I had sex for the first time. Afraid.

He stops and looks at me. "You have done this before?"

"Yes, just...not in a while." I can't hide my embarrassment.

"How many men have you been with?"

"Enough. That's not important."

"You work in a strip club." His voice sounds slightly accusatory.

"Just because I work there doesn't mean I sleep with every man who walks in the door!" I shout, trying to hide from his hurtful accusation.

"Beverly, I'm right here; you don't have to shout at me, and I'll never shout at you. I didn't mean to upset you. I was just curious. I don't think anything less of you, okay?"

I nod. His words made me feel bad.

"Joseph." I whisper softly, "I really like you but I'm feeling a little scared."

"Why?" He puts his arms around my waist, holding me.

"I just...can't." He tilts my head up and stares into my eyes.

"Can't what?"

I can't help the tears sting at my eyes. "Trust."

"Trust what?"

"Trust you."

"Why?" He whispers softly, leaning his head in to my face.

"You're a man."

He stops, frozen. Then whispers, "Kiss me."

"I can't!" Oh God, if only you knew how much I want to!

"Kiss me!" His voice is deeper, his breathing heavier. I can't help myself. The dark puddles of passion in his blue eyes are intoxicating. I kiss him and warmth floods into my body. All of my fear suddenly vanishes.

Heart of Gold

"Do you feel that?" He whispers.

"I do." I sigh, still reeling from the passion.

"How can you be afraid of that?"

I look into his eyes. "I'm not now."

He smiles and kisses me. His hands move to my waist, under my shirt. I run my hands up and down his back and around his waist. His breath is hot against my face as he moves down to kiss my neck. I lean my head back, sighing with pleasure as I take off his shirt. He unbuttons mine and slides his hands up my stomach to my breasts. I lean back against the wall as he kneads them like kneading dough. His hands are so firm and strong! I run my hands up and down his sides softly, then let them slide down to the middle of his stomach. I can feel his muscle as I tug gently on is pants. I slowly put my hand into his boxers.

"Oh, God!" He moans as he presses my hand against his shaft, letting me feel him. I unbutton his jeans and slowly unzip them. He kicks them off, along with his boxers. He pulls me into him, kissing my neck as he takes my bra off. Before I can blink he's unbuttoning my jeans and pushing them down. I kick them off and grab his face, kissing him desperately. He pulls me to the hot tub and turns the water on then steps in and helps me get in. I gently push him against the side of the tub and climb on top of him, making sure he feels me against him.

"Are you comfortable?" He whispers as I kiss his neck.

"Mhm. As long as I'm with you I'm wonderful."

He smiles and kisses me. I wrap my arms around his neck and kiss him back, lost in him. he shifts, pushing his manhood against me. I shift so his manhood is underneath me. I squeeze my legs, hearing him gasp with pleasure. I kiss his neck and let my hands roam up and down his chest.

"You're so perfect." He whispers.

I smile. "So are you." I kiss down his chest to his stomach, where the water is rising. He reaches over and turns the water off. I slide my hands to his lower back and push him against me. I kiss

Rebecca Nietert

down his stomach slowly and inch my way to his waistline. I move my hands down to his butt and massage it as I look up at him and press my soft boobs into his hardness. He leans his head back and gasps, his whole body moving with each breath.

I slowly slide my body down and kiss his shaft lightly, smiling as he jumps with pleasure. I take his shaft into my mouth and work my magic. His moans of encouragement keep me going. I finally stop, feeling him about to burst. I look up at him and smile, then slide my body up his and kiss him passionately.

He pushes himself against me and I bite his lip while slowly moving myself off of him.

"You okay?" He looks at me, concerned.

"Yeah, let's get in bed." He smiles and gets out, taking my hand to help me out, and lead me to the bed. I push him on the bed and climb on top of him, kissing his neck as I press myself against him. He puts his hands on my lower back and pushes himself against me. I gasp as I feel him wanting me. I slowly push against him, moaning at his touch. He presses against my lower back, guiding me deeper.

"Joseph!" I can barely say his name as I let him push deeper, letting him into parts of my soul; places where no man has ever been before. I let him push against the tight defenses, letting him get a glimpse of sweetness. His heartbeat racing at a hundred miles an hour mirrors mine. We are one. His soul is my soul. I lay on top of him, letting him roll me over to get on top of me. His touch is setting me on fire! I look at him, watching his beautiful muscles constrict and expand, watching him work. I feel him in me and gasp as I finally let loose.

"Oh, Beverly!" He collapses on top of me, trying not to put his full weight on me. I let out a sigh of relief. I've never felt so…good before. Especially after sex.

After we calm down I look at him. "Do you remember earlier when I asked what you do?"

"Yeah. I'm a general contractor for construction." He answers and kisses me, then quickly stands up. "I have to go now."

Heart of Gold

"Go? Now?" I look at him as he starts getting dressed, confused.

"I have a meeting." He stammers as he looks at his watch. "Honestly Bev, I didn't think we would be doing this—here—this long. I hope you understand."

"Do you always have meetings this late in the afternoon?" I looked outside the window. The sunny day has already disappeared into early evening.

"Yeah. We're adding a room onto this house. I have to meet the carpenters there." He finished getting dressed..

"Oh. Okay, then how about tomorrow?"

"Tomorrow?" He looks at me, surprised.

"Yes, silly. You asked me get free for a week so I could get to know you better. Since we were together today I figured we could start our week tomorrow."

"Oh, but I can't tomorrow. The next day will be better. Okay?"

"Promise?"

"Promise." He kisses my forehead and hands me my clothes.

"Can we pick up where you ran off?"

He laughs. "Yes."

"You're going to take me back to my car, right?" I quickly get dressed.

"Yes of course. Then I have to go, okay?"

I nod. "I had a great day."

"Me too. This is only the beginning though." He walks towards me and kisses me deeply. I don't want you to go!

"You are so dangerous!" He whispers.

I smile and whisper back, "It's only the beginning."

We check out of the hotel. The drive back to my car was too short. After a long, sensual kiss I get out of his truck and into my car. I wave good-bye as he drives off. I head in the opposite direction. I can't wait to get home and tell Lana all about my day!

Rebecca Nietert

19

When I arrive home, Lana is busy in the kitchen. "Hey there!" I smile as she turns around.

"What's up with you?" I can't help but tell her all about my day with Joseph. I'm bursting with happiness!

She sighs and turns off the stove. "Beverly, come sit down." Huh? Isn't she happy for me? She walks into the living room and I follow. We sit in the only two chairs in the room, covering ourselves with two Afghans my grandmother had made. She looks up at me.

"So, tell me about your trip to Chicago." I sigh. Guess not. The weeks passed slowly after I left the Gentleman's Club and Phillip. I don't know if it was the intense loneliness or the fact I feel I need to reconnect with whatever I broke within my family. My mother and I are building our relationship after what we've been through so it gives me hope that my brother and sister will forgive as well. I'd gone to Huntley, my small town where I went to high school.

I went to visit LaNette, who was getting married to her high school sweetheart. Of course the best man was my first boyfriend. Talk about awkward. My sister's husband to be asked me what I remember about my first love, but I couldn't remember more than the notes we wrote each other and the horrible way he broke up with me. It seemed as though whatever I said was confrontational? I didn't know how I was creating so much drama because I was desperately trying not to, but the end result is by the time I left it was clear that everyone thought it was time for me to go.

The man believed to be my biological father showed up to the events. Even worse. I sat there imagining what it must be like to be walked down the isle. I couldn't imagine, but one thing I did know

Heart of Gold

what that he would never agree to walk me down mine. I couldn't wait to leave.

"Not much to tell. It was pretty much all about LaNette, like it always is. I thought it might be fun to go back but nope. My father was there. They think I'm a bad person just because I work at the topless bar. The tension was so high. It was terrible."

"Did you really expect that your family would respect you now?" Lana blurts out. After seeing the look on my face she softens her voice. "Sorry. I mean, if they never have before do you really think that they would start now?"

I shake my head. She's so confusing at times. Why can't she accept me being happy for once instead of bringing up this kind of crap? "I think they resented me for being at her wedding."

"Why is it so important to you that your family accept you and what you do?"

"I don't know. I've done everything I can think of to win their love."

"So are you angry because no one is doing what you want or feeling the way you want them to feel?"

"No, I just want some to love me the way that I love them. I want my family to respect me like I respect their choices."

"Your family is exactly what they are. I find that in most families whatever position one person is in, they stay that way their whole life. It never changes. They aren't going to miraculously get you. Life just doesn't happen that way. You'll always be a little off or weird to them and you need to accept that." I flinch as the weight of her words hit me like a slap.

"I guess you're right." I mumble, looking down at the floor remembering how often they labeled me 'weird' while I was there.

"My point is, are you sure that you're not going to try and get that respect from this new guy since your family won't give it to you?"

I can't understand why she's merging Joseph with them! "No. Joseph respects me."

Rebecca Nietert

"Beverly, come on! If he respected you he wouldn't have offered to pay you."

"That's not true! He was just taking care of me. He respects me and that's why he paid me money. He said it's for missing work. He wants to take care of me."

"You want so badly for someone to take care of you and to respect you that you don't see what is really going on! You're so desperate that you're not thinking right!"

I sigh. I'm glad that she's looking out for me, but this guy really is different. Why won't the words come out? "I have grandparents that care about me."

"And where were they when your mom beat the crap out of you?"

"They helped when they could. What were they supposed to do? There isn't a foster care system in Huntley. I never told anyone until I was a teenager, and by then it was too late. Besides, children were seen but not heard."

"I'm not trying to make you angry, but why didn't they have someone keep an eye on you?" I shrug, unable to answer that question.

Lana reaches over and put her hand on mine. "You're a great story teller and I want to believe that what you're telling me is the exact truth. Sometimes when we're young we have a different opinion of what truth is. If what you're telling me is true, you really need to face the real truth. The truth is that your family knew about what was happening and did nothing about it."

"Lana, I know they loved me; I know it for sure. I think they were just afraid of my mother."

"So the grandparent who gave birth to your mother is now terrified of her? I'm not buying that."

"Do you really think they didn't care enough to do anything?" I can't keep the sadness out of my voice. What if she's right? Has everything I've grown up believing been one huge lie?

Heart of Gold

"What I think doesn't matter. It's what you think; what you've spent your whole life searching for."

I'm starting to see where she's headed with this. Sort of. Have I really been searching my entire life for some knight in shining armor to rescue me from the life I was born into? I explain to Lana my confusion of having a mother who professed to love me yet beat me, and the family who had apparently protected her instead of saving me.

"I really don't think they knew how severe the beatings were. I always wore long sleeve shirts and pants. I was so afraid to let my bruises show. Even my sister's didn't know about it."

"I think everyone knew. You told me that Shirley tried to kill herself. You even said that when she died you whispered to her that she had gotten her wish. It seems that she knew something. So why then do you think that no one knew?"

"I don't know. All I know is that when I was young I was using a pretend iron because I wanted to help mom iron some of my father's military clothes. I ended up undoing all of her days' work. That was the first time I remember her losing her temper so badly."

"Was that when your parents were married?"

"I think so."

"And did you not meet your father at LaNette's wedding?"

I sigh, exasperated. "Where are you going with this?"

"Your parents split when you were three."

"Meaning?" I asked.

"The first incident happened when you were three years old." I pause, thinking about how if, as a grown woman, I hit a small child like my mother did. I can feel hot tears burn my eyes. "Okay, I got it!"

"No, I don't think you do. How old were you when you left?"

"Fourteen." I choke out.

"Beverly, for fourteen years you were beaten in the middle of the night, you had bruises on your arms and legs and you went to school every weekday. Surely the teachers noticed something they must have known what she was doing, and no one did anything? If all that happened the way you say it did someone had to notice."

"Lana, they must have known all along!"

"Whether or not they did is irrelevant. What is relevant is that you have always known the truth. You may have buried it deep inside but you did know the truth."

I shake my head trying to rattle the thoughts in it.

"Don't you see? You want so much to be loved that you're willing believe that you are in love with any guy who shows you affection."

"If that were true I would've been in love with a lot of men. I might be a whole lot better off than I am right now."

"Can't you see that you're being manipulated by them? From what you've told me, this one is very, very good. It's too soon to feel that way about someone. Just take it slow."

"Lana, you're wrong. He's a gentleman. He's smooth, charismatic and intoxicating. He asks me what I need. He tells me that I have to ask for what I want and not just take what I get. He won't ever take from me what I don't want to give."

She shakes her head. I shrug. She doesn't have to believe me. "Just be careful." She says softly.

"I promise." There's an awkward silence between us now. I look at the kitchen.

Lana clears her throat. "Well...I have some news of my own."

I look at her, waiting. "Yes?"

"I met someone. His name is Rod."

"And?"

"And...you know the passion you have with Joseph? Well...it's the same that I have with Rod."

I roll my eyes. Oh, so it's oaky for HER to have a love life but I can't? I lean back in the chair, mocking her, pretending to listen.

"Beverly, it's the first time I have ever been so completely overwhelmed by a guy!"

Heart of Gold

I can't help the words come out. "Why can you have something like that but I can't?" Who does she think she is?

She looks away. "It's possible for you. I can't get enough of him! We are always driving off to meet up with each other and I think about him all the time! I can't wait to be with him either."

"So..."

"So I'm moving out with him."

I look at her, incredulous. All I had said was I had a fun day. I wasn't planning on moving out with the guy!

"Really?"

She smiles. "Yes."

It seems as though the light came in today. I was buried in some darkness and for the first time I feel genuine hope that I can feel happy again. I love Lana. I do. However, I am consumed with confusion about what just happened. I wanted to continue the butterflies that I felt earlier. I wanted to share that with Lana, but now my mood... I'm hurt all over again and I am angry.

Was she just trying to warn me about the thing Joseph was doing in the beginning of our relationship or was she making a parallel between Joseph and the behaviors of my immediate family? I cannot figure out why someone would not jump right into the celebration of my happiness rather than bring me down with a reality check about how I might get hurt. I just met Joseph for Pete's sake!

I'm happy for her I really am. I just wish that she hadn't criticized what she knows nothing about. I feel so much passion for Joseph unlike I have with any other man, and I am sure that I know myself too much to think for one minute that I am not going to pursue this.

Rebecca Nietert

20

I've thought a lot about what Lana said over the past few days. Lately she's spent most of her time away from home because she wants time with Rod. Of course happiness is okay for her. Clearly I have a chip on my shoulder put there by our talk.

I walk out onto the balcony and look out over the Houston skyline. The view is beautiful, full of nights against the dark sky. I look around at the city below, reflecting on what I truly want in life. Joseph. He's what I want. Those eyes. The mental pictures keep coming up, pushing away any other thoughts. I can't help but feel alive when I'm with him.

Lana comes home to get ready for work. I turn to face her.

"Hey there." She looks at me.

"Hey? Do you want marriage, kids and a family? Or is this new guy just for fun?"

"Beverly, I don't believe in your fairy tales. I like this guy a lot. I want to be with him all the time and he makes me feel good. For me, that's enough." She goes into the bedroom while she's talking and comes out with clothing. She slips on her leggings. "By the way, Rob and I are renting a place that offers weekly rent."

I can't help but feel like I've offended her by asking about her plans with him. I can't help but feel like I have the right to ask, but shouldn't I be the one who is offended? After all, all she thinks I want is a fairy tale. I actually want a family while she just wants a boy-toy. How come my situation is so repulsive to her?

"Well, you're always welcome to come home when he can't be with you. Just keep the key." I say trying not to judge my best friend.

Heart of Gold

"I'll do that." She smiles as she grabs her keys from the kitchen table.

"When are you leaving?"

"Next week if I make enough money for one week's rent."

"I think it's great that you know who you want."

"Yup." The door slams shut behind her.

We work at different clubs. The days of working together in friendly competition are long gone; nothing but a memory. I've tried to get her to come work with me but she said something about "being comfortable there." I almost laughed. Whatever that means. There's no such thing as comfort in a job like ours.

At work, I grab the drink from the bar and take a sip, looking around the room. It's a full night. I let my mind wander, thinking of the good ole days at the hottest club in Houston. We made a chunk of cash! Until I was kicked out for "inappropriate actions". Lana left also, saying that she couldn't handle the pressure and wanted less stress. She ended up on the north side of town at a bar I've never been to. Even with her tall figure, blonde hair and blue eyes, the quota wasn't worth the effort. Now she comes and goes as she pleases. We barely talk. I can't help but stare at the design on the floor feeling lonely.

I look up and see Joseph approaching the bar and force a smile.

"Hey, what are you doing here?" He looks over and smiles.

"You." I laugh and shake my head as he leans in and kisses me.

"You wish." The smell of his aftershave is so tempting.

"Take off work tonight." He whispers. I feel his hands move to my sides, gently caressing me. "I can't spend another minute without you."

I laugh and shake my head. "I can't. I have to make a living."

His lips are on mine again. "I'll cook dinner for you." I look up at him wearily. It's been a long time since someone's cooked for me. Phillip used to in the beginning. Would this be any different?

"You want to cook dinner for me?"

Rebecca Nietert

He nods and brushes his hand against my cheek. "Yes. You can toss your things in the truck. Let's go. Right now."

I look over at the dance floor, at the sea of people. There's so many clients to entertain tonight. I look at him. But this one is the most important. "Okay, but can I follow you? I can't just leave my car here."

His face lights up and I feel amazing as he takes my hand. "Come on!" I feel like a little rebellious kid again, sneaking out. Can I really make a man this happy? This is so surreal!

Driving behind Joseph is a nightmare! If I thought I drive fast, well, he's got me beat. Weaving in and out of traffic, dodging cars, honking horns. Farmhouses whiz by. The drive seems to take forever, even at top speed. We finally stop at the entrance of a red dirt road. I can see the A-frame house in the distance, covered with a metal roof. As we drive down the driveway, I notice a wraparound porch with dim lights. The house seems to be well taken care of. That's a good sign. The house looks like something out of a Louis L'Amour storybook. I can't believe he's asked me to come here!

I park behind him in the circle drive. He hops out of his truck and comes to my side, opening the door.

"Thank you." I smile reaching for his outstretched hand.

"What do you think?" He turns to look at me as we walk to the front door.

"I love it! I've always dreamed of a place like this in the country; a house with a wraparound porch. It's the picture-perfect home!"

We walk into the living room. It's huge! The stone fireplace extends from the floor to the ceiling. Did he make the home himself? Joseph gives me a tour of the house, showing me the loft above where we are standing. Then he takes me into the kitchen, which has the most beautiful hand-crafted table. It's big enough to seat six people. Maybe he has guests over often? The stove is old and black but fits in with the rest of the décor.

Heart of Gold

"I love the table!" I run my hand over the surface, feeling the smoothness of the wood.

"Thank you." His face is beaming. "I made it myself."

I look around the kitchen, seeing the workspace already prepared. Phillip used to have things prepped in the beginning. Could this really be different? Joseph reaches into the refrigerator and takes out a carton with green things sticking out everywhere.

"What is that?"

He looks over at me and laughs. "Green beans silly. Can you snap them please?" He hands me the carton. I just stare at it and shake my head. The only green beans I've known have come from a can.

"Snap? What do you mean?"

He looks at me. "You're kidding me, right?"

I shake my head and can't help but let out a nervous laugh. "No, I'm totally serious."

He laughs and reaches from behind me, taking a green bean in his hands. "Like this." I can feel his breath against my ear as he takes my hands and helps me snap the ends off, then snaps the thin green stick in half. "Got it?"

I nod and smile. No one has ever been that…gentle with me before. I feel his hands run back against my waist as he steps away. I can't help but blush. Is this what love really feels like? I get to work on the green beans. There's enough to feed an army!

"So, are we expecting company?"

"Yes, it's about time for Trent and John to come home."

Wasn't this just supposed to be us? "Those are your roommate's right?"

"Yes. They are big boys who eat a lot. Neither of them can cook though."

That's surprising. "So you cook all the meals here?"

"Yep, except once a year for our annual barbecue. Every year Houston has a celebration when the rodeo comes to town. This year I'm going with them. Then the weekend after the big barbecue

Rebecca Nietert

we have our own cook off with everyone I've known since I was a small boy."

"So you were raised here in Houston?"

"Yes, downtown near the projects. My mother was single most of the time. The man you saw at the bar with me when we met is the man who pretty much raised me."

"Wow, and you still know him? That's incredible! Do you keep in touch with everyone you grew up with?"

"Yes for the most part. Don't you?" He glances over.

I shake my head. "I don't know anyone I grew up with. We moved too often."

"That's too bad." His voice is full of sympathy. I'm not sure if I like that or not.

"But I have a lot of friends where I work."

"Yes, but nothing is better than a lifelong friend."

He rinses the beans and puts them on the stove to cook. He adds sugar, bacon, and onions in the pot and covers the pan. Next he puts what he calls "field peas" into another pot of water and turns them on as well. He squeezes some juice from banana peppers into the pot with the peas. I watch him prepare the meat and bread.

"So…when is it going to be just us?" He stirs the peas then looks at me and smiles.

"After dinner." I can't help but smile back. I walk up behind him and wrap my arms around his taunt waist. He puts one hand over mine as he stirs with the other. I put my head against his back, never wanting to let go.

The sound of a roaring engine makes me jump. I let go of him and we both look out the window to see two trucks racing down the dirt road. They both slammed on their brakes and skid to a stop, one of them almost hitting my Porsche. My heart skipped a beat. If they had hit that car…

Joseph walks back to the stove as if this kind of thing happens all the time. The front door slams.

Heart of Gold

"Who won?" Joseph looks over his shoulder at the figure emerging.

"John!" Came the reply.

"You're Trent?" I can't help but ask.

"Yes." He nods, and then looks at Joseph.

"This is Beverly."

"The girl from the club?" Trent's eyes widen.

John bursts in the room, almost knocking me over.

"I'm so sorry!" He grabs my arm to steady me. Joseph puts the spoon down and walks over. John quickly lets go of my arm.

"It's okay." I look at Joseph nervously.

"I'm John." He extends his hand.

"Beverly." I shake his hand then quickly drop it.

"Beverly from the club?" His eyes widen also. I almost roll my eyes. They both seem to know me as the woman from the club. I'm not sure how I feel about that. On one hand, it means Joseph has been talking about me, which is really good. On the other…it makes me feel disrespected.

As if he can read my mind, Joseph speaks up. "Guys, it's Beverly, not Beverly from the club. And yes, she's the girl I told you about."

"Thank you." I whisper up at him and smile. He nods and smiles back. They leave to get changed. I sigh in relief as Joseph and I get to have a little more time together. When dinner is ready, Joseph calls John and Trent to come eat. They both pile their plates high with food threatening to spill over the sides as they sit at the table. Joseph and I fill our plates and sit down as well. I haven't sat down family-style like this in a very long time.

Rebecca Nietert

21

After dinner is over and everyone leaves the table, I ask Joseph for directions back into town. "Good night!" John and Trent call out from the other room. "Night!" Joseph and I shout back.

"Go back to Hockley Road and then left on Highway 290. It'll take you back into town."

"Thank you." I kiss his cheek. "Better get going." He grabs my hand, looking confused.

"What is it?"

"Are you thinking you have to run off and go home?"

"Well, yes." I look at him. "Do you want me to stay?"

"Yes I want you to stay. You can follow me to town in the morning."

"Okay." I can't help but feel a little nervous. "That'll be fine."

"That doesn't sound convincing. Do you really want to stay?" He looks into my eyes. I look back at him, unsure how to answer. I want to be with him but I'm not sure about being with him while there are two other people in the house. I look down. He stands up and lifts my chin, making me look back at him again.

"Do you want me?" He wraps his arms around me tightly and kisses me gently.

I nod. "Yes." How can he not believe me? Doesn't he feel that heat between us?

I did not know how to answer him. I wanted to be with him, but I was uncomfortable staying there with the other two guys in the house. Without more of an answer for him I just lowered my head. Joseph came over to me, lifted my chin and asked,

"How many men have you really been with?"

"Not many." I answered honestly.

Heart of Gold

"I can tell." He answered. Then he wrapped his arms around me tightly, brushed his lips against my neck and asked, "Are you comfortable now?"

"Yes." I answered breathlessly.

He leads me to the bedroom, kissing me feverishly as we inch our way past the door. He lays me down on the bed and climbs on top of me, kissing up my neck to my face. I grab his face and kiss him, then run my hands up and down his sides. He sits up and takes off his shirt, then presses his body against mine. I can feel the heat building up inside. I want him. I press myself against him as he kisses my neck. I gasp as I feel his hands start to caress my boobs, fondling and touching me all over my body. I can feel him wanting me. He presses his lower body against mine. I lean my head back and moan as he starts to move against me.

"You're so beautiful." His breath is against my ear as I feel his hand move lower down my body, resting lightly on my stomach.

"I want you so bad." I can barely get the words out.

"I want you too." I swallow hard as I feel him touching me through my pants. I'm going to explode!

The sound of an engine's roar fill my ears. I look up in surprise. Joseph sits up, alert. Tires screech as the car slides to a halt. Joseph bolts from the bed and looks out the window. Footsteps march on the porch.

"Come here, Beverly!" Joseph reaches to grab my arm.

"What's going on?" I follow him down the hall.

He quickly walks to Trent's room and opens the door. He throws me on top of the bed, almost hitting Trent.

He then bolts out the room, shouting loudly behind him, "If anyone asks, you're his girlfriend!" The door slams. I look at Trent, who looks back at me. I hear him exchanging words with a female voice.

"Well this is uncomfortable!" I growl in shock.

Trent laughs a little. "Yes it is. That's his girlfriend, Sally."

"His what?!" I shriek, whipping my head to look at him square.

Rebecca Nietert

"He didn't tell you?"

"No! Joseph did not tell me." I spit out, then make myself take a deep breath as tears start to stream down my face. "How long have they been dating?" I sigh, feeling like I'm being played again. Will my life constantly be a Soap Opera?

"Quite a while. Honestly, he has been trying to leave her. It's just she's not that strong." He stops short, as if he's already said too much and doesn't want to say anything more.

The door bolts open, slamming against the wall. It startles us both as Joseph appears.

"Beverly." Joseph said softly. His face was riddled in anguish.

"Joseph." I said as I stood up from the bed. I walked past him and through the door, "Why didn't you just tell me about her?"

"I've tried; I really have. Listen, I'll explain everything tomorrow, but tonight you have to go." He answered.

I gather my things from his room, tears stinging my eyes. I look at him sadly then walk out the door. As I walk down the steps, I look back at his figure in the doorway. "Call me then."

"Of course I'll call. I'll explain everything tomorrow." The door closes as I turn away. I don't see another car when I leave, but as I drive down the street I notice a small red vehicle almost spin out of control. It pulls into a driveway, waiting for me to pass by. When I do pass it peels out again and heads back towards the house.

I can't help but cry all the way home. How could he do that to me?! I feel humiliated! Once again, I'm treated like a common tramp. He pawned me off on a man I just met to save his sorry ass!

Once home, I throw my showgirl-backpack against the wall and head straight to the liquor cart. I pour a glass of straight vodka and chug it. I need to stop the pain! I need to be numb. No olives this time. I open the door to the balcony of our twenty-first floor apartment and let out a scream. I don't care who thinks I'm crazy! Lana races into the room.

"What in Heaven's name happened?!" She shouts.

"That son of a bitch has a girlfriend!"

Heart of Gold

"You're kidding, right? When did he tell you? Did you not go to work tonight? Did he-"

I cut her off. "No, Lana! I let him take me to his place about an hour from here!"

"He took you to his place to tell you he had a girlfriend, but I thought you were supposed to be working?" She squints as she asks seemingly confused.

"Yes, I mean no." I stop to gather my emotions and take a deep breath. "Lana, he was at the bar when I got there. He asked me to leave and have dinner with him. He cooked me dinner at his house." I can feel the tears coming back.

"Did he tell you after dinner?"

"No! He told me after his girlfriend found us in his bedroom, but not before he threw me into another man's arms. He was trying to pretend I wasn't his guest."

"Another guy? What other guy?"

"His roommate! He threw me into his roommate's bed, and he was in it!" I shout, frustrated that she isn't catching on.

She laughs and shakes her head. "Oh honey. I'm sorry. I thought he might have a girlfriend because he sounded too good to be true."

I look at her in shock. I can't believe she's actually laughing! I can feel a wave of rage begin churning in the pit of my stomach. I throw my glass, almost empty of vodka at her, screaming. I look at the brass liquor cart next to me, picking up a one glass at a time. I throw another one at her, then another.

"Damn it, Beverly! Calm down!" She shouts, ducking behind the kitchen wall to avoid the glasses flying toward her. Telling me to calm down only infuriates me more.

I am not sure if I am more angry about our previous conversation or the fact that she just told me she thought he had a girlfriend. Why didn't she tell me that instead of the drivel the other night? "How in the world does everyone know what is going on in my life except me?!" I grab a bottle off our liquor cart, jerk it open

Rebecca Nietert

and take a large gulp. As I take a drink, Lana inches her way onto the balcony. I slam the bottle down and look up at her. The look of shock on her face enrages me even more! I pick up the bottle and throw it at her. It misses and flies over the balcony railing. I pick up the remaining bottles, one by one, and throw them at her. She lunges for me, trying to get me to stop. I'm not giving her that chance! One by one the bottles fly past her and drop from the twenty-first apartment floor to the ground below. I can hear the sounds of crashing glass below.

"Beverly, stop!" Lana shouts, looking over the rail. "You're hitting people below!" She tries to maneuver me into the other room but I'm not letting that happen.

"You want to see me hit people below?" I run over to the VCR, yank it out and threw it over the balcony before she even has a chance to shut the doors.

As I run down the hallway to grab more things to throw, Lana closes the doors and follows me. I fall forward as I realize she just pushed me! Oh, she's going to get it!

"You are going to regret this!" She hisses.

"Regret? What the hell do you know about regret?!" I scream back as I stand up.

"Yes, regret because I'm fixing to kick your butt, little lady!"

I looked into her eyes and fall to my knees. I'm acting just like my mother! I put my hands over my face, feeling ashamed of what I've just done. I don't know what just came over me, but I couldn't help it. "How does all of this shit happen to me!"

"I don't know, babe. I don't know." Lana kneels down and hugs me gently. "It's going to be all right though." She paused and then quietly asks, "Is that what happened when your mother got mad?"

"Yes!" I put my head into her shoulders. "Yes and I'm just like her too!"

"Beverly, honey, you can be anything you want to be. You don't have to react this way. You haven't known Joseph that long so why on earth did he have this effect on you so quickly?"

Heart of Gold

"I don't know, Lana. I'm just so mad! It hurts so badly and I'm so tired of hurting! I'm always the one being lied to and always the one getting jilted. Why can't people just tell me the truth? Why can't I win just for once?"

"I'm sure that's how your mother felt too."

"Do you really think that's how she felt?"

I look up at her with tear-stained eyes. "Really?"

"Probably. She loves you just like I know you love me but you have got to get a hold of yourself. This is just one man; one guy in the big scheme of things. You've known him for what, a couple of weeks? Does he really deserve this much emotion from you? See, he's already controlling you."

"No, he's not. But you were right about one thing, my mother was selfish and I am too. Will you forgive me for what I just did?"

She nods and helps me up. We walk back to the living room. There are fragments of glass all over the room. We walk out onto the balcony and look over the rail. The remains of our belongings now lay scattered in the street below. People surround the piles of debris, looking around. Wondering where it had come from. We look at each other, both thinking the same thing and promptly return to the apartment, shutting the doors silently.

"Beverly, we're in such trouble!"

"I know. Me more than you, as usual."

"I'll get the vacuum. You start picking up the big pieces of glass." She commands and we got to work.

"I'm so sorry, Lana" I repeat.

"Well." She sighs, "I did learn something from all this. I will never laugh at you again."

"I never want to hurt you. I promise I will never do that again. Sometimes we hurt the ones we love the most. Good thing I was here; no telling what all would be in pieces in the street by now! Although I have to tell you, I wish it was Joseph dodging your glass bullets!"

Rebecca Nietert

"Me too! Bam! Right in the jaw!" I laugh, wishing it was true. We finished sweeping all the glass up. We finish giggling over the mental pictures of Joseph dodging glasses. We sit on the floor. I tell her what Joseph had said about a cook-off at the rodeo.

"Beverly, he participates in the rodeo?" I nod. "That's next week, right?"

"Yeah. Joseph said he goes with his roommates."

"Roommates?" We look at each other at the same time. "He might be going with his girlfriend."

"Maybe. I don't know."

"Are you going?"

"I don't think so. As far as I'm concerned it's over. I don't need the heartache."

"I'm so glad to hear that."

"I may be forgiving, but I'm not stupid." I add, trying to convince myself it's true.

"No ma'am1 That you are not!" Lana laughs loudly. "You never went to work did you? How are you doing with money?"

"I have a few bucks. Why?"

"Lately I haven't done so well. I was wondering if you could loan me some money so that I can get a room?"

"Oh great Lana, rub it in! You have a boyfriend and I don't." I laugh, trying not to show how much that comment hurt. "Of course I'll loan you the money." I grab my purse and pull out what she needs.

"Thank you." I nod as I hand it to her. We sit back down on the floor and talk until we both fall asleep.

We wake late in the afternoon, stiff and sore. I get up and walk around the apartment trying to get the soreness out. Soon after Joseph calls.

"What do you want?"

"We have to talk."

"Yes, we do. Last night was horrible."

Heart of Gold

I sighed heavily, and said, "Do you want to explain or just say good-bye now?"

"Not on the phone."

"Then when do you suggest? I have to work tonight because I'm out of money."

"Fine. I'll just see you at work." He snaps.

"Fine." I snap back.

"See you there. Bye." Click. I look at my phone in disgust. He just hung up on me!

Lana looks up at me, half-awake. "That was him?"

"Yes. He said he's coming in to work to 'talk'. Now what do I do?"

"Go to work and act as if nothing happened. At least you'll have "Barbie" there to help you."

"You're right! I can do this. Thank you."

She giggles, "Never a problem. He's in for it now!"

"You got that right!" I laugh and walk down the hall to take a shower.

I leave the house for work, transformed into Barbie. I make sure to put on my best look; a slinky, tight fitting dress. I look around the bar and see Joseph already there, waiting. I almost laugh. He can wait. I head to the dressing room to finish my stage makeup, and then head back to the bar and order a drink.

"Hello Joseph." I smile and plant a kiss on his cheek. I'm going to win this game.

"What's that for?"

"In here, Darlin, that's what I do. I'm nice, simple little Barbie." Joseph looks at me sadly.

"Beverly, put Barbie away. We have to talk."

"Barbie is here as long as I'm here. Why didn't you tell me you were still attached?"

"I told you I had a girlfriend who is like a little girl. I've had to teach her about the world. She's fragile. I'm sure I remember telling you that."

Rebecca Nietert

"Joseph." I clear my throat, forcing the lump to go down. "If you told me you would have refereed to her as an ex or I wouldn't have dated you."

"Yes, I did. She has a small apartment in town. I've been trying to leave her for some time now, and I think last night finally did it." He looks down, obviously embarrassed.

I have such mixed feelings! I'm so angry for being tossed away and abandoned. However, I believe his sincerity. I remember what it was like to be fragile. Suddenly I'm feeling guilty for how I must've made his ex-girlfriend feel.

"I'm sorry for you." I shrug.

He looks at me, confused. "You're sorry? Why?"

I can't look in his eyes. It must have been hard for you to hurt her like that."

"You have no idea!" He shakes his head.

"What is it that you have a problem with Joseph? Is it that I'm not so fragile or that I have a heart?"

"Both." He smiles.

I smile back. "I do have heart you know? I really would've hated to be you last night."

"I hated to be me last night. Beverly, I'm so sorry I threw you at Trent. My God, I never wanted to hurt you."

"I believe you, Joseph. Believe it or not I'm not hurt anymore. I'm fine. I'm not some baby you have to explain things to over and over again. Once I decide that I want something I go for it. If that doesn't work out, I still end up okay.

"You're one tough cookie, Beverly."

"You have no idea!" I mock him. That felt nice.

Feeling like the next sentence is going to be a subtle good-bye, I stand. Time to end this. "I have to go to work."

"Don't go." He pleads.

"Why not? If you're trying to decide which one of us you should end it with, I'll help you out. Since she's so fragile, you won't even have to make that choice. I'll take myself out of the equation."

Heart of Gold

He reaches out gently for me. "Beverly, don't go." He stands up, towering over me. He presses his chest against mine and wraps his hands around both of my arms. I look up at him as he whispers, lips inches from mine; eyes staring into mine. "I still want you so badly."

I look into his eyes. Those eyes. His charm. Maybe just one more chance. After all, he did leave her, right? "I do too." I cannot help myself. I am literally melting into liquid in his arms.

He lowers his head and kisses me softly. "I need you." He seems so...vulnerable.

"I can see that." I need you too.

"What are you doing later?"

"After work?" I laugh.

"Yes, after work."

"I'm going home to bed. You've never dated a dancer have you?"

"Obviously not." He sounds hurt and then releases me so abruptly I almost fall over.

"It's not you, silly. After 2:00 a.m. and after the last drunk is gone, the last thing I want to do is be with a man. I want to sleep."

"Oh." He looks down, deflated.

"But if you want to come sleep with me that would be fine." I offer, keeping my tone light.

"Sleep is not what I had in mind."

"No kidding. Well then maybe tomorrow?" I offer with a raised eyebrow.

"No, tonight will be fine. I'll come to your place and we will." He laughs softly, "'sleep'."

"What's so funny?"

"The most beautiful woman in the world has invited me over to sleep in her bed, and we're actually going to do nothing but sleep."

"Oh. Well, thank you for the compliment." That was very nice.

Rebecca Nietert

"Now you're thanking me! God woman you are incredible. I have to run now to let you work. I have some things to do anyway. What time later?"

I reach over him for a napkin, pull the pen from his shirt pocket and write down the time and directions to my place. Then I fold it gently, place it in his pocket and give him a gentle kiss on the cheek. I'm still reeling from his compliments. He said I'm incredible!

"I will see you later then." I wink.

"I love a woman who knows what she wants." He kisses me on the cheek, gathers his change from the bar and leaves.

As I watch him leave, I can't help but feel completely overwhelmed. He intrigues me and I can't wait to experience the fire between us again. How can I sleep next to him with all that heat? "I love a woman who...." Ah, the possibilities! Suddenly I realized I have to call Lana to let her know I'm having a houseguest.

When the answering machine picks up, I listened to the message Lana had left. "If this is Beverly, because she's the only one who calls here, this is Lana. I will not be available for consultation this evening. I am so sorry to inform you that I will be getting laid by the most handsome man in town. However I will be available tomorrow afternoon. If you need me, leave a message and I will check this machine after 2:00 a.m."

I laugh. "No ma'am, I will be with the most handsome man in town!" I hang up.

Heart of Gold

22

I wake with Joseph in my bed. True to his word, all he did was hold me throughout the night.

"Good morning." He whispers gently.

"Good morning. How did you sleep?"

"Great! Listen, I have to go meet a contractor early this morning. Afterwards can we get some breakfast?"

"Yes, but what do you plan on wearing?" I tease, looking him up and down.

"I have extra clothes in my truck." He sits on the side of the bed.

"So you expected me to say yes last night and get what you wanted?"

"No. Sex was my goal and I didn't get that." He kisses me on the forehead and walks out the room to find his clothes.

"Good because I hate to be predictable." I yell behind him.

"I bet you do!"

I laugh. "While you're going down to get your clothes I'll hop in the shower."

He appears in the doorway. "I wouldn't mind seeing you hop in the shower."

I roll my eyes. "Go get your clothes. I'll be showered when you get back up. Take the key above the door."

"Okay." He smirks.

I sit on the bed for a moment, thinking. It feels wonderful to be happy in the morning. I shake my head. I hurry up and get in the shower. After several minutes I hear the front door open and shut. Suddenly Joseph opened the door to the shower and stares at me with another broad smile on his face.

Rebecca Nietert

"Mind if I join you?"

"No, but please close the door. It's cold." In seconds the door opens again. Joseph steps into the shower, completely naked. He pulls me to his chest, lowers his head and kisses me while the rain of the water pours down our faces. I can feel his body shaking as he softly moans. The heat of his body against mine has me reeling. I can taste the desire on his lips. He reaches behind me and picks up the bar soap from the tray. He then starts to rub the soap all over my body; caressing my back, inner thighs and then my breasts. I can feel my desire exploding. He's so gentle. My mind goes blank. My body is his. I melt into him, letting his hands touch me freely.

Half conscious I am aware he put the soap in my hand. I lather the soap on his whole body. We caress each other in the shower for only a few minutes but it seems like a lifetime. He put his hands though my hair and gently pulls my head back, kissing me softly. His crystal blue eyes are deep blue, shining with desire.

"I have to go." He kisses me again.

"I know." I moan, not even realizing it. He smiles.

"So you feel just as much desire as I do?"

Still under his spell, I mumble "Uh huh."

"I want to stay but I have to go." His words bring me back to consciousness. I look up at him and blink a few times.

"Huh? You have to do what?"

He laughs. "Just meet me for breakfast okay?"

"Okay." I exit the shower.

He stops me and gently kisses me. "It's exactly how I thought it would be." He turns off the water and kisses me quickly again.

"How you thought what would be?" I press my body against his. It's either really cold or he's really warm. Or both.

"I can't be near you without feeling like I have to have you. I feel like you were meant to be with me. I knew it from the moment I met you." His next kiss makes me weak at the knees again. When he lets me go I can't say anything. I know that letting a man know how much control he has over me is never in my best interest. If he

Heart of Gold

can't tell though? I reach for a towel, feeling uncomfortable for appearing vulnerable.

"You don't give yourself easily do you?" His eyes narrow as he tilts his head.

I grab a towel and wrapped myself in it, feeling exposed and uncomfortable. "I have never truly given myself to a man before. Not completely." I shut the door and dry off.

He speaks above the water pouring. "Have you had an orgasm?"

"Yes. I think all men are selfish in bed." I snap. His questions are starting to make me feel trashy. Why are all men so condescending? He seems to recognize my discomfort. He cracks the door, puts his arms around me and pulls me close to his soaking wet form. I almost want to jerk away, to be left alone. He looks down at me, his blue eyes meeting mine.

"Oral or intercourse?" He whispers, his lips just inches from mine.

I sigh and pull back from him a little. "Joseph, this is making me feel really uncomfortable."

"Can I help you climax?"

I can't believe he's being so blunt! Obviously this cowboy has fewer manners than I thought. Still, my shyness can't cause him to not want to date me anymore. So I blushed when I said, "Maybe someday."

"It will be possible someday."

I can feel my face heating up against my will.

He looks into my eyes. "Beverly, I want you to be happy."

I nod. "Thank you." I just want to get out of here.

He snatches my towel. "You don't need this anymore." I look down, realizing that I'm dry except where he's touching me. Whether it was the heat from the embarrassment or his body, I'll never know.

"I'll get dressed then."

Rebecca Nietert

"Don't on my account; I love seeing you naked. You're one beautiful woman."

"Thank you." I pry myself away. I reach for my robe and slip it on, feeling his eyes on me the entire time.

"You're shy? That's a first." He laughs as he exits the show. He grabs a towel and then he grabs his clothes.

I walk into the kitchen to make some coffee, leaving him to finish dressing alone. That is a first? A first for who? How many times has he been with a dancer? I grab the morning paper from outside the front door and walk back into the kitchen, needing something to distract me. I hear footsteps heading towards me, then stop. I look up to see Joseph leaning against the doorframe. I almost drop the newspaper. He looks just like one of those cowboys in a movie. The kind with the wide smile, lean muscles and incredible jawline.

"You read too?" He gestures at the paper. I look down at the paper and nod.

"Every day. Haven't you noticed my books? I read all the time." I can't help but feel a little upset. Does he not think I'm capable of reading? Just because I'm a dancer doesn't mean I'm stupid.

He must have noticed my face drop. "I meant it as a compliment." I nod. Joseph clears his throat nervously. "May I share a cup of coffee with you?"

"Sure. How do you like it?" I reach up to get him a cup.

"Just a little sugar please." I look at him, catching the reference of 'sugar' to me. He's grinning from ear to ear. I can't help but smile a little as I pour the coffee.

"I'm looking forward to getting to know you better." I walk over and hand him the cup. I want to press my body against him but I don't.

"Me too." He takes a sip and nods in approval.

I look at him, then grab the paper and sit down. I start to read. "You know you didn't have to say that." I look up at him.

"I know. I wanted to."

Heart of Gold

"No, you didn't. Do you think I don't really want you?"

I shrug. "It's not like you've done this before." I passively suggest... interrogating.

"Don't mix words, Beverly. If you think it say it." He moves over and stands next to me. I look down at the paper. "I've never dated another dancer."

"Never? Then why did you say that my shyness was a first?" I can't even look at him.

"I said that because I've been to plenty of topless bars all over the country and I haven't met one girl like you."

"Thanks." I try not to show that his answer makes me feel better. He pulled me up to him and when his lips brush my cheek I can't help but smile.

"You're welcome. Listen, I have to go." He hands me the cup. "See you for breakfast?"

"What time and where?" I mimic his question from last evening.

He smiles. "Is the Kettle Kitchen at ten okay?"

"Sure, but where is a Kettle Kitchen?"

"You've never been there?" He smiles through his shock.

You're mocking me?

"No. It's on 290 at Hempstead."

I laugh to myself. Why would I know where a breakfast place was? I work nights in a bar. The last thing I want to do is get up early for breakfast.

"I'll find it and meet you there." I place his cup next to mine in the sink. I feel his arms tighten around me as he kisses me on the cheek. I grab his hand as he lets go, intertwining our fingers, and follow him to the door. As he opens the front door I jump back when I see Lana standing there, key in hand, about to enter.

"Well, hello." He sounds as startled as I am. He turns around and kisses me again, then picks up last nights' clothes he laid by the door. He tips his silver Stetson at Lana and, without a word, walks off.

Rebecca Nietert

"That him?" Lana looks at me in shock as she steps in the apartment.

"Yep." I smile and nod, closing the door behind us.

"Did my two-a.m. call interrupt anything?"

"Your call?" I look at her, confused.

"Yes, silly. You must been very busy to not notice that I left a message on the recorder."

"Oh, that. Well we weren't here yet, so no, it didn't interrupt anything. I thought you said you would be gone until noon."

"Well..." She laughs, looking toward the door. "He's as cute as you said he was when you left that message on the answering machine."

"I did not!"

"I want details! And you did! Your message said that he was cuter than my boyfriend. I don't think so but if you do, then hats off to you. And by the way, I checked the messages at two; that's how I know about the recording. I'm here because I need some new clothes."

"There's nothing really to say. We came back here and slept."

"There is no way that he just slept in your bed without touching you. Your hair is wet and he looked freshly showered. Oh, what did I see in his hands? A change of clothes?"

"No, really! All we did was sleep! And he even asked me--" I stop mid-sentence, not sure how to say this.

"Asked you what?"

"He asked me if I ever...umm..." I pause, shaking my head. "It's nothing."

"If you ever what?!"

"If I ever...climaxed." I can't help but look away, embarrassed I had even told her that..

"Climaxed?! You're kidding me!" She gasps as her hands flies to cover her mouth. "Oh Beverly, he's a keeper!" She laughs. "Anyone who cares enough to ask that question is definitely a keeper!"

"We even showered together! I haven't done that with anyone!"

Heart of Gold

"In broad daylight?!" She's mocking me. "You have got to be kidding!"

"I know! It was awesome but embarrassing at the same time."

"I bet! That's way too open for you. You can't even undress your G-string in front of the women you work with every night; I've seen disappear in the bathroom stalls. You're so shy at times, it's funny." She laughs and looks at me. "So...did he try to do anything in the shower?"

"No, but I wanted to. God, I wanted to!"

She smiled broadly.

He really knows how to warm a girl up." I can't help but smile at the thought of his hands all over me.

"You're in love!" She blurts out. "I can see it all over your face!"

"Love?!" I look at her, incredulous. "I am not 'in love'!"

"Lust or love; what's the difference? You've got it bad for this guy."

"I know." I feel like my face is on fire. All of this smiling is so foreign to me.

"So you decided to forgive him for the girlfriend thing?"

"Oh yeah!" I almost forgot to tell her about that. "Come to find out, she's an ex-girlfriend. He has been trying to get rid of her without hurting her since she's fragile. He rented her an apartment in town and moved her in; he said he was trying to get her to live on her own. When I was over there she showed up at his place for some reason. He said that finding us together really made her mad and now it's definitely over for them."

"You believe him?" She asks gently.

I nod. "Yes. I do. He's gentle and kind to me. He wouldn't lie."

"Okay, if you say so." She seems unconvinced.

I jokingly punch her arm. Don't forget the last time you laughed at me. I say mocking her this time. "Oh Lana, stop being my mom. I have a lot to tell you!"

She laughs a little. "Okay, okay. Tell me everything." So I did.

Rebecca Nietert

23

A few weeks pass. Lana and I are sitting at my home, exhausted. The Houston Livestock Show & Rodeo brought out all kinds of wannabe heroes, looking for girls like us to 'rescue from distress'; leaving Lana and I with more money than we have made in a long time.

"What should we do tonight Lana?"

"We could watch some TV." She plops down on my new couch.

"Nah, I don't feel like sitting down for so long. Want to go clubbing?"

"What's wrong, Beverly? You've been antsy all day."

"I don't know Lana. I feel like a cat on a hot tin roof!"

"Is it Joey?"

"God, I hate it when people call him that!" I shake my head and shrug. "I just don't know."

"Why do you hate that?"

"Because it makes him sound like such a boy. He's a real gentleman."

"One night together and you're already swooning over him?" Lana lets out a sigh.

"I guess so." I smile at the thought, and then plop down next to Lana. "Ugh! I hate how I can't get him out of my head!"

Lana nudges me gently. "Feeling a little vulnerable?"

"No. I mean...I can take it I guess. It's just that I haven't heard from him. I thought that evening meant a lot to him. He hasn't even stopped by the club!"

"I'm sure it meant a lot to him, Beverly. Want to go to the park and talk?"

Heart of Gold

"Nah, too cold. Sushi?"
"Nah, just ate." She exhales a big sigh.
"I think I know." I announce.
"Know what? What's bothering you?"
I nod. "Yeah."
"Well then spill it!"
"Tonight is the Rodeo kick off barbecue."
"Okay..." She looks at me, confused. "I'm not getting it?"
"So...that means he's right down the street. It's only two blocks from here."
"You're angry because he's down there and you're here?"
I shrug and let out a sigh. "I don't know. I think I'm pensive because he hasn't called. He's not with his friends; he's with her."
"You're jealous." I look over at her and finally nod slowly.
"I know. I hate it." She looks over at me, eyes searching for the truth. "I know, I know...I never want to be like this but after Phillip...damn it, I can't be lied to again!"
"So you need to be in control?"
"I don't want to get hurt again."
"Well, you're not hurt now right?" I nod. "See? You're fine. If you go over there and see them together then you will be hurt."
"I know; that's why I have to go."
Lana lets out an exasperated sigh and rolls her eyes, shaking her head. "Then it won't be him that hurts you. If you go down there you will catch them together and you'll just hurt yourself."
"I know, but at least I will know why he didn't call." I said exasperated.
"It doesn't matter why he didn't call; it hasn't even been a whole week. Give him a break!"
"I can't!" I walk into my room to get ready.
"You're not going to rest until you know are you?" Lana' shouts from the other room. "I came over here to see you!"
"No! I am sure I won't be long."

Rebecca Nietert

"Then go, but don't stay all night. I'm leaving tomorrow, remember?"

"Yes, I won't be long." I walk into the bedroom, pick out a killer dress and high heels, put them on and leave to find out if what seems to be eating me alive is the truth.

I walk briskly, the winter air chilling my face and arms. I knew I should've brought a coat! I finally arrive and pay for my entry and walk down through the crowd, recognizing a few people from the bar I work at.

"Where have you been?!" I turn around, looking at a blonde girl I used to work with at the Gentleman's Club. Oh God, help me.

"I'm at The Rocky Mountain Men's Club now. What have you been up to?" I strain my neck, looking for Joseph.

"One of the girls at the club told me you had moved again. Said some trashy babe was dating your ex. That true?"

"Yes I guess so. Look Liz, I really don't care about any of that right now."

"Obviously. So who are you trying to spot?"

I laugh and shake my head. "I'm looking for a long tall cowboy whose here with some guy friends and maybe a girl."

"Checking up on him then?"

"Yes."

"I wish I could help, really I do; nut you just described every man here."

"I know; thank you. I really need to continue my search."

"Okay. Hey Beverly, come over to my part of town sometime, okay?"

"I'll think about it. Thanks!" I shoot her a fake smile and nod, then walk off.

I walk a little farther and see Joseph leaning against a tree, much like he did in my kitchen doorway. The dim light behind his Stetson hat illuminates his silhouette. He's so handsome. I smile broadly as I approach, noting that all his friends are male. Receiving my answer, I turn to leave but look back one more time. Then I see. Or rather,

Heart of Gold

her, step out of the shadow of a tree and face him; her tiny body standing near his. I guess he smiled at her, from the look on her face. Something must have made him look around, because when he did his eyes meet mine.

I turn briskly and start to walk away, until I feel a hand grab mine. I turn around. "What are you doing here?"

I look up at him. "I missed you, and I thought--" I blink, trying not to cry, "Never mind what I thought."

"It's not what you think!"

"It's exactly what I think." I look into his eyes, "You lied to me."

He sighs and reaches out, putting his hands on my arms and turns me to face him. "I didn't lie, Beverly. I just omitted that Sally was coming with the guys."

"Trent and John?"

"Yes."

"Omission is a lie, Joseph. What did you think I was going to do if you told me? Kill myself? Throw myself at you?" I jerk free from his grasp.

He grabs me again. "It's not a lie! I had to bring her. All our friends are here and it would embarrass her if she weren't invited. You just don't understand!" He lets me go abruptly.

"What I understand is that you haven't been honest. I've been completely honest with you. You're playing the games I play at work all day long. I know a game when I see it, and I don't like it. You don't have to lie to me!"

"I'm sorry. I felt I had to."

"There's no excuse. Sorry doesn't cut it, Bud."

"I get that now. You're not like most girls, Beverly."

"Most don't know they can take care of themselves. If you want me to trust you then you have to be honest with me."

"I'm sorry I haven't called."

"Now I see why!" I gesture at Sally.

Rebecca Nietert

"No. Really I felt guilty about not telling you. I didn't want you to hear it in my voice."

I shake my head. Unbelievable! "If you felt guilty then it's wrong. You should've told me! I would've understood."

"Now I know."

"Now may be too late."

He grabs my shoulders, looking into my eyes. "No it isn't. Tell me it's not true. Let me see you tomorrow?"

"No." I shrug him off an turn to walk away. Of course I understand what he said; it isn't about that. It's about the fact that I'm not the only important woman to him.

"Don't do this, Beverly!" He insists.

I spin back around to face him. "Do what exactly? Joseph, you have two seconds to tell me what I want to hear before I'm gone forever."

"I'm sorry!"

"Not good enough. I just told you that!" I snap, rolling my eyes. What a waste of time.

He walks up to me and grabs my face, pulling me close while staring into my eyes. "Please forgive me?" He whispers as he kisses me softly.

I can feel myself melting inside as I kiss him back. I nod. "I will."

"What do I need to say for you to forgive me?" He kisses me again; asking as if he had not heard me.

"I need to know you feel the same way I do." I can barely breathe.

"How do you not feel that I do! I never want to let you go. It's tearing me apart to be here with her, feeling the way I do about you."

"Really?" I stare into his eyes, searching the the truth.

"Can't you see that?" He presses himself against me. I can feel the familiar warmth and passion in his touch.

Heart of Gold

I surprise myself by laughing. "Yes, I can feel that." Beverly! You're supposed to be mad at him!

"Are we okay?"

"Yes. Thank you for telling me." I kiss him again.

He smiles broadly and chuckles. "You sure are something, Beverly."

"I have to go. Seeing you with her unsettles me." I look toward Sally. He grabs my hand and leads me off a few feet, away from the crowd.

"Please see me tomorrow?"

"I can't. I have to help Lana move out."

His eyebrows shoot up. "Your roommate? Is there a problem?"

"Yes, it's Lana. No, there are no problems but I'm busy tomorrow." I turn around to walk off. He grabs my hand.

"Okay. Will you at least call me?"

"I will." I say over my shoulder as I let go of his hand and walk off.

I walk home; the air seems even colder now that I'm not with Joseph. There is electricity when we seem to connect together. Now I'm convinced he feels it too. Is this what love feels like? I walk inside the apartment and see Lana standing on the balcony.

"I'm back."

"I know." She turns to face me. "I saw you coming."

"Oh." I walk over to the balcony where she is standing and look out into the distance. "Could you see the party?"

"Yes, kind of. I could see you leave but I couldn't see into the party. So what happened?"

I nod and turn to face her. "I saw Joseph." I take off my jacket.

"Was he alone?"

"No. He was with her and their friends."

"So how are you?"

"He told me it meant nothing."

"Nothing? You have found him with her twice now and she means nothing?"

Rebecca Nietert

"Well, he said he had to take her because all their friends were going."

"Really. Did he say he still wanted to see you?"

"Yes."

"And you're going to?" Her tone changed from interest to disapproval. I can't help but feel a twinge of anger at her tone.

"Yes, Lana. I am!"

"You are an idiot! For Pete's sake, Beverly, how gullible are you?"

"I'm not gullible! I hear all the time from men about how they want something from me. He isn't like that!"

She puts her hand over her mouth in shock. "Beverly! You're really in love with him!"

"Yes." I can feel the tears, unable to keep myself from crying.

"I'm so sorry, Beverly. I did not believe it before now."

"How did you guess how I feel?" The tears won't stop!

"Because you will stand by or die for someone you love. You will fight me with all your power to be loyal to him. That's just how you are. There's no sense in telling you that he is manipulating you; or for that matter that you're a fool for loving him. You're going to do it anyway."

"I'm a fool!"

"And you will be for some time. Maybe he's sincere and the rest of us are just making judgments of what we see."

I know she's trying to make me feel better, but the sarcasm in her voice makes me feel even worse. She's supposed to be happy for me! Isn't that what a true friend does? "Lana, why are men such cads?"

"I don't know, Sweetie. I don't know." She gives me a hug. "Are you going to be okay?"

I shrug, crying softer. "I don't know."

Joseph calls the next day and asks if I will go with him to the Cattleman's Restaurant for lunch.

"I would love to." I admit.

Heart of Gold

"Great. Be there in half an hour. I'm on my way downtown."

"That's fine. See you there."

The Cattleman's is a popular restaurant in Houston where all cowboys frequent. I've heard a lot about it over the years but have never actually been there.

I enter the restaurant and notice Joseph sitting at the bar. I walk up behind him very slowly.

"What's up, Darlin'?" I mimic a country accent. He turns to face me and smiles.

"Hi Darlin'." He pulls out a bar stool for me to sit on.

"Thank you. How's your day been?"

"Awful! I have a lot going on. I have contractors who've made bad decisions, Sally on my back; you name it!"

"Sally?" I'm getting really fed up with that name! "What's she doing now?"

"She's been really hurt by me. I've decided that it's in both of our best interest if I move out of the ranch."

"Really?" My eyebrows shoot up. That's the last thing I expected to hear. "Does that mean you're putting it on the market?"

He laughs, "I don't own it, Beverly. I lease it."

"Oh...well I just assumed I guess." I grab the drink the bartender hands me and smile. I love how Joseph remembers the little things, like this Crown. Even in the morning it's helpful.

"I just rented an efficiency apartment off Westheimer."

I take a sip of my drink and almost spit it out. "An efficiency? Kind of drastic change isn't it?"

"I don't think so. I was willing to live in a trailer once so this is better than that." His idea of living quarters is....simple. I'm not sure how I like that. Simple means poor. There's no way I'm going back to being in a place of financial ruin – the same situation my mom and went through.

I guess my discontent shows on my face, for he looks at me carefully. "You think I'm dropping my economic status don't you, Beverly."

Rebecca Nietert

"Well, yeah. What are you going to do with your toys?"

"I'll sell them. I've owned a lot of toys in my life, Beverly. They come and go. Everything comes and goes. It's not about what you own, it's about what you have with someone. I thought you understood that. Joseph seemed to be scolding me as if I didn't comprehend that basic thought."

I fight the urge to roll my eyes and take another sip.

"I get what you're saying. Are you moving your beautiful table and everything to the efficiency?"

"No, it won't fit. That stuff is going into storage. I'll have a furnished apartment."

"That sounds nice. Expensive? Not too much." He shrugs.

I eye him while sitting back in the stool. "And Sally? What's going on with that?" I almost laugh at the term I used: 'that'. Good one, Bev.

"I'm trying so hard to be her friend right now. I care so much about her but she's making it difficult. Besides-" He leans over and grabs my waist, "I need more time with you."

I can't help but smile. "I would like that too. You're sure you have the time?"

"What I'm sure about is I have too many dogs in the woods right now. I can't see you for about a week or so. I need to get some things together and get moved. I have a lot to do."

After a hard swallow of the Crown and nod, "I understand, that's fine. Go do what you need to do."

"You're so strong." He interjects.

I look at him, wanting to tell the truth. I want to say that I'm not strong. I'm not 'something' as he likes to say. I'm a little girl who's scared of being alone. Truth is: I am afraid to be poor. I feel as though I already need him. His voice breaks my reverie. "Hey, why don't you lose that no paying job at the Club and go to work at the Baby 'O Club? I hear those gals over there make a killing."

"I didn't know it was finished yet."

Heart of Gold

He nods. "It is. It's up off Westheimer close to everything I do. It's even close to the new apartment." He looks at me and winks. I can't help but laugh. That look in his eyes gets me every time.

"I'll check it out. Who knows, maybe some of my friends from an old club will be working there."

He nods. "Are you going to keep your fancy car?" Huh? Where did that come from?

"What is wrong with my car?"

"It's a foreign car. Your ex's idea I bet?"

Not wanting to go there I shrug, "Yes."

"That has to go first. When I'm free next week we can change that."

"I can change my own car. I bought this one."

"Fine."

"I have to run." I stand up.

"What about lunch?" I put my hand on his forearm and give him a quick kiss on the cheek.

"You do whatever you need to do Darlin'. When you're all done, I'll catch up with you."

He looks at me, confused, "What happened?"

"Nothing." I squeeze his arm and walk off. His voice trails behind me.

"Okay."

I don't even know what to think of that conversation! Who does he think he is; thinking that he can control me like that? Yes, I'm not with Phillip, but still; did he have to bring it up? On the way home I drive by Landmark Chevrolet. Cruising along, I spot a beautiful Silverado in the driveway. I pull up next to it and get out, admiring it from all angles. The midnight blue paint is beautiful. Out of the corner of my eye a salesman approaches.

"Hello Beverly." That voice. Oh perfect...This is just what I need! I stop myself from rolling my eyes and finally manage a, "Hello Lance." Lance had come in one night and had tried desperately to get me to date him. He even proposed while he was drunk! Of course I said no. I'm not attracted to him at all. But maybe in this case I can get a good deal out of him.

"You want this pretty truck?" He gestures toward the vehicle.

I shrug. "I'm thinking about it."

"That Porsche yours?"

"Yep. How much do you think it's worth?"

He raises an eyebrow. "Well...pricey. With what you do, really think you want it?" I smile and walk slowly towards him, not even caring that he's totally checking me out. As much as he disgusts me, right now I can handle it.

"I have great credit and-" I pause, letting him hang on every word as he stares at me. "-no one knows what I do."

"What do you tell the creditors when they contact your work reference?"

"I tell them I work at a Restaurant. Bookkeeping."

"They buy that?"

"Mhm. It says it on my credit report, which by the way, is perfect."

"Really?" He looks at me, amazed. I almost laugh. I'm outselling a salesman! This is too easy.

"Look, can you help me get this truck or not?" The change in my tone surprises him.

"No, but I can help you buy that red and black two-tone over there." He points to another truck. "This one is sold."

I thought about what he offered. I said, "Oh. Well...I'm not sure about the two-tone paint. I want a shorter box too."

"I have the perfect truck then. It's a red truck with a black under bottom. It's a short bed, 350HP-V8 engine with lots of power. You will love it. It has luxurious cloth on the bench seat, lots of leg room, which it looks like you need."

"Let's check it out."

When we walk into the showroom he stops to asks for my keys. "May I please?" He extends his hand.

Heart of Gold

I look at him, then remember I have to be nice to him. For now. "What for?" I force a smile.

"So someone can look at your car to find out how much it's worth."

Oh, yeah. I slowly place the keys in his hand, making sure that our hands touch for a few seconds before I let go. "Great, thanks."

He laughs and announces proudly, "This is my area of expertise." The comment ends with him looking into my eyes. I know what he's thinking and want to throw up. Be nice, Beverly. Maybe he can cut you a deal!

I smile politely and follow him to a large red truck in the center of the showroom floor. I'm in love! "I love it! Can I see the inside?"

He smiles and nods proudly, "Of course. Go on in." He opens the door for me. I peer inside. There's a plush, red bench seat as he said. The carpet is black.

Okay, I really want this truck. Maybe... I turn around and look up at him. "Do you happen to have one of these like the blue one out there?"

He thinks for a minute, and then shakes his head. "Just the lower sports model. Nothing nice like this."

"Bummer!" I look back at the car, knowing full well that his eyes are all over me.

"Let's see what I can do, okay?" He asks.

"Really?" I say excitedly.

"I'll go run the paperwork but I can't promise anything."

"Well, thank you for trying. That's the least I can ask. I really appreciate you helping me."

I take another look at the bright shiny truck.

He nods as he leads me back to a desk. "Come on over here and sit with our finance department so they can check everything out for you. I'll be out shortly okay?"

I smile and nod. I just want the truck. forget you coming back out. "That's fine." Within an hour I'm driving my beautiful new

234

Rebecca Nietert

truck out the parking lot. Sure it's red, but it represents a fresh start. What better way to start than with a power color like red?

Later that evening I drive my new truck to work. I walk in, face glowing, wanting to show it off to everyone. Suddenly, I realize that I don't know anyone here. Not on a personal level anyway. Then I remember what Joseph said this morning. I need to make a change. Without telling anyone I'm leaving, I walk out the door.

I head over to Westheimer Road and Sage where I see a brightly lit, elegant building. I park the truck and walk in, not bothering to wait for an escort. I'm happy to see someone I know, a DJ, working behind the counter.

"Hello Max!" I shout above the music, glad to see a familiar face.

He smiles broadly. "Barbie! How are you?"

"Great! I'm looking for a new place to work. Are you bartending here now?"

"No!" He steps out from behind the counter, showing off a pricy suit. "I'm the manager here."

I raise my hands to my mouth. "Congratulations! How did that happen?"

"Well, Tony, the owner, decided that this job suits me much better. I'm hoping to make a difference here; to weed out some of the riff-raft."

"That's quite a task."

He asks, "What are you doing here?"

I would think that was obvious.

He blurts and option I had no idea existed. "Did you come in to see your pictures on our walls?" He starts to walk towards the bathroom, where it isn't so crowded.

I follow.

"I came here to go to work." I say looking over the pictures that lined the walls.

"Really?" He turns to face me.

"If you will hire me?" I smile innocently.

Heart of Gold

He laughs. "Of course! It's good to have you here."

"It feels good to be here. How much on average does a girl make here?"

"Day or night?"

"Day? Men come in here during the day?"

"Yes. The day the girls actually do better. The men are older and have more income."

"You have got to be kidding me!" I'm already in love with this place!

"Nope. Best thing is that girls don't have to be here for work until 11:00 in the morning. But the very best thing is that I work here during the day. I only work nights on occasion."

"Can I work some days and then some nights?"

"Babe, it's days or nights only. The girls get pissed off if you switch."

"Just days then?" I can spend my nights with Joseph!

"Sounds good. Welcome aboard!"

"Hello Norma!" I recognize the girl coming out of the bathroom.

"Barbie!" She squeals and runs up to hug me. "Oh my gosh it's been forever!"

She turns to Max. "This is Barbie. She used to work with me."

"I know who she is, Norma." He snaps.

I shrug my shoulders, not sure of what to do or what to say. Although I know Norma, I've never really hung with her much before. I've always felt comfortable around her.

"How about showing me around?"

"Sure!" She nods and takes my hand, leading me to the dressing room. I wave bye to Max as he nods and walks off. She shows me around and introduces me to everyone. It's nice to see a familiar face and hear a familiar voice, even if I don't know her that well. Needless to day, this job looks a hell of a lot more promising than the last one.

Rebecca Nietert

24

I've already made a lot of money at the new club. I like working during the day. When I go shopping in the evenings I feel normal. No one looks down at me. For the first time in my life, I feel like a normal human being. Is this really how people actually live? I notice their clothing and decide to try to fit in. My clothes are becoming more "conservative" as someone pointed out to me recently. I'd rather be 'conservative' (whatever that means) than looked down upon.

It's been a while since Joseph has called. When I finally call him, his tone is not as pleasant as I had hoped.

"Meet me at the Waterford Apartments at 10:00 p.m. Apartment 4124." I look at the clock: it's 9:00 p.m. It's late...but I haven't had the chance to tell him about the new job at Baby 'O Club. I gather my things and quickly get dressed to please. Familiar with the Waterford Apartments from touring myself, I head out in search of the apartment number he left on the machine.

These apartments are where Phillip and I had stayed when we first met. Will anyone recognize me? I shake my head. It's been too long for that. I hope. I reach his apartment door and knock.

Joseph opens the door slowly. "Come in." His voice is flat. Is something wrong? I mean, his voice wasn't that bad earlier was it?

"Hello Joseph?" I stutter.

"Sit down, Beverly. I have something to say to you." His voice is calm. Too calm.

"Joseph, what's wrong?" I sit next to him on the couch. He shifts away from me.

"You're scaring me."

Heart of Gold

"I went to Paradise tonight." His expression is blank, his tone flat.

"The topless club?"

"Yes." He looks at me. "Heard of it? Know anyone who works there?"

I pause for a moment, then shake my head. "No."

"Some dancer there knows you. Very well actually." His icy blue eyes are staring into mine.

"Oh really?" I raise an eyebrow. As if he knows anything. Rumors happen all the time. "What does she know about me?"

"She knows about you and Phillip."

I look shocked and I know it. Especially by the way his eyes turn into slits of distrust. What...how? How could he have found out about him this way? All I can do is stare back numbly, unable to speak.

"I knew she was telling the truth! She knew about Phillip."

I regain my composure. He can't know that much. "What did she tell you?"

"It's not what she told me as much as how she told me. You left me wide open!"

I look at him, confused, "I don't understand?"

"Let me spell it out for you then. I'm sitting there with Trent, John, Dillon, Jerry and a friend you haven't met. I was telling them all about you; how in love I am with you, how wonderful you are. Then some trashy babe named Cathy comes up. The guys ask her if she knows you and she said she does. She knows all about your black boyfriend and how you supported him!"

I can feel my mouth hanging open and quickly cover it with my hand, embarrassed. "Oh my God!"

"Yes, 'Oh my God' Beverly! Why didn't you tell me?"

I shrug and look away. "I got played. Would it have made any difference?"

"No."

"So that's it? It's over because I dated a black guy?"

Rebecca Nietert

"No!" He stands up. "It's over because you lied to me!"

"I never lied, Joseph!" I stand up also. "Okay, so I omitted the fact that my ex was black. This is exactly the reason why! Most people can't handle it and it seems like you are one of them!"

"You were the one who once yelled at me about omission!" He shouts back.

I roll my eyes. I'm so done with this! It is about the color of his skin. Both Joseph and I know it. He's not fooling anyone.

"I have to go to the bathroom. I've been working all day."

"Working all day? Where?"

"Not that it matters now." I push past him to the bathroom. Once inside, the tears start to fall. I let them. I look at my tear-stained face and wipe my eyes. I can't stop crying! I'm so angry. I need to calm down. I smell his cologne and look around. He isn't in here? I then notice his closet and open it, inhaling his intoxicating scent. Then I notice it: women's clothes mixed with his. Huh? I take a closer look through the array of clothes, unable to believe my eyes. There's someone else he's seeing? And he has the balls to fuss at me for something that happened a long time ago! What the hell?

"Oh, that's it!" I storm out the bathroom. Whatever shame I had felt has been replaced with betrayal.

I walk up to him, now sitting on the sofa, and look down at him.

"You have some nerve to get onto me about my ex when you have another girls clothes in you freaking closet?!"

He jumps to his feet. "Like you know everything! She's coming to get them soon."

I cross my arms and roll my eyes. "Uh-huh. Look, I didn't tell you about Phillip because I knew it would change things between us. He used me. I didn't find out until the end of whatever I thought we had. It was my mistake and I have to live with that."

"I don't. You have to leave."

I look at him, incredulous. Is it really this easy for him to dump me? "So that's it?"

Heart of Gold

He nods. "Yes."

"Fine, good-bye Joseph. It was nice while it lasted." I open the door and walk out of the apartment, but not before looking back. He's looking right at me when he slammed the door angrily.

I drive for an hour, going nowhere in particular. After I got home, I notice I"m not alone. Lana is here, gathering the last few things for her apartment. She bounces into the hallway.

"Hi!"

"Hello Lana." I can't keep the sadness out of my voice.

"Not again!" She sits on the sofa, "What happened?" Her voice is deflated.

I can feel the embarrassment on my tear-stained face.

"He found out about Phillip." I answer softly.

"Found out? So what?" She looks at me, confused.

"He found out when he was with his other friends and now he's humiliated and embarrassed. He left me, which by the way is ridiculous, because he called me. Of course, I drive over there all too happy to be dumped again." I can't keep the anger or sarcasm out of my voice.

Lana shakes her head. "Okay, let me get this right. Someone told him about you and Phillip around his friends..." She looks at me for confirmation. I nod. "And now he won't see you anymore because you dated someone whose skin is black?"

"Yes!" I yell, exasperated.

"He told you that it's unacceptable to date a black man?"

"Pretty much!" I hiss annoyed.

"Prejudice Bastard! Who the hell does he think he is?"

Confused, I look at her. "What?"

"You feel like he has a right to judge you for dating a black man?" She shouts.

I flinch. "Yes. I mean I gave all my money to Phillip."

"The two are not exclusive, sweetie. He's black and that should have no bearing on what you did or didn't do to you!"

"I don't get what you mean."

Rebecca Nietert

"You're so upset that Phillip happened to be black and with that comes this stigma you feel attached itself to you. It's as if you wear some sort of scarlet letter for your choices. Regardless of what he did to you, with or without your permission, the fact is that he could have been white but no, he just happened to be black. You need to stop putting the two in one category. It's not about him being black. What he did to you was wrong regardless of his color. You were the victim in all this. God, why can't you see that?!"

I think for a moment, contemplating. Slowly, it starts to make sense. "Yeah...I think you're right."

"I know I'm right! He should have said he couldn't be with you because you're too damn gullible. He could have stated it's because you made a huge mistake. For that matter, he should want to date you if you're that gullible. Whatever his reason was, it shouldn't have been because you were with a black man."

"So...he condemned me because of the pigment in Phillip's skin and he's not upset that was stupid enough to waste my fortune on a manipulating bastard?" My brain is mush. I'm still trying to process all of this.

"There you go, Girl! Finally! You're the one who should be embarrassed."

"What?" I look at her, shocked.

"You should feel embarrassed for dating some senseless jerk who thinks that your one mistake, not because it was with a black man, but your one flub up is any less than any one of his flaws! Men like that push me to the limit."

"I can see that." I look at her and can't help but smile. She's so cute when she's mad. I laugh a little. "You always put things into perspective for me." She did too. I don't know if the hurt from Phillip made me a little tougher or if I chose to deny my feelings. She made me feel at ease. Justified for being angry. I need that and somehow just having her understand allowed me to put my feelings aside for now.

Heart of Gold

"I should hope so! Don't let anyone reject you for a mistake. Don't do that."

"Thank you, I won't. By the way, what are you doing tonight?"

She looks at me, "Sushi and beer?"

"Wonderful! The Captain's Boat Restaurant?"

"Yes, let's go there."

I grab my things. "I'll drive. Are you staying here tonight?"

"Tonight yes. Tomorrow no. I've got a uh...hot date." She winks and giggles.

I laugh, completely understanding what she means.

"Good. Hey, did you know I'm working at the Baby 'O Club?"

She shakes her head as she opens the door. "Tell me all about it at the restaurant."

We spend the rest of the evening talking at the restaurant. I try to convince her to join me at the new club but she refuses.

When we return home, Joseph had left a message on the answering machine. "I was wrong."

Lana and I look at each other, bewildered.

"What do you suppose he's wrong about? Loosing you? Judging you? What?"

I shrug my shoulders. "I don't know. Honestly, I am not sure if I can jump onto another roller coaster? This emotional whiplash is killing me."

"Oh who are you kidding? You want to know and I don't blame you. I suppose if it were me and Rod going through this I would hear him out."

"Call him. I'm dying to find out."

"Me too." I pick up the phone and dial.

"Hello, Beverly."

"Hi?"

"I'm sorry, I need some time to get over this."

"Time? Sorry? For what?"

"Look, I never want to bring this up again. I just feel like I think I can get past this."

Rebecca Nietert

"Awful big of you." Of course I'm going to be sarcastic. Especially after the stunt you pulled. Idiot. "Yes I know." I roll my eyes. He didn't get it. I sigh, too tired to fight. "I'm really glad you can just get past this." I look at Lana, whose face is frozen with disbelief.

Then she laughs and walks out of the room, whispering under her breath, "Son of a bitch!"

I laugh also but softly.

"Someone there with you?"

Well, no sense in hiding it now. "Lana."

"Oh. I'll let you go. Can I see you tomorrow?"

"Yeah I suppose so."

"You really are something else."

"I know. I hear that a lot."

"See you tomorrow then?"

"Call me." I hang up.

I walk into the room where Lana is. "Can you believe him?"

"Yes. But you're still going to meet him."

"Yes, I am. I'm hooked. Absolutely head of heels hooked. All I need is that voice talking to me and I feel like I have no will of my own."

She sighs. "You will never meet your Mr. Knight in Shining Armor as long as you waste your time with these guys who keep putting themselves first."

I laugh at her warning. "I know. But hey, at least I'll have a lot of fun along the way?" I honestly said thinking of the heat between us.

"He will hurt you." Her tone is sad but I shrug.

"He already has."

We both look at each other. "That's true. As long as you know what you're in for."

"Lana." I look her in the eye. "I know I really love this guy. When I'm with him he makes me feel so special."

"Yeah but when he's away from you he breaks your heart."

Heart of Gold

"He has his reasons."

She shakes her head. "You've got to find out on your own, don't you?"

"I guess I do." I laugh nervously.

She looks at me with the most sorrowful face I've ever seen.

"Lana, let me explain it this way. I want to be happy. If that means I am not always going to go the safe route, then so be it. I have never felt this kind of passion with a man. Not ever. It's not easy for me. I thought I had something like it with Phillip, but when I found out how played I was it left me beyond consolable. I managed to live through that. I don't know because I honestly believed that if Phillip left me I would die. I would starve. I wouldn't be able to wake a morning without him. I lived. I got through that and that let's me know I am pretty tough. I may not seem like it to you, because I show you how they hurt me. I will not show a man though."

"I think that you have to be friends. You have to be able to talk through things. You have to have mutual respect and I am afraid that as long as we're dancers that is not in the cards for us in our near future."

"You may be right." I respond thoughtfully.

"Okay." She sighs heavily. "I'll be there when the chips fall okay?" She walks over to me and gently caresses the hair out of my face.

"Thank you." We hug and her warnings stop.

Rebecca Nietert

25

Joseph and I make up the next day, agreeing to never speak of Phillip again.

Time seems to pass quickly when Joseph and I are together. Every night after work he picks me up and takes me all over town; mainly to his favorite restaurants. Once he took me to a local hangout where he met some friends that he told me about the night of our fight. One of them he called Buddy. He was boisterous and loud, which it was probably because of his intoxication.

While playing darts, he tried a couple of times to mention the Paradise incident (only when Joseph was out of earshot). I tried to keep Joseph close, not wanting to hear anymore about how I apparently would never be half the woman to Joseph that Sally was. As long as I could keep Joseph by my side, I was able to prove that I have the power, not her. Days later, I still can't get that out of my mind.

Joseph and I always seem to have a lot of fun doing whatever we want. Of course, the only requirement of us being together is always formed around the alcohol we consumed together.

Our life together is party central with both of us as the two main players; the stars of our own world. Sure we get drunk a lot, but at least it's fun. What's even more fun is the sex. Every night we have more passion than the next. Every event we go to, every conversation we have is all geared toward the foreplay that leads to the most ultimate connection than either of us could have ever hoped for.

Life at a hundred miles an hour is great! It's not like I'm trapped with nowhere to go. All I want to do is go out and be with Joseph. Nothing matters anymore, not even work. I look over at Joseph

Heart of Gold

sitting in a chair and smile. He's so handsome. He takes a swig of his beer.

"Beverly, what would you think about living with me?"

I laugh and take a sip of my Crown. That hit the spot. "I would love it!"

"Really?"

I get up and walk over to him. He looks up at me with those gorgeous eyes. I sit in his lap, almost dropping my glass, and kiss him. "Really!"

He smiles and kisses me back, one hand already feeling my lower back. "Then let's do it. I'll find a place for us as soon as I can."

I put my glass on the floor. He hands me his beer, which I also put down. He grabs me as I'm sitting up and pulls me against him. I can't help but laugh. He's perfect! I kiss him softly and whisper, "Fine with me."

I open my eyes and see him staring at me. I look around, realizing that we are in bed. How did I get here? I look back at him. Oh, yeah. He carried me. I'm kind of surprised I don't have any hangover after all of the drinks from last night. I guess I've built up a tolerance of some sort.

"Good morning roomie?" I offer. He laughs and shakes his head.

"Roomie?" I almost roll my eyes.

"Last night? Your proposition? Come on! You never forget."

He reaches over and before I know it his lips are on mine. "I did not forget." His whisper calms me and I smile.

"You're such a tease." I comment

"You're the tease." I feel his hands moving slowly up my body. I push them away.

"Can we just cuddle for a bit? Still tired from last night." He nods and warps his arms around me, using my chest as a pillow. I run my fingers through his hair.

"I like this."

Rebecca Nietert

"Me too." He looks up at me with that broad smile I love, "And we can have this every morning now."

"Well you have to find the place first."

"I know. Hey, I have to go riding with some guys this afternoon. Want to come?"

I look down at him, "Motorcycle riding?"

"Yeah, my friends have lots of them. I'm thinking about buying a Yamaha V-Max. What do you think?"

"I love bikes! That would be so cool."

"Really? Come with me today. Take off work."

"I have already taken off so much. My bills are being paid late."

He leans up and kisses my neck. "So? I don't even have credit cards." I can feel the need coming back as his lips move up my neck to my jaw. "Come on." His lips are on mine now; so intoxicating. "I don't pay bills, never paid taxes, and don't care too much for credit."

I lean my head back a bit and look him in the eye. "You don't pay your taxes? Seriously?"

"Seriously. Now tell me you're honest." He looks back at me, eyebrow raised.

I look down. "I am. I mean...I have been, but I'm losing a lot of money these days hanging out with you."

His lips are on mine again. "Let them go." I can't help but be enchanted by him. He's everything I've ever wanted in a man! "Pay them when you have a good day."

I nod, feeling breathless from his assault. "Okay, I'll go." I grab his face and stare into his eyes. "I think you might be bad for me."

"Good." He smiles and slaps me playfully on the backside. "Let's go."

We took a long shower and then we head out to his friends house. After a brief introduction, Chuck takes us on a long journey into Waller County and some nearby local bike hangouts. Riding was fun, fast and dangerous. I've never been so thankful for a helmet in my life!

Heart of Gold

When the day ended, both Joseph and I were exhausted. He brought me to my place. Even though he said he will collect me after he gets a place, I can't help but wonder if he never comes back. I call Lana; I hate being alone. I leave a message and look around. The apartment seems colder since she left. It's no wonder I miss her. I fall asleep, exhausted from the weekend's adventures.

I wake up at the sound of knocking on the door. I look at the clock: it's noon. I get up and hurriedly get dressed and open the door. Joseph is standing there with a huge grin on his face.

"I found a place!" He announces proudly. I can't believe it! That fast?

"Yep?!" He nods and takes me out to see his brand-new V-Max, purchased right before he stopped here.

The new apartment is on the north side of town, quite a distance from my apartment. When we arrive, I notice that it's a small townhouse. We walk inside and Joseph gives me a tour, specifically of the one bedroom that has burnt-orange colored carpet. I can't help but wince a little.

"This is...quite a bit different from my taste."

He nods. "I like it. My table will fit nicely."

I look around. He's right about one thing at least. Still... "If you like it I love it."

He walks over and picks me up off the ground, swinging me around in circles. "Honestly?"

I laugh and nod. "You sure you're ready for this?"

"You sure you are?"

We both laugh; the memory of that question isn't far off in our past. "Yes."

"You know, you could work at Paradise. It's closer to here."

"Joseph." I look at him sternly. "First you want me to work at the Baby "O Club, which by the way, is working out fine. Now you want me to switch to another club? I'm doing well at Baby 'O's."

He shrugs. "Wherever works better for you. Do you like days?"

Rebecca Nietert

"Love them. I just need to get my stuff moved in and work a few days for our rent."

"Rent? No, I'll pay for our rent."

I smile, remembering of the old days when I used to pay the rent while Phillip would sit there and be lazy. Never again. "Great."

After about a month of talking about living together the day has finally arrived! I move a few things from my apartment but most of it goes to my grandmother.

We merge what I've brought over with his. When Joseph puts all the pictures of his ex-wives and girlfriends on the wall, it upsets me. I decide to confront him about it.

"Why do you keep those around with a new girlfriend?"

"Remember what I said? Just because you can't respect someone you once loved doesn't mean the love ends."

"Yes, but isn't that kind of rude to the new love?"

"It's who I am. Either you accept it or you don't accept me." His answer is emotionless. I guess that means he's really over them? After all, he would have been upset by my asking if he really cared. So that's it. I accept it.

The first few weeks are amazing! We purchased a burnt-orange sofa; Joseph's taste of course. His contemporary style is very unlike my Victorian taste. Even though the couch matches his things, it's okay. I still love being with him. Every night brings new adventures; whether it's some new element to our sex life or just us watching TV on a lazy afternoon. I can't help but fall for him all over again. Nothing seems to get him cross. He's so gentle and appears to truly care about me. He opens doors for me, takes me out to romantic restaurants and dinners. Last week he talked me into going fishing! Sure I missed some work, but who cares? He's perfect! He even takes off work for me, so why can't I do the same in return?

Sure sometimes I get mental images of Phillip; after all, he did similar things when we started dating. But being with Joseph is so...different. He makes me feel different. Special. Like I'm the only girl in the world. The only girl in his world. I adore him.

Heart of Gold

The phone rings. I look up, watching Joseph answer. It's nine at night! No one ever calls this late. I watch him answer politely, then his smiling face turns into a frown. I listen closer and I can tell it's a woman's voice on the other line. I can feel the jealousy creeping in as he sits down, holding his head in his hand, rubbing his forehead with his fingers. Finally, he hangs up. I walk over to him, curious. I've never seen him like this before. As I sit next to him he turns to face me, his eyes echo sadness.

For the first time in a long time I feel completely helpless. I want to take his sadness away.

"That was Cherry." He's told me about his two sisters, Cherry and Candy. Cherry seems to be the maternal one while Candy seems to be flighty. I nod and sit silently, waiting.

"My brother's dead." I can feel my jaw drop in shock. I cover my mouth with my hand, hoping he doesn't notice. He doesn't seem to. I can't help but think of my sister. I'm at a loss for words.

He reaches his hand out for me. "Come here."

"Of course." I sit on his lap. He holds me tight against him. He doesn't cry or move, just sits there, holding me. I let the silence hang for a while, then decide to break it.

"How did it happen?" I whisper softly as I kiss his forehead gently.

He shakes his head. "Don't know. His wife, who is a great woman, said he dropped dead before he hit the ground."

Oh my God! "A heart attack?"

"Apparently a heart implosion."

"I'm so sorry. I lost my sister so I understand the pain of losing a loved one."

"Thank you." He lifts me off his lap and heads into the bedroom. I let him have his space and sleep on the couch.

"Beverly, I love you. Thank you." I open my eyes to see him sitting next to me, fingers caressing my cheek. I smile up at him.

"I love you too." We say nothing more.

Rebecca Nietert

At the wake Joseph got to say a final goodbye to his brother. I meet his mother, sisters, and brother's ex-wife, who is crying hysterically. It wasn't until the band played, "The Cowboy Rides Away" by George Straight that Joseph lost it.

After the ceremony Joseph looks at me, "We used to ride on the Rodeo Trail Ride together." He reminisces.

"You will always have that?" I know I'm awkward at funerals; I never know the right thing to say. Especially after my sister's death. I just want him to know that I'm here for him. I still can't help but feel powerless.

"That and much more." He grins at the memories. "We used to ride these old wooden horses out back our house together. Mom didn't have much money and my Dad wasn't around. He was a tough old bird though. I suppose that Jason is with him right now."

"Jason? Who is that?"

"I've been married before. I told you that?" He waits for confirmation and then once he has it he resumes. "I was married to a woman named Connie and we had a son named Jason." I choked with his word 'had.' "Jason was the most amazing little boy but he died in a car accident. He was burned to death."

"Oh my God Joseph. I had a sister who died that way too. She was only 16 and her name was Leslie."

He looked at me with tears in his eyes. "I'm sorry."

"Joseph, do you believe in God?"

"I want to. At times like this I sure wish there was a God. I would like to see him again one day."

"I know. I feel the same way."

"We used to pretend like we were dead when we were kids. He always let me shoot him with my toy gun. He was the oldest so he really taught me a lot. I learned how to ride horses, rope, and take care of myself because of him. He truly was my friend." Tears start to fall down his face. I can feel them falling down mine too.

"He will always be your friend. That'll never change."

Joseph grabs my hand and smiles. "I know. I love you."

Heart of Gold

"I love you."

"I love you too."

"You're a very lucky man to have so much family now when you need it."

"Are you coming back to my mothers' place after the funeral?"

"Only if you want me to."

"I do."

"Then I'll be there with you."

"Good, I don't think I can make it without you."

"Yes, you could. You're a rock but I will be there nonetheless."

The next day we arrive at the funeral. It's held in a beautiful chapel. It feels like Deja Vu from my sister's funeral all over again, minus the emotions. The only emotions I have are the ones I have for Joseph. I never knew his brother so I can't cry for his brother, but I cry for him and try to help the best way I know how.

I look around at the crowd of people crying. Everyone seems to have loved him. I look over at Joseph, who is now sobbing. I reach over and hold him. It's all I can do.

After the funeral is over we head over to his mothers house for a buffet-style dinner. Everyone seems to accept me, even as an outsider. For the first time in my life I feel at home. I look over at Joseph. He is my home. We belong together.

Rebecca Nietert

26

It's been weeks since the funeral. Somehow, the funeral connected Joseph and me on a whole new level. I don't talk to Lana that much anymore, or anyone really not associated with the Baby 'O Club.

The door slams shut. I look up from the TV to see Joseph walk in, looking perplexed. He sits on the sofa next to me. I know better than to ask, so I wait.

"Guess what I found out." He asks.

"What?"

"It seems my ex-wife, Connie, got herself in a fix. The guy she left me for left her high and dry with a kid. She's pregnant."

Knowing that Joseph found it difficult to talk with me about one of his ex's, I responded lovingly, "What does that have to do with you or us?"

"Nothing. She called me to ask for my help."

"What does she want you to do?"

He shrugs. "She didn't know I was with you."

"I understand. Tell me what she asked of you?"

"She asked if I could help her out of the mess she's in."

I eye him carefully. "What mess?"

He shrugs again, unresponsive.

"Don't dance around it! Say it!"

"Okay." He sighs heavy. "She ran off with this guy who tried to shoot her. She's so wrapped up in this guy that she can't think clearly. She thinks if she keeps this kid he'll marry her. I told her I don't think so but it hurts my heart that she's in such a bind. Anyway, this guy told her he doesn't want the kid. He claims it isn't his."

Heart of Gold

"Sounds like the losers I choose!" I laugh. The look he gives me says that he doesn't think the joke is funny.

"Sorry, go on. What does that have to do with us?"

"Me. Not you. Me." He reinstates. I roll my eyes.

"Okay, you. Go on!"

"Well, she was beginning to believe he wasn't going to come around so she started fooling around with her boss."

"That's the guy he thinks is the father?"

He nods. "Yes. Of course, she got pregnant. The boss thought it was his. Apparently she says its Curt's. She tells her boss it's not his and he fires her. Nice, huh?"

"She gets what she deserves? What's she going to do?"

He shrugs. "She spent all her money on this Curt and has nothing left. She bleeds when she moves so she has to be confined to bed. She can't work."

I raise an eyebrow. "And she wanted you to come to her rescue? Why would she think that you would if she is the one who left you? Oh, that's right. The whole 'love and respect thing'. I get it. She needs you to rescue her from her choices?"

"Yes."

"Okay well let me ask you something. Do you feel obligated to help her?"

"Obligated? No. I feel like she is a friend in need. I want to help her but I don't know what I can do."

"She can't move, can't work or even care for herself. How will she manage a kid?"

He shakes his head. "Wish I knew. She may have to terminate the pregnancy."

"Joseph." I look him in the eye. "Did I ever tell you I terminated a pregnancy?"

He thinks for a moment, and then shakes his head. "No, but I believe it. Who's was it?"

I ignore the first pat of what he said. "That doesn't matter. What matters is that I had to make a choice directly after a horrible

Rebecca Nietert

car accident. I chose to abort. I don't want any woman to have to suffer through the guilt of that. Not if I can stop it."

"So what can you do?"

I think for a moment. "What if she lived with us?"

"What?"

"Hear me out! What if you and I both helped her? You love her right?"

"Not like I love you, but yes."

"So, what if we asked her to come live with us? Think she would?"

He slowly approaches, wraps his arms around my and stares into my eyes. "Are you sure?"

I nod and smile. "Yes."

"That is the most benevolent thing anyone has ever done for me."

"I'm mainly doing it for you but also for her. A little."

"But you don't even know her."

"I know she's a woman in need. Sometimes that's just enough for a woman to help out, you know?"

He shakes his head and laughs, "You're incredible! I'll call her right away."

"Wait!" I scream, not meaning to sound that loud. He jumps in surprise.

"What? Change your mind?"

I laugh, "No, silly! I was thinking I should meet her first or she'll think I'm crazy or something."

He stops to think for a moment, "You're probably right."

"What should we do?" I ask.

"Maybe throw her a shower? Not a girly one though; she doesn't like those. We could throw her a shower at the Baby 'O's. A baby shower where only men can come."

"What?" I'm so confused! I watch him pace back and forth, thinking out loud.

Heart of Gold

"An all-male shower with all her male friends and father at the Baby 'O's Club in the middle of the afternoon."

"You have got to be kidding me!" I can't believe he's actually planning this out! He's more excited than me – the one who started this entire idea!

"Nope. She'll love it!"

"Won't she be intimated by me?"

"Nope!" He shakes his head. "There hasn't been a woman who can intimidate her yet. She's very successful."

"Oh. I didn't know." I can feel my confidence deflating.

"There's no way you could have known." He continues to pace back and forth. He finishes formulating his plan then walks off and calls Connie. I hear faint laughter coming from the other room. He's laughing? I wonder who else has made him laugh recently. After some time, he finally comes back in the room.

"She said she would do it."

"Good." I pause, hesitant. Just say it! "Sounds like you two are close."

"Not as close as we are." He warps his arms around me and kisses my cheek. "One thing: she doesn't know she's going to meet you."

I look at him in shock. "You're going to just spring it on her? This should be fun."

He laughs and picks me up, spinning me around. "Don't worry, love. She's going to see what I see and love you to pieces." I smile and kiss him. It's not long before we are in the bedroom.

I walk into work, not sure if this plan of bringing an ex-wife into our home is a great idea after all. An eerie feeling starts to creep into my gut but I push it down. Joseph and I are happy. If helping out a friend will make him happy, I'm all about it. I glance at myself in the dressing room mirror. I can't help but smile. I have to admit, I look hot! My black cocktail dress with a velvet halter provides a stark contrast to my blonde hair and blue eyes. The contrast is complementary. I spin around. My tan legs are barely

Rebecca Nietert

visible through the peek-a-boo lace bottom half of the dress. The dress cuts a long v in the back and a shorter v in the front, showing just enough cleavage to get anyone's attention. I take one last look in the mirror and put on some lipstick. Sure he said that no woman intimidates her. Was she pretty the last time I saw her? I shrug. Can't remember. Guess I'll find out. I look myself over once more, "It's go time."

As I walk out the dressing room I see Joseph walking in with two of his friends I haven't met before: Mike and Mike Jr. It turns out Mike is Tommy's younger brother, which I find odd because they don't look anything alike. Still, you never know these days. Joseph also introduces me to Connie's father, Sam. After some chitchat and a few drinks, Trent and John show up. I look around, searching for any sign of Connie. Nope. Not here yet. I look at Joseph, who is going to escort her in. I shake my head and walk to the front counter. Why is he escorting her? Can't one of her other friends do it? I let the girls at the front counter know to look for her. They're good spotters. I take another swing from my Crown and look at Joseph and his friends sitting at the table, talking about what a louse Curt is. Maybe it's the alcohol or the fact that she's having a baby, but I feel a sudden urge to protect Connie; a woman I haven't even met!

I pass by the DJ who pulls me to the side, asking if I want to get on stage. I agree, needing the distraction. I walk up on stage, feeling the music start to run through my veins. I look out over the crowd and see Joseph and his friends turn around to watch me. I smile at Joseph, determined to make sure I'll be the talk of the night. I love being on stage with courage running through my body. I feel powerful. Invincible. Nothing and none can touch me on stage. I love the feeling! It's been far too long since I've had this much fun. The song ends too soon, followed by the clapping and hollering of males. They try to get an encore but I smile and gracefully exit the stage and head to the table, fixing my eyes on Joseph There's only one person I'll do an encore for now. When I

Heart of Gold

get to the table, Connie is sitting at the end of it and smiles at me. Good to know she feels comfortable at least. I look at the table and notice that gifts brought by the men lay open, tissue wrapper is scattered everywhere! I feel an arm circle my waist and look up to see Joseph gesturing to me but looking at Connie.

"Connie, this is the girl I've been telling you about."

"Hello." She stands up and holds out her hand.

I shake her hand, unable to notice that she doesn't look pregnant. "It's nice to finally meet you."

"I've heard a lot about you." I smile and nod, determined not to let her get to me.

"Likewise."

"Dance for Sam?" I look up at Joseph in shock. I don't know if it's the whisper or what he just said that threw me off guard more.

"What are you talking about?" I whisper, forcing a smile.

"Just do it. She'll see why I love you."

I titled my head and look up at him. That hurt. "Joseph, I can't dance in front of Connie. I just met her. I would like to talk a little first."

He grabs hold of my arm, "Just do it."

I jerk my arm away, "How much have you had to drink?!"

"A lot, why?"

"I need a drink to catch up, Sweetie. I'm not where you are yet."

"Okay." He walks off to catch the waitress. As I sit in idle conversation with Connie I can't help but feel the pain form deep within me. Did he just show me off like a trophy? I can't believe it! That's something Phillip would do, not Joseph. I look at Connie. This isn't about me, it's about her.

"Did Joseph offer to have you come live with us?"

A hush falls over everyone at the table. The music seems to stop. Every eye is on me. After what seems like an eternity, Tommy speaks up, "Did you really just ask her to move in with you two?"

Rebecca Nietert

"Yes. What's wrong with that? I heard she needs a place to stay." Sam lifts his drink as a toast to me. "You are one tough little lady." He lets out a laugh. "And beautiful too!"

"Thank you." I respond shyly, unsure of what to say.

"Yes, Joseph did ask me." Connie looks around the table at the men, then settles her gaze on me. "Was it his or your idea?"

Everyone looks at me, waiting for an answer. "Mine."

Everyone at the table starts laughing. Joseph returns and looks at me. "What's going on?"

I shrug so Connie speaks up.

"Apparently the boys here find it funny that Beverly asked me to move in with both of you."

Joseph looks at me and laughs, then starts to high-five the guys. "She's a fine filly isn't she?"

The guys keep laughing. Tommy chimes in, "Oh yeah! You're one lucky dude!"

I look at Connie, "Men! They can be so boyish and crude. Don't let them get to you!"

She looks at me, bewildered. Almost like I had said the most preposterous thing. "I needed that!"

The music blares again. "Needed what?" I try to shout over the music.

I needed to know it's not just me. Other women think they are all just boys too!"

I nod and smile, "They are!" I lift my drink in a toast.

Connie, Joseph and I talk for hours before everyone leaves. I know I've drank to much. Joseph and I stumble home. I feel sick. How could he have treated me like a trophy all day? I thought the only man who would ever do that was Phillip. Maybe I was wrong. I don't even know what to think anymore. I feel more confused than I've felt in a long time.

It's been a few days since that night. I head to Connie's place using the directions Joseph gave me. As she shows me around, her obsession of Curt is obvious. The rooms are filled with artificial

Heart of Gold

flower arrangements and pictures of their life together. She shows me the place where he broke in and tried to kill her. I shake my head. How can she still be into this guy? He tried to kill her! I help her pack and load everything into my truck, shaking my head. If she's so successful how come she has so little possessions? I look at her, noticing for the first time what she really looks like. She looks like the girl next door, only slightly more refined. She has large hands for a woman and big bones that is masked by her slender form. How in the world am I supposed to be intimidated by her? Her light brown eyes match her calm demeanor. I slam the door shut and press on the gas pedal. At least we're friends. I think?

Joseph and I have the entire house sanitized for Connie's homecoming. We baby-proofed everything. Since Joseph has experience when he had kids, he knew what to to. I just helped in any way I could. We decorated Connie's bedroom as well as the baby's.

When I get home from work in the evening I come home to Joseph cooking dinner. At breakfast, they talk non-stop about their old life together. I look down at my plate. He seems to make her favorites. Maybe he's doing this because she's new.

As the days pass I realize that isn't necessarily the case. After learning that they had been married for only 60 days (but best friends prior to that), Connie decides one evening to pull out their old wedding album. I can't help but feel like an outsider as they continue to reminisce together. They're so comfortable with each other. I can tell they genuinely love each other. Still, I can't help but feel like they're bringing up their past as part of a future foreplay.

Joseph has told me all the reasons why he would never get married again, especially the part about him not wanting to disappoint another woman.

"Here's that stupid dress I wore." Connie laughs.

Joseph chuckles and shakes his head, "You were beautiful."

After a while, Connie calls me over to look at the picture of their rings. As she points out hers, Joseph stands and retrieves his

Rebecca Nietert

notebook, something he carries with him wherever he goes. He opens it and pulls out a gold band dangling from the top of the spirals. I haven't seen it before, thought I had seen him open the book many times. Connie waves her left hand in his face and laughs. It's the same ring from the picture. Both rings are. I look at them smiling at each other and it hits me.

I run to the bathroom and shut the door behind me. I feel sick! I can't help the tears from falling. Am I really just a second choice to him?

I hear a knock on the door followed by Joseph's voice, "You okay?"

"Fine!" I didn't think any man could devastate me the way Phillip had. I thought I was smarter than that! Once I made that mistake with him, why would I make it a second time? Wouldn't my instincts have saved me from making the same bad choices, like when they've saved me from many men in the club? Maybe moving her in with us isn't such a good idea after all.

"You sure?" Joseph's voice is full of concern.

"Yes! I'll be right out." I compose myself, open the door and walk past Joseph into the living room.

"Let's put that book away, okay?"

Joseph walks behind me. "That isn't nice Beverly."

I whip around to face him, about to give him a lecture on how I don't need to hear any more of their past life and how he doesn't need to be defending her.

Connie chimes in, "It's okay."

Joseph begrudgingly picks up the notebook and walks off.

I stand up and walk to the TV.

Connie walks into the living area after talking to Joseph in the other room and notices me on the couch. "You okay?" She seems sincere. I nod.

"I'm fine."

"Good. Hey, what are you watching?"

"Some stupid show." I look up at her. "Why?"

Heart of Gold

"Can we talk?"

I turn the TV off. "Want some hot chocolate?"

"That would be fabulous." We enter the kitchen and see Joseph doing the dishes. As we gather the necessary ingredients Joseph turns to face us.

"What are you two up to?"

"Hot chocolate." Connie responds nonchalantly.

"Sounds like you girls are getting along." He laughs nervously.

Connie nods. "Yes, I need to talk to Beverly. That okay with you?"

"Fine." He shrugs. "I need to go to bed early anyway. I have a big day tomorrow."

"What you doing tomorrow?" I can't help but ask.

"Fishing with Mike."

"Can I come?"

He looks at me inquisitively, "Can you get up at 4:30 in the morning?"

"I think so."

"Then don't be too late tonight, okay?"

I nod and look at Connie. "Is that okay with you?"

She nods, "Great! Come on, lets go sit down."

With our cups of hot coco in our hands we sit down. I can tell it's going to be a long night.

"When did you start dancing?"

I take a sip and tell her my story. For some reason I even mention that Phillip was African American.

Her hand flies to her mouth, as if the cup burned it. I know better. "Does Joseph know?"

"Yes, he knows everything."

"Wow." She takes another sip. "He must really love you."

I shrug and look uncomfortably at my cup. "I love him."

"I know. I can see it." There's an awkward moment of silence. She breaks it. "Where do you see you and Joseph going?"

Rebecca Nietert

"Anywhere we want to." I answer flippantly, trying not to seem emotional about what happened earlier. I feel she's judging me.

"I'm glad you're a tough cookie. He usually recycles his ex-whatever girlfriends. You need to be tough with him."

I look at her cautiously, "What do you mean?"

"I mean he generally doesn't leave until he has another to run to. In his past it's always been an ex that was waiting for him to come back around. When he gets bored he pushes us away but he'll never leave. He'll make it so damn hard for you to be with him that in the end you'll leave."

I almost laugh. A trick like that won't work on me. "Well he's going to stick it out with me, so that won't be a problem."

She nods and I know I've made her uncomfortable. Good. She deserves it after how she made me feel earlier.

"So, what did you do when you found out that I was a dancer?"

She laughs, "I didn't believe that he was leaving Sally for a dancer."

I almost spit out the hot chocolate. "You know Sally?"

She nods. "We're friends. I never understood why he was with her though. I like her but Joseph needs a little more from a girl. I grew past him, which is why I left."

"I can tell he loves you still."

"We've been through a lot together, especially when he found out he couldn't have me." She laughs.

But it's for the best. I don't feel romantically for him anymore. Like I said, I grew past him. But you find him attractive, right?"

I nod and can't help but giggle. "Very much so!"

"Good, then it'll last as long as you want it to."

"You have a good point."

"Yes, I do."

We laugh and talk until the sun starts to rise. I wonder what future hot chocolate talks will bring.

Heart of Gold

27

After driving in Houston traffic for over an hour back one-way to work, I decide to take Joseph's advice and leave Baby 'O's for The Paradise. When I walk in I see Erin, an old friend of mine who was a bartender at a club I used to work at. When I walk up to him he presents himself as a manager.

I'm impressed. "Who owns this club?"

"You know Tony, the customer you would met at Mack's?"

"Tony?" I shake my head, unable to put a name to a face.

"He used to hang out with Sonny from Mack's."

"Oh my Goodness! Really?!" I can't believe it!

He nods, "I thought you would know him." I remember Tony being gentle with nothing rude to say. I'm glad that Joseph pointed out this club to me.

Just then Tony came up from behind me. "Brooke?"

I turn around o see Tony standing there, facing me.

I turn to face him. "How did you know that it was me?"

"I can tell it's you a mile away. Are you coming to work?"

I smile. "Only if you let me?"

He throws his arms around me. "Of course you can work here Sweetie. My club is your club!"

"Thank you, Tony!" I hug him back. "Do I have to do stage?" I look at Erin and smile.

"Not unless you want to. Here you are royalty Sweetheart!"

"Thank you." I giggle. I love having connections.

"Can you get Lana to come here?"

"I bet I could. She might be working tonight. Should I call?"

"Please, come on to the back. I'll let you use my phone."

Rebecca Nietert

"Great!" I follow him back to a plush office. "This is a great club."

"Thank you." He hands me the phone and leaves, giving me privacy.

When Lana answers I can't help but scream in excitement. "It's so good to talk to you!"

"Oh my goodness! Where have you been?"

"Paradise! Want to come?!"

"What?" Ignoring her confused tone, I keep on talking.

"I'm working at Paradise and Erin, the old bartender, is the manager. Anyway, he asked if I could get you to consider working here. Guess who is the owner? Tony from Mack's!"

"You're at a new club again? What's going on?"

"It's a traffic thing. Please say you'll give it a shot. I would love to work with you again. Besides, we don't have to do stage here and knowing the guys can really help!"

"You working days or nights?"

"Days, why?"

"I don't know if I can work days."

"Please? Come on! Tomorrow come down to see and then you can decide."

"Okay...see you at what time?"

"Just before lunch. We can come in late too."

She laughs. "It's good to see you happy. Okay then, I will see you tomorrow."

I hang up the phone and hurry over to Tony to tell him the news. Both of them are very pleased. I walk to the dressing room and get changed into some clothes that I obtained from the tailor selling dancer items in the dressing room.

I look at myself in the mirror. I have to admit, I look hot! I stare at my body, unable to believe what I'm seeing! I know I look good but I haven't felt this god in a long time. The high cut tattered denim shorts and black-and-white polka dot 50's style tight top fit

Heart of Gold

just right. I apply on some red lipstick and look in the mirror, smiling. I feel...

"Beautiful." I look up and notice another girl staring in the mirror, looking at me.

I smile, "Thank you." She nods and quickly turns around, as if she hadn't meant to say that. I shrug. To each their own.

Although I hate the whole stage thing, I decide it will acclimate me quicker. Being on stage is amazing! I can feel the energy bringing life back into me. I love the attention from the men in the crowd. I catch one man's eye and smile playfully. He puts a few bills on the stage. I can't help but feel beautiful. I see Tony and Erin watching from a distance, nodding in approval. It's nice being around Erin and Tony again. It almost feels like home. Joseph was right about this one; it's the place to be! I'm so glad that he convinced me to come here. I dance a little more then head off the stage. I'd forgotten how much fun dancing can be! I've been so worried about Joseph and Connie that I never realized how much stress and pressure dancing takes off.

As I walk towards the bar I notice a man watching me. Normally, I would've barely paid him any attention but there's something that seems familiar about this one. I look at him, searching his face for any trace of familiarity. Who is he? As I get nearer it hits me.

"Phillip."

"Beverly." He nods. "How are things?"

"Good. You?" Is this really happening?

"I'm driving the red Porsche outside. Did you see it?"

"No, I don't pay attention to sports cars. Who is she?"

"She?" He barks a laugh. "No one. I made it big."

"Big?" It's my turn to bark a laugh. "Really?"

"One of my songs sold. I told you I would be big someday."

"Phillip, you could lie to me then but you can't now. There was a girl at Mack's that was hot for you. What's her name? Cherry?"

He shakes his head, "So."

Rebecca Nietert

"I wouldn't want anyone wasting their life just like I wasted mine on you."

"Wasted? That's harsh. Hey, how about a dance for me for old times sake?" He asks playfully.

I almost choke. "Not a chance in hell! I don't feel anything for you anymore."

"Who's your new black man?" He hisses. I know that look, I've seen it way too many times; the look of jealous anger.

"He's not black, he's a cowboy who is a much better man than you any day of the week and twice on Sundays!"

"You're kidding right?" His face droops in shock when I don't answer. "You and a cowboy?!"

"Anything that's not remotely like you."

He eyes me carefully, "You're in love with him?"

"Love, lust, all of it. I don't care enough to listen to what you have to say about it." I turn to walk away and hear a "Hello Sweetie!" I look back and see one of the girls hanging all over Phillip.

I roll my eyes and laugh, "What a surprise."

The room is so dark that the girl looks at me and squints, as if she can't see me. Something in me tells me that she recognizes me.

"Oh how the mighty have fallen..."

I look at her and shake my head. Point proven.

I look her up up and down and stifle a laugh. "Cathy I presume?"

She looks at Phillip uncertainly. "How does she know my name?"

I clear my throat and look her in the eye. "He doesn't speak for me. Besides, your little rumors with my cowboy didn't work." I lean in closer. "If you ever say anything else about me again, I'll rip you to shreds!" This time I walk off.

"Bitch!" I heard. I shrug, ignoring her comment.

I find Erin and Tony at the bar. "Thank you for the demo but I've got to run. Fishing tomorrow with my boyfriend."

Heart of Gold

Tony smiles and gives me a bear hug, "Good luck to you then. Hey, that guy over there giving you any crap?"

I look over and see Phillip sitting at a table with Cathy, watching me. "Yes, as a matter of fact he is. He thinks he he's my boyfriend or something?" It isn't a total lie...just a small one. They don't need to know that.

"You want me to get rid of him?" Erin asks.

I thought about what Phillip might tell him and then I decided it would be best no matter what. I did not want him here if I were working. That might be too difficult. "Yes, can you make sure he never comes back?"

"Will do. Be right back." Erin smiles and starts to walk away. I see Cathy wondering what I have just done.

"Erin?" I shout. He turns around.

"Yeah? What is it?"

"That girl Cathy? She important here?"

"Cathy? Who is Cathy?" He looks confused.

"The dancer all over that guy. She called me a bitch." I motion over to where Phillip and her are sitting.

"Man, you really make enemies quick."

"No. I know her from somewhere I can't place." Well...I can't tell them the exact truth. "Can she leave with him?"

Erin and Tony both look at each other. I can see that Erin gets it. I'm not sure about Tony though. He doesn't say anything.

"Sure. Consider them both banished." Erin leaves to finish his promise.

I hug Tony tight. "Thank you, Tony! Thank you."

"Anytime Darlin. I'll always take care of you!"

"Thank you." I can't help but smile. "This is going to be so great!"

When they leave Cathy walks past me with her head hung low. "Yeah, that's right. Who's the bitch now?" I hiss.

Four-thirty A.M. comes early. "It's time to rise and fish with Joseph." I giggle. A hand covers my mouth.

Rebecca Nietert

"Shh! Don't wake the fish!" Joseph jests. I turn around, grab his face and kiss him.

"You 'shh'!" He laughs and pokes me. I yelp.

"Hey, not fair!" He pokes me again and starts to tickle me. I kick him lightly in the stomach.

"No! Off!" He finally stops and lays next to me, both of us laughing. I look over at him. This is going to be a fun day. I'm ready to see what this fishing stuff is all about. "What do I wear?"

"Something warm. Even though it's Spring it will be cold at six on the lake."

"How do we catch these fish?"

"I thought you said you went fishing with a guy from high school?"

"I did, but that was a million trillion years ago. I don't remember. Besides, it was a small lake with only perch, I think."

"Well, that's okay, but you're in the big leagues now, baby. We're going to catch large-mouth bass."

"Large mouth what? Do they bite?"

He laughs and shakes his head, "Put a move on it hun, we have a good ways to travel before we get there. Bring a blanket and pillow. You might fall asleep in the truck."

I stifle a laugh. I drive myself everywhere; it's highly unlikely that I'll fall asleep in a truck. Even though I'm not used to letting someone have this much control over me, it is his fishing trip. He knows what he's doing. "Okay."

After staying fully awake for the hour and a half drive, Joseph pulls up to a tackle shop. "You want to come in to meet Vern and Selma?"

Before I can say anything Vern runs out of his shop, "Beverly!" Oh God!

I can feel my face heat up so I cower behind Joseph, who laughs at my shyness.

"Be proud of who you are girl!" He pulls me out and points to me, "Hot isn't she?"

Heart of Gold

Not sure how to feel about that, I sit in the boat and wait to go to our private cove. When we get there I look at Joseph, "Teach me what to do."

"Throw this out." He put's a slimy thing on the end of a hook. I can't help but feel a little disgusted but I do what he says.

We cast the line. It isn't long before I feel a nibble on the end of my line. I almost drop the fishing pole. "What do I do when I feel something?!"

He looks over at me and laughs. "You have to set the hook. Does it feel like grass when you reel it in or do you feel a bobbing on the line?"

I steady my grip. "Definitely a bobbing."

He walks over to me. "We need to set the hook, which is when you put the hook through the fishes mouth. Now listen Beverly, this is crucial to fishing. You don't want to do it too early because if you do the fish will spit it out."

"Typically at you and that'll piss you off." I look up to see Mike in a boat next to us. I look over at Joseph, surprised that Mike is here. He looks at Mike disapprovingly and continues.

"If you do it too late then kiss your lure good-bye because he swallowed it. It has to be at the perfect moment." He teases the fish with the lure while talking. Suddenly, the fish bites and Joseph jerks the line upward towards the sky. He sets the hook in the fish's mouth and gives me the pole back while holding on from behind. "Reel it in."

He helps me reel it in and I can't help but be amazed at how much strength fishing takes! It's awesome! It reminds of me baiting guys back in the club; only they never get to reel me in fully. I look up at Joseph. He's the one who caught me. Once the fish is on the boat Joseph reaches over with his bare hands and grabs the fish by the mouth.

"It looks like it has teeth!" I screech, dropping the pole.

"It does." He laughs. "Now, this is a slot lake. That means that we can keep anything under fourteen inches and anything over

Rebecca Nietert

twenty-one inches. Between that is prime breading so we have to release it back. Mike and I don't keep a lot of fish. We generally come to catch and release. This baby looks like it weighs in at around two pounds." He looks over at the other boat, "What do you think Mike?"

"Bout that." He grimaces in concentration.

Joseph looks at him and laughs. "What's the matter? Are you mad she caught the first one?"

"Damn rookies! Of course. First you whip me very time we fish together, then a girl out-fishes me!"

I shrug, "I'm sorry?"

"It's okay."

"Come on, let's take a picture of your first fish." Joseph whips out his camera, "Put it across your forearm so you'll know how big it is. That way when you tell your fish story everyone will believe you."

"How long is it?" I look down at the fish uncomfortably.

 He lays it across a ruler on the boat. "Bout sixteen inches I would wager."

He looks up at me and I can't help but smile. I actually caught something "Now we need to release it, right?"

"Yep." He releases it.

"Tell me more."

His eyes light up. "I'm glad you love doing this Beverly. This is my heart's desire." I smile, wondering if he really means that. I watch as he reaches in his tackle box and listen as he explains what each lure is for. He explains when to use it and what temperature the water has to be. He goes on to talk about the differences in fishing lines needed to be used, depending on conditions of the water. Well, this is educational to say the least.

Joseph catches several five-to-six pound fish while Mike doesn't catch any. I catch a few more but release them. By the end, we are all exhausted and hungry. Joseph takes me back to the docks where the truck is, with Mike following behind. Joseph reaches inside the

Heart of Gold

truck and grabs a bag of charcoal. He lights a tiny Smokey grill. While waiting for it to heat, he shows me how to clean a fish. He clears one side of scales and places the other side with scales on the grill. Before long, lunch is served. It tastes wonderful! We talk about this mornings missed injuries and the one I almost had wrestling with a fish. I take a bite of our catch. I've never known fish could taste this good! I feel like I belong here. Just like one of the guys.

On the way home we stop at Vern and Selma's tackle shop to get more beer for the trip back.

"Hello there, Beverly!" Vern shouts when he sees me.

Selma races in from the back of the room. "Well, first day out here and you already have quite a reputation!" She looks at me.

I look at Joseph and hear Vern whisper, "I told you everyone was talking about it."

"We had quite a morning." Joseph replies.

"I heard we have a new name for that cove that you guys were at. They call it 'Beverly's cove' now." Selma looks at Joseph then at me. "Must have made quite the impression. No wonder you haven't brought her before. Get any fishing done?"

"Caught a few." He responds, not paying much attention to her words. I look at him. He seems to be actually amused by her. I feel my face get red with embarrassment. I'm not drunk enough to write this one off. The sting of shame washes over me. I need to get out of here.

"The sandwiches are great but I have to go." Before anyone can say anything I walk away and head to the truck, slamming the door shut. After a few moments of idle conversation, Joseph gets in the drivers seat. I watch Mike's tires spin against the road, following his vehicle with my eyes until it disappears.

"You okay?" I can feel Joseph's eyes on me.

I look over at him and smile, "Terrific!"

"Great!" He smiles and starts the engine. I don't bother telling him that I just lied.

272

Rebecca Nietert

28

Work over the past few months has been a blast! Whenever I make a few hundred, Joseph and I go off fishing or go out for a weekend to the coast. It's always nice to have fun in the sun. My free time seems to be filled with drinking parties. Everything is so surreal. At times, I feel like time spent with Joseph seems too good to be true. The one thing that does bother me though is the excessive amount of alcohol we consume. At first, it wasn't such a big deal. Now, it's starting to get to me and I'm not entirely sure why. Sure Joseph becomes a different man when he drinks, but don't we all become a little different? Besides, if I don't participate, would he still love me?

"Come with me." I look up at the man who has my heart. I look back down at the pile of bills scattered about the desk. They're screaming my name, begging to be paid. I used to be on top of things when it came to paying bills, what happened?

"Joseph, I can't. I have to work and pay some bills."

"Let them go. My God girl, you have to live. If all your life is about is acquiring things you're going to be pretty miserable."

"I can't. Until I met you I had really great credit. Now I have collection agencies calling me all the time."

He looks me in the eye. "Listen, you could die tomorrow. You can either say you had fun with me or you can say you paid a bill."

"I have to pay for my car!" I burst out, the frustration threatening to boil over.

"I won't be able to go anywhere without it. I'm already a month behind."

Heart of Gold

"So what? They'll let you slide for three months and when you have a good night's pay at work you can pay them back. Come on baby, come with me?"

I look into his eyes, knowing full well I shouldn't be looking at him. Those eyes pierce my soul every time I look at them. I'm reminded of the first time we met in the bar, where his eyes met mine over that spilled drink. I didn't know it then, but I had fallen in love with him. I can't help it; I'll do anything for him. Maybe tomorrow will be better. I nod. "Okay."

After a long day of fishing Joseph pulls into the driveway and I almost want to scream bloody murder. There's a tow truck in our driveway! Joseph gets out the truck, slamming the door angrily and walks up to the driver of the tow truck. I follow right behind him. After a few short words, the truck driver looks at me.

"We're here to repossess your truck."

I look at Joseph, alarmed. "My truck? Why? You have no right!"

The man pulls out a clipboard and starts to read down a list. "Continuous missed car payments, not paying annual maintenance fees." He looks up at me. "Yup, that about does it."

I look from him to Joseph, and then back at him.

"You can't be serious! What am I going to do?!"

I look over at Joseph, frantic. "I just spent my truck money fishing!"

Joseph holds up a hand to stop me, then takes out his wallet and pulls a wad of bills. "I got it." He shoves the money in the man's hands. I can see the dollar signs reflected in the man's eyes. Greedy pig.

"Have a good day!" He gets in his truck and drives off while Joseph escorts me inside.

"Thank you, that was a close one. I softly say." Where did all that money come from? Why didn't he offer to make my truck payment? I am paying for our fun?

"You should probably go to work." I look at him and nod, smiling sarcastically.

Rebecca Nietert

"Yeah, I probably should."

Lana is at work when I arrive. Even though we don't have matching schedules anymore (Lana usually works nights while I work days), I'm glad I get to see her tonight. We have a lot to catch up on.

"It's so good to see you!" She turns around, surprised.

"I had no idea you were working tonight!" She smiles and runs up to hug me.

"Yeah my life is kind of that way now. I come, I go, and I have no idea when or where."

"Quite a ride!"

"Yeah!" I force a smile at a customer who walking by. "They almost repossessed my truck today."

"What?!" She looks at me in shock. "You're not doing well here?" She holds up her hand to get the bartenders attention. "Two Long Island ice-tea's." He nods.

"I am. I just end up spending everything on fun with Joseph. I didn't even realize I was a month late for a bill till this morning!"

She takes a sip of her drink the bartender just dropped off. "He knows about this?"

I nod and take a sip of mine, feeling the familiar rush of courage ease its way into my body. "Yeah, he's the one who says I should live my life now and not worry about paying for it. 'Just have fun' is his motto."

"Fun is good but there comes a time when you have to pay the tab for it."

"I know. It's just that I want to please him and we have so much fun together."

"What are you spending all that money on?"

"Booze mostly. You know how I get my courage." I take another sip.

"He likes you to be wild?"

Heart of Gold

I shrug. "He likes me to be uninhibited. I admit, I like his reaction when I get that way. He seems to be more into me in those moments than at any other time. But..." I shake my head.

"But...?" Lana presses.

"But honestly, all this alcohol is taking quite a toll on me."

She nods. "I understand. I drink now too."

"What?! You're drinking too? What's going on?" I'm shocked. Usually I'm the one with the issues and she's the sane one.

"I'm in love!" She blurts out, then slouches on the bar stool. "Damn it Beverly, I can't do this anymore! Everything's changed!"

"Rod?"

She takes a swing of her drink and nods. "I work nights because he needs to be with me during the day. Every time I take my clothes off for other men I want to throw up."

"I always feel that way, boyfriend or not."

"Well now I know what you mean."

"Well, if we have to drink to get by then let's do it."

She smiles a little. "Yeah...but hey, don't let him ruin your credit, Bev You've got to stop him. You're too good for that."

"I know but it's too late. I'm not myself when I'm with him. I feel weak I can't say no."

"He isn't right for you."

"I know, something deep in me tells me that. I can't help but hang on, clinging to the possibility that maybe one day he will love me the way I need him to. Maybe he will need me as much as I need him."

"What if that never happens?"

I pause for a moment. "It will devastate me." That can't happen again; not after Phillip. I won't let it.

"I know." She flags the bartender down for another drink

"Hey, want to just have some fun tonight?"

She looks at me cautiously. "What are you conjuring up in that imagination of yours?"

Rebecca Nietert

"I'm thinking about playing with the men here. Let's make a game of it; pretend like it doesn't matter! I'll dance the stage and we can see who gets the most money."

"How?"

"Just like the old days! You go up to guys in the audience to tell them to come tip me. I'll do the same for you and we can see who wins."

"Kind of like who can get the most phone numbers?"

"Yeah! What do you think?"

She smiles, "I'm in. Anything to get out of this funk! I get to pick your music though."

"No way!"

"Or I'm not playing." She grins and I can't help but laugh.

"Fine, let's do it. I get to pick yours too. I go first."

"Deal." She runs to the DJ to select my music while I run to get changed into my cutoff shorts and daisy may top on. As if Lana read my mind, she asks the DJ to announce me on stage. "Here's Daisy May!"

I laugh, not caring what everyone else thinks. I dance as if I've never danced in my life. It's so much fun! I look over at Lana in the DJ booth. She smiles and gives me a thumbs-up. I can barely contain my laughter. I don't even notice the crowd anymore; all I want to do is get lost in the music, not caring about having the perfect form or pose. Not caring about who's watching or not. Not caring about any of those men and how much they'll be giving me. Not caring about car payments or bills. For a moment, I'm not even caring about Joseph. I just want to leave it all behind, even for a moment.

I spot Lana walking around, talking with different people. One by one the men she speaks to walk up to the stage. For some reason, a guy wearing glasses catches my attention. Maybe it was the fact that he stood up on his own, without prompting from Lana. Or maybe it's because he's tall and handsome, walking with a confident

Heart of Gold

stride towards me. Whatever it is, I'm intrigued. I can feel his gaze slowly taking my body in. I focus my eyes and senses on him.

He shouts up at me on stage. I lean down, trying to hear him above the music. He tries again.

"You a real cowgirl?"

I laugh. "You a real cowboy?" I respond flippantly.

He laughs also and returns to his seat. I notice him motion a waitress over and watch him whisper something in her ear. After my dance is finally over I get off stage. The waitress approaches me.

"That man wants you at his table."

"After Lana dances. I have something I have to do."

"I'll tell him." I nod and she walks off.

I run to the DJ to tell him to play some country music for Lana too. She never dances to country so this will be fun. As she gets up on stage she shoots me a dirty look. I burst out laughing as I give her a thumbs-up.

Lana dances. I walk around, mingling with the crowd.

Before long, I have several clients headed in her direction, spurring her on. I take the time to finally approach the gentleman with the glasses who had tipped me earlier.

"Barbie, right?"

"Yep. Got a buck or two?"

"For you or her?"

"Depends."

"Two of those twenty's came from me."

"Thank you."

"What kind of game are you two playing?"

"Game?" I feign innocence, which seems to amuse him.

"Yes, Barbie, what game is this?"

I laugh, "You're smarter than the average bear."

"I've been around."

"Me too."

He nods. "I can tell. What ended you in this place?"

"I did."

Rebecca Nietert

He laughed. "No, you didn't do this but I would wager you feel like you have to."

"Okay bud, are you a psycho-therapist or something?"

He smirks. "Hit too close to home?"

"I've got to go."

"I understand." He tips his beer to toast me.

"You're rather arrogant."

"So are you, Little Lady, so are you." He walks off toward the men's restroom.

"What's your name?" I shout at him.

"You already said it." He shouts back.

I think for a moment. "Bud?"

"Buddy!" He disappears.

After Lana exits the stage we meet up in the DJ booth and decide to get more drinks at the bar.

"This was fun!" I shout over the music as we take our seats.

"Yes it was!" She laughs

"So how does it feel to make all your money on stage?"

"Good! I can go home now?"

I laugh and nod in approval, "Yes you can."

She hugs me tight. "Thank you. I needed this!"

"Me too. I don't get to see you enough anymore."

"I know!" She shouts above the music. "It's not fair!"

"Well the only way we could get away with it would be to leave town..." I offer with a smile.

"Yeah! Remember that one time you asked me to go to Chicago?"

"Yes. Why?"

"Let's go! I want to take a road trip."

"Really?" I look at her, surprised she even remembered!

"Really! It will give me a break from the stupid hotel. I always feel like a real person when you're around."

"Me too! I'm so glad you feel that way and I'm not the only one!" I smile and take a sip of the drink the bartender brought.

Heart of Gold

"What we have isn't right is it?"

I look at her, confused. "What do you mean?"

"I mean our men. They aren't right. If they were, we would want to be with them, right?"

"No, I think we just enjoy each other more. We can still have them but let's not lose us okay? I'll organize the trip."

"You will? You'll go?!" She smiles that smile that lights up the room. I remember wanting to protect her way back when we first became friends. Part of me still wants to.

"Yes! Now all I have to do is convince Joseph..." We both look at each other, knowing how hard that's going to be. We nod and say in unison, "Good luck." We both burst out laughing.

Going back home will be bittersweet. The few memories I have from my childhood aren't ones I want to hold on to. I especially don't want to remember my mother's bursts of outrage that led to abandonment of her family and abuse of every male relationship she's ever had. Yes, she rescued me from Phillip, but that was a one-time deal. I still remember her being immensely self-centered and extremely demanding. She was outraged because the choices that she made left her abandoned and fraught with challenges she didn't want or expect.

Lonnie, my stepfather and she were married for about a few years. He wasn't there long and she controlled him thoroughly. They had a son and named him Eddie. My mother didn't want any extra burden and ended up abandoning both of them as well as she did my sisters and me.

I've heard is that Lonnie has tried to make his son feel valued. Secretly, I've always wondered what it feels like to have a father who wants you to feel valued. It's not like I've had any male role models in my life. Or good ones at least.

My father left my mother when she was just a teenager. He saddled her with three babies before he did. That and the fact that her immediate family lived well beneath the poverty level left her a nervous wreck. So much that when I was a small child she did have

Rebecca Nietert

a breakdown. She spent 14 years of her life ruined by what that man did to her.

Yes, she married Lonnie for the security that her first husband didn't give her. Lonnie is a good man, but not good enough to make her happy. She wanted the passion I believe I have with Joseph because she desperately sought sexual rendezvous with men.

Her hypersexual behavior created a reputation that I couldn't escape and I've never wanted to go back to that small town because of it.

Lonnie adored their son. When Eddie was about nine, mom decided she wanted a whole new life. She was evolving and as she did she left her son behind with Lonnie.

My mother told me that she had an affair when she was married to the man who believed he was my father. He abandoned her when he found out. There's a whole story behind all that I am not privy to.

My father married Mary and they had 2 children, Lisa and Daniel. Lisa died in a fiery auto accident at the age of 16. That marriage didn't last. He married Cathy but they never had children and then he married Brenda and adopted a baby girl.

My father and my mother had Lynette, me, and my sister Shirley who died in a car accident at the age of nineteen.

I remember my family being trashy. Honestly, I am not quite sure I am any better than any one of them.

Heart of Gold

29

"Joseph, I need to ask you something."

"What is it?" He looks up reluctantly from watching TV, sounding annoyed.

"Lana and I are driving to Chicago to see my family. Want to come?"

He looks at me as if I'm insane. "I don't want to see your family."

Confused, I blink a few times, unsure if I heard right. "But...why not?"

He turns back to face the TV. "Have no desire to meet them. That's your deal."

"My deal?" I walk to the TV and shut it off, then turn around to face him.

He looks up at me and sighs, "Look Bev, we are together as long as you want to be here. I told you that, remember? You can share my life as long as you want to and I won't ever ask you to leave. I just don't really want to meet your family."

"Oh." I look down, taking the full weight of the conversation in. "Then you won't mind if I go?"

"Nope."

"Wow." I whisper, mostly to myself.

"When?"

"When what?" I look at him, confused.

"When are you going? Goodness, you have to keep up!" I flinch at the frustration in his voice. Maybe he had a bad day at work...

"Hello." I look over to see Connie walking in the room.

"I'm going to Chicago in a few days."

"Oh?" She responds then looks over at Joseph, "Are you going too?"

"No."

Connie looks from him to me, "Why?"

"To see my family."

"Why aren't you going?" She looks at Joseph. He looks at her as if she's lost two heads.

"Because your classes start soon, remember?"

"Classes?" I look at both of them.

"Connie asked me to be her birth coach in the delivery room."

"Really?" I look at Connie.

She nods, "Yep." She answered without feeling any guilt about it.

I'm not sure what hurts more, the fact that she doesn't seem to feel guilty at all or the fact that Joseph obviously picked her over me. Either way, I'm not happy. Doesn't she have some other girlfriend who she can call to take the class with her? I'm not opening that can of worms. I just shrug and walk out the room, leaving them alone and call Lana.

"How does Friday sound?"

"We really are going?!"

"Yes." I can't help but smile at her excitement.

"I'm so excited! Can I bring my dog? I won't be able to leave him alone."

"Absolutely! Make sure to get some doggie downers though."

"I'm on it. This is going to be so much fun!"

"Yes, it will. I've got to run and make some stay-over plans."

"Okay! See you tonight?"

"I'm only supposed to work during the day, Sweetie."

"I know, but please. I miss you!"

"I'll see what I can do. See you then." We both giggle and hang up.

Next, I call Lonnie. "Hello?"

"Well a fine howdy-do!" He answers. I laugh.

Heart of Gold

Eddie picks up the other receiver, "Hello sis!"

"What would you two think about me coming to stay with you for a few days?"

"LaNette won't let you stay with her?" Lonnie asks.

"Maybe. Should I call her?"

"You called us first?" Eddie asks.

"Yes, stupid!" Lonnie growls over the other line. "It's fine if you stay here. Is it just you or is that cowboy coming too?"

"Well..." I sigh, "He's not coming but a tall, six-foot blonde friend of mine is. That okay?"

"Great!" Eddie shouts. I can't help but laugh.

"Hormones?" I ask Lonnie.

"Yep. Sixteen and got them bad."

"Hey!" Eddie shouts over the receiver.

"I'm leaving on Friday so I will be there some time on Saturday."

"Sounds good!" Lonnie responds.

"Great! See you two then. Hey Eddie, how's it been going? Have you talked to mom lately?"

"No. I want to but I never know what to say to her."

"All you have to do is say you miss her. That will open up a conversation."

"Are you two getting along now?"

"Sort-of. We're working on being friends again." I'm not about to tell them what happened when I left Phillip. They probably wouldn't believe me anyway.

There's an awkward silence on the other line. "What's she like?" Lonnie's voice is soft.

"She's happy. I'm so sorry, Lonnie. I didn't mean to imply she wasn't happy with you."

"I'll let you two talk." I flinch as he hangs up the phone. Oops.

"I'm so sorry. I didn't mean to hurt him."

"He's mostly over her. What is she like?"

Rebecca Nietert

"Well, as far as I know she's really happy. She smiles all the time and seems to have more patience. She asks about you a lot."

"Really? Or are you just saying that?"

"Really! How can a mother not miss her only son?"

"I get mad sometimes because she just gave me up without a fight. I was just a kid."

"You wanted to live with your father and she wanted a new life. She let you make a decision that would make you happy."

"I know." His voice is soft. "I hurt her when I said I wanted to live with Dad."

"Yes, but no one blames you. She's had to make some changes to her life, just like the rest of us."

"I guess so...I miss her."

"You two really need each other don't you? How long has it been anyway?"

"Well she left when I was eight."

"You need to call her."

"Why? It's not like she sends me birthday cards or anything."

"Maybe the pain you are feeling is exactly what she feels. She's human you know." I want to say that men have been her greatest disappointment, so she feared that she might as well lose him too, but I shut my mouth. That will only cause more damage. "Maybe. I'll call her." I can hear his voice cracking.

It breaks my heart to hear him cry. I sniff and force myself to pull it together.

"No tears when you do. Stand firm when you speak and she'll respect you more for it. She doesn't handle crying well."

"I know. You ever think about Shirley?"

"Yes, why?" I shut down the painful memories that threaten to arise. I'm not going there right now.

"Cause I do too. I think about when we all lived up here while you and LaNette were in Houston."

"Really?" I haven't thought about those days in a long time. "What do you think about?"

Heart of Gold

"All the nice times we had."

That's funny, I don't remember many nice times growing up. I'm glad he can remember some though.

"You can have them again, Sweetie. Just call her okay?"

"I will. So I will see you Saturday then?"

"Yes. Are you excited?"

"Yup, I can't wait! You were always there for me sis."

I can't help the pain from starting to form in my chest. The regrets and lies start to form in my head. All the times I've had to lie to him because of Phillip's controlling nature. All the times I wasn't really there but pretended to be, just so he could have a lifeline that I never had. All the times I had to cover for why I couldn't call back or talk late. If only you knew...

"Hey, maybe you can come see me play in my band?" His voice breaks me out of my reverie.

"You play in a band now?"

"Yep! Remember that first guitar you bought me? You were with Phillip. I used it and taught myself how to play."

"Phillip. Yeah I remember."

That guitar had been one of the rare presents I've been able to give him. Since Phillip wanted a studio, I found two guitars for the price of one at a garage sale. He wasn't happy at the quality but I used the low quality as an excuse to "give it away to someone in need." Little did he know I gave one to Eddie and kept the other one.

"Yes, I will come see you play."

"Awesome! See you then Saturday."

"Tell Lonnie I'm so sorry again okay?"

"I will. Bye sis."

I lean my head against the wall and sigh, needing to breathe for just a moment, to clear my head. Yes, I told Eddie I think about her often. Truth is, I don't. I haven't thought about her in a long time. Honestly, I don't know why I said that I have; it just slipped out. I didn't have the heart to tell him that since mom had difficulties with men, she thought it would be better off for the both of them if he wasn't around. I feel the tears stream down my face and wipe them with the back of my hand. Pull yourself together! You can't live like this! She's gone and there's nothing you can do about it. Focus. Focus! I look at my phone and dial Lana's number.

"It's all set up. We can stay at my ex-stepfather's place. It's just him and my younger half-brother living there."

"Good! I'm glad we don't have to stay in a hotel. I, for one, won't be able to afford it anyway."

"Friday we'll leave early, okay? I'll pick you up."

"That sounds great. See you then!"

After hanging up with Lana, I realize that I need to at least tell my mother about the conversation with Eddie. She deserves to know. I stare at her number in my phone, contemplating how I'm going to go about this. She needs to talk with Eddie again but she's stubborn. Looks like I'm going to be walking a tightrope with this one. The phone rings for what seems like an eternity. Finally, she answers.

"Mom, I have some news."

"What is it?"

"Well..." Here goes nothing. "I just got off the phone with Eddie."

Time seems to stop. I can feel the tension from the weight of what I just said.

She finally answers softly, "Yeah?"

"And he really misses you."

"Really?" She sounds surprised. "What about his father?"

I roll my eyes. Why is it always about men? "It's not a contest. He loves you too."

"It was once, Beverly. Besides, Eddie chose his dad and didn't want anything to do with me."

"Well, actually that's not exactly true. He did choose to live with Lonnie but he never thought you would move twelve hundred miles away either."

Heart of Gold

"What does it matter? He doesn't care."

I can hear the frustration in her voice rising. I've got to calm her down. "He does, mom. He cares more than you know. This isn't a husband who abandoned you; this is your son. Your only son."

I can tell that softened her mood.

"I know. I just feel like so much time has passed. He probably hates me now."

"Remember your dad?"

"Of course. What does he have to do with this?" I say wondering why she changed to another subject.

"He abandoned me. Yet after all this time I have no hard feelings. I didn't need him then and I don't need him now. You didn't need him either."

"Mom, that's not true! Look, Eddie doesn't need you to tie his shoes or pick out his clothes, but he does need you to be his mother."

"And just what can I do for him? After all these years?"

"Let him know he's loved! He's sixteen now. He needs it now more than ever"

There's a moment of silence. "Is he really that old?" The sadness in her voice breaks my heart.

"Yes," I respond softly, "He is. Please call him?"

"He really wants me to?"

"Yes, he even cried."

"Oh my God...I don't want to hurt him anymore than I have."

"I know. Just call him, okay?"

"Okay, I will. Thanks honey."

"Not a problem. Listen, Lana and I are taking a road trip to see him. I told him you would call so do it before I get up there okay? I don't want to break my promise to him."

"Okay I will. You and Lana have fun. When are you going?"

"This weekend."

"Is Joseph going? I heard Don won't let you stay with them. Where will you stay?"

Rebecca Nietert

"No, Joseph's not coming but we are staying with Eddie." I ignore the comment about LaNette's husband not wanting us to stay over. I never liked the guy anyway.

"Good. Don't let Don get to you!"

"I won't. He can't hurt me anymore. We're leaving Friday so if you need me call up there, okay?"

"I will. Thanks for calling, Bev."

"You're welcome. Now call Eddie." I hiss facetiously, trying to provide some much-needed humor.

She laughs and agrees. I hang up and sigh. Well, that went better than expected.

There isn't much time to get ready for the trip. Over the next few days I scramble to get a manicure, go tanning and get some much-needed things for the car ride. I get my truck looked at, making sure that we won't end up stranded in the middle of nowhere. Good thing I got it checked because it's been a while since I put oil in it.

The conversation with Eddie keeps ringing in my ears. I've come to the conclusion that the reason I can't trust my gut feeling is because they've always proved to be wrong. Since I come from a family who abused trust time and time again, it's natural to feel comfortable knowing that I need to watch my back, no matter what happens around the corner. It's what I've done all my life and I'm not sure how to stop.

This trip will give me pause to think. I can already tell it's going to be more than just some fun in the Sun with Lana. It's going to be a trip that will change my life. I can't wait to see my life through Lana's eyes. Maybe she will be able to help clear some things up.

Heart of Gold

30

Over the past few days Joseph has been moping around the house. I've been working nights with Lana to make some extra money for our trip to Chicago. He doesn't seem to be liking the fact that I'm making money and that I'm taking it all with me on the trip. I look over a Connie who looks at Joseph leaving the room, then back at me.

"What's up with the tension between you two?"

"Yeah. I guess he doesn't want me to go."

"Why do you think that is?"

"Because he wants me here with him?" I offer.

"Well, he's a control freak, as you already know. It doesn't help that you're going with Lana either."

"What do you mean? He's okay with Lana. He even said that it's fine for us to go together, so I don't know why there's such a problem."

"Is that what you think or what he told you?"

"Well...both. Why?"

"He told me he doesn't care for her too much. He doesn't say anything because he doesn't want to hurt you."

"He doesn't like her?" I can't help but feel the hurt start to set in.

"Nope. Can you understand why?"

"No. Stop beating around the bush and tell me."

"Lana doesn't like Joseph and he knows it. I don't think she's as great of a friend to you as you think she is."

"What?! You don't know what you're talking about."

"Listen, any woman who doesn't understand that her man comes first has no business being a friend."

Rebecca Nietert

"Lana has never come between me and a man and she never will. What happens between Joseph and I is our business."

"You'll see, Beverly. She isn't all that you think she is." I look at her. Why does she sound so jealous? Lana and I are always going to be close. Is she jealous of that? I decide to change the subject.

"When are you moving out after the baby is born?"

"Joseph has given me six months after Jeremy is born."

"Jeremy? When did you know it was a boy?"

"Since my Amniocentesis test."

"Are you excited?"

"Yes and no. Curt always wanted a little girl. I want to have part of him. A girl would have put us back together. A girl would have fixed everything."

"I'm sorry he left you here. Do you miss him?" Wondering if she knows that I know about the boss. The whole story.

"God Beverly, sometimes you can be so cold. Of course I miss him! We're having a freaking baby together!"

I decide to turn the other cheek with that comment. "Have you talked to him?"

"Yes. He doesn't think it's his."

"Is there a chance he's right?"

"A chance, but I know in my heart it's his. I only wanted his children; I never wanted my boss's."

"Well, sounds like you really have done it to yourself."

"Yeah, I guess." She starts to cry. I roll my eyes.

"What did you do to her?!" I jump at the sound of Joseph screaming, footsteps pounding the ground as he walks to Connie.

"I didn't do anything!" I shout back.

Connie is just sitting there, sobbing.

"I swear!" I roll my eyes again.

"Well then, why is she crying?!"

I look at the two of them. Joseph bends down to hold Connie and looks into her eyes, "What did she say?"

Heart of Gold

When Connie tells him, his eyes fly up to focus towards me. "How dare you!"

"Look, Joseph. I love you. I love her and this baby. I didn't mean to hurt her! She's crying because of what this Curt did to her, not what I did. If she has anyone to blame it's herself!" I storm out of the room and head into my bedroom.

A few minutes later Joseph walks in, seeming much calmer than before. "You don't have to do that. She already feels bad enough."

"Joseph, if it came to her or me which woman would you choose?"

"I won't make that choice. I'm her friend and always will be."

"And what am I to you then?"

"You're part of my life."

"Well, I have feelings too."

"I know you do but you're being a big baby. You think I need to tell you all the time that you matter to me. I told you once. I'm not your babysitter nor am I the person who should be picking you up emotionally all the time. What you did to Connie was plain mean to make yourself feel better. Does that work for you?"

"All I did was talk to her. I asked her questions; that's what friends do. I didn't want to hurt her and she knows it. Besides, I think she wants you back."

"She wants me to take care of her and that's exactly what I'm doing."

"And if that requires more?"

"Beverly." He walks up and puts his hand on my chin, making me look into his eyes. "I love her but I love you too."

His gaze melts me. "I know, I love that about you. But I can't help but think that you two have something going on. You came to her rescue as if I wounded her. We both know I never would because I care about her. You have never rescued me and you never will."

"You don't know that. I haven't had the chance."

Rebecca Nietert

"No! You charged me guilty before the trial. You always do that with the two of us."

"I promise I won't do it again."

"Look, I know better than anyone else about how guilty you feel for your relationship with her. You have got to get passed that."

"I know. I feel like she needs this from me."

"I know you do. I'm happy to help but my God, Joseph! She eats us out of house and home. We pay for her room and board and everything else. All she takes care of is her medical insurance for the baby. I can't cut anymore for her. My benevolent act is going to end us in the poor house."

"No it won't. I'll do more jobs. The air conditioning season is approaching. I'll go into that and make us some money. Before long all our bills will be paid off."

"That would help. It would help too if your attitude towards me going to Chicago would improve too. You're walking around like you've been wounded."

"I don't want you to go."

"Why not?"

"Because I don't think you should be around Lana that long. That's all."

"Lana can't influence what happens between you and I. Only you can do that."

His blue orbs meet mine. "You mean it?"

"Absolutely. I love you." I give him a quick kiss, which he returns.

"Thanks, love you too. Listen, I've got to run. I'm meeting the guys for a beer."

"Have fun. I'm packing and will leave first thing in the morning. If I don't see you tonight, be careful."

"Will do."

I walk out into the living area and spot Connie reading a book. I walk quietly, not sure if I should say anything or not. Better to be safe than sorry.

Heart of Gold

"I'm really sorry if I hurt you." She doesn't look up.

"That's fine, I'm okay. I'm going to call him and try to work things out. Frankly you helped. I've been so mad at him, I couldn't even think about him. Now I can at least do that."

"I'm glad. I'm leaving in the morning."

"I know, Joseph told me. Are you going out with him tonight?"

"No, I need to pack."

"Oh? I thought..." She let's the thought trail off.

"Thought what?"

"I thought that you would want to go since Sally will be there."

"What?!"

"Well, Joseph's friends and family are gathering. Tommy's wife, Sara, asked Sally to come too. She doesn't exactly like you."

"Exactly? What does that mean? She doesn't know me."

"Well, she hates that Joseph gave up Sally for you. She hates that you take off your clothes. To her, you're nothing more than a common whore. Of course, she doesn't really care about Joseph either."

"Then why does it matter who he's with? Why is she there then?"

"You know Joseph; All the women of his past are in his present too. He loves them all. He told me that he doesn't care if Sally goes or not, that he loves you and that's all that matters."

"Still, she's going to be there. This is so wrong! Joseph said he was going out with the boys. He lied!"

"Yes, Joseph lies. You should know that by now."

"Did she have a problem with you?"

"No one ever has a problem with me. The difference between you and I is that you say what is on your mind. I'm more purposeful about my words."

"Sounds like you're more manipulating about what you want."

"No, I just get what I want because I'm not immature about it." She retorts.

Rebecca Nietert

"Okay, so Sara hates me. Joseph is going to a party with Sally and a woman who hates me. Why are you telling me this as if it's something that's okay with you?"

"Joseph would tell you if he intended to do anything."

"What's your relationship with Tommy and Sara now?"

"After our affair ended we all became the best of friends."

"Affair? You and Tommy slept together? While he was married to Sara?"

"Yes, I thought Joseph told you that already or I wouldn't have."

"Did she find out?"

"No, she never once suspected. I gave myself to him one night for his birthday and then after that a few times. He was fun but I didn't want him permanently."

"And Sara is your best friend?"

"She is now. She wasn't at first but after I moved in to their house we became friends. I decided if we were sleeping together it would be in all of our best interest if we stopped."

"Wow. I don't think I would've had the courage to do something like that right under someone's nose. But I have to say, after hearing she hates me without even knowing me, she probably deserved it."

"No, she doesn't. She's conservative but she's really nice. Give her a chance; you might like her."

"I doubt it. I can't be a friend with someone who judges me so unjustly, so quickly. It won't happen."

"Whatever. I have to go to bed. I'm exhausted."

"Okay, I'm going to finish packing. Thanks for the information."

"Not a problem. Goodnight." She walks off to her room.

I go back to my room and sit on the edge of the bed, lost in thought. Why would Connie tell me such stories? For a woman who's rumored to be put together well, she seems a bit shady to me? I can't imagine that a woman would let a man shoot at her.

Heart of Gold

Phillip had threatened me many times but that was it. Also, how can she be so passionately obsessed with him? Add to the pile that she slept with her best friend's husband, and I can't seem to trust her judgment. Joseph is out with Sally and "the guys." He just lied to my face, as he's done many times before. I can't help but be reminded of Phillip when thinking about him. How has my life come to this, with this kind of people in it? I don't know who to trust anymore.

Rebecca Nietert

31

Friday morning comes and I still haven't talked to Joseph. I pick up my small suitcase and head out the door. I feel a wave of excitement course through my veins as I close the truck door. This trip is going to be exactly what I need! I need a fresh perspective; a fresh start. I just want to feel free again. I roll the window down, enjoying the rush of wind blasting my face. I can't wait to be away from every shackle that binds me down. Away from a life of chaos. Of confusion.

I pull up in the driveway and honk the horn. Lana pushes back curtains and motions me inside through the window. As I walk in I notice the place is a mess! The kitchen is filled with empty dishes stacked in the sink haphazardly. I notice Lana's bags are packed by the door, ready to go, but can smell the lingering passion hanging thick in the air.

"Had a great time last night, eh?" I tease.

"You bet I did! I'm going to think about him the whole time on this trip!" She blushes.

I look at her, Is she going to back out? "You have to go."

"Oh, I'm going. I'm not happy about it but I'm going."

"We are going to have such a great time!"

"I know, but we both know I could be getting laid every night!" She sits down in a kitchen chair and sighs longingly.

"Poor you. You have to go on a road trip with your best friend." I mock and laugh.

"He'll be here when you get back."

"True." She stands up and grabs her bags.

"So, guess what?"

"What?" She looks at me as I open the door.

Heart of Gold

"I had the most powerful feeling of freedom when I left to come here."

"Really? That's interesting."

That's all she has to say? I unlock the car. "What does that mean?"

"Wait! I forgot something!" She throws her stuff in the back of the truck and runs inside, appearing moments later. She has a can of dog food and a spoon in hand, along with a bottle of pills. In the other hand she has her dog, Alphy, and a bowl. She puts the bowl on the ground, opens the can and puts the pill in with the food.

"I forgot Alphy hasn't eaten yet. Poor baby." After Alphy finishes eating, Lana picks up the bowl and dog and runs inside. She runs back out with the dog in one arm and opens the car door. "Sorry about that."

I shake my head, "Not a problem. What was that pill anyway?

"Doggie Downers!" She puts Alphy in the backseat. We both laugh as I exit the driveway.

"So really, tell me what you think the feeling I had means."

She sighs as she adjusts her seat, "We've been over this; you know what I think. You want to be free of Joseph and you know it."

"You really think I want to be free of him?"

"I think you're tired of being his little sex toy and you're beginning to see the light."

"Okay, what's the difference between me wanting to be with Joseph sexually and you with Rod?"

"I don't want anything more from Rod. I'm fine with what we have. I don't have any illusions about how this should all turn out."

I reach back to pet Alphy, keeping one hand on the steering wheel.

"Since Connie moved in you want a kid now don't you?"

I look over at her, shocked that she would mention that.

She laughs, "I know you better than anyone."

"Well, who says he can't give it to me?"

Rebecca Nietert

"He does. He told you nada, nothing, never going to happen. What part of that don't you understand?"

"Like that makes me feel any better!" I snap.

"I'll do anything to break into that outer shell you have towards anyone who tells you the truth!"

"Is that dog going to sleep?" I ask, trying to change the subject.

"Not going to work, Bev. While we're this truck you're all mine so you're going to listen."

"Fine. Whatever! But is the doggie downer going to put him out or just wipe him out?"

"I don't know since this is the first time I've used them. I hope they'll make him sleep but he's pretty tough."

Silence fills the air so I focus on driving, trying to block out the nagging voice in my head that knows she's telling the truth. We start to talk about work, clients and people in cars passing by.

"What do you think my problem is?" I finally feel comfortable enough to try to finish up our prior conversation.

"You don't have a problem, Beverly. You think you're the only one with a rough road."

"I do not! There are others who have it harder than I do."

"But you're always so surprised when things happen to you. It's as if you think you have nothing to do with your choices. I don't mean to be harsh. I really don't. You're always so darn surprised when bad crap happens to you."

I'm taken back to when I was little, hungry and crying, begging my mom to let me come back inside. The door slams shut. Meeting him. The love in the air, the nice presents and fancy cars. The money. The luxury. For a brief instant, I'm back in time. Back to Phillip.

"Sometimes I didn't."

Almost as though she read my mind, Lana asks, "Why did you start dancing?"

"Because Phillip and I made a deal." I say softly, barely able to get the words out.

Heart of Gold

"No!" I jump at the sudden outburst, "You started dancing because you were starving and without options. You chose what you thought was the best option at that time. Look what it's done for you!"

"Oh yeah, done for me?" I hiss. "I'm with a guy who sees all his ex-whoever they are. I dance for a living. I hate what I do but can't get out because nothing else I could possibly do would make me this much money."

She sighs, frustration laced in her words, "You don't get it. I can't understand how you just don't get this stuff on your own."

"What is it that I don't get?"

"That you're confident now and weren't back then. That no one can tell you to do something you're not willing to do. You're pretty, nice, and smart. If you chose to you could accomplish anything. Probably better than anyone else I know. Heck, even better than me! Phillip gave that to you and you chose to let him. You danced Beverly. It's not like he put a gun to your head."

The memory of that one time echoes in my mind. The gun. The threats. His voice. If you leave I'll kill you! I shake my head, blurring the memory from existence. I've never told Lana or anyone. I like to pretend that it never happened. Maybe it really is my imagination? Maybe that's something I wish I had gone through, just so I'll have a way out? I'll never know. I look over at Lana.

"He might as well have," I lie. "I believed what he told me and trusted him when I shouldn't have." At least that part is true. "I thought he wanted to help me because he loved me."

"You painted a picture in your mind that wasn't there. You want to believe that your romantic visions in your own head are reality and they're not. When you realize that your goals or dreams about your relationships don't iron out, you're dumbfounded. Can't you see the pattern?"

"I see that I'm goal-driven. I mean...I try to get men who choose me for me."

Rebecca Nietert

    You've spent your whole life letting people come to you, telling you what you need. Then, because you want to be accepted and feel guilty for not being able to repay them, you try to help by fixing their issues. It's like your benevolent acts are going to put them in your debt, which would make them stay. It's like you want to earn eternal love from them. You haven't learned anything! The men you choose aren't worth the time and effort you give them. Once you realize that you don't have what you thought you did, you try to wipe the slate clean and start over."

    "I do get a lot out of helping people. It just...makes me feel good I guess."

    "Yes, I do know, but you're helping people because it helps you."

    "How in the world did helping Phillip ever help me?"

    "He made you who you are today. Do you think anyone can tell you now that you can't take care of yourself?"

    "No."

    "Are you afraid of any man now?"

    "No." I laugh at the absurdity of her question.

    "See! He gave that to you."

    "I can see that but what about Rob, the one who was Jewish?"

    "I don't know what happened there. I think he took advantage of you. Wasn't he a lot older or something?"

    "Yeah, he was."

    "Did he choose you or did you choose him?"

    "He chose me."

    "Did Joseph choose you?"

    "Yes." I lean my head back against the headrest, thinking.

    "You let guys tell you what they need and you bend over backwards for the, You think you're earning their respect but you're actually losing it. They know you'll do anything for their 'love' so they use you. The fact that you don't respect yourself makes it easier on them."

    "I respect myself!"

Heart of Gold

"No, you don't! It's as if you don't have a mind of your own once a guy has you.

Would you honestly let Joseph treat you the same way if you really respected yourself?"

I think for a moment, knowing full well that she's telling the truth. I need to get my thoughts lined up with hers. I shake my head in defeat, "What exactly does he do to me?"

"From what you've told me, he parades you around in front of his friends. It's as if he only likes to be seen with you when he's with his friends."

I shrug; we are with his friends a lot. "And why is that bad?"

"He's showing you off! You're his possession, not his girlfriend. You allow him to treat you that way."

"I'm just trying to be sensible, honest and trustworthy."

"And when you are you lose their respect. You have no backbone and don't tell them what you want."

"Why can't I get past this?"

"Because you fear their abandonment more than you fear being their personal doormat."

"Do you really think I'm a doormat?"

"I think you are a personal trophy for Joseph."

A trophy? "Really?" Her words sting as if she had slapped me in the face.

"Yes, and until you believe in yourself you will let him treat you anyway he wants."

"I don't think so."

"Oh you will; I know you. What scares me about all of this is that you're asking for friends to tell you but when we tell you, you refuse to listen. You're not paying any attention to any of us! You just don't want to accept the fact that Joseph isn't perfect for you."

I flinch at the weight of her words, "You're right."

"And when you're much older, your chance for real marriage and children will come along. Too bad you;ll miss it because you'll be too hurt and angry with me and everyone else for 'not helping you'. When, in reality, we've been here all along."

"I will never be angry with you Lana! I can see us sitting on some rocking chairs when we are eighty and laughing about stupid jerks like Joseph." I laugh at the thought.

She smiles, "You finally admit it! He's a jerk. That's the first step to recovery! Well done my friend!"

"Recovery?" I pause for a moment then laugh, "Oh, I get it! I'm a love-a-holic."

"More like a princess-a-holic. Man, you've you got it bad!"

"Do you really think Joseph won't ever marry me?"

She laughs, "You've got to be kidding."

I laugh too. Up until now, I didn't think of the possibility that Joseph and I would never have a life together. If we aren't going to have a life together, why am I wasting my time on him? Because you love him, dummy! It's true; I love him. I love how magnificent he is in my eyes. He makes me feel special when we're alone together. He's different than other men I've dated, especially Phillip. He doesn't talk bad about people. He doesn't hit or verbally abuse me. He's so down-to-earth and doesn't care about putting on airs. He's all about love and making someone feel special in the moment they are together. I can't help that he makes me feel like a princess; the very thing I've longed for ever since I was a little girl. He's my Prince Charming. I glance over at Lana. Is it possible that she's right?

Heart of Gold

32

Before long we are crossing the Illinois state line. It's dark by the time we get close to the Chicago area. Once we connect with Route 47 towards Wisconsin, I wake Lana up.

"We are almost there."

"How much longer?" She yawns, wiping the sleep from her eyes.

"Not much." I glance in the back, "The dog has been great."

"Yes, he has. Thanks for bringing me."

"No, thank you for coming. For your advice too."

"It helped?"

I nod and smile at her, "Immensely."

"Good. Are you thinking about leaving him?"

"No, but I'm definitely thinking about an ultimatum."

"Like what?"

"I'm not sure, still thinking about it."

She laughs which makes me laugh. "Another time, let's just have some fun."

She looks around. The darkness covers the sky, shrouding the fact that one can see for miles on these Illinois streets in the daytime. I can barely make out the beginning of row-to-row corn stalks.

"Having fun now? There's absolutely nothing but farm houses out here!"

I laugh, "You haven't seen anything yet."

Finally, we arrive at Second Street. I park in Lonnie's driveway. It's good to be back. We bring our things to the front door.

"There isn't anything here. This is...desolate!"

Rebecca Nietert

I laugh again. "This is huge compared to when I left. I think only eight-hundred people lived here back then."

Lana shakes her head in amazement, "I don't know how you did it." I knock on the door. Lonnie answers and smiles as the door opens.

"Hello Beverly!" He wraps me in a bear hug. I hug him back.

"Hello." I step inside and gesture towards Lana. "This is Lana, the one I told you about."

"Hello Lana." He said extends a hand to greet her.

"It's a pleasure."

"Is Eddie still up?" I look down the hallway longingly.

"No, but you can see him in the morning. I have blankets and pillows all ready for you on the couch."

"Great! We can get settled in ourselves. Go back to bed."

"I will. I'm tired." He laughs modestly.

"Good night." Lana smiles and waves as Lonnie walks away.

I take Lana into the living room where two vinyl-orange sofas are set up, the bed part open with pillows and blankets intact. "These were in Lonnie's mother's basement when I was a kid."

"You don't call him dad?" She starts to unpack some things from her bag.

"No. Once I called him dad when I was a kid but when he and mom got divorced, I didn't really know what to call him. We both ended up settling on just calling him Lonnie. It's just easier that way."

After some idle chit-chat we lay down for some much-needed rest from the long ride.

"Oh my God!" My eyes snap open to the sound of a scream, "I'm so sorry!" I listen, quickly realizing that the voice belongs to Lana. I get up and run down the hallway and stop when I see her walking towards me, hand over her mouth.

"I walked in on him!" She mouths. I look at her and can't help but laugh a bit.

"It's okay. Lonnie you okay?" I shout towards the closed door.

Heart of Gold

"Yeah, not used to ladies here that's all."

I wave her toward me, "It's okay. Did you see anything?" I giggle.

"No!" She hisses and softly hits my arm. "Gees, Beverly. I swear!"

I laugh, "So what are you doing up this early anyway?" I look at the clock: it reads 6 A.M.

"Well, Alphy kept me up all night with his constant whining and wanting to go outside." She rolls her eyes and glares at the dog, who looks up at her innocently. "Yeah, that's right. I'm talking about you!" The dog just sits there.

"Then you walked in on Lonnie?"

"Yeah, I had to go to the bathroom..." She looks away, face starting to turn red.

"I'm so embarrassed!"

"No need to be." In the corner of my eye I see a silhouette at the edge of the room. I turn around, recognizing the deep voice as one I heard days ago on the phone.

"Eddie!" I can't contain my excitement and run up to him, squishing him in a hug. He smiles and hugs me back.

Before he can say anything back, Lonnie walks up behind him.

"Looks like everyone's awake. Let's get some breakfast."

"Fine with me." I look at Lana who smiles, "You need help?"

"Nope. You don't know how to cook anyway."

"Would you believe I know how to cook a lot of things now?" I offer.

Lonnie leers at me, trying to see if I'm telling the truth or not.

"You're kidding, right?"

"Nope! Joseph taught me new tricks." I look into his eyes, challenging him.

"Joseph, huh? Well, we will have to test that out." He walks to the kitchen. Score!

Lonnie, zero; Beverly, one. I smile and follow him.

Rebecca Nietert

"Well, even if you don't believe me, you should see Lana! Her soup is out-of-this-world!" Lana giggles modestly.

Lonnie looks at her.

"That good? We'll certainly let her cook if she wants to."

"I'm sure you'll love it! What can I do?"

"Go take your shower, I'm fine here. If Eddie gets in there first neither of you will have hot water."

I laugh and walk back toward the living area where Lana and Eddie are conversing.

"I need a few more things out of the car that I forgot to get earlier. Eddie, will you help?"

"You Texas girls can't do anything for yourselves can you?"

"Fine!" I walk out the door and grab a few things that had fallen out of my bag. One of them was shampoo. I noticed last night, but was too tired to go back and grab it. When I return to the door Eddie is holding the screen door open.

"Sorry, I didn't think you would take me seriously. "

I walk through the doorway.

"Become kind of aggressive, have we?" He laughs as I dump my stuff onto the sofa bed.

"Nah, I was kidding. I can't be mad at you."

"I know." He smiles, then looks towards the doorway to the kitchen, "She's really nice."

"Lana?"

"No, the dog." He says sarcastically.

"The dog is a he. And yes, she really is."

"And pretty." He adds.

I look at him, "You like her?"

"Who wouldn't? She's gorgeous."

"Yes, she is."

Lana walks into the room and I smile at Eddie, who gives me a "better-not-say-anything" look. I look back at Lana, "Get your stuff to shower. Lonnie says we won't have hot water if we don't do it now." I pat Eddie's chest as I pass by him. Lana looks at me,

Heart of Gold

confused, then shrugs and grabs her bag. As she heads to the shower I shout behind her,

"Oh by the way, you're cooking soup tonight."

She stops, turns around and briskly walks back towards me. "I'm doing what?"

"Cooking soup." I laugh at the look on her face.

"How did I get roped into cooking? You know how to cook too!"

"I told Lonnie how good your soups are?" I smile apologetically. She steps back and narrows her eyes at me.

"Really?"

"Yep, he wants to sample it."

"And she cooks?" Eddie tries to push past us.

"Not so fast, buck-o!" I stop him as Lana walks to the bathroom and shuts the door.

We pretend-push each other. Wrestling is something we always do when we're together.

"Want some of this?" I challenge.

His eyes light up, "Do you?" Before long, we are both piled on the floor. I finally get on top, holding his arms behind him.

"Okay, okay, I give!"

"Always could whip ya!" I laugh.

"You work out or something? That's not fair!"

"No, I just know where your weak points are." I tease and let him go. "You're right, it's not fair. Plus, I know you don't want to hurt a girl." I punch his arm playfully.

"Ouch, that hurt!" He turns his head and looks up at me.

"Sorry." I get off and walk to the bed, sitting on the edge. He joins me, laughing.

"I lied, it didn't hurt." I punch him again, just for good measure. He laughs, "So how are things, sis?"

"Good, for the most part. Traveling with Lana clears things up a bit."

"She seems like a good friend."

"She is. You're going to love her."

He looks towards the bathroom door, "I think I already do."

I grab his face and turn it towards mine. "Hey, get your head out of the gutter."

"Can't help it."

I look into his eyes, "Yes, you can. You're just choosing not to."

"So what?" He shrugs. I sigh and roll my eyes. There's no reasoning with a hormonal sixteen-year-old.

I change the subject.

"What's the agenda for today? Remember, we're only here until Monday."

"I know. We're going to see LaNette today."

"Really?" I look at him in shock. I wasn't expecting that answer.

"Yup, 'bout time you two patched up whatever broke."

"Nothing broke Eddie. I like her, I just don't like her husband."

"Well, it's mutual. Don doesn't like you either."

"Why? What did I ever do to him?"

"It's because you're a dancer. He doesn't want her anywhere near a dancer."

"But doesn't he go to strip clubs?"

"I don't get it either, Beverly. Just go to see LaNette and don't pay him any attention."

"I will. It will be nice to see her again."

"I know, it's so cool. We'll be The Three Musketeers again."

I laugh, "Maybe so."

We laugh all the way to LaNette's new home, remembering fond memories. I can feel the anxiety rising as we pull into the driveway. Walking up the steps of her porch feels like climbing a mountain. The knock on the door sounds like a boulder tumbling down, bouncing off the surface and slamming into the ground, to bounce back off again.

I feel a sense of relief when LaNette opens the door, smiling as she sees us. I step inside and gesture to Lana. "Hey, LaNette. This is Lana."

Heart of Gold

"Hello Lana, it's nice to meet ya." She replies as she holds the door open, letting everyone in.

"Hi sis." Eddie hugs her on the way in. She closes the door behind him. She gives us a brief tour of the house which ends in the living room.

"Where's Don?" Eddie asks as she sits in a plush chair.

"He's working but he'll be home tonight." Lana, Eddie and I exchange glances of relief.

As we talk, I notice that LaNette's demeanor is different than when we last saw each other. She's considerate and hospitable. I even notice sparks of her old, bubbly self. Just like when we were little. She has the American Dream: the big house, fancy cars, and a husband who comes home every night. Who wouldn't want a life like this?

As LaNette leaves to get some drinks Lana leans over and whispers, "She's not so bad."

"I know." I laugh, remembering the awful perceptions I've given Lana of her over the years, "This is how I remember her. Ever since she married that loser she's changed. When he's around, she can't talk the way she wants, all of her excitement goes away. It's like she's his robot. It just blows my mind!"

"She's married and in love. That's what married people act like." Lana comments nonchalantly.

"Not my Uncle Jack!" Eddie pipes up defensively, "He's been madly in love for over 50 years. When I fall in love it will be just like that, forever."

I wave my arm at him, "He's the quintessential romantic."

"Don't worry it runs in the family." Lana quips. I looks at her suspiciously as LaNette walks back in the room and sets a tray of drinks on the coffee table.

She stands up straight, "I have an announcement."

All three of us look up at her, waiting. "What is it?" I ask impatiently.

"I'm pregnant."

Rebecca Nietert

Eddie and I look at each other, shocked. "Really?!"

"Yes!" She beams. We all get up simultaneously and give her a giant hug.

"Oh LaNette, I'm so happy for you!" I shriek.

"I'm going to be an uncle." Eddie shouts. We laugh at his enthusiasm.

"Tell us all about it!" Lana says as we sit down.

She sits down and tells us all about her excitement when they first found out. She tells us the due date and how happy she is. I can't help but smile. Even though we have our moments, she's still my sister and I'm happy for her.

"I don't mean to ruin the moment but we have to go now."

"Why so soon?" She asks, surprised. "You all can stay for dinner if you like."

"Thank you but Lana is cooking soup for us tonight. We need to get to the store on the way home."

"Oh, okay. Will I see you again before you leave?"

I shake my head, "I can't come back out this way since we are leaving late Sunday or early Monday."

"That's a quick trip for such a long way." She seems genuinely disappointed.

"Yes, but it's worth it. I'm so glad I got to see you."

"Me too." She hugs me.

On the way to the store I can't help but think about what a nice visit that was. She acted just like when we were teenagers; not intentionally condescending or hurtful. When I said I had to go she didn't act like I had some personal vendetta against her and actually listened.

Memories of our childhood float to the surface. Memories of all the guys who adored her, and all the girls who wanted to be her best friend. She fit in wherever she was at the time. She was the life of the party, the humor, the challenge, and the mystery all wrapped in one fine, tiny, perfect little package. I recall there wasn't a star or

Heart of Gold

adult that was cooler than my sister. I wanted to be just like her. Idolized her.

"We're here."

"Oh?" Eddie's voice snaps me out of my trance. They both turn to look at me, "Sorry."

Lana looks at me, and laughs, "Where have you been this whole drive?"

"Thinking about LaNette and the new baby."

"I know. Isn't it cool?" Eddie comments, "I'm actually going to be an uncle. I can just see it. Uncle Eddie." He smiles and laughs.

"Yes, it is. I'm going to be an Aunt!" I pretend to shiver.

"Oh, who are you kidding?" Lana retorts, "You have babies all around you now. Still want one so bad?" She teases.

"Well, let's see how happy they are after the kids are born." I look at Eddie, "I used to dream all the time about her getting hurt."

"Really? After Shirley died I used to dream about her getting hurt all the time too."

"Weird. I don't want to feel that way." Lana comments.

Eddie and I laugh as we walk into the store to get what we need for dinner tonight. Lonnie is already home and welcomes us with a smile. It's good to be back. Alphy barks, greeting us while dancing around our feet.

"He needs a walk." Lana sighs as she carries an armful of groceries inside.

I look at Eddie, "Let's bring him for a walk." I grab the dog leash from the back of a chair and clips it to Alphy's collar.

"You're not leaving me here alone!" Lana looks alarmed.

"It's okay, Lonnie is here."

She looks at me wearily, "Fine but be back soon."

"I will." Eddie follows me out the door.

We head to a small park behind the apartments.

"I remember that Grandma and I used to walk her dog Tiffany when we lived up here."

Rebecca Nietert

"I remember that dog." Eddie smiles, "She was well-trained. Do you remember that cast she had to wear when she broke her leg after falling off the bed?"

"Oh, I remember that." I giggle.

"This park holds a lot of memories." He adds, looking around.

I nod, "Sure does. I look at the back of the apartment and remember when you weren't around yet. We lived in those apartments," I point to an apartment complex to the right. "I remember the torment that took place there." I say softly, not meaning to say what's really going on inside.

"Torment? What are you talking about?"

"Well, we moved into the apartment 'cause we didn't have a lot of money at the time."

"I know. Dad told me how mom used to complain about how hard it was for her back then."

"Well, we had to wear clothes from neighborhood kids because mom usually spent all her money on herself."

"She did?" He looks at me, surprised.

"Well, she always managed to provide but we wore a lot of hand-me-downs from other kids. We were made fun of a lot because we didn't have the 'latest fashion.'" I shudder at the memory.

"That's not nice."

"No, it wasn't. LaNette could hold her own but Shirley and I couldn't and therefore, got the brunt of the teasing. They would throw food at us so we usually stayed out of the lunchroom and just stayed hungry." "That sounds awful."

"It was but I survived. Do you remember mom's violence?"

"Not really. I remember she used to beat the crap out of you but I don't remember her touching any of us."

"I don't think she did hurt the rest of you. I think I used to set her off because I was confrontational."

Eddie shrugs, "Maybe, maybe not. I know she loves you very much. She told me the other day on the phone."

Heart of Gold

I smile and lean into him, "She loves you very much too."
After hugging we head home to help Lana cook dinner.
"What can I do?" I walk into the kitchen.
"Nothing. Just set the table." I notice her face is red.
"Lana, what happened while I was gone?" I ask as Eddie walks off to find Lonnie.
"He embarrassed me!"
"How?"
"He said I was beautiful. Your stepfather, who is twice my age, said I'm beautiful!" She looks at me in disbelief.
I laugh, "Well, you are!"
"Oh, get out of here!" She mocks.
"Have you tasted it yet?" I gesture towards the soup.
"Now, you know I never do that. I will tell you though, that they didn't have what I normally use so I had to use some beef bouillon cubes."
"What's the difference?"
"It isn't supposed to be this dark, but it will be fine I'm sure."
"Great! Well, the table is set. Let's eat!"
"Lana!" Someone screamed.
We both jump.
Hard to tell which male is shouting.
She runs down the hall and finds Alphy throwing up on the carpet.
"Damn it!" She shouts, embarrassed.
"Lana, it's okay. "I answer, stopping briefly after she does.
"I'm so sorry!" She looks at Eddie.
"Not a problem. I didn't know what to do but he wasn't looking too good."
Lana looks at Alphy, "Yeah, you really don't look too good do you?" She asks the dog.
"Dinner ready?" Eddie asks as she heads toward the kitchen.
"Yep, go ahead and pour some. I will be back after I take him out." Lana picks up the dog and starts to walk away.

Rebecca Nietert

As she takes the dog outside, Lonnie, Eddie and I head for the kitchen to taste the soup.

Lonnie pours Eddie and I a bow, then sits down to eat his own. I watch him taste it, smiling. He smiles back.

"Good?" I pick up my spoon.

"Taste it, Beverly." He's still smiling.

I taste it and look up at him, shocked. "I'm so sorry."

Eddie takes a gulp and jumps in his chair, "This is nasty!"

"Sh!" Lonnie looks at him sternly.

"Beverly, this is too salty!"

I know! Oh my God, what are we going to do? She will be humiliated! I swear to you that her soups are normally tremendous. I'm so sorry guys."

"We're going to eat it." Lonnie slaps Eddie softly on the head, "Eat!"

"I can't eat this dad!"

"Yes, you can and you will! She went through all this trouble so don't let her know you won't eat it. Here, pour some in my bowl so when she comes back it will look like you ate some."

He puts his bowl next to Eddie's. Eddie does as asked then swallows more of what's left, "Beverly, you can't tell her okay?"

I looked at both of them trying so desperately to be chivalrous, "You two are so awesome!"

"No, we are crazy!" Lonnie laughs loudly.

"What's going on?" Lana asks as she enters the kitchen.

"How is it?" She walks to get herself a bowl.

"Salty but good. I ate some, see?" Eddie brings his bowl to the sink, showing Lana.

"Glad you liked it." She answers, smiling.

"I have band practice. See you all later okay?" He said heading out the door as fast as his feet would carry him.

"Be home early!" Lonnie shouts after him.

"Will do!" The faint answer is followed by the door slamming shut.

Heart of Gold

Lonnie looks at me and takes another painful bite, "This is nice Lana. Thank you."

Lana looks in his half-empty bowl, "Want some more?"

"Nope. Full." He answers without hesitation.

She look at me, confused. "I thought you said he ate a lot?"

"He does. Did you eat earlier Lonnie?" I ask, shaking my head yes at him.

"Yes, that's it! I just had a snack while you were cooking and the kids were taking a walk. I didn't think. I'm so sorry." I can tell he's trying desperately to be as honest as he can be.

"That's fine." Lana answers, a little distraught.

I watch Lana sit down and prepare to eat, horrified that if Lonnie is still sitting here she would be utterly humiliated. I fumble in my mind, searching for something, anything to say.

"Lonnie, would you mind taking us out for some drinks?"

"Sure." He looks at me, sounding surprised. Oh, just go with it! I snap on the inside.

"Great! Why don't you go get ready and we can go after dinner?"

He looks at me and nods, understanding what I'm trying to do. "Okay, see you in about twenty minutes?"

"Will that be enough time for us to get ready?" Lana looks at the clock.

"It will be plenty. It's Huntley; No one here dresses up. What we are wearing is just fine."

"My kind of town." She giggles. Lonnie walks off to give us some privacy.

Lana takes a bite of her soup. She sips slowly, letting the juices stay on the tip of her tongue, sure it's going to be perfect. I watch her face crinkle as she stands up from the chair, face red. "How does this happen to me?!"

"What?" I ask, alarmed.

"This crap is so salty I don't even know if I can finish it!"

"I'm sorry." I look at her empathetically.

Rebecca Nietert

"They ate this?!" She looks at me, mortified.

"They really didn't notice."

"Oh come on, Beverly! This is completely gross! You can't tell me that they didn't notice."

"Well, they must not have thought it was that bad. Look at their bowls – they're empty!"

"Yeah, but they could have poured it down the disposal." She gets up to look.

"Nope, they just ate it."

"There is no disposal?" She looks at me, shocked. I laugh and shake my head. She looks back at the soup, "They...actually ate it."

"Like I said, they didn't think it was that bad."

"Oh my God, I'm so embarrassed!"

"Don't be! They both like you. Plus, they respected you enough to eat it."

"No one should have to eat this stuff." She laughs, calmer now. "Thank you." She pushes the remainder in the trashcan. "Let's go get ready okay?"

I put mine in the trash as well, "Sounds like a plan to me!"

Heart of Gold

33

The remainder of the night is spent in a bar, eating and drinking way too much. When I wake, it's late in the afternoon. Lana is up and packing.

I sit up, "What's going on?"

"We have to go home. Alphy is really sick and I need to get him to a vet."

"Okay, I'll let Lonnie know."

"He already knows, we've been talking all morning. Eddie is still sleeping."

"Well then, I'll get ready and go tell him."

I pack up my belongings, take a quick shower and poke my head in Eddie's room. He's fast asleep. I can't help but smile at the innocence laying before me. I hate to wake him up but I have to. I shake his shoulder lightly. "Hey dude, I have to say good-bye man."

He stirs in his sleep, slowly becoming conscious. "What?"

"I'm leaving."

He wipes at his eyes, "You're leaving?"

"Yeah, I have to. Alphy is really sick so we need to get him to a doctor."

"What time is it?"

"Almost one. I'll miss you kid." I ruffle his hair, "Can I have a hug?"

He reaches up and I wrap him in a huge hug, never wanting to let go. "I'm going to miss you too." He mumbled.

I laugh softly and give him a kiss on the cheek. "Tell LaNette I'm happy for her. I'll see you when I can okay?"

"Okay..." I quietly close the door behind me, and head to the living room where Lonnie is sitting in a chair.

Rebecca Nietert

"Can you watch Alphy ? I have to load the car."

"Why don't you watch him and I'll load the car?"

I smile gratefully, "'Cause I know where everything goes and you don't."

"Good point." I can feel his eyes on me as I start to pick up some bags. "I'll miss you Beverly."

I look over at him, drop my bags and give him a giant hug. "I'll miss you too."

I gather up my bags and head to the truck, determined not to cry. I grab Alphy as Lana is finishing putting on her make-up. She hugs Lonnie goodbye, we promise him we will be back and head back home.

The feeling of heading to home away form home is bittersweet. I want to see Joseph again of course but I'm also realizing that maybe, just maybe, my family has changed. Maybe there's something different now than there was back then. Is that really possible? Have they grown up and matured just like I have?

"Sure are a lot of corn fields here, Beverly." I look over at Lana and nod.

"You're not used to it after being here a few days?"

"Well, yeah. But I still can't get over how many there are!"

I can't help but laugh, "That's about the sum of it. We used to have a lot of fun in them too."

"Sex in a cornfield?" She looks over at me, eyes wide in a mixture of shock and amazement.

I burst out laughing, unable to control myself at the thought, "No, silly! We used to drink ourselves into oblivion at high school parties. That's all they do here is drink."

"With drinking usually comes sex." She retorts flippantly.

I shrug, " Good point, but back then I personally never had sex."

"I figured. There isn't much to do in this small town."

"Nope. That's why I couldn't wait to travel twelve-hundred miles to Texas right after I graduated."

Heart of Gold

"Takes a lot of courage."

"Or stupidity." I laugh.

"So, I noticed you didn't call Joseph once."

I shake my head, "Don't care to talk to him right now. This trip is about clearing my head."

"Good." She takes a look at a Rand McNally's U.S. map, "Let's go through Arkansas instead of straight down 55 to Texas."

"Lead the way Co-Pilot!"

Before long we are headed into the lower Missouri border. We've driven about eight hours with one short trip for gas, and Alphy apparently has had enough. He starts hyperventilating as if he's going to throw up. Lana and I look at each other, confused.

We haven't fed him anything. I decide to stop anyway, just in case. Good thing I did — he's barely out the car when he chucks some stuff nasty mucus stuff.

"That is so gross!" Lana shrieks as she gets a towel from the car and cleans him off.

"I agree. Can you give him one of those pills again to sleep?"

"I don't know, can I?"

I shrug, "I would try it. We have about another ten hours to go."

"Fine, hand it to me."

I retrieve the vile from her purse and hand her a pill. She puts one down his throat, which he hacks back up.

"Damn it, dog!"

"Okay, just let him walk around a bit. That might help?"

She lets him walk around, watching him carefully as he tips from side to side.

"Why can't he keep his balance?" I shrug and watch also. Thankfully, he seems to start breathing much better after taking a few steps.

"Okay, let's try this again." We load him back up and head to Arkansas as fast.

Lana notices Alphy and utters deeply, "We need to stop."

Rebecca Nietert

"I know, there should be a hotel up here."

"Stop!" She shout.

I jump at the shout and slam on the brakes.

We are parked alongside Highway 7 somewhere in Arkansas. The scenery is beautiful! Majestic trees are abundant with leaves, tall grass blowing softly in the wind. It's almost a picture-perfect image, until Alphy gets out and starts hacking up again.

I roll my eyes, "This dog is a lot of trouble..."

"It's not his fault!" She defends.

"I know but you have to admit, the drive up was a lot easier. Maybe we can try the pills one more time?"

She shakes her head, "No can do. He won't even drink water – look!" She starts to show me how he don't drink the water she tries to give him when she lets out a scream, "Oh my God!"

"What?!" I lean in closer to where she's pointing. The white fur on his neck is turning brown with black spots. "Oh my God, Lana. That isn't an allergic reaction – those are tics!"

Lana jumps up, hysterical, "Get them off! Lime disease!"

We try to get Alphy back into the truck but he resists.

"Why does your dog decide to be stubborn now?"

"I don't know!" She picks him up and throws him in the back. "Step on it!"

I slam on the gas and fly down the highway, looking for a place to stop.

"They're in your hair!" She shrieks.

"Yeah, probably in yours too."

"What?!" She begins to complain and whine.

I pull into a parking lot with a grocery store, ignoring Lana's complaints about what an awful situation this is. She can be such a drama queen at times! I slam the door and run into the store and buy the only thing I can think of that will work: bug spray. I run out and see Lana placing Alphy on the ground. I uncap the spay.

"I can't use that on my dog!"

Heart of Gold

"What's the alternative? Lime Disease? Come on, just do it!" I snap while spraying Alphy. The little critters start jumping off of him.

"This is so gross!" Lana wails as some of the bugs get on her. She swats at them.

I finish spraying Alphy, "I know. Here, let me help."

"Oh, please do." She sighs, exhausted.

"Take off your shirt."

"Here?" She asks. She looks at me like I'm crazy.

I roll my eyes. "Look, I need to spray your clothing. Just take it off."

"Okay...Okay!" She takes it off and hands it to me. I spray it thoroughly and check for tics. Not seeing any, I hand it back to her. I take mine off and do the same for myself.

I sprayed the shirt thoroughly checking it for tics. When I did not see any left I put back on my own shirt. "Make sure none of them made it to your shorts."

"This is so embarrassing..."

She takes them off. Her eyes grow wide as some tics fall off.

I spray them as well. I look at her, I hiss, "See?"

I do the same for myself and sure enough, some fall off as well.

After spraying our clothes, Alphy and even the inside of the truck, I sit down, the adrenaline starting to wear off.

Lana approaches, "I have to look in your hair."

I nod and let her. She pulls a few out. I do the same for her. We sit and watch Alphy heave a bit from the bug spray.

"We need to find a hose and clean the dog off."

I nod in agreement, "Go look at the map and see where we are while I shake out our shorts to dry."

"Sounds like a plan." She gets up and reaches in the truck for the map. "Um...Beverly?"

"What is it now?"

I look up at her, my eyes following her finger to land on four men who are obviously farmers. They're staring at us, eyes as big as

Rebecca Nietert

a bug's. They've obviously been watching. I stand up and put Alphy in the back of the truck. I toss Lana her shorts and put on mine. Well, they've obviously been watching this whole time... I get in the car and slam the door.

"Standing here half naked, pulling tics out of your hair with a heaving dog in the back. Weren't we a sight to see?!"

I pull out the parking lot, laughing, "This is the most ridiculous thing that has ever happened to us Lana!"

She starts laughing too. Just the thought of what must be going through their minds is enough to send us both over the edge laughing. "We didn't even get a tip!" She laughs. We head down the road to find a gas station with water.

"There's one!" I follow her direction and pull in next to the hose.

I jump out, "Get some clothes out of the suitcase to change into."

"Okay, but they're all dirty."

"Seriously?! Dirty is better than this nasty smelling stuff." I start to spray myself off with the hose but it isn't working as well as I had originally thought. "There's not much water here."

She grabs Alphy and brings him over. It takes a while but she finally washes him off. After that, she washes herself off and puts him in the back of the truck.

I notice that she seems to be feeling a bit faint from the bug juice also, "What can I do?"

"Spray me with the hose?"

"Not a problem." I spray her with the hose to which she shrieks.

"I didn't think you'd actually do it!"

"Well, you're already wet! What's it matter?" I drop the hose and we both laugh.

We change into some dirty clothes from our suitcases and get back in the truck. While driving, Lana brings up the men watching

Heart of Gold

us again. We laugh, needing to let out the stress of Alphy and our potential Lime Disease.

"Hey, it's getting late. Think we can stop somewhere and take a quick shower?"

I look at the clock, "Yeah, good idea. I think there's a hotel around here somewhere..."

After a few minutes we spot a Travel Lodge. I park as Lana grabs Alphy and heads to the reception desk. As we enter the room I plop my suitcase down, exhausted.

"I'm going to take a bath." She commands.

I look at Lana, "Just don't turn on any lights. I have a migraine from the smell of this stuff!"

"I won't. Sleep. I'll be out in a minute."

I nod, slowly falling asleep on the bed next to Alphy.

I wake the next morning, realizing I need a shower. "Ugh!" My head is pounding; feeling like a weight keeps dropping on it with every thump. I just want this spray stuff to be off!

"There's just a tiny bar of soap. No shampoo or anything." I hear Lana's voice from the other room as I enter the bathroom. I stop, turn around and poke my head out the door. I hold the soap up.

"You're kidding me! Please go downstairs and buy some."

"I can't. We don't have enough money for that and gas on the way home."

"Guess I'll do without."

I turn back around, get everything ready, look in the bathtub and let out a scream, "Lana!"

I hear her jump to her feet. "What is it?" She runs into the bathroom, looking around wildly. "Oh my God!" She shrieks.

I look at her, her hand covering her mouth. I look at the tub which now has a ring of mildew on it. "Did you shower in that?!"

She shakes her head with a look of pure disgust, "I took a bath!" Then, she looks at me and gasps, "What are those?!"

Rebecca Nietert

"What?" I follow her finger pointing to my legs and see red dots all over them. "What is it this time!?" I growl and walk out the bathroom and look at Alphy who jumps off the bed, wagging his tail. He has dots too. I look back over at Lana, who doesn't have any red dots.

"Alphy and I have the dots but you don't. Where did you sleep last night?"

Lana walks in the bedroom, "On the chair. I didn't want to wake you or Alphy."

It dawns on me. "Chiggers!" I shout victoriously.

Wait... I look at Lana, talking slowly, "Alphy and me both have chiggers." I look from her to Alphy to my legs. "How do you get rid of this?!" I can feel the panic coming on.

"Nail polish." I look at Lana as if she's lost her mind. She rolls her eyes, "Just trust me, it works. Be right back." She walks out the door.

I begrudgingly get in the shower, careful not to touch the sides of the tub. After I get out I pack up all of our things, making sure nothing will be left behind. The door opens and Lana walks back inside.

She hands me the polish, "The office said they're not going to do anything about the tub or sheets. No refunds." She shakes her head and looks around, disgusted. "I knew we should've stopped somewhere else other than this dump."

"Well, we're leaving anyway."

She nods, "True."

"Do we have enough money for some breakfast?"

"Very little. Let's hit the road. We'll have to hit up a drive-thru. It's already going to be late by the time we hit the Texas border."

"Fine." I pick up my bags and we haul out to the truck.

We drive past lunch. Alphy seems to be doing much better. Exhausted from the earlier commotion, he falls asleep finally! As we drive up Highway 7 I can feel my eyes getting heavy. I pull over.

Heart of Gold

"Take the helm." We switch seats and within minutes I'm out like a light.

I wake to Lana unloading the car. I look around, realizing that we're in a garage.

"Home?" I yawn.

"Yup!" She opens the door with my keys and walks inside. I get out and help unload.

"You can stay and wear some of my clothes if you want."

"Thank you!"

"I'm going to shower first while you get settled." When I get out I study my reflection in the mirror. I'm still looking good. I smile to myself, looking myself up and down. My gaze stops on my legs. What?! I take a closer look. I have bruises all over! I turn around. Yep, on my back too. "Lana!"

She runs in with Alphy in her arm, "My turn!"

I stop her. "Why do I have bruises?!"

She looks at me, "Oh, that. Well..." She smiles sheepishly, "When I was driving you kept bumping all over the truck."

"And?"

"And... I was driving through a lot of curves?" She offers with an apologetic smile.

I sigh impatiently, "Why didn't you wake me?"

"You wouldn't wake up!" She defends, "I figured after the embarrassment of that dinner, the road trip from hell with bugs, and a heaving dog, the least you could have is a few bruises. Now go!" She pushes me out the bathroom and closes the door.

"Okay, I guess I deserve that!" I shout through the door and laugh.

"You bet you do!" I can hear laughing from the other side of the door, "Oh, guess what?"

"What?"

"You're working tonight. You're running on fumes and we have no more money."

Rebecca Nietert

I sit on the bed, thinking, "Makeup will cover the bruises at least."

"Yeah." Suddenly, I hear a scream, "Beverly!"

"What?" I open the door.

"Grab the dog!"

Alphy is covered with water from head to toe. When I pick him up he looks at me with pleading eyes. He looks so pitiful!

I look at Lana, "You took a shower with your dog?!"

"Yes, he feels better. Just dry him off and lay him down, please."

"Okay." I take Alphy out and do what was asked.

Within a few moments she walks out of the bathroom, "That was some trip!" She comments as she walks into the bedroom.

"It sure was. I'm glad I'm back though."

She nods, "Yeah. Hey, will Joseph be here soon? Can I still crash here?"

"Yeah, that's fine. I'll go to work but leave some cash for you on the dresser okay?"

"Thanks." I watch her lay on the bed, asleep in minutes.

I'm making a sandwich in the kitchen when Joseph walks in.

"You're back!" I look up to see him smiling and smile back as he hugs me.

"Shhh! Lana is here. She's asleep on the bed."

"I've been replaced by her?" He teases as he kisses my cheek.

I laugh, "No, silly." I tell him briefly about the trip back.

"So, you don't have any money now?"

I shake my head, "Not a penny."

He reaches for his wallet with one hand and hands me ten twenties, "Here."

"Thank you." I lean forward into his chest and look up at him, "I love you."

"So the trip was good for you, huh?"

"In more ways than one." I smile and kiss him softly, "I've missed you."

Heart of Gold

He smiles and kisses me back, "I've missed you too."

He's so charming! For a moment I lose myself in his arms only to be brought back to reality when he lets go.

"I've got to get some paperwork done for work." He insists.

I nod in understanding. He walks away and I head to the bedroom to wake Lana.

"Here's some cash. You still want to stay or do you want me to take you back to the apartment?"

"Apartment." She answers softly, still waking up. She picks up the phone and calls Rod, asking him if he'll be there. She hands me the phone to hang up.

I grab Alphy and put him in the car. Moments later Lana gets in the car. I drive them to the apartment. When I pull up to the driveway Rod's car is already there.

"Thank you." She yawns and reaches out for a hug.

I hug her back, "You're more than welcome. I love you."

"Me too." She smiles, "You're a great friend."

"You Darlin', are the best friend anyone could have. Thank you for going with me."

Rebecca Nietert

34

Joseph talks me out of working again so we meet Connie for dinner at a local steak house. Of course, she brings up their past history. I roll my eyes. Sure, she may need some closure but this is getting really annoying. It's just...rude. I kind of feel like she's trying to let me know she'll always be most important in his life no matter what!?

When we got home I look at Joseph, "Why do you think she keeps bringing the past up?"

"Because she wants to feel loved I guess?"

"You think she knows you love her?"

He looks at me, "Not the same way I love you. While you were gone I told her I will always love her but need her to leave."

I look at him, confused, "Need her to leave?"

He nods, "Right after the baby is born."

"Why so soon? I thought you loved that baby too. Didn't you want to be part of raising it and seeing the baby grow?"

"My needs changed."

"What does that mean?"

He walks over to me, "Sit down, Bev. We have to talk."

I sit down, feeling extremely uncomfortable.

"Connie has been talking to Curt again. They are making plans to move to Dallas."

"You're kidding! Is he going to marry her?"

"No, I lost respect for her when she told me."

"Respect?" I look at him, puzzled. Then it dawns on me, "...You're still in love with her! You're jealous?"

"Yes, I always will be in love with her. No I just don't like the choices she makes. Something has changed."

Heart of Gold

I roll my eyes, "What exactly has changed, Joseph?"

He looks at me carefully, weighing his words. Finally, he speaks, "I ran into Sally recently." He looks at me, waiting for my reaction.

"I know." I look at him nonchalantly, as if it doesn't faze me one bit.

His eyebrows shoot up in shock, "How did you know?"

"A woman always knows. What's wrong?" I lied.

"You know I love you, right?"

"I know. Did you sleep with Sally?"

His head jerks back, insult written all over his face, "Why would you ask me that?! No, of course not!" I wait. He continues, "But she's really hurt by what I did and can't seem to get her life together." He seems to have some inner anguish about that.

I look at him, confused, "What do you mean can't get her life together?"

"She asked me to take care of her."

"But you're already taking care of Connie and me?"

"Yes, but when Connie moves out I told Sally she could move in. I didn't think you would mind."

"Joseph!" I stand up, unable to contain my anger any longer, "Sally is a lot different than Connie. My God! I took you from her didn't I?"

"No, remember I left her before we met."

"Whatever! Listen, I get that you want to help her and I believe you when you say that you love me, but all this 'helping the ex' thing is just too much."

He stands up, looking down at me, "Don't you want me to be happy?" I look up at him and sigh in defeat. How can I say no to that? Seeing him happy is what I live for! I nod as he hugs me tight.

"If you really feel like this won't hurt us then go for it." Do I mean that? Of course not! Why can't one man put me first?! I wanted him to tell me that I'm more important than Sally. I look up at him. He kisses me softly but doesn't say what I need to hear. Lana's words echo in my mind: You're his doormat. It's true.

Rebecca Nietert

He lets go abruptly and picks up the phone to call Sally. The tone of his voice is too happy. I sit down, unsure of what to think about this. As I listen to their conversation I realize that he can convince me so easily. And he knows it too. I'm hooked, line and sinker. I have no clue what to do next.

When he walks back into the room I look up at him. I take a deep breath, trying to calm my nerves, "Joseph..."

He looks at me, "Hmm?"

"I'm thinking about getting a real job." The words come out in a rush before I can stop and think them through.

He looks at me and starts to laugh, "Seriously?!" I nod. "Doing what? You are not qualified to do anything but take your clothes off."

"I could be trained to get another job." I can't keep the defensiveness out of my voice. I'm arguing with him trying to help him see I am growing and see that I cannot keep living the life we are living, but he doesn't see it.

"Why would you do that? You make enough money to do anything you want to do. Any time you want to leave, you just hop in your little red truck and go. You can't do that with a normal job."

"I think it would be worth it."

"What's wrong with you? You can't honestly think you have the brains for a real job?"

"If Sally has one a brain for a real job I can too. I can only imagine what she thinks about me. After all, I'm just the dancer who lives with her ex."

"She thinks like I do. If not, I'll convince her too." He walks over and looks into my eyes, "You may be just a dancer, but you're my dancer."

His words make me feel sick to my stomach. "I have to go."

"Where?"

"To work."

"Are you okay?"

Heart of Gold

"Yeah, I'm fine. Bruises are covered. I'll catch you later." I walk towards the door, grabbing my work bag on the way out.

"Remember, you're here as long as you want to be Bev. I don't want to hold you back." He yells from behind.

"I know, thank you." I shout back, not bothering to turn around and walk out.

I slam the door shut. For some reason, I feel like I have overstayed my welcome. I'm playing a hand I'm never going to win. I'm playing his game on his terms. He doesn't want to marry me. I'm just his trophy, put on a shelf for the world to see. Nothing more. Just like Phillip. I bow my head and shake it in disbelief.

I arrive at work but don't feel like getting out right away. I stare out the windshield, unsure of what to do. I want to talk to Joseph but every time I try, he hypnotizes me with those blue eyes.

I'll do anything for the man. I love him. I hit the steering wheel. "It's not fair!" I want him! I don't know what to do? I slump back into the seat, defeated. Guess not...

I walk in and notice Buddy sitting at a table, looking at the stage. For some reason I walk over to him.

"Hey."

He turns around, "Hey there! They told me you weren't working."

I shrug, "I changed my mind."

"Have a seat." He gestures to an empty chair. I sit, "Wow! You look normal."

I look at my street clothes and have to laugh a bit, "I guess so. I'm usually called Beverly but here it's Barbie."

"Thank you for telling me your real name."

"I honestly don't know why I told you."

"When you never let men get that close it's a good thing."

I look at him, surprised at what just came out of his mouth, "You know a lot about dancers?"

Rebecca Nietert

"No, I never really come into these places. I did that one time when I saw you on stage. I came here today to look for you. You don't seem like the kind of girl that should be in here."

"That's what they tell me but if you have no skills then this is what you do." I gesture up at the stage.

"So? Save your money to get some skills. You've got to make a fortune here."

I shrug, "I guess some call it a fortune."

He nods, "I thought so."

"What does that mean?"

"Seems to me that you don't really know what you want."

"Why do you say that?"

"You're too confident not to get what you want."

I laugh softly, "No, I never get what I want." If only you knew.

"Want to know why?"

I look at him smugly. I'll play this game. "Why?"

"Because you don't know what to ask for."

Oh, really now? "I get what I need on my own. I don't need a man to give it to me."

"That's part of your problem. I can help."

I sneer at him, "What do you mean you 'can help' me? I've helped myself this far, I think I can go farther." I start to stand up, tired of the accusing. What a waste of time.

"If you ask me for anything, I'll give it to you. I'm not dumb enough to break your heart." His words stop my in my tracks. My body moves on its own, sinking back into the chair.

"How do you know so much about me?" My voice comes out in a whisper. I don't know how he hears me but it seems that he does.

"I know about girls like you. I have a daughter not much younger than you. If it was up to me, I would want some guy in place like this to tell her what I'm telling you."

"That's nice." I replied honestly.

"You don't have a father either do you?"

Heart of Gold

"Why do you ask that?"

"Because no father worth a damn would let his daughter do this!"

"Maybe you're right." I push the thoughts about my absent father out of my mind. Not going there tonight.

"You seem to be on edge tonight."

"I think my life is about to change; I can feel it. I'm just not sure I'm ready." Why did I just tell him that?

"Sit with me. Have dinner. Don't work tonight."

"I need some cash." I may be upset but I'm not stupid.

"Alright, go get some cash then come back to talk?"

"Okay, I can do that." I nodded glad he didn't offer me cash to sit.

I walk off to the dressing room. Lana is in the back, putting on last-minute touches to her makeup.

"Hey there!" She smiles when she sees me.

"Thought you would be tied up for a while." I say mockingly knowing she's probably spent the better part of the day in the sack with Rod.

"What's wrong?"

"How do you do that?" I grab some clothes out of my bag and start getting dressed.

"What's wrong with you, Beverly?" She insists.

"I think I'm going to have to leave Joseph."

"You already knew that."

"Yes, no... I mean, but I love him so much. It breaks my heart to hurt him."

"What about what he's doing to you?"

I shrug, "I can't wait any longer can I?"

"No, I don't think so. Not if you want a real man in your life."

"He's so real to me. Why doesn't he want just me?"

"He does. Just not for forever." I nod and wipe at my eyes, trying not to cry. "I know it hurts, I'm so sorry. Listen, I don't want

Rebecca Nietert

to add to your bad day but I have some news." I look up at her, "You too huh? What's wrong?"

"Nothing's wrong." She smiles as she raises a leather necklace up to me with a ring around it, "Look!" I reach out and touch the ring.

"It's beautiful! Who gave it to you?"

"Rod. He asked me to marry him!"

"Oh my God!" I look at her in shock, "You're kidding!"

"Nope! I don't want to hurt you though."

I shake my head, "I'm not hurt, don't worry about me for Pete's sake. I'm so happy for you!" I look at the necklace, unable to contain my excitement any longer, "When? Where? Am I going to be a bridesmaid?"

She laughs, "Slow down! We can't afford a wedding so I'm going to the Justice of the Peace this weekend. Then I'm going to Corpus Christi to live with him and his family in some mansion they own down there."

"You're leaving me?!" I look at her in shock. I can feel my heart sinking.

"Not for forever! We'll always be friends."

I shake my head, unable to believe what's happening, "No, you can't go."

"I'm going. I was going to pop by and see you this evening after work to tell you."

"This is sudden."

"Come on! We have one more night together before I leave. Let's go make some money."

"Okay." I wipe at my eyes, trying to compose myself, "I'll be right there." Watching her walk away breaks my heart. Is this where it all ends? After all we've been through? God, are you really going to take her from me too? First, it's my family, then my baby, then the love of my life and now my best friend? What's the meaning of all of this?! I finish getting ready furiously. I'm sick and tired of losing everyone I love! I storm out the dressing room and walk

Heart of Gold

around aimlessly, trying to clear my head. I spot Lana and Buddy in a deep conversation. I walk over to them and sit down.

Lana looks up at me, "Hey, we were just talking about you."

I figured that much. "What about?"

Buddy reaches in his pocket and pulls out a business car. He gently hands it to me, "Before long you'll need this. I can't give you money in here. I won't do that for you but I will rescue you when you're ready. Whenever you want to change your life you just call me."

Rescue me? I let that thought sit around in my head for a while. I hurt deeply and I don't want to manipulate men anymore. I can't have him believing that I could be anything other than exactly what I am. "You would be the re-bound guy. I will use you and spit you out." I said as a matter of fact. I don't love him. I know myself.

"I know. If using me is what it takes to get you out of here then I'm here for you."

I nod and walk off, Lana hot on my heels, smiling.

"He cares about you."

"He cares about me? He doesn't even know me!" I hiss.

"He does now! We've been talking for a while."

"Whatever, I need to make some money. I'm going on stage."

I dance to a soft melody. I can feel it inching its way through my veins. I usually don't dance to the slow songs but tonight I need it. I need the sadness to be poured out of me. I'm feeling hurt, fearful. What am I going to do without my best friend to keep me out of trouble? I look over at Lana talking to some guy. I can't help but feel like I'm losing a lifelong mate. I get off stage, feeling abandoned. I head over to Buddy's table and talk for a bit. He's arrogant, that's for sure. He also seems to have a need to be needed. Don't we all?

I wrap things up with him quickly and head to the dressing room where Lana is telling her good-bye's. I walk up and hug her tight, tears stinging at my eyes. She hugs me tight.

"Beverly, take advantage of it."

Rebecca Nietert

"Take advantage of what?"

"Buddy." She says softly.

"What do you mean?" I ask. "Last year you would have told me not to do what you're telling me to do now." I lift my hands up. "This is all so confusing!"

"Look, you're in a relationship that's wearing you down. You and I both know you love Joseph more than you have loved any one else. We also know that as long as you're with him you'll never get what you want."

I nod, "Sometimes I believe that. Sometimes, Lana, I just need him to hold me." I can feel the tears falling down my face.

"I know. When you've had enough, call Buddy and he will rescue you."

"Rescue me?! I don't want him to rescue me! I want Joseph to!"

"Listen, he wants more; we both know that. He also wants to help you do whatever you want to get you out of here. Can Joseph say that?"

"I can't sleep with someone I don't feel anything for. Yeah, I am a dancer but I can count the number of my men on one hand! I can't do it, I tell you, I just can't!"

"Yes, you can. Just this once, think of your future. Stop thinking that your pride is worth more than getting the hell out of this business. Whatever you do from now will determine the rest of your life. It's your choice. What's more important: your pride or your future?"

I don't have an answer. "I know, you're right. I can't do it. I love Joseph so much!"

"Tonight you can't, but there will come a time when you will. Heed my advice if only this once, Bev. Use that man to get what you want in life. Maybe he can love you and give you what you need. You'll never know if you don't try."

I look at her and laugh, "Now you're just crazy!"

She shrugs, "Nothing new, right?" We both smile.

"Would you do it?" I asked her.

Heart of Gold

"Never. I have too much pride. But then again, I'll never want the things you do. That's the difference between us: You'll get what you want and I will too, just not the same things you get."

Neither of us say anymore. We hug tight then Lana walks away. I feel like time is running out. I need to make a choice: stay with Joseph or leave. I hate being in this constant state of turmoil! Fighting for a way out yet needing him like I need my air to breathe.

I am sure that when I am away from Joseph I get clear and then the moment I come back home all I have to do is look at him. I love the man, with my whole heart and yet I feel as though he might just be the wrong man for me. The constant confusion makes me exhausted. I get home. I want to crash.

Rebecca Nietert

35

The next morning I check in on Connie. She seems to sense my bad mood,
"Are you okay?"
"Yeah. Want some coffee?"
"That would be great but I'm going to get Mexican for lunch. I want the labor to start."
"Mexican food brings on labor?" I laugh.
"I heard it does. I'm willing to do anything! Help me up please."
I help her up and we walk into the baby's room. I look around at the blue and yellow-themed room.
"It's going to be so weird leaving here." She sighs.
"You think that you and Curt will be happy?"
"I'm not sure. I know I have to try."
Trying to make things less awkward, I change the subject, "Let's get going."
"Yeah, I'm starving."
I laugh, "When are you not hungry?"
She laughs also, "Never!" We both get ready and head out.
Soon we are seated at Connie's favorite Mexican Restaurant. A friendly waitress takes our order.
"This is great!" Connie looks around the restaurant. "It's been a while since I've been here."
"I bet! You haven't been out in a while huh?"
"No, laying in bed all day gets lonely.."
I nod in understanding, "I guess I will be alone a lot now too."
"What do you mean?"
"Lana's getting married."
"That doesn't mean you won't be friends anymore."

Heart of Gold

"I know, but she's moving to Corpus."

"Oh. Well, you'll be fine. It's only 4 hours away. I heard Sally is moving in."

"Joseph told me." I shake my head, "Unbelievable."

"What? That he rotates his ex-girlfriends?"

"Yes! That he puts them before his new ones."

"Shouldn't you be used to that by now?"

I shake my head, "Am I supposed to get used to something like that?"

"Well, they were really happy. She even packed up everything and quit her job to move to to a trailer in Florida with him." She responded.

"She was going to go with him? She was going to live in a trailer? How does one compete with that?"

"Yes."

"This is who he wants me to share his house with?"

"His bed too I assume?"

"What?!" I shout, not caring who hears.

The waitress walks up, asking if everything is alright. I nod. She walks off again.

"Calm down! You told Joseph that you were a lesbian once, right?"

"No, I never told him that!"

"Well, he's under the assumption that if he moves the pregnant lady out and moves this hot young chick in, he can have his cake and eat it too. Then you, her and him can live as one big happy family. Just think of what shock his friends would go through, not to mention how good that makes Joseph feel." I can hear the bitterness and pain in her voice.

"You really believe he would do that? Think that?!"

"What part of you doesn't? You're his play toy. He doesn't care enough about you to consider your feelings."

I can't say anything so I just sit quietly, absorbing the conversation.

Rebecca Nietert

"You'll be okay, he knows that."

"Do you think he wants me to leave?"

"All I know is that when Joseph wants out he makes it so difficult for us to stay that we leave him. That way, he doesn't take any of the responsibility for the pain. He accepts it and moves on. If it helps, no. I think he wants you to share in his twisted fantasies."

"And the ex's keep coming back out of guilt?"

"Yep."

"Not you. You're way to smart to fall for that."

"I fell for letting him be the one to help me. I had no one else and he knew that. Of course, he took advantage of that and decided to throw me out when it isn't convenient to have me there anymore."

"You're okay with that?"

She shrugs, "I've learned to accept it."

"I'm sorry, I didn't know."

"You never do." She laughs, "Then you wonder why you're a victim. You make yourself one."

I look at her, shocked that she would say such a thing. Is it true? More importantly, why isn't she angrier with him?

"it's not all your fault though. You're just looking for something that he won't give you. Joseph will never marry you."

"I suppose."

Our food finally arrives. Connie devours hers within minutes.

"I guess you were hungry huh?" I watch her devour her food. She nods and smiles, then spits out her food as her eyes grow wide.

She puts her hands on her stomach, "Ouch!"

I look at her, alarmed, "Are you going into labor?"

"I think so...ouch!"

I call the waitress for the check and help Connie into the car. We take off for the hospital. When we get there I call Joseph and tell him what happened.

Heart of Gold

"Be right there." He hangs up. They admit Connie. I walk into the room after she gets into her gown. I watch as the nurses hook her to some monitors.

"How're you feeling?"

"Hurting." She winces in pain, "The doc says I have to walk to break my water."

"Can I do anything for you?"

"No, just walk with me."

I help her up and we walk down the corridor. She has me call a few people to tell them she's at the hospital. She attempts to call Curt but he doesn't answer.

Joseph finally arrives after we get back to the room. He barrels through the door, shouting orders, "I'm here, everyone out! I have it handled now." Connie doesn't say or do anything. She let's him throw me out. He tells me to go home.

I leave. Instead of going home I drive to work, needing the distraction. When I get there, I get straight to work.

I don't think about Connie or Joseph, I just do my job. I rake in a few bucks. To me, it's a successful night since I haven't gotten personal with anyone. It's nice to be able to numb out your feelings and just forget everything for a while. It's been a long time since I've felt this ability, but I kind of like it.

When early morning arrives my shift is over. It's been a grueling day. Hours at the hospital with Connie and then a full twelve hour shift at work. I tip the bartenders, my favorite waitresses and proceed to leave the building.

On the way to the truck I notice Phillip standing nearby. I don't think anything of it, walking as briskly as I can. I look around, as usual, for anyone who might approach me. It never occurred to me that Phillip would.

"Beverly, I'm so sorry about what I did."

I shrug, "I'm fine."

"I know. I see how you do each night when I can get in."

"How long have you been coming?" I ask a little apprehensive.

Rebecca Nietert

"I've been watching you for a few days now."

Is he stalking me? Suddenly I get a horrible feeling in my gut and I know the answer. "I don't think that's such a good idea."

"Why? Are you afraid our past in going to embarrass you? Are you ashamed of me now?"

"Yes! I'm ashamed of myself for allowing you to use me for years. I would have done anything for you. I respected you that much. I was so loyal because you were the only man who ever believed could take care of me. But that's not true! Not only did you not take care of me, you broke my trust. You used me!" I dig in my purse for my keys.

In an instant he's at my side, grabbing me forcibly. "Come with me for a minute!" He starts to pull me towards the back of the building. I struggle to get a hand free and slap him as hard as I can. It lands on his face. "Let go of me! Don't you ever touch me again!"

"You've had your fun. Now, it's time to come home." He grabs me again and pushes me against the wall. "You've had your time to yourself but guess what? You're mine! I own you! I made you what you are and you still owe me!"

I try to push against him but it's no use. He's too strong. "Get off me! Help!" I scream as loud as I can before feeling the blow land on my jaw. My head reels back, slamming against the wall.

"You bastard!" Suddenly, I'm reminded of all the people who have hit me in the past. All of the blows I've endured, especially from Phillip. "I can take a punch! There hasn't been one person who can knock me down and keep me there yet!" This time, I'm fighting not only for my life but for my right not to let another man beat me. I kick him in the groin. He screams in anger and lets go. Now's my chance! I run towards the cars.

He grabs me and pulls me backwards. I turn around to face him with his face right in front of mine. Those black orbs burrow into my soul. Something in him looks so...wicked. For the first time in a long time I feel not only vulnerable but also fear for my life.

Heart of Gold

In the distance through the fear, I hear an engine roar in the gravel parking lot. Someone's here! I scream and kick, trying to create a scene, hoping the driver will notice. I hear the screech of tires coming to a halt.

All at once I'm forcibly pulled form Phillip's grasp. I'm free! My hair whipping in front of my face, without bothering to look at who my savior is, I grab my keys and purse from the ground, get in the car and speed off. I have to get home!

Right before I get home I park on the side of the road, unable to control myself any longer. A song on the radio echoes my thoughts and feelings: "Ace In The Hole" by George Straight.

My pensive thought is how did I get here?

I'm not who I once was. I'm crippled by my fears. How in the world can I expect any man to want this? Heck, I don't want me. The tears won't stop! I'm still not making any of my own choices. Why am I not making my own choices? Why don't I speak up? I needed Phillip teach me. I need alcohol to give me courage. I need Joseph in every way a woman wants a man. I wanted it all. Everything. I didn't get anything I wanted.

I have to give it all up. Everything I've ever wanted, and for once just surrender to the fact that I have made an absolute mess of my life.

Rebecca Nietert

36

Joseph isn't there when I get home. Joseph told me about a new contraption that he just bought. They call it a cell phone. It is about as big as a blow dryer and as uncomfortable to carry, but I try to reach him by cell phone. It doesn't go through. I take a shower, trying to get the loneliness off my mind. I fall asleep.

The next morning, I lay on the bed, not sure of what to do. Something in me says to call Connie at the hospital.

"Hello?" Her answer is groggy, as if she's just waking up.

"It's Beverly. How are you feeling?"

"Tired. What time is it?"

"That doesn't matter. Do we have a young man to celebrate?"

"Yes." I can hear the sleep smile in her voice, "Jeremy's sleeping well. He's in my room with me."

"Jeremy is such a great name!"

"Thank you. Listen, I have to get some rest. He wakes every hour."

"Okay, but really quick, have you seen Joseph?"

"He left last night. He wanted to share the news with you. Isn't he home?"

"Don't worry about it. Good night." I hang up. I get up to look around the house and don't see any lights on. I start turning them on in each room. When I reach Connie's room I hear a sound.

I turn on the light. What would Joseph be doing in there?

"Turn it off please." I look at where the voice came from; it's Joseph. I start to walk in when his voice stops me in my tracks.

"No, don't! I just need some space from you right now."

I can't believe he would ever speak to me like that! I turn away and walk to the comfort of my own room; the comfort that he was

Heart of Gold

supposed to have provided for me. I get dressed and put some make up on.

The sun shines through the window of the kitchen where I get my coffee. I'm all alone... Again.

I look around the house, unable to find Joseph. Maybe he left for work early? I put on some Country music. I can't help thinking about what Lana said before she left. I try to focus on the music, urging it to sweep me away into the romance many songs portray. I can't help but feel like I'm missing out on relationships and life. I don't feel loved, wanted, needed or protected. I just feel undeniably alone.

I pick up the phone to dial my mother. For some reason I feel the urge.

"Hey."

"Hey. What are you up to today?"

"Bev, what's wrong?"

"I don't know. I need to go shopping. Want to come with?"

"Sure."

"I'll be there as soon as I can." I hang up.

The drive there gives me time to think. My mind is a whirlwind of thoughts. I need her to clarify some things for me. I pick her up and we head to the local wholesale trade company. I like this place because it has anything needed for home décor. I love looking at the variety of glass, pictures, plants and furniture.

We walk inside, "Tell me what happened."

I let her in on what happened at the club.

"Oh my God!" She looks at me, incredulous, "And this man who helped you out - do you know who?"

"I have absolutely no idea. At the time I just wanted to get away. I didn't care about who was behind me."

She nods in understanding, "I'm just glad you're okay."

"Well, that's not all. When I came home and showered, Joseph was in Connie's room with the lights off."

She looks at me, puzzled, "What was he doing there?"

Rebecca Nietert

"I'm not sure. He said that he needs time away from me. So, I left the room and slept alone. Now I haven't seen him."

"Hmm...Maybe he feels like he should be married to Connie again?"

"Do you really think this is all about Connie?"

"Well, yeah." Her face says 'of course', "I mean he's in her room with the lights off. What else could it be?"

"I'm not sure." I shrug and pick up a pretty piece of glass, then put it back down, "That makes sense though. Sometimes I wonder if he's the man for me."

"Honey, he may or may not be. I can't tell you what and what not to do." I shoot her a look and she laughs. "I know, I know. I used to be so demanding."

"And demeaning." I mumble. She ignores the comment.

"Still, he doesn't seem to be making you happy. You know what I think?"

"What?" I look at another piece of glass, trying to distract myself.

"I think he loves you but only thinks about himself. That isn't real love." I can't help but cringe. She continues softly, "Think about it: He doesn't consider what you've been through. He wants you to continue dancing because he's afraid for you to do anything else. He won't be able to control you. He doesn't want you to rely on him, but for some reason he needs you to need him."

"He said as long as we're together we'll be happy. I am not happy!" I can feel my voice cracking. I blink a few times, trying not to cry.

"Those games might be fine when you're dating but you two are living your lives together. It's a whole new ballgame now."

"You're right."

"It's not about just having fun anymore. He's your life now. It seems like he doesn't want this to be permanent either. You can't see that despite what everyone tells you because you don't want to see it?"

Heart of Gold

"I'm beginning to." I can feel my heart sink.

She looks at me, unconvinced, "Beverly you have to consider your future. Do you always want to be a dancer? What about when you're thirty and your body changes? What about when you have had enough? He's not going to be there for you. Don't you want to be married? Don't you want children some day?"

On the way home I think about what she told me. I didn't know if I truly ever wanted marriage and children, but what I did know was that I didn't want that choice taken from me.

I know that I need to talk to Joseph as soon as possible. This can't wait any longer. I park in the driveway. I want a life with him and I want him to want that with me. When I walk into the kitchen Joseph looks at me but doesn't say anything. Sally is sitting on the other side of the island on a barstool.

I let out a gasp. He looks like he's been in a bar room brawl. His eye is bruised and cheek is inflamed. "Oh my God! What happened to you?!" I pay absolutely no attention to the visitor.

"I don't believe you!" He shouts and slams his fist down.

My eyes widen. "What is it now?!"

"Never mind!" He hisses.

I take a deep breath, realizing that I need to calm down. We need to have this conversation. "Listen, I have to go to work. I know I have to get some money together but I've been thinking-"

He interrupts abruptly, "I don't give a damn right now what you do, Beverly!"

All I can do is stare as he turns and walks away. Tears sting at my eyes; I can't breathe. The pain inside my stomach hurts worse than after I had the abortion. My heart is literally breaking in two. I grab my bag and head out to the car, slamming the door. I stare out the windshield, struck with disbelief.

He really doesn't care about what I need. I look towards the doorway, knowing full well that leaving means never coming back. I can't help the feeling of dread that suddenly washes over me. I can't keep doing this.

Rebecca Nietert

He will never give me what I need and I will never be enough for him. I will never be the only woman he wants. A woman was sitting in the kitchen with him. He talked to me that way in front of her. It has to be Sally. Who else could it have been?

I will never be the kind of girl he respects enough to keep around forever. Not like he does Connie. I wipe at the tears rolling down my face.

I know that when he holds me, he owns me. One look into those blue eyes and I'm suddenly his puppet; a trophy to be put on display for the world to see. He can command me to do anything and I'll do it. Just like a puppy. I silently weep for lost dreams; the dream of a life together, happily married.

I whisper softly, "You're my addiction." There, I said it. I actually...said it. I can feel my circulation stop and for a moment, the world is still. Joseph shows up in the doorway and I do nothing. I back the truck out of the driveway.

There's a sort of...peace that surrounds me. I'm going to be okay. I've got to get out of here. From now on, it's me first. I crank up the radio and drown myself in the music. A song by Reba McEntire is on; it echoes what I know in my heart but can't bring myself to say. You came along a little too late. Maybe if I was in my early 20's I would have the time to waist on waiting for him to love me, but I know that I don't have that kind of time now.

When I get to work Buddy is sitting at a table near the exit of the club. I walk up to him and toss my backpack on the table. He jumps and looks up, surprised. He tries to hug me, but his welcoming smile vanishes when he sees my face. I'm sure my eyes are red from crying and my makeup is all over the place. Right now, I don't care. I just want to get out of here.

I look at Buddy, realizing that this hero won't be around for long. I'll take up his offer to educate me then he'll probably vanish. It doesn't matter. I need to make the best choice for me. I will never allow a man to put me second on his list ever again. Either I'm his first choice or there will be no choice. If a man truly cares

Heart of Gold

for me, he won't put my feelings on the line, especially for another woman. Does such a man exist? Can I really desire someone else as much as I've desired Joseph? Can I really love someone like I loved him? I shake my head, bidding the thoughts to leave my mind. Of course not. Joseph is the love of my life. A life without him just saddens me to a point I don't think I could come back from if I allowed myself to wallow in the truth of it.

What matters most right now is the opportunity to have options. I'm still young enough to have a family if I choose. I can turn my own life around. I feel like I don't want anyone's help, but I know I need someone's help. It's ironic how I'm asking a stranger, a potential client, to help get me out. For the first time in a long time I feel like I have control. What I want actually matters. I can plan my own future.

I look at Buddy. I say firmly, "I'm going to school. If you care about me, you'll send me."

He looks at me for a long time, contemplating. Finally he speaks, "It's about time. Let's go."

I smile; feeling he genuinely wants to help me. For the first time a man wants to help me become who I want to be, not who he wants. He takes my hand. I look at him then back at the stage, at the crowd. My eyes glaze over the bar and the drinks.

I begin to feel a new surge of courage wash over me. This is the last time I'll ever end up in a place like this again. I look at the other dancers up on stage. This is the last time I'll ever put on a show for money; the last time con game I'll ever play for cash. Oddly I believe I will miss this.

I know I'm trading my heart for my future and my pride for my freedom. I don't care. I decide to believe in myself, finally feeling hope again.